The Martian Marauders
Book One
of the Jack Commer Series

Michael D. Smith

Sortmind Press, 2020
press.sortmind.com

For my wife Nancy

CHAPTER ONE
Survey
Thursday, June 8, 2034, 1000 hours

The five-hundred-mile-wide crater had been thoroughly radar-mapped, though nobody had ever seen it. They all knew the ground was still burning eight months later. Copilot Joe Commer looked away. All he could picture was the red-orange lava beneath all that soot.

"You know, I still can't believe it," he muttered. "Those were the *Himalayas*."

His older brother Jack shrugged from the command seat to his left. "Are the sensors deployed?"

Joe took a breath. "Yep, they're out. All five up and running. No problems." Far to starboard hung the icy white fragments of the moon, beginning its eons-long spread into a complete ring. Joe listened to the whirring of the ventilation fans and the beeps of the electronics. The Control Room of the *Typhoon I* was brilliantly lit, and the reflections of its interior curved through the cockpit window, obscuring the line of twilight on the ruined planet below.

It was the first run where they hadn't come to pick up a passenger shell. Nothing to do but drop off a few sensor satellites. Nobody else to rescue, nobody who wanted to be rescued. They were really saying goodbye.

Joe shuddered at the charcoal blanketing most of the planet. He could all but smell the death below. How could he ever have lived there?

The United System had declared June 5th the final day for mandatory evacuation, and three days ago the USS *Celeste* had picked up four hundred refugees, all against their will. There were only handfuls of human beings left down there anyway, all doomed, but they'd made their choice. What good did it do anymore to send USSF troops into the refugee camps, taking casualties fighting the diehards, just so they could haul a few survivors back?

Captain Jack Commer punched an orange square on his

1

console. "Jim, prepare standard navigation program for the ride home."

"Up and running," came the crisp voice of Jim, the third Commer brother, from his workroom down the fuselage. "Tell me when you're ready and I'll lock 'er in."

"Stand by," Jack said, his face solid and square, his deep-set brown eyes intent on the readout panels. "First let's download some sample readings from New Orbiter 1. John?"

"Got it, Jack!" came John Commer's high voice. "This is an amazing interface! The satellite's actually *talking* to us! That's incredible! And the software was so easy to set up! All I had to do was flip a switch!"

Jack sighed. "Fine, John. Go ahead and patch it through so we can all hear it."

"Okay, Jack! Fine, just fine! It's so easy! All you have to do is *activate* it, and the default settings are *perfect!*"

Joe watched Jack struggle whether to reprimand or indulge the fourth and youngest Commer. Jack finally shook his head with a half-smile. "Just patch it through. If there's a problem, talk to Ken."

"No problem," came the voice of communications officer Ken Garrison. "Downloading to all crew now."

"Wait! I was programming the *voice!*" John cried.

"Forget the voice! Just patch the damn thing through!" Jack snapped. Joe caught his disgusted glance. How many times had they had the *John* discussion, alone here in the Control Room?

"General Summary, Planet Analysis Report One," New Orbiter 1 spoke to each of the eight *Typhoon* men in their compartments. "Atmosphere poisonous for human beings. Cloud cover has destroyed most plant life. Radioactivity levels in major urban areas and in Central Asia fatal to human beings. Planet still experiencing magnitude four earthquakes at all locations. Entire planetary surface deadly to humans. 40,500 humans estimated left on Earth, all expected to die within two months. Specific data totaling 1,200 petabytes feeding into crystal storage."

"A couple months," came Harri McNarri's voice over the

intercom's ship-wide circuit. "Wow. There were six hundred thousand in March."

"Guess next time we're back those last people will be gone," Joe sighed. "If we ever come back. What's the point?"

"We aren't gonna try to convince 'em to evacuate?" McNarri said.

"The computer automatically radioed messages to the various refugee camps," Jack said. "No replies. They were serious when they said they'd die on Earth. The Evacuation is officially over, and I'm going to respect their wishes."

Joe scanned the garbage below. "Well, sometimes I wonder."

"About why anyone would stay?" Jack said.

"About why anyone *ever* stayed. What the hell did we think we were doing down there for five thousand years? Just crashing around through one war after another?"

"You mean millions of years, don't you?" McNarri put in. "Millions of years of human evolution led to *this*."

"Well, I was talking about recorded history. Seems to me that once we started recording it all, we should've grown up somehow. Was all that *crap* down there just a training ground for space? For getting us off the stupid planet?"

That silenced the crew.

No, nobody was supposed to say that. You were supposed to say how sad it all was and how grief-stricken you were. Hell, Joe wasn't grief-stricken. He'd been kicked out of the damn nest and now he had a new life in space. Sure, it had been a painful kick, but he guessed it needed to be.

"Well, people just want to forget," McNarri finally said. "Can't say I blame 'em. Won't make much sense coming back here until a couple thousand years or so. And even then, this place will still be a godawful mess."

Joe shook his head. The ship's engineer still didn't get it. He thought somebody would really want to come back. In a thousand years people would've put this disaster way behind them. Earth would be a polluted curiosity, a place where daredevils in rad suits might climb Mt. Everest for kicks. Well, not Mt. Everest, that one was gone, maybe some other slag heap.

"Well, there's still the concept of planetary engineering," Jack said, evidently deciding to let the discussion flow on ship-wide intercom. "That's why we're deploying these upgraded sensors. The USSF wants current data for research purposes."

"C'mon, Jack, you don't really believe that stuff, do you?" Harri said. "Planetary engineering? In our lifetimes? It's just too immense a task."

"Look, Harri, if we can start terraforming Mars, who's to say that in a few decades we might not terraform the earth as well?"

"Sheesh, you sound like that Frankston quack."

"He can't be a total quack. He designed some of the Mars projects, after all."

"Can't be done, Jack. At least not in our lifetimes. Maybe in a couple thousand years. We don't have the technology or the means. This whole planetary engineering crap is just nonsense the media shoves down our throats. And anyway, we can never replace the moon. Why would anyone want to come back here if there isn't a moon?"

"C'mon, Harri, you're an engineer, you know there'll be advances in the field."

"Forget it, Jack. I just hate quackery. That Frankston guy is one of the worst. Or was. He decided to stay behind and die down there, after all."

Jack shrugged. "All I'm saying is he may have had some good ideas."

"If you say so, Captain. I need to check the reactor. We can continue our debate later."

Jack sighed. Joe grinned back. Debating the argumentative Major McNarri was always difficult, mostly because Harri was always right. Joe had no idea where Harri had picked up his vast expertise. In a way he was the most important man on the ship, because he knew how to repair every system on board. In addition, he was an M.D., their ship's doctor. He would be irreplaceable if he ever resigned. Not that any man aboard the *Typhoon* would, of course.

Communications Officer Garrison came over the intercom. "We have a communication from General Scott, Jack."

"Thanks, Ken," Jack said. "What's the clearance?"

"Standard."

Jack leaned back. "Well, if it's not Secret or Urgent, let's let everyone hear it. We need a little entertainment here today anyway."

Joe nodded. A communiqué from Mars, even one that took twenty-one minutes to get here across the current 232-million-mile distance, was a living contact from home. The five sensor satellites they'd deployed were just ghosts talking about the ghosts below.

"Patching it through," Ken said.

"Jack," came William C. Scott's clipped baritone, "when you're through with your deployment I've got another little assignment for you. Since the *Typhoon's* due for a two-week inspection, you and your crew will have plenty of time to attend to it."

Jack grinned. The two-week inspection was news to Joe as well. They hadn't had one of those in a couple years. Maybe the *Typhoon* was due, but McNarri surely would've been the one to suggest it. More likely it gave Scott the opportunity to send them on another demented special ops mission. The last had involved coordinating the rescue of two hundred tourists stranded in the Vallis Marineris a few weeks ago.

"The matter is this," the General went on. "Something's--I don't really know how to say this, but something's come up at this end."

Joe caught Jack's puzzled glance.

"And unfortunately, it's dovetailing with all these stupid rumors over the past few months. The entire population riled up, and over nothing. But I say this is really an opportunity to put all this talk of native Martians to rest once and for all."

"Oh, no!" Joe groaned. "Not the *native Martians* again."

"Quiet, Joe," Jack said.

"--reports of noises at night, vibrations in buildings, strange footprints, all these little bits of so-called *evidence*. And this idiotic talk of *Martian spirits*. Like that video of that dark shape prowling around the Armstrong Center, with AresNet blowing the whole thing out of proportion. Interviewing housewives living behind the Center, as if they're experts! Turned out to be a dog somebody strapped an EnviroField on. And riffraff like Huey Vespertine say there must be some ancient Martian culture we're trampling on! I don't have to tell you that all of Marsport's getting edgy. Of course, it's got to be that we're seeing some long-term effects of relocating our people to Mars. Some people are spooked and their ears and eyes are playing tricks on 'em, that's all."

"Sheesh," Joe said. "What people will--"

"That is, until now." General Scott's voice got heavier. "I thought it was all in people's imaginations, until now. Boys, I need you back here immediately. There's been--I really don't know how to say this--"

"What?" crackled the voices of several crewmembers simultaneously.

"--been a discovery. In--in the Kilpatrick Desert."

"What?" Jack cried.

"--still can't believe it. But I've seen the footage, men. On AresNet, right after you left for Earth this morning. We're all dumbfounded here at HQ. Dammit, it can't be possible! And in the Desert! The Kilpatrick Desert!"

"Right where he crashed!" John broke in. "In Hellas Basin!"

"Quiet, John! We know where he crashed!" Jack snapped.

"Where Colonel Kilpatrick died! No wonder the General's upset!"

"John, let's listen for God's sake!" Joe said.

"All I'm trying to say--"

"Cut it, John!" Jack cried. "We want to hear--"

"Nobody listens to me!"

"--of the ruins. It's unbelievable," Scott went on. "We have no idea how far underground some of these--these *temples,* I guess you could call them, may go. And they're covered with things like hieroglyphs, for want of a better term. We're flying out more teams of specialists, but so far we haven't cracked this--this language, if that's what it truly is."

"Damn," Jim Commer put in. "Can this be real?"

"I know, I know," Jack said in shock. "Ruins? Martian ruins?"

"So as soon as you're done, get back here at full speed," Scott said. "I'll fill you in more when you return. Out."

"Wow ..." Joe said.

"God, he's right," Jack said. "All those crazies who think there are native spirits prowling around are going to go into high gear."

"Yeah, the same idiots who've been accusing us of covering up data about life on Mars," came the voice of turret gunner Mickey Michaels.

"Yeah, so we could evacuate to Mars without worrying about what stupid bacteria we might be doing a genocide number on," complained Craig Reynolds, the other turret gunner.

"Scott's probably already feeling the pressure," Jack agreed. "He and Kilpatrick spent five months in Hellas. Never came up with anything."

Joe nodded, mind racing at the thought of ancient ruins. It was a measure of how upset Scott was that he hadn't thought to send along any downloads from AresNet. For the next four and a half hours the *Typhoon* was cut off, unless someone at the USSF got his act together and sent more data. "Well, the old man will make it through."

"Yeah, sure," Jack said. "Still, I can't wait to get back and find out what this stuff's all about. He's obviously going to send us to the Kilpatrick Desert for a couple weeks."

"You think so? Yeah, you're probably right."

A light blinked on Joe's console for the Navigation Room. Jim Commer was on the line.

"Yes, Jim, what is it?" Jack said.

"When I was loading our course, I got a flag. NAV4 says there's an asteroid-sized object near our flight path. We don't have it in our databanks. All I can think is that John's sensors must've picked something up on the way over and just stored it in memory, but on the way back we're close enough to trigger the alert."

"Huh," Jack said. "It's getting damn rare to find new asteroids these days. Hey, John, check with Jim on this object. Let's compare data and see what's there. We might have a little time to go after the thing on the way home." Joe knew they were all eager to get back to Mars and the news from the Kilpatrick Desert. Still, they were under standing order to check out every new asteroid.

"I've got it, Jack!" John called. "Jim was right. It wasn't close enough on the way over to abort the nav program, but it'll come within two million miles on our way back. I'll bet it's a new asteroid! The computer doesn't have anything on it. I'd say it's not too large, maybe a chunk a couple hundred feet wide."

"Fine," Jack said. "Jim, I'm taking us out of orbit now. Plot me an intersection course with that thing as well as its orbit. We'll name us a new asteroid and we can get back to Mars in a hurry after that."

"Roger," said Jim.

"Joe, prepare to increase to maximum thrust. You take her this time."

"I've got 'er," Joe replied. "Inertial dampers on."

As Jim's new course fed into the computer, maneuvering jets turned the *Typhoon* in the proper direction. Joe hit the throttle and the inertial compensators cut in, keeping the interior gravity at 1G under any acceleration. Within a minute Joe had the *Typhoon* at top end, 49.8 million miles per hour.

"We'll intercept in five minutes," Jim said.

"Fine," Jack said. "How far will this take us off our course to Mars?"

"Not too far. Won't slow us up for more than a few minutes."

"Jack! Jack! I--I can't believe it!" John shouted, voice breaking into distortion over the intercom. "The--the thing--I thought it was moving in an elliptical orbit, but--"

"What's the problem, John?" Jack snapped, his irritation evident to everyone.

"Well, I don't know how to say this, but--"

"But *what?*"
"Well, the thing's changed course! It's moving *towards* us!"

CHAPTER TWO
Saucer

Joe gripped the console joystick, adrenaline surging. The *Typhoon* was supposed to have all records of USSF, scientific, and commercial craft throughout the solar system. He scanned his console for a plot of the object, but John had neglected to feed it to the Control Room.

"Jack, it's a ship! It has to be a ship!" John cried.

"I know that!" Jack yelled back. "What else can it be? Get me precise measurements on that thing! The pilot needs information, John, information! You know that! You've had pilot training!" He turned to Joe. "Joe, you keep piloting command. I need time to think."

"Sure," Joe said. "Jack, do you think this thing could be AC?"

"Well, who can--hell! John! Configuration on that object! Does it match Alpha Centaurian?"

"Well, *I* don't know," John muttered. "How'm I supposed to know?"

"John, get on top of this! Is that an AC ship or not?"

"Uh--sorry, Jack, I guess I got carried away. It's just that I've never seen--"

"Measurements!"

"Uh, sorry, uh, let's see ... length is 205 feet, width is, uh, looks like its width is also 205. Wow, it's perfectly circular! Man, like a classic flying saucer!"

"Hmm," Jack said. "Joe, what do you think?"

"Not one of ours, that's what I think."

"Not any AC design I know of. Their ships are thousands of feet long with all sorts of crap stacked on 'em."

"But we can't rule it out on those grounds. And for all we know, John's misread the sensors."

"Don't get me started," Jack sighed, then spoke into the intercom: "John! Double-check configuration and please send detailed plot to command and copilot consoles."

"I didn't misread the sensors!" John shot back. "The thing

is circular! Why does Joe always assume--"

"John! Double-check it anyway! That could be an AC ship invading our solar system! We don't have any time to waste!"

"Okay, okay, I'm doing it, I'm doing it! Calibrate zonal sensor A ... long range scanner override ... c'mon, scanner, override ... okay, press F3 to override ... dee dee dee ..."

"Jeez ..."

"While he's doing that, I've downloaded you the plots," Jim broke in.

"Thanks, Jim," Jack said as a 3D plot of the alien object's trajectory appeared on Joe's console.

"Jack, Jim grabbed my sensor output for his NAV4 Cluster again!" John complained.

"Look, it's okay this time," Jack said. "We know you're busy, and we're having a little emergency here."

"But I always have to recalibrate the matrices if NAV4 intervenes!"

"I don't care, John! We'll recalibrate them later! And go for visual as soon as you can! Dump it on our screens in the Control Room!"

"Man, the goddamn ACs can't be in our solar system, can they?" Joe said. "They aren't supposed to be able to *get* here. Their ships are too unreliable."

"We just don't know," Jack said. "This could be it, Joe. This really could be it."

"Dammit, after all we've been through," Joe muttered, ashamed of himself for succumbing to one second of whining. Still, after the end of Earth, after the Evacuation, after the solar system had *chopped itself in half,* weren't they entitled to a break?

Jack jabbed a blue square on his command pad. "Weapon turrets."

"We're here, Jack," spoke Mickey Michaels, commander of the turrets.

"What's with that thing?" asked Craig Reynolds, the second turret operator.

"We've got an unidentified spaceship heading our way.

Pick up the heading from John and set blasters to maximum power. If and when I tell you to, destroy it."

"Wow …" said Michaels. "I mean, roger. We can hit it."

The two turrets, mounted on the back of the *Typhoon I,* each contained a swiveling PlanetBlaster capable of hitting any object within 10,000 miles of the ship. Michaels liked to say that these guns could hit a dime at 7,000 miles and remove one letter from it, or slowly melt the entire surface of a planet, but they'd never tried either experiment.

"Okay, I guess it's standard procedure for your first officer to remind you that there's no reason to suppose that ship is actually hostile," Joe said.

"Forget it," Jack said. "We don't know that. I'm not taking any chances. That thing changed course and it's heading right at us. I want you to aim the *Typhoon* at top end straight down that thing's nose. If it has one."

Joe grinned. "You got it. I was just reminding you of USSF First Contact Policy One."

"Piss on USSF First Contact Policy One. This could be the start of the AC invasion. They're crazy, they hate our guts, and they'd give absolutely no warning." He punched another square on his console. "Garrison, any contact?" Jack called to the communications officer.

"None, sir," came the reply. "I'm sending out standard messages."

"Turrets, when we're within firing range we're going to veer sharply to starboard. Be prepared to shoot to port when I tell you." He jabbed his pad again. "John, is that thing still on a collision course?"

"Well, I don't know if I'd say *collision,* Jack, but--"

"John! Does it show any sign of getting out of our path?"

"Uh, no, Jack. It's like it's heading directly for us at 10.6 million miles per hour. Distance: 2.148 million miles. Time to intersection: 2.13 minutes."

Joe tensed his right hand tight around the joystick as the seconds passed.

"Is it showing any signs of slowing down or changing

course?" Jack called.

"No," came John's reply. "Time to intersection: 1.89 minutes."

"Systems checks, everyone. Battle status. Turrets ready. McNarri, come forward and man the Xon bomb command station."

As the crewmembers checked off their systems over the intercom, Harri McNarri entered the Control Room and took a third seat behind the Commers. He swiveled to face a small console at the rear of the cabin.

"Well, Harri, how's the reactor holding up?" Jack said.

"Running perfectly," McNarri said over his shoulder. "Jack, are you really sure we'll need an Xon?"

"We just may. I'm not sure what that thing's capabilities are. Maybe it's not at top end, maybe it'll take evasive action. If we can't get within ten thousand miles and have to have the Xon bomb radiation take it out, so be it."

"Right." Harri went through the Xon arming sequence. Joe could tell Harri was shocked. The last time they'd armed an Xon was eight months ago.

"Turrets, are you ready?" Jack called.

"Ready," said Michaels. "We have maximum on both blasters. Our computers are locked onto the object."

"Jack, are you sure we should fire at that ship without making contact?" Joe said. "If it turns out to be one of ours, with some weird computer error causing it to do this--"

"I won't blast it if it tells me it's one of ours. Garrison? Any contact?"

"Still none, Jack."

"John!" Jack said. "Do we still not have any identifiable configuration on that thing?"

"Uh, no, nothing," came John's reply. "Um, time to intersection, uh, twenty-five seconds."

"Tell me at ten."

"Jack, my reflexes don't mean anything at this closing speed," Joe said. "The computer will have to take the evasive."

"I know that," Jack said. "Get the backup autopilot online

too. Set it to auto-evasive at eight seconds if main doesn't confirm at ten."

"Got it," Joe said, punching in commands. "You know, it'd be great if we could disable this thing and capture the crew."

"Forget it. No time. I'm not taking chances."

"Okay, just giving options," Joe grunted, tensing on the control stick.

"Ten seconds!" John cried.

"Blasters, fire!" Jack shouted. Joe felt the slightest computer-aided quiver in the stick as a massive white streak flashed by in the sun's glare. From the rear of the ship came the tremors of the dual PlanetBlasters.

"We are blasting!" cried Michaels. But thousands of tiny lights blossomed everywhere.

"Bombs, missiles--something!" John babbled. "We--"

The cockpit canopy showed nothing but white. Without waiting for orders Joe shot the ship further right and down, so fast that the inertial compensators had trouble keeping up. He could feel the computer aiding his movements, which were probably wildly exaggerated compared to what the system thought necessary to avoid whatever was exploding out there.

"Tiny little *missiles* ..." John said dreamily. "Thousands of 'em, none over a foot long. Who ever heard of that?"

"Turrets--results!" Jack yelled.

"We--got it, Jack," Michaels said, voice drained. "Both PlanetBlasters caught it before the evasive. It's gone."

"John, give me a view from the rear. Patch it to everyone's console."

Joe's console showed a jagged glowing red cloud of debris fading behind them. "Wow ..." he whispered. How quickly they'd gotten into combat, how quickly it was over. He exhaled, heart racing, feeling relief and disgust at the results, along with an uneasy mix of pride and shame in his own reactions.

To his surprise Jack was on his feet, pacing. "Yeah, wow. Hard to believe, isn't it?" He turned to McNarri. "Harri--ship's status. Any damage from the missiles?"

"None, sir," McNarri replied. "That copilot of yours has

good reflexes. We avoided 'em all."

Jack grinned at Joe. "We'll keep him on for now. Harri, let me know if you find anything to the contrary. We'll give the ship a thorough going-over once we get to Mars. Scott wants a two-week inspection anyway."

McNarri whistled. "We're not due for any inspection!"

Jack laughed. "I knew it! We'll discuss that later. Joe, turn us around. We'll sift through the debris, see what we can find. John!" he called back to the sensor officer's workroom. "Feed Joe's console the coordinates of the debris field. Jim, plot us a course back to Mars from there."

"Roger, I'm on it now," Jim said as Joe slowed the ship to twenty million miles per hour and swung it in a wide circle.

"Listen, Jack ... that was real great, what you did back there," came John's voice.

"John, are you feeding Joe the location of that debris field?"

"Well ... okay ... let me try ... grid zone Alpha, standard pulse ... dee dee dee ..."

"Harri," Jack said, "stand down the Xon and let's do a diagnostic on the solar rechargers. That was a fast acceleration to top end and we probably used up enough drive to slow us down a bit on the way home."

"I'm on it," Harri said. "They're at 89%. Not bad. Got 'em recharging now."

"Anyway, what I wanted to say is, I'm sorry I wasn't a little faster back there," John said. "I guess it all happened a little fast."

Jack exhaled. "It's okay, John. You did okay." He walked back to the command console and looked out the front window of the *Typhoon*. The glowing debris field came into view. "Let's just cruise right up to it so we can take some samples."

"Got it," Joe said, slowing the *Typhoon* to a few thousand miles per hour over the unknown ship's last known velocity and activating the sample tubes under the nose. Anything they got would be sealed in lead and stored in the compartment under their feet. Meanwhile the debris field, the remnants of a ship that had been traveling 10.6 million miles per hour, spread further and further apart.

"Garrison, was there ever any communication from that ship?" Jack said.

"None, sir."

"John, did you get photos and detailed scans of that thing?"

"Well, Jack, to tell you the truth, in all the excitement I guess I forgot to set the main analysis program in gear."

Jack pursed his lips. "Hell, John."

"Sorry, Jack. I guess I just ... messed up. But I do have the long-range scans. They still show a lot of detail. I'll send them through now."

Seconds later a radar image of the other ship showed on both Jack and Joe's computer screens.

"It sure doesn't look like any AC ship design I've seen," Joe said. "Look at that thing. Who the hell would build a military *flying saucer?*"

"Well, there are those stupid little circular civilian ships."

"You think this was an oversized Mercedes PleasureCraft?" Joe hooted. God, what if some billionaire really did commission some oversized space yacht? How many innocent people would they have just blasted? And for nothing? For some communications glitch?

"No, nobody'd use that design for military work," McNarri put in, getting up from the Xon bomb console. "Too inefficient if you need to cruise in a planetary atmosphere. Unless they have one heck of a power source."

As McNarri opened the Control Room hatch to move down the ladder into the fuselage, Joe became aware of the chatter from the open doors of the various workrooms on the catwalk behind them:

"--got to be Centaurian! How else did it avoid our databanks?"

"Hell, there could be all sorts of rogue ships we don't know about."

"But I do have this radar image of one of the missiles launched at us," John said over the intercom. It came to Joe's screen, a foot-long cylinder with rounded ends.

"Not exactly fascinating," Jack said. "We'll let headquarters examine all this data. We ought to be able to get something out of the debris as well. John, please scan ahead and identify interesting pieces we might want to take back."

"Uh, roger," John said. "Let me shift to that module. I'll have to figure out how it links up to the sample tube interface."

Jack sighed and, still on his feet, punched a square on his console for ship-wide contact. "Men. You did great. We certainly didn't expect this attack, but you all did extremely well. I know we're all curious about the source of that craft, but it'll have to wait for USSF analysis back on Mars. Our next task is to pick up as many samples as we can from the debris field. As we do so, and on the trip back home, everyone will stay on alert for any other intrusions. Thanks. Out."

Joe noted the tone in his older brother's voice when he spoke of the trip back. Home. Mars was home now. This short meaningless battle reinforced that. Whether they'd just blasted some foolish rogue ship that had no idea what it was taking on, or an Alpha Centaurian battleship invading the solar system, the crew had further bonded. They'd survived, they had a home to return to, a home to defend.

"Sorry this is taking so long to set up the sample tube interface," John said. Joe noted that John had decided to broadcast this to everyone on board. "But whenever Jim patches in his NAV4 Cluster to my sensor array I have to recalibrate the whole thing."

"John, we're in a combat situation here," Jack said, also choosing to reply to the entire crew. "Harri can look into that glitch when we get back. All we need is a simple pickup of twenty or thirty pieces of debris off that ship. If you can find anything organic, so much the better. You don't need to recalibrate your entire sensor array now."

No reply from John.

Jack switched to John's workroom only. "John, answer me! We're in the debris field now. You're the one who should be telling *me* that! I need you to zone in on likely debris candidates! Do you hear me?"

"Yes, Jack ..." came a tiny voice. "I'll get right on it ... I'm so sorry ..."

"Patching ship's controls to Sample Collection Mode," Joe said. John's sensors would now aim the ship toward promising pieces of debris.

"Yes, Joe ..." came John's petulant whimper. "I'm really sorry ..."

"*Dammit,*" Jack muttered as he shut the intercom off. "You know, this just can't go on, Joe. We've got to do something about John. Despite what I just said about the entire crew doing an excellent job, John could have gotten us all killed."

"Look," Joe said. "I agree. I mean, I know we have to talk about it sometime."

"He just doesn't belong on the *Typhoon*. Why can't we all just admit that?"

Joe turned back to his console, shocked. Had the battle upset Jack so badly? Could he really think of splitting up the Commer brothers?

"Look, Jim's a damn navigational genius. We couldn't possibly function without him. But John? I mean, they just about cancel each other out!"

Joe winced. In all the *John* discussions, Jack had never gone quite that far.

"I don't care what Dad thinks!" Jack fumed. "We nearly lost the *Typhoon* due to John!"

"Look, Jack, why don't we discuss it with General Scott when we get back? Maybe he'll have some insight. I mean, everyone's edgy right now. We can't think properly. This is the first time any of us have seen ship-to-ship combat, after all."

Jack exhaled. "I know. I know."

"Meanwhile, maybe everyone ought to try and relax. We just had a scrape. But maybe if we just spend some time picking up debris, we can all relax again. Might take anywhere from a few minutes to a couple hours to get what we need. Then we can head for home. Fill in on all the news. Find out about those ruins and all."

"Home ..." Jack sighed, pulling himself back into the

command seat. "Yeah, Joe, let's get on home."

CHAPTER THREE
Standdown
Thursday, June 8, 2034, 1700 hours

The automated bus came off the Upheaval Freeway and onto Jupiter Boulevard. Jack tried to will the tension out of his neck, his forearms, and his back. He checked his watch. Twelve hours since they'd lifted off this morning for Earth. The other seven crewmembers were sprawled in their seats. Michaels, Reynolds, and McNarri were asleep.

Jack supposed they should all be excused that sloppy *Typhoon* standdown. They must've spent all of ten minutes closing down the ship after putting her in the hanger. Jack had informed Facilities of the load of debris to send to Investigation, then he'd run a Quick Mode AutoDiagnostic and walked out. He hadn't even asked the other seven if they'd shut down properly. He probably should mention that when they got to the hotel.

Two 4.67-hour journeys. Although at 49.8 million miles per hour it no longer mattered where planets were in the solar system, and they no longer had to calculate orbits and conserve fuel, Jack knew his entire crew vastly preferred the runs where Mars was within forty or fifty million miles. Nobody wanted to sit still for over four and a half hours, twice in one day. They'd left at 0500, arrived at Earth 0940, spent an hour deploying the five satellites, then *fought that ship*. And surveyed the debris field to noon.

Jack had ordered himself not to even think about the attack until some analysis of the debris was complete. He wished he could pretend this was all a pleasant normal work day. Wasn't it time to grab a few beers and relax with the boys?

Mars' one-third gravity lessened the fatigue. His back already felt a little looser. Beside him Joe yawned. Ahead Jim studied the high glass boxes of downtown Marsport connected by thin skyways, some architect's idea of an homage to the classic science fiction stories of Mars from the previous century. The pink sky was failing, but the lighted boxes of the city glowed yellow in the coming sunset.

All built by robots within a few months. Most of those skyscrapers were still going up. In the lower Martian gravity, they'd be much taller than on Earth. The city also incorporated two lovely pedestrian pathways circling downtown. The outer ring, Earth, was raised, resembling the Great Wall of China, and you could see the entirety of downtown from all angles as you went around. The inner ring, Venus, was a sunken pit filled with geologic specimens from around the solar system, and thousands of different kinds of Earth trees kept alive in their own EnviroFields. Jack loved to explore both rings.

The bus rolled to Canal Street, passing the United System Building, two hundred stories tall and headquarters of the USSF. Jack noted the silent gratitude of the entire crew that he hadn't programmed a stop at HQ but instead allowed them to ride a couple more blocks to their hotel. Nobody wanted to be debriefed; nobody wanted to think of the journey, or the attack. Everyone was anxious to be home. There was so much going on here, like the Kilpatrick Desert discovery. He was so tired, and hoped Scott would never send them back to Earth again. Who wanted to visit a dead planet? Then again, Easterling, Deputy USSF Commander, was so gung-ho for missions back to collect artifacts from libraries and museums. There was a big political push for that, but couldn't they send some slower, nonmilitary ships for that stuff?

Jack could also feel the men's relief at riding a civilian bus back from the spaceport. They often avoided taking a USSF jeep to their hotel. The bus was charmingly slow, removed from any military duty of even returning some ensign or airman's salute, and it also gave a great view of Marsport as they came down the Upheaval.

Up on the right was the tall black tetrahedron of the Marsport Hotel. The officers' quarters at the spaceport weren't due to be completed for a few months, so the *Typhoon* crew had their own rooms at the hotel. Here again they enjoyed the respite from military life, and all eight men would be sorry to be assigned their new quarters, even though they'd be getting single rooms.

"Wake up, Harri, we're here! Mickey and Craig, you too," Jack said. "How can you guys sleep through the attractions of Canal Street?"

"Aw, jeez," Harri said, stretching. "I was trying to *demonstrate* how."

"Marsport Hotel!" came the automated voice from the front of the bus. "Warning! Depressurization at stop! Sensors show all passenger EnviroFields set to activate. If for some reason you think yours is not ready, please press the HELP button on the seat in front of you. Thank you. Depressurization *now*."

Jack felt his own EnviroField click on as the bus sucked all but a fraction of the air out of the bus and stored it in canisters atop the vehicle. In a moment the front door opened to the outer Martian environment.

"Those are the Commers!" came a child's whisper through a suit radio as the eight men of the *Typhoon* made their way down the center aisle and out.

They strode across a plaza filled with sculptures carved from pink rock. In the center of the plaza workmen were constructing one of those new giant information screens. They seemed silly to Jack, who was accustomed to processing his information through his personal USSF Comm, but he understood the emotional need for people to congregate at information sites and read the day's news in letters a foot high. Or input their own news into AresNet if they desired.

So far the only information available on the ten-by-twenty-foot slab was a sign that said "Information Kiosk Under Construction" in numerous languages. Jack's goal was to learn Chinese. English and Chinese were the two big languages on Mars, although Jack supposed a lot of those ideograms were languages other than Chinese. Still, so many USSF personnel were Chinese that a working knowledge of the language would come in handy, despite the ongoing refinement of translation software.

Jack felt himself slipping into his command role even in the act of walking across the plaza with his crewmates. He noted which ones seemed most tired or edgy, and guessed which ones would be most receptive to discussing the sloppy ship standdown, and which ones might have the worst problems dealing with the spaceship attack. Which, again, he wasn't going to think about right now.

And here he was herding seven grown men through the hotel airlock, across the lobby and to the elevators. When two elevators came, the four Commers took one and the other four took the second. That was unusual, as the four Commers liked to make sure the groups mixed, that the Commer brothers didn't become some upper hierarchy.

"Tired," was all Jim said as the four brothers avoided looking at themselves in the mirrored elevator.

"Me, too. Man, what a day," Joe said. Jack knew the saucer was on everyone's minds. The Kilpatrick Desert curiosity had been pushed to the back of their fried brains.

"We'll need to look at that NAV4 cluster glitch first thing in the morning!" John said. "Do you think it could be a central server problem? Maybe the new sensor alignment package wasn't compatible with--"

"Later, John," Jack said. "We can deal with it later. And our two-week inspection ought to include some overall computer upgrades."

"Still, you'll never know when we'll fight another *saucer* like the one we ran into today!" John said. "Do you think maybe the ACs could be jamming our sensor modules, and that it's only *apparently* a NAV4 cluster glitch?"

"Look, we don't know it's Alpha Centaurian," Joe cut in wearily. "And that NAV4 glitch has been with us for a couple months now."

"Let's just drop it for a while, shall we?" Jack said. "Everyone's tired, John, let's just relax and think about this tomorrow."

"Okay, okay, I was just trying to be of assistance here."

Jack shook his head. With the four of them in the elevator, he was again reminded of that crack about "the Commers decreasing in size." Every Commer wound up two inches shorter than the last. Jack was the tallest at 6'1", although Joe, who

worked out a lot, was the most physical of all of them at 5'11",
with huge biceps and pectorals straining out of his tight red
tunic.

Crew-cut Jim at 5'9" was of medium build, but his body
was a highly efficient tool. There was nothing spare on him, and
he looked ready to attack any problem instantly. He had sharp
features, a pointed chin, intense blue eyes and a confident, direct
voice. Jack had always wondered why Jim had never expressed
interest in ship's command. There was a slightly dark
complexion to his face, somewhat like Joe's, in comparison to
John's milky one. Jack supposed his own complexion was
midway between Joe's and Jim's.

At 5'7", John got by on his high-energy charisma. At least,
he was charismatic up to the point where he crossed the line into
irritating. More than once Jack had heard John described as "the
small cute one." His thin blond hair brushed the tops of his
eyebrows. His blue eyes were somehow brighter, bigger, and
airier than Jim's. Jack and Joe shared the brown eyes in the
family, Jim and John the blue.

Speaking of cute, John had a lovely girlfriend, Laurie, red-
haired, petite, an airman first class at the USSF Spaceport. No
one could explain how John had snared her, except to consider
that the youngest Commer could be charming when he wished.
Joe had cynically said that he himself would act charming if it
would get him into Laurie's tiny pants. That had earned him a
rare rebuke from Jack: "For God's sake, respect his girlfriend!
This is probably the first one he's ever had."

They came up to their rooms, 1001 through 1004 at the end
of a sunlit hall. As Jack unlocked 1001 and watched Joe sail
through the open door to flop onto his bed, he berated himself
for paying too much attention to these trivial concerns. Why had
he pulled rank on his own brother and told him to mind his own
business about John's girlfriend? Who cared? Why was Jack
involving himself in such nonsense? This wasn't a game. Jack
Commer had more important duties, such as being responsible
for the USSF's most powerful spaceship.

Jim and Harri, Mickey and Craig, Ken and John were

getting into their rooms, groaning and sighing. "Let's call up for some margaritas," Craig said.

"Later, lemme sleep," Mickey responded. "We'll hit the bar later, man."

Before their door closed Jack could hear John eagerly biting into the NAV4 problems with Ken Garrison, who was already asleep or faking it. Jack wondered if now might not be the best time to chat with John about his performance during the saucer attack. Sure, he was exhausted, but maybe it was best to get this unpleasantness out of the way now.

He was distracted by a USSF corporal exiting the elevator.

"Oh, there you are, sir," said this corporal, saluting. "General Scott noted that your USSF Comm was off."

"What? Really?" Jack said, returning the salute and then pulling his comm from his pocket. "Well, I'll be. I've had it off the entire mission." He knew what was coming next. No wonder they'd remained unmolested during their bus ride back.

"General Scott wishes to see you and Commander Joe Commer immediately," the corporal said.

"I see," Jack said with a sigh. "I should have figured he'd still be in his office, what with all the Kilpatrick Desert news. Well, then, dismissed." The corporal saluted and left. Jack turned to the other men who'd managed to get off their beds and hang in the doorways. "The rest of you are off the hook. For now at least. Come on, Joe."

*

Jack checked his watch as the express elevator shot to the USSF Command Suite on the 130th floor, developing 1.5G as it did so.

"Worried about time?" Joe said, steadying himself under the acceleration. "We could've had that corporal take us back in his jeep. I saw him duck down Neptune to the parking garage as we were coming up."

"Nah, I needed the walk. Unkink my legs," Jack said. "I was just surprised it's still so early. 1730 hours. Feels like it's about

2200 or so."

As the elevator decelerated there was a brief moment where Jack's feet almost left the floor. Then they returned to one-third gravity and the elevator doors slid aside to reveal the red, white and blue-tinted glass of the sprawling USSF Headquarters lobby.

Lieutenant Larsen of USSF Security was on duty at his command station. "Just you two here today, sir?" Larsen said, saluting.

"That's right," Jack said as he and Joe passed through the DNA scanner. "You know Scott doesn't like crowds. I can't remember the last time we had the whole crew in his office."

"We heard about that ship that attacked you," Larsen said. "Great work taking it out."

"Thanks. Couldn't take chances. Can't wait to see the debris results."

"Would you two get your butts in here?" General William C. Scott rasped over the intercom. "Wasting the entire damn night out there! And I can't believe the security officer on duty is babbling United System *secrets* to anyone who walks up."

"Well, uh, sir!" Larsen said, coming to attention even though Scott was nowhere in sight. "Uh, really, sir, I saw it was the Commers, you know!"

Jack grinned at Larsen, put a finger to his lips, and mouthed: "He's kidding." He pushed open the heavy oak door to Scott's office.

"That's better," Scott snarled from behind a titanium desk that seemed as large as *Typhoon I's* wing. "Larsen, secure the door and initiate a full-scale security sweep of this entire floor. We can't chance any slip-ups."

"Oh, yes! Yes, sir!" Larsen said, throwing Scott a salute that almost took his own forehead off. "I'll get on it right away, sir! Security Sweep Bravo underway, sir!"

"Sheesh," Scott said. "The man has no sense of humor. But the security sweep should keep him busy for a while. Well, sit down, boys." Scott gestured from behind piles of paper at two large blue chairs. Jack had always wondered about the old man's affinity for paper reports. Jack had all that stuff accessible, and better organized, on his USSF Comm.

"First of all, General, I'm sorry about my comm being off," Jack said. "I had some problems with the battery last night and I guess I forgot to turn it back on."

"No problem," Scott said, picking up a long heavy wedge at the front of his desk that spelled out SCOTT - SUPREME COMMANDER USSF (SCUSSF). "The man who has this thing on his desk can certainly take the time to order a corporal to drive over to the spaceport to find you, and then chase you all the way back to your hotel room when he doesn't find you there. We only wasted an hour or so. No problem."

Jack swallowed. "I--I--"

"You could've always called me on *my* comm," Joe pointed out.

Scott swiveled his small powerful torso in his adjustable gravity chair and fixed Joe with a long silent stare out of his black eyes. His face was a weathered Martian boulder catching the dying sunset from the thirty-foot-long floor-to-ceiling window. He let the silence go on long enough for a few Martian dust storms to etch new lines into the rock. "Commander Commer," he finally spoke, "I believe my primary contact on the *Typhoon* would be its captain, not you."

"Uh ... sorry, sir," Joe gulped.

"What he meant, sir, I'm sure," Jack said, "was as backup, in case of--"

"You boys are as bad as Larsen!" Scott laughed, shaking his name plate at Jack. "No sense of humor! Commer, I ought to lay this piece of crap on *your* desk when I retire! Pass over a few hundred eager generals and admirals and make *you* the damn SCUSSF! You could see what it's like to be surrounded by people with no sense of humor."

There was a long silence as Jack and Joe avoided Scott's eerie laugh. Jack focused on the view of Marsport and the sunsetting desert from 130 stories up, wondering once again if General Scott wasn't quite unhinged at the bottom of it all.

Jack had always wondered if the Evacuation didn't snap the

old man. How had he hauled two billion people to Mars? What about his order to drop the Xon? Wouldn't that snap anyone?

Or maybe it was the *Triumph* disaster. To be the second man to step on Mars and have your inertial dampers fail on the launch for home. Watching your best friend Kilpatrick get killed. Crash-landing in Hellas and living in the wreckage for two months. What had that done to his mind? Scott's back was so crippled that all he could do was sit in that adjustable-gravity chair all day and run the damn bureaucracy.

"Well, to be frank, sir, sometimes it's hard to tell whether you're joking or not," Jack finally spoke.

Those obsidian eyes set deep in the Martian boulder fixed Jack again. "That's how you get to *be* SCUSSF, you know. Keep 'em guessing."

Jack nodded. "I--I guess so, sir."

Scott let his name wedge thump back onto his desk. In one-third G it didn't pack the wallop it would've on Earth. "Well, enough pleasant career counseling, boys. Let's get to work. We've got problems, as I'm sure you know. How's your crew holding up after that attack?"

Jack blinked at this tidbit of solicitude. "Well enough, I guess. They're all exhausted, though."

"You included?"

"Uh … no, sir."

Scott cocked his head. "Get some sleep tonight. That's an order."

"Well … yes, sir."

"Commander," Scott turned to Joe. "How about you? A little tired?"

"Well, now that you mention it …"

"Rattled by that ship, no doubt. I bet you all are."

"Well, I guess we're all worried it was an AC ship."

"We won't know until they analyze the debris," Scott said. "They'll be able to tell us which solar system the metal is from. My guess is AC, but I still maintain the Centaurians don't have the technology to mount any sort of full-scale invasion on us. Not yet at any rate. This was probably just a scout."

"Still, it's sobering to consider that they might be in the system," Jack said. "But the only other explanation is some unregistered civilian ship. I'm just hoping it's not that."

"Well, all we can deal with is reality. All I know is that no ship outside the military can do 10.6 million miles per hour."

"That we know of," Joe interjected.

"Well, we'll deal with whatever comes up, that's all." Scott leaned on his huge muscled forearms. "As we'll deal with this goddamn archaeological dig in the Kilpatrick Desert. Wish to God those science types would just back off for a while, but they had to go discover this thing and now we have to deal with it. Dammit to hell!"

There was a silence during which Jack contemplated the lights turning on in skyscrapers across the panorama of downtown Marsport.

"So now we've got to deal with the fact that the public is already tying the Kilpatrick ruins into those strange noises in southwest Marsport that AresNet's been hyping. The entire population's on edge. And the mayor's a total idiot. Plill's babbling about poltergeists, about spirits of ancient Martians, dammit, he'll babble anything! I should never have gone along with his appointment."

Jack shrugged. His own dealings with Anmond Plill, mostly ceremonial, had been anything but pleasant. Plill made no secret of his distaste for "militarists."

"And now these damned Martian ruins." Scott picked up a report in a thick plastic binder. "Latest data." He tossed the heavy binder at Jack, who snatched it out of the air with difficulty, loose pages spewing into his lap. He scanned the color photos of strange structures amid sand, boulders, and what looked like caves. Now he realized how exhausted he was, because he couldn't make sense of what he was seeing and worse, he didn't care.

"Well, in short, gentlemen, we have a public relations problem here," Scott said. "We've got to convince the public we're on top of this. Which is why I'm sending my war heroes, all eight of your crew, to the Kilpatrick Desert tomorrow morning at 0800 hours.”

“Uh, yessir,” Jack said, hopes of sleeping well into the afternoon evaporating. “But of course, we’re not archeologists or anything like that.”

“Of course not. We’ll be inserting our own USSF archeological team there in a day or two to keep those civilians from the University of Mars in line. But I’ve also sent a Star Drive communication through to Alpha Centauri and I’m recalling General Douglas. First he can tour the ruins, then he can analyze your ship debris in full detail. And we plaster his picture all over AresNet.”

Jack nodded. “Wow, the Alien Hunter himself.”

“Batty but brilliant,” Scott rejoined. “Weird how he can sniff out those Centaurian hiding places and find those damn spies. It still amazes me how we can call him back from four light-years away in just a few minutes. He’ll be arriving on the *Cloaked Vengeance* at 2000 hours. Your first assignment will be to accompany General Douglas to the hotel when he lands at the spaceport. Then you and your crew will accompany him for a *Martian hunting expedition* at 0800 tomorrow.”

Jack and Joe dully absorbed this news of even less sleep. Jack found himself transfixed by the changing light outside. It was only when Scott slammed a few binders on his desk that Jack understood he’d fallen asleep in his big blue chair.

“That is all, gentlemen. Dismissed.”

CHAPTER FOUR
Aboard the MATS

It was getting dark at 1830 hours, and Jack felt chilly despite his EnviroField as they waited at Canal and Neptune for the bus. EnviroFields weren't designed for the deep cold of the Martian night. He'd need a full Mars suit for that.

"Here it comes," Jack said, pointing to the green bus rolling up on oversize deep-cleated tires. In an emergency these city buses could handle the rock fields of the open countryside. Buses riding on cushions of compressed air had been tried in Marsport, but they kicked up too much dust. "We can requisition a jeep from Ground Transport once we get to the spaceport."

"Yeah, I'm sure the Alien Hunter won't want to ride the bus," Joe said. "Sheesh, what are we, his chauffeurs?"

Jack sighed. "I guess so. My guess is Scott wants us to brief him on everything we know about the saucer we destroyed, and as soon as possible."

"Yeah, but I'm about to drop dead. I don't want to deal with some weird general from Alpha Centauri. The other guys are all sacked out by now. Or else getting good and drunk with the prospect of sleeping it off."

Jack winced. He might have a couple sociable beers with the men, but he wasn't the kind to take part in the major *Typhoon* drinking bouts. Joe didn't participate much himself, but more than once Jack had noted Joe's hangover on a preflight check. He'd let the crew know this behavior was unacceptable, but they apparently still needed to indulge in it now and then. At least it had scaled back drastically from the first few weeks after the war, and the start of the Evacuation. Then it had been every night.

He didn't mind whatever festivities his crew decided on tonight, though, after what they'd been through.

It had only lasted a few minutes, the actual battle just a couple seconds. But they could've all been killed. The *Typhoon* could've been the one destroyed. The crew had a right to feel spooked.

He'd been right to blow the thing to atoms, even though they hadn't been positive it was hostile until they saw those bombs coming out of it. How many people--aliens or whatever--had Jack just killed? Could it possibly have been a completely automated ship?

"So what are you up to?" Jack said as Joe punched in something on his Comm.

"Reminding the crew to be ready to leave their rooms at 0715," Joe replied. "If they're awake they can read it now, or they'll get a pleasant little alarm buzzer at 0630 and *then* they can read it."

"Sheesh. Well, thank you, Mr. Executive Officer, for remembering the obvious. I'd hate to be the one rousing those six guys awake tomorrow and telling them we have an expedition at 0800."

The thirty-foot-long bus stopped in front of them. "USSF Spaceport," Jack said as they entered. "Two of us."

"Thank you, Captain Jack Commer," the bus replied, picking his voice out of its database. "Two fares have been charged to USSF account 3394514."

"Thanks," Jack said. God, he was so exhausted he was thanking a stupid bus. He and Joe made their way to the back and plopped into their seats as the bus repressurized.

"Well, we have maybe a half hour to relax a bit," Joe said. The interior of the bus was illuminated in dim emerald green. Only a few passengers were aboard.

"Route 014, USSF Spaceport," the bus said. "You are leaving the United System Building. This bus will circle through and south of downtown Marsport. Stops for this bus: 1) Marsport Hotel. 2) Earth Museum and Memorial Gardens. 3) The University of Mars. 4) USSF Spaceport via Upheaval Freeway."

Joe closed his eyes and settled back in his seat. But Jack was on edge. He had a lot of catching up to do on that Kilpatrick Desert expedition tomorrow. He knew nothing about the dig, the discoveries there, or how Douglas would take charge of it. And as the high-profile captain of the *Typhoon I* assigned to this mission, Jack might be called upon to give an interview tomorrow morning.

He'd put off prepping for the Kilpatrick mission in favor of worrying about the saucer. Why was he obsessing over it? He'd spent the entire four and a half hours on the return journey brooding about the attack. It wasn't as if he'd never been in combat before.

Well, he'd never been in *ship-to-ship* combat before. Did all the years of training for ship-to-ship mean the same thing as actually having done it for the first time? Jack was just a novice compared to those crews in Alpha Centauri who did it on a daily basis. So he could swoop down from orbit and drop a bomb. Was that combat? Sure, the *Typhoon* had been in some danger during the war, but not like today. That saucer had been an enemy ship, designed to kill other ships. How had Jack held up? Was he too cruel? Too easy? How had the men taken it?

The bus came to a halt on Saturn Boulevard. To their left rose the dim dark blocks of the University of Mars. Everyone but the Commers got off.

"Looks like we'll have the bus to ourselves," Joe said, woozily coming awake for a moment at the sound of air depressurization and his own EnviroField clicking back up to one hundred percent.

"Yeah, it's nice seeing people go off to night class," Jack remarked, then cut himself off as two seedy characters climbed aboard.

"Donbottor Street," muttered the first one. He was a scrawny, short, wiry middle-aged jerk in a scruffy denim jacket and jeans, with a dirty baseball cap to hide his balding head. Jack had reported to a guy like that during the first phase of the *Typhoon* project, and he instinctively distrusted the type. Closet alcoholics, always on the make, manipulative, lying cheaters, eager for any advantage …

Jack was surprised at the invective flooding him. Was he really so exhausted that he was judging people so severely?

"This bus does not stop at Donbottor Street, Mr. Al Carson," the bus said. "You may transfer to the Donbottor Street route at Saturn and Ceres."

"This *is* Saturn and Ceres, you piece of crap!" yelled the second man. He was short like Carson, but heavyset, with puffy hairy hands. He was younger, with a full shock of dark hair sticking straight up, and stubble-bearded. He had large white teeth and sneering rubbery lips. To top it he wore a filthy, battered crimson and chartreuse plaid suit coat above dark blue nylon gym pants. Jack shuddered. They certainly hadn't evacuated only the decent people to Mars. The United System mandated that everyone go. Still, Jack could think of a few that should've been left behind. They didn't need these whiners on Mars.

"Hello, Mr. Samuel J. Hergs," the bus said. "Do you have a question about the Donbottor Street route?"

"You're damn right I do!" Hergs snarled. "That's where the damn whorehouses are, ain't that right?"

The bus considered this. By this time Joe was awake, hitching himself up in his seat. Then: "No information about *whorehouses* is present in the Marsport Automated Transport System database. MATS suggests you wait for the Donbottor Street bus at the corner of Saturn and Ceres. The next bus is due at 7:10 PM, about fourteen minutes from now. Thank you."

"Jeez, okay, whatever," Carson said, with a sour look at Jack and Joe in the rear. "Okay, okay, we'll take your pissing bus wherever it's going."

"Fares charged to Al Carson and Samuel J. Hergs for the USSF Spaceport. Caution to passengers: foul language is taken by most citizens as a sign of incivility. Prepare for pressurization."

"Inciba' wha'?" Al said, swaying in the center aisle as the bus moved off. "Whaz it sayin', Sam?"

"It says it don't want us to use words like crap and piss and sh--"

"Okay, enough, gentlemen," Jack found himself barking down the aisle. "We've had a hard day and don't want to listen to any of this."

Next to him Joe grinned in surprise. Jack himself certainly hadn't expected to open his mouth. But the point was that nobody who had the slightest sense of civic pride wanted the new Martian culture to slide downhill the way Earth culture had gone the previous sixty or eighty years. After the Evacuation, people were grateful to be alive, to start anew. They were pioneers, and pioneers didn't whine and complain or spew obscenities. Courtesy and cooperation were resurgent not only in Marsport, but all over the planet, and the remnants of a civilization that had been through disaster didn't want to lose that again.

"Hey, it's the pissin' Commers!" Carson cried.

"You're right, dude!" Hergs yelled from behind him. "What the hell they doin' on our bus?"

"An' lecturin' us like schoolmarms!" Carson snickered, pulling out a nine-inch knife. "Let's carve up the stinkin' militarists!"

"Yeah!" Hergs flashed another long knife.

Jack and Joe stood instantly. "Are these guys crazy?" Jack said, pulling his USSF heat blaster as Joe had already done.

"Crap!" Joe said. "What is this?"

Sure, Jack knew people in this city were edgy, just settling into life on an alien world and now being hyped by AresNet about all those strange noises. But personal attacks were so rare in Marsport that they made it to the top AresNet news. Not only were people more cooperative and friendly than they'd ever been in human history, but the consequences of even a schoolyard fistfight on Mars could be deadly. An EnviroField torn off one's belt would kill in seconds.

"Cowards!" Carson snarled, slashing his knife through the air. "Damn cowards!"

"Carve 'em, Al!" Hergs yelled from behind him. "We don't hafta listen to their militarist BS!"

"Crap, I don't wanna waste *civilians*," Joe complained, training his blaster on Carson's nose.

"Joe, hold up," Jack began. "We don't want--"

The explosion yanked Jack off his feet and knocked him into his brother. They both grabbed for railings as the wind rushed past them. Jack saw his blaster--no, two blasters--

tumbling towards the front of the bus.

"*Dammit we decompressed!*" Joe grunted through his EnviroField radio as the last of the air blasted out of the bus.

Explosive decompression. They'd experienced that on the *Typhoon* a year ago when the escape craft hatch failed. Fortunately, nobody had been blown out into space, and the men's force field spacesuits had kicked in properly. But most of the crew had been pretty banged up.

"Where the hell did they go?" Joe said.

"There," Jack said, pointing at two figures sprawled on the sidewalk beneath a streetlamp.

Meanwhile the bus spoke over their EnviroField radios: "The Central Processing Unit has determined that decompression was mandated as the solution to prevent violence aboard a MATS bus. Violence is not permitted on MATS buses. If you have questions about this action, feel free to email us at MATS@AresNet. In the meantime, please exit the bus. Your fare will not be refunded. Police have been notified of this action."

"Damn right I'll exit your stupid--" Joe said, then yelled: "Jack! Our blasters are out on the sidewalk!" He pointed to Hergs and Carson crawling to the weapons.

Jack bounded out of the bus behind Joe. "Let's get 'em before those jerks do!"

Behind them the bus roared off. "This bus will protect itself by moving to a safe location," it broadcast to their EnviroField frequencies. "Thank you for your consideration."

Getting to his feet, Hergs swung a vicious punch at Joe. "Pissin' militarist!" he grunted as Joe sidestepped, sending the man stumbling to the concrete. Jack felt Carson leaping on his back, tearing at his EnviroField belt. It was easy to flip the lout over his head, but as he swung his opponent through the Martian night Jack saw that Hergs was up again, training one of the blasters on an oblivious Joe.

"Joe!" Jack shouted, changing the course of Carson's arc just enough, as Hergs pulled the trigger--

"Militarist! Damn militarist!" Carson snarled, upside down,

twirling between Hergs and Joe. "We'll sue the fartin' pissin' USSF! We'll--*aioyieeeeee!*"

The blaster's brilliant white beam connected, and Al Carson was sundered into two twitching legs and a flailing upper torso spinning in the thin Martian air. All three pieces plopped sickeningly on the ground amid a shower of blood.

Joe's fist connected with Hergs' bloated purple lips as the strobing orange light of a police spacecopter flooded the scene. Jack plucked the Hergs blaster out of the air as Joe scrambled for the other weapon.

"*Police!*" the spacecopter broadcast as it landed. "*Police!*"

"Where the hell is Hergs?" Joe cried, pointing to where he'd just decked the man.

"He was here just a second ago!" Jack said. "He couldn't have run anywhere!"

"Aw, hell." Joe pointed to several men exiting the spacecopter, then at the pieces of Carson on the sidewalk. "Looks like we've got some explaining to do."

CHAPTER FIVE
General Douglas

Jack slouched in the plastic lounge seat and checked his watch again. 2200 hours. "Man, is that ship ever going to get here?"

"At least *we're* not the late ones," Joe pointed out. "From what I hear the Alien Hunter would flay us if *we* were the ones who were late."

"Thank God Yao was there. Or we'd be in jail now."

"Yeah, but it was really the stupid bus confirming it that got us off."

"I'm sure you're right," Jack said, feeling berserk at the entire day. He was so glad Joe at least seemed balanced.

They'd wasted two hours with the Marsport police, but not as much as they would have if Yao Xing, a Marsport police lieutenant who knew the Commers, hadn't been aboard the spacecopter. He'd believed the Commers' story and unsuccessfully sent men to find Sam Hergs. At police headquarters they'd downloaded the entire exchange aboard the bus, confirming the existence of Hergs and the beginning of the attack. The knives of the punks on the sidewalk, complete with fingerprints, capped the evidence. Unfortunately, General Scott had to be called, and it looked as if there would be no way to keep this incident out of AresNet. And at 2100, already stretched to his limit, Jack had been floored when Scott said that General Douglas's ship had been delayed and that the Commers still ought to be able to pick him up.

This time a USSF jeep came to take Jack and Joe to the spaceport. To their astonishment the driver was John's girlfriend Laurie Lachrer, airman first class. In contrast to their deep fatigue, Laurie was pert, lovely in her light blue hanger technician's uniform, slender and sexy and distracting. Though she was normally involved with ship storage and security, somehow she'd been released for driving duty.

John, it turned out, had already emailed her about the saucer attack. Jack could tell she was shy about questioning Captain

Commer about her boyfriend's well-being, but Joe got her to open up and she in turn had soon pulled every aspect of the attack out of him. Jack had finally changed the subject by asking Laurie her opinion of their messy standdown this afternoon. Now that she was warmed up, Jack heard a few things about the ground crew's view of *Typhoon* landing procedures that made him want to pull out his comm and dictate harsh orders to his entire crew. Yet Jack noted that neither he nor Joe wanted to allude to their fight with the two bums and the death of that Carson character. It was as if they couldn't believe it had happened.

Now Jack and Joe, wiped out, lay in their hard seats while Laurie perched with feminine grace on her chair, hands clasped over a crossed knee, long red ponytail flowing out of her blue USSF technician's cap. Somehow that reassured Jack that the universe was functioning correctly, here, in this quiet spaceport lounge in the deep Martian night, as he spiraled into welcome unconsciousness.

He was jolted by a sharp kick to his ankle. "Dammit, ya bahstads, on ya feet!" came a voice like a stick of dynamite in his ear. Jack tried to make sense of his environment: to his right, Joe scrambling for footing, Airman First Class Lachrer stiffly at attention, right hand glued to her forehead, and in front of Jack--

A middle-aged wolverine with a white handlebar mustache drooping to his chin, his blue-gray USSF uniform, spangled with dozens of medals, stretched tightly across his immense chest.

"Ya bloody bahstads! Don't you salute your superior officer? Or do I have you busted down to privates, eh? Salute, dammit! Don't you Navy goons know how to salute? Or do you just fiddle with yourself in your pants? Look, your damn airman knows how to salute! *She's* not fiddling in her pants! At least I don't think so!"

"Uh, yessir ..." Jack said, struggling to piece it together. Yes, the Australian accent, the attack Doberman Alien Hunter himself, General John J. Douglas. Jack looked over to Laurie, who was doing a superb job of having not a shred of expression on her face.

"Damn!" Joe said, finally making it to his feet. "Man, I was zonked!"

"Salute, dammit! We'll have military discipline here, by God!" Douglas roared.

Jack managed to shuffle upright and throw a salute. He waited a few seconds for Joe to join in, then Douglas snapped off a millisecond return salute, allowing the other three to finally pull their arms down. Jack blearily fixated on the big medal across Douglas's breastbone that said ALTROUDA DEATH SQUAD.

"That's better, ya damn bahstads," Douglas nodded. "Must be you're getting soft here in the Sol system, what with this comfy life you have here, eh?"

"Uh, yessir. Uh, possibly, sir. I hadn't thought of it that way, sir," Jack said. He'd found long ago that it was preferable to roll with this sort of attitude than fight it. After the Alpha dog barked a few times and marked a few corners, he usually settled down to business. Meanwhile Jack could remain secure in the knowledge that he commanded the most powerful spaceship humanity had ever developed.

"It's probably that slothful Navy background of yours," Douglas went on. "You, sir, ought to be a colonel," he said, stabbing Jack's chest. "And you," he jabbed Joe, "ought to be a lieutenant colonel. Your pretty little Air Force accomplice here--" he considered jabbing Laurie's chest but decorously declined-- "would be a private first class. That sounds sane to my way of thinking. Why they didn't merge all the ranks properly I'll never know. Captains in particular mix me up. Why, in the Army, a captain is nothing! Nothing!"

"Uh, yessir," Jack said. "Uh, actually, Airman Lachrer is here to drive you to the hotel. In fact, all of us. We can brief you on the spaceship attack we had earlier today as we drive into town." That was, if he could stay awake.

"Yes, yes, I read the report on your little skirmish," Douglas said as Jack indicated the way out. "Not an AC tactic to come head-on like that, it's not. Took an easy shot and destroyed the evidence in the bargain, eh? I'd say you've wasted some millionaire out on a pleasure cruise, eh?"

Jack looked away. He wasn't going to let this son of a bitch get under his skin. "Well, sir, let's make sure your EnviroField is properly tuned for the Mars environment, shall we?"

"By all means, gentlemen, make sure your superior officer isn't turned into a pile of writhing guts outside, eh? The least you could do, you know."

Stifling a curse, Jack examined the general's EnviroField, and Laurie gave it another look, perhaps suspecting that Jack might not mind if the general had an unfortunate accident outside the airlock. The four made their way through the lock to the curb where the USSF jeep was parked. Here the general sniffed at the chilly night sky and spat: "And you don't even ask me why I was delayed! You don't even ask me why my ship is two hours late!"

"Uh, sorry, sir," Joe said as Jack stared blankly into Douglas's fierce gray eyes. "We just assumed you'd had a delay."

"We were attacked!" Douglas boomed. "A *real* attack, not like your little skirmish with a civilian! A saucer-shaped ship came right up on our tail!"

"What?" Jack cried.

"The *Cloaked Vengeance* couldn't hail it, so I've been told, not that those Air Force bozos would think to tell the Alien Hunter anything!"

"A ship? A saucer-shaped ship? Like the one we fought?" Joe said.

"So the damn thing cruises up on us dropping these teeny little bombs! It would've destroyed us if I hadn't ordered the captain to pay some damn attention! Caught napping, he was! But finally he put the *Vengeance* into these evasive maneuvers that left everyone puking except me."

"Little missiles?" Jack said. "About a foot long, rounded at both ends?"

"That's what the scans showed later." All four got into the jeep, Laurie driving, Douglas in the passenger seat, Jack and Joe in the back. "Now if you'll stop interrupting, gentlemen.

Naturally, I knew they had to be Centaurians infiltrating our system, no doubt out to get *me*. At first I was puzzled by the new ship design. The ACs don't like rounded shapes, but I figured they'd do anything to get me, even build a new design to throw me off balance."

"A saucer!" Joe said. "Just like the one we blew away!"

"But curse it, the *Cloaked Vengeance* is Air Force and the captain wouldn't obey my order to prepare for boarding and hand-to-hand combat! The Army knows hand-to-hand combat now, by God, not like you Air Force and Navy wimps! Anyway, the bahstad captain just keeps going through these pointless evasive maneuvers instead of turning around and attacking! All right, so I did blow my beets once! Everyone did! Most of those twerps were accountants back from auditing HQ, if you must know!"

"Wow, that has to be the same kind of ship that attacked *us*," Jack said.

Laurie had the jeep out on the Upheaval. Douglas raised an eyebrow at Jack's interruption and went on: "Finally the damned thing shot on past us. And the idiot Air Force captain and his idiot Air Force crew lost it on their sensors! Said it was headed straight into the sun if you can believe that! But my theory is that the ACs now have a base on *Mercury*."

"Crap," Jack said. "We can't have that. We can't have ACs in our system."

"Maybe now you boys'll get a taste of *real* combat!"

"So you're saying that was an AC ship?" Joe said.

"Yes, yes, you stupid twits, haven't you been listening at all? What do they teach you at the Academy? Do they teach you how to listen to a normal conversation in English and make sense of it?"

"No, sir, they never had classes in how to understand a bombastic jerk!" Jack cried.

There was a long silence in the jeep as the lights of downtown Marsport came into view.

"What--what Jack means to say," Joe said in a small tortured voice, "is that we ourselves must've fought an AC scout ship this morning, and we're really tired after spending all day in the ship, and that battle, and then there were these two *idiots* on the bus who--"

Douglas cleared his throat. "I say, from the very first, I would've thrown you chaps in irons. For not saluting your superior officer, you know. But then you *are* the Commers. And apparently General Scott's finest pets. But don't think you're going to get away with it. After jailing Senator Johnson for treason at Alpha Centauri, I think I'm ready for the *saviors of the human race,* or whatever AresNet calls you."

"Uh, yessir, I'm sorry, sir," Jack said, brain shorting out. It made no difference to him whether he shouted at Douglas or licked his boots or fell asleep. He was exhausted, physically, emotionally, morally. So what business did he have commanding humanity's most powerful spaceship?

"Anyway, here we were, about to have hand-to-hand combat with *aliens,* my little saviors! So naturally I tried to save the ship, except this blasted stewardess strapped me in my seat, and tightly too! I could hardly breathe! Well, I know she wasn't a stewardess but another one of your blamed airwomen first class! If I could sue the Air Force I would, but dammit, I have to work with those fools! We're all USSF now! I have to work with you Navy types as well! Disgusting! Absolutely disgusting, and that's the end of it!" He folded his arms and glared out the window as Laurie navigated the Upheaval and took the Jupiter Boulevard exit.

"Whatever you say, sir," Jack said, comatose.

"Again, what Jack means to say," Joe said, "is that we're very tired. Not only did we fight a space battle, but there were these two derelicts who tried to kill us on the bus tonight. We wound up killing one of them!"

"Really?" Laurie said, looking back at Joe.

Douglas raised both eyebrows. "Really? Perhaps there's hope for you bahstad gentlemen yet. As long as we have to spend some time together wasting our time looking at your silly Martian ruins, I suppose I could teach you some of the more advanced hand-to-hand combat techniques."

"Oh, I'm sure we'd love that, sir," Jack said amid a tremendous yawn.

"One time there was a spy at USSF HQ at the Military Intelligence Office. In fact, he'd been working for Senator Johnson, passing secrets on to the damn ACs. We all sat down to dinner when he received the order to blow us all away. Pulled out a blaster, the bahstad did. But, with a toothpick, with a bloody *toothpick,* mind you--"

"Yes, sir. Fascinating, sir," Jack said.

"Jack!" Joe hissed, punching him.

"--successfully penetrated directly up his left nostril and into--"

"Yuck!" Airman Laurie put in.

"He expired fairly quickly, but not before barfing copious amounts of foul, half-digested wine directly onto--"

"Right, right, we get the picture," Jack said.

"--and soiling his pants all over the table as well. The entire ballroom was *puking* at the smell! They thought I'd done it just because I was unbalanced or something. They were too stupid to even see his blaster, just the body. Dreadful business, the whole thing was. I eventually got the Crimson Cross for wiping out that cell, of course. But it all just goes to show that, with the ACs, you have to be superhumanly alert at all times." There was a pause as everyone struggled to process this wisdom. "Well, I guess I've been called back at just the right time, then, mates! Looks like I'll be hunting down Centaurians in our home system!"

"Sheesh," Jack said.

"What I don't understand is why Scott wants me to waste my time on aliens who're *already* dead! Imagine me, kicking around some old ruins! But I'll bet Scott's pissing in his drawers now that they've discovered a civilization here. He was so sure there could be no life on Mars!"

As the jeep continued down Jupiter Boulevard, Jack decided that the best thing to do was let Douglas ramble without interruption, as he himself oozed into a twenty-five percent semblance of consciousness.

"Of course, that raises the old jibe that Scott's suppressed any talk of Martian life because all he's wanted to do from the very beginning was colonize the place and wallpaper it with nasty American cities!" Douglas laughed.

"Well, sir," Jack heard Joe put in from far away, "from what I understand, General Scott wants you to put an end to any connections between the weird noises people have been hearing and the archeological dig. I guess it's all about rumor control now."

"Nonsense! I saw the AresNet headlines myself. Bleating about *Martian marauders!* That's just like you soft colonists, to worry about imaginary *Martians* when you should be worrying about Alpha Centaurians! I can't believe people are taken in by these things."

Laurie stopped the jeep. "I could take it around to the lobby airlock, if you want," she said.

"Wait, what is this?" Douglas said, craning his neck.

"The hotel, sir," Laurie said.

"Wait!" the general said. "I don't want this crummy Marsport Hotel!"

"Uh, sir?" Joe said. "We do have a room reserved."

"I want the Space Carpet at the edge of town. Quick, tell your driver to go there."

"Man, the Space Carpet!" Jack mumbled. "The most expensive place in town! Of course the general wants it!"

Another long silence.

"Excuse me, sir," Joe said, leaning forward to General Douglas. "What Jack means is that it's late, it's 2245 hours, and everyone's really exhausted, if you know what I mean, and we'd like to turn in."

"Driver, the Space Carpet! Now! And for your information, my wimpy Navy brothers-in-arms, I am going to the Space Carpet because it's smack dab in the middle of where all these so-called noises have been heard! And the Alien Hunter will place himself at the center of danger! He'll get to the bottom of your mysterious *Martian marauders!* Is that understood, ya bahstads?"

"Five thousand dollars a night," Jack mumbled. "Don't charge it to *my* account."

"In any case I'm going to the Space Carpet. Driver, the Space Carpet Hotel, quick."

Laurie got the jeep rolling again. Jack peered at his watch but couldn't decide what any of the numbers meant, and then he didn't register any more of the journey. He just became one with the feverish tires rolling forever in the night.

CHAPTER SIX
Noises in the Night

General Douglas unloaded his heat blasters, EOS pistols, neural stunners, and combat knives onto the smooth marble bathroom counter and stood back to admire his nude forty-five-year-old body in the floor-to-ceiling mirror. His pectorals bulged with wiry dark hair. His thighs were thick, his ass blunt and hard, his dark groin powerful and rough, male and ready.

He pulled out a pair of thirty-pound barbells from the weight room and went to work in front of the mirror. Overhead, to the side, forearm curls. He'd forgotten how good the new beer breweries on Mars were. Had to work some of those calories off. That amazing steak dinner in the lounge as well. Steak was astonishingly expensive. Only a few cattle had been evacuated to Mars, and the breeding farms, equipped with one-gravity fields to keep the animals in as Earthlike conditions as possible, were only now getting into gear. Oh well, charge it to the USSF along with this fantastic sixty-foot-long suite.

He had to clear his head. Of course it wasn't the beer. He'd only had three glasses. He knew why he was so unsettled. The damned Star Drive. It made anybody crazy. Sure, the Earth-Alpha Centauri journey only took fifteen minutes, but you felt you were under the dentist's drill the entire time. Everyone remarked on it, though most pretended it wasn't too bad. It wasn't considered manly to admit that Star Drive freaked you out.

Well, Douglas was man enough to admit it. He was flat out of sorts from the Star Drive. No matter how many times you did the Drive, it was always the same. You never got used to it. Those fifteen minutes seemed like hours. That little dust up with the mysterious saucer wasn't half as bad as Star Drive.

Of course it was a piddling AC scout ship, no doubt sent from Alpha Centauri to assassinate him. He was the ACs most feared adversary, after all. Douglas wondered if the saucer had somehow latched onto the *Cloaked Vengeance* when it went into Star Drive, because God knew the ACs own version of Star

47

Drive was problematic to say the least. They'd warp a fleet of a hundred kill ships into the middle of a battle, but maybe only forty would get there in one piece. The ACs maintained their tenuous hold on their sprawling seventeen-sun empire by that sort of overkill, happy to train a hundred warriors so that forty might arrive to do the job. The consensus had always been that the ACs were too weak to take Sol.

But they could've sent scouts ahead. The hundreds of fancy automated USSF surveillance craft orbiting out in the Jovian or Saturnian Fragment Fields couldn't possibly detect everything that came through. That would explain the other saucer the Commers had fought this morning. Douglas had jazzed them about it being a civilian ship, because he was damned if the Commers were going to get credit for discovering the first AC scout in the solar system. Of course he'd read their report. After his own attack, as the *Cloaked Vengeance* made its approach to Mars, he'd caught up on his paperwork. The head-on attack was anomalous, but by damn it looked like the same type AC scout that took on the *Vengeance*.

Douglas dropped to the floor, using the barbells as handgrips as he shot himself through sixty pushups. Stood and held the barbells at arm's length for two minutes. Damn, that felt good. His heaving chest was red and hard beneath the hair. His arms ached. Good. He had to be alert, he had to be strong for the fight ahead.

He pressed the intercom for room service.

"Service Desk, how may I help you?" came a sensuous feminine voice.

Douglas glanced at his formidable male self in the mirror. *Honey, you could send yourself up to me,* he thought, imagining that slender red-haired airman first class who'd driven him over here. Then, realizing he couldn't be sure the voice was that of a real woman or another one of those damned clever AI interfaces, he said: "I'd like six bottles of that Red Desert Pilsner I had for dinner sent up immediately to room 1870. It was damned good."

"Very good, sir. For your information, the time is 11:33 PM. At midnight will follow the usual thirty-nine-minute time skip."

It was probably Artificial Intelligence after all, Douglas thought ruefully. She'd sounded as if she'd have been good if she'd been real. The clock on the bathroom counter was no doubt also set up to skip thirty-nine minutes at midnight, to keep Mars time synched to a regular Earth day. Tomorrow he'd download a program into his watch to do the same. Not tonight, though. Tonight was for shaking off that Star Drive, getting his brain unscrambled.

Sure, he was pissed at being recalled for this idiotic *Martian marauder* business. This ruins on Mars crap. He wasn't surprised at the discovery. Of course there were probably ancient Martians. Who cared? Two years in Alpha Centauri had taught him that life was more surprising, tenacious and deadly than anyone could ever have guessed. It was everywhere, in hundreds of different forms. He'd lost count of the number of species the Alpha Centaurians had managed to assemble into one empire.

The door buzzer rang, and Douglas strode across his vast suite, past ten couches, a pool table, a twenty-foot-long oak table covered with flowers, and a wet bar the size of a downtown restaurant. He opened the door without thinking. Fortunately it was a service robot that didn't care in the slightest that Douglas was naked.

"Your Pilsner, sir. Enjoy!" said the robot, and whirred down the empty corridor.

Douglas set five bottles inside the wet bar's refrigerator and opened the sixth, then settled into an adjustable gravity chair and played with the controls for a while. Two gravs … one grav … one-sixth. One-eighteenth was as low as it would go.

He needed this luscious beer. The Star Drive still dug into his nerves. The entire universe was singing in his ears. This immense room, with the baby blue canopy bed on a dais thirty feet away, nevertheless felt as cramped as a coffin. Sixty feet of floor-to-ceiling window displayed an astounding vista of nighttime Marsport. Or was it just a clever brochure pasted on the inside of his coffin lid?

Sure, he was used to strange hotels and barracks, to living on the edge. He was constantly being reassigned in Alpha

Centauri, training new battalions of USSF soldiers in the most efficient ways to hunt down and kill Centaurians. He'd been to all seventeen AC systems, and had known the Star Drive hysteria on every transfer. Yet this Drive had hit him harder than any he could remember. He was keyed up in a way he couldn't fathom.

Was it because he was angry at Scott for ordering him here for this ruins idiocy? He'd been summoned from Proxima Centauri just a few hours ago, where he'd been working on a pleasantly strong margarita, jotting down notes for a series of speeches on alien hunting he was to give over the next few weeks. Scott could wreck his schedule, all his plans, just like that. Within an hour he was on the *Cloaked Vengeance,* then fifteen minutes of shattered nerves later he was back in Sol, helplessly strapped in his seat as that idiot Air Force captain cowardly dodged an AC death ship. And shortly after that, Douglas was enduring the prattle of those wimpy Navy Commer brothers. He knew Commer hadn't properly checked his EnviroField. Only that Laurie creature had saved him.

That Laurie woman … fascinating. Douglas regarded the tall golden bottle of Red Desert Pilsner coldly sweating next to his hairy maleness. Yes, he could picture Laurie kneeling here, right now, right between his knees.

Abruptly he was on his feet, finishing off the Pilsner and yanking a new one out of the big black refrigerator. Ice-cold electricity shot through his body. There was no way he could sleep tonight. Maybe he should review all those reports about the ruins. But hell, he'd read them once already. Nothing new. Ruins, so what? He'd seen ruins of dozens of empires in Alpha Centauri.

This noise business, ditto. These soft Martian colonists were on edge. Have a noise complaint? Hell, call the damn cops.

Half the second beer poured down his throat, Douglas turned to the expanse of downtown Marsport and shuddered. Without knowing why, he spoke: "Kill all lights," and the room plunged into darkness. The skyline glowed with fresh intensity. A voice came into his head:

This is eternity.

Douglas shook off the new shiver, then rapped out a defiant laugh. Look at him, as spooked as these soft colonists with their fancy super-modern city and their service robots and their easy lives. So the fools thought there were Martians prowling around their houses. But here he was hearing voices himself.

He had to prep for the morning. He needed sleep. If he finished this second beer it might calm him down. He had to take charge of the Kilpatrick dig, otherwise he'd be in an endless tussle between the civilian archeologists and General Scott. Get in there, take charge. Issue a definitive report within a week. Calm all these fools down, take a ship back to Alpha Centauri, get back into the war and get some *real* work done.

Unless they assigned him here. It was possible. If the colonists felt there were ACs close to home, they'd go berserk. They'd want the best. They'd want the Alien Hunter. But then Douglas would have to compete with those damned saviors of the human race, the Commers.

Jack Commer was a wimp, unfit for command. He was supposed to be a war hero, but all he'd had to do was push a button. Sheesh. Let him come out and fight the Zarj in AC.

Yet Commer had potential. At least Jack if not his brothers. Anyone could see that. The way Commer had sassed Douglas tonight and somehow gotten away with it. That showed a high level of personal power. Was Douglas losing his touch? Or was it that Jack Commer was somehow fated for great things? If so, maybe the best thing to do would be to have Jack attached to the Alien Hunter. Yeah, defuse the situation, control the bastard from the beginning.

Douglas could train him. Commer had that ship that could do 1/13th light speed. And its sister, the *Typhoon II,* had Star Drive. It was supposed to be ready soon. It had been designed for the AC war but Douglas might need it here. He'd command it, Commer would be his first officer, they'd cleanse Sol of ACs first, then return to Alpha Centauri. Return to AC and everything Douglas had left behind.

Coerjen. Douglas smiled, and took his naked male body to

the bed, pushed the covers down, and lay with his masculinity pointing to the gentle canopy above. When would he see his mistress again? When would he grasp those delightful breasts? Coerjen Wilder. Admiral Wilder's wife. The best woman he'd ever had. And what a last name, even if she did take it from old Jeremy. She was *deliciously* wild. Just last night was the first time they'd been able to get away for long hours of love. The dozen encounters before had, of necessity, been furtive and hasty. They made it twice last night. The second time, after the most sensuous soapy fondling shower he'd ever had, Coerjen had climbed onto him and writhed in ecstasy for half an hour.

Now, in the hotel darkness, he finally was able to close his eyes, to feel Coerjen atop him, rubbing across him, reaching down to take him in hand.

"*Quar zee X domic glos.*"

"What? What?" the general cried, eyes flung open to the dark shape straddling him. "My God! Coerjen, you scared me!"

"*Merk sno zee don gabs X,*" said--

The *thing*. In the eternity light of downtown Marsport shining into his vast coffin, Douglas saw the *creature* squatting on his crotch. Grasping Douglas's member in one hand and a long silver knife in the other.

The creature had a fish head. A long fin down its back.

Old reactions set in. Douglas yanked free of the fish man's intimate clasp, swiped the Electron Oblivion Sequencer pistol from the bedstand and turned back to--

The *alien*. The fish man regarded him with unblinking eyes two inches wide. Douglas felt the thing's *thoughts*. The alien knocked the EOS pistol out of his hand with a *thought*.

CHAPTER SEVEN
At the Carpet, or, Is This the General?
Friday, June 9, 2034, 0200 hours

"I'll need you boys for some identification," Lieutenant Yao Xing said, motioning Harri McNarri and Mickey Michaels over. Harri shook his head at the idea of the slender young Chinese police lieutenant calling any of the *Typhoon* crew "boys." But he picked his way across the glass shards, the smashed furniture, the scattered kitchen utensils and torn linen, towards three bodies beneath sheets.

"We'll need to get Jack or Joe," Harri said, pointing to the two older Commer brothers craning at the hole far up the side of the Space Carpet Hotel. "They were the only ones who actually met the general. I suppose I'd recognize him from a photo, but--"

"Perhaps not after decompression," Yao finished for the *Typhoon I* ship doctor, who'd seen enough decompression deaths to last a lifetime. "Jack? Joe? I need you over here to ID the body."

Jack and Joe nodded and came past a battered PhoboStar limousine with a pool table upside down across its hood. Searchlights played up and down the sides of the Space Carpet and the other buildings in the area. Dozens of Marsport police walked the grounds. Red and blue lights strobed relentlessly from the tops of police jeeps.

"Hello again, Lieutenant Yao," Jack said, extending a handshake.

"Maybe you shouldn't be shaking my hand," Yao said ruefully. "You guys seem to be at the center of a lot of trouble tonight."

"Those guys on the bus attacked *us*," Jack said absently, focusing on the red-stained sheet across the largest body. "And this--I had no idea. I guess Joe and I should've stayed with him, made sure he was okay here instead of going back to the Marsport and crashing."

"It's not your fault," McNarri said. "You couldn't have known."

"Why did he *insist* on staying here?"

"If it's any consolation, the attack came long after you'd dropped him off," Yao said. "We think somewhere around the midnight skip."

Jack shook his head. "Well, I'm awake now, at least." Although he maintained he was fully alert after a couple hours sleep, Jack looked a hundred years old to Harri. Joe only seemed seventy-five. The rest of the *Typhoon* crew appeared to have gotten enough rest after the ordeal yesterday. But now this on top of it.

"Anyway," Yao went on, pulling back the sheet on the largest body. "Is this the general?"

"God … yes," Jack said. "That's him."

"Yeah …" Joe added.

The other *Typhoon* crewmen came up to view the body. A hundred yards past them, at the edge of the parking lot, a police force field glowed bright blue. Dozens of Marsport citizens behind it strained to see what was going on. Harri turned back to the body of General John J. Douglas with professional interest. The blood had dried to a crimson crust in the virtually nonexistent Martian atmosphere, but Harri could tell that a lot of it had come out of the general before decompression had blasted his features into spoiled meat. Further down, on the naked torso, were numerous stab wounds.

"Under this second sheet," Yao went on, "is the body of one of the *things* the general killed." He whipped back the sheet.

The men gaped. Before them lay a small pinkish creature, its head curved back into a long fin running down its translucent white back. The entire body was no more than four feet in length. Not that the resemblance was exact, but Harri was reminded of human fetuses in the early stages of development. He mutely pointed to what appeared to be a missing eyeball in one of the two eye sockets.

Yao nodded. "Douglas apparently gouged one of the eyes out. We haven't found it yet."

"Sheesh," Ken Garrison put in for all of them from behind Harri.

There was no apparent sign of clothing on the alien. The body was humanoid, but Harri had a hard time deciding if there were genitalia between the legs, and if so, whether it was male or female.

"What *is* this thing?" Joe said, staring.

Yao shrugged. "Some of the civilians over there who first saw it in the parking lot have been calling it a Martian."

Harri scanned the growing crowd behind the force field. "So they've seen it," he said, letting the implications sink in for all the men. The noises in the night, the unease throughout the city ...

"When a hotel room decompresses and everything gets blown all over the parking lot, we don't really have much control over who sees what," Yao said.

"You guys don't really believe this is a Martian, do you?" Joe said.

"For want of a better term. You do realize that all police have to memorize the *United System Classification for Alpha Centaurian Species?* Just in case we do get jumped by an AC invasion?"

"Well, it doesn't look like any AC species I've ever seen a picture of," Harri said. "We have to memorize the damn thing too, you know."

"But we can't rule this thing out," Joe said. "And that first edition's out of date already. They say they're revising it in light of all the new species we've been running across."

"Well, we won't know until we do DNA tests," Jack said.

"We've done a preliminary DNA sampling," Yao said. "On the spot and sloppy, but it also confirms this isn't an AC species. At least, any that we've ever gotten a sample of."

"Well," Harri drawled, "I'm sure this is something that pathologists and exobiologists and politicians and AresNet pundits are gonna be debating for a long time."

"If there really is an AC invasion underway," Jack said. He took a deep breath. "What about that third body?"

"Not so interesting after the other one." Yao pulled its sheet back. At first Harri thought he was looking at a cow carcass.

Then he saw it was a creature identical to the first one but missing a head. And drenched apparently in dried blue-purple blood.

"We haven't found that yet, either," Yao said, pointing to the stump between the frail shoulders. "God knows where all the evidence has been blown to from eighteen stories up. But it was obviously cut off by a knife."

"In about three or four quick motions," Harri said, kneeling. "I'd say Douglas at least avenged himself." He looked back to the *Typhoon* crew. None of them had been able to stay away when Jack had gotten the call from General Scott. Jack, bleary from a couple hours sleep, had neither ordered them along nor forbidden them to come. All were unable to take their eyes off the three bodies. Harri pointed to the general. "He put up quite a fight."

"He definitely killed one of them outright," Yao said. "As for the other, with the missing eye, we can't know if that was fatal. The fight apparently went on for a long time, maybe ten minutes. The entire place upstairs is bloody, with both kinds of blood. Can't tell much from what little is left in the room, after the decompression. Maybe the general was trying to finish off the second alien with his EOS pistol. There are several EOS scars on the walls, then …"

"Then he blew out a few dozen feet of window," Harri finished.

"Whether or purpose or by accident we'll never know," Yao said. "We can possibly conclude there were only two aliens involved in the attack, unless we find other bodies out here."

Harri surveyed the parking lot covered with the smashed miscellany of a luxurious hotel room. He wondered how that heavy pool table had been blown out, then saw it had wheels. A sudden hurricane force might've rolled it nicely. Douglas must have realized that firing an EOS gun in a pressurized civilian hotel room was bound to lead to disaster. On USSF ships the hull interiors had coating that absorbed such rays, just in case.

"Did the other rooms hold?" Harri asked.

Yao nodded. "Yes. No further casualties up there. Luckily

nobody was in the hallways at the time."

"Well, that's good. If they didn't have failsafes the entire hotel could've been at risk." Harri bent down to the two aliens again. "But this is interesting." He pointed to the alien missing an eye.

"What's interesting?" Jack said.

"Well, neither of these alien bodies seems to exhibit any damage due to decompression. Harder to tell with this headless one, but I think it holds in both cases. It seems to me that if Mr. Eyeless here wasn't killed by the eye gouge, it was the fall from eighteen stories in .38G that did him in."

"So?" Joe said.

"So these creatures must be adapted to the naked Martian environment. I see no sign of spacesuits or anything that would pass for an EnviroField on them."

"Hmm …" Jack said, as everyone thought that over.

"Then again, they were also in Douglas's room when it was fully pressurized. Can they somehow handle *both* extremes? I wonder if it's possible they have some sort of internal EnviroField to enable them to survive in various kinds of atmospheres and densities."

"Well, that's all right for speculation now, but the first thing is to get these bodies back to the Exobiology Lab for analysis. And, of course, to properly take care of General Douglas's body." Jack cocked his head at something beyond the sheeted forms. "Wait a sec." He moved to a broken coffee table and pulled out what looked to Harri like a man's belt. There was something small and black attached to it.

"It's like a holster," Joe said.

"And there's a gun of some sort," Jack said, withdrawing a small silver weapon with a bright blue ring around the end of what appeared to be a gun barrel, and odd hieroglyph-like symbols on a rubbery purple handgrip.

"Whoa!" Yao said. "I can't believe we missed that!"

"Is it a weapon?" Jack wondered. "Or some plastic toy?"

"Look!" John broke in. "The belt would just fit around that Martian!" Without asking he pulled the holster and belt out of

Jack's hands and draped it around the one-eyed Martian's waist.

"John, we don't know it's a Martian," Joe began, but everyone stared at the perfect fit the belt made on the alien.

"And that gun looks like it would fit in one of those small hands," Harri said.

"No, you're jumping to conclusions," Joe said. "That could easily be their version of the EnviroFields you were talking about."

"But it looks like a gun!" John maintained. "And if it quacks like a gun--" He paused as even Lieutenant Yao laughed with the others. "I mean--"

"There's no trigger," Jack said, standing and sighting along the barrel at a small pine tree forty feet away shimmering within its EnviroField. "Joe may be right. It must just look like a gun, and we're all assuming--"

A blue-purple ray shot from the barrel and an eerie whine overwhelmed the men's EnviroField comms. Harri felt his mouth drop as the ray enveloped the pine's EnviroField, which glittered bright pink for a moment, then cut off.

And the tree itself shattered like a giant collapsing chandelier, the men's comms amplifying that smashing out of the thin Martian air.

"My God!" Joe gasped, pointing. "That--that--"

"It *is* a gun!" John cried. "I told you so!"

"It doesn't have a trigger!" Jack said. "You squeeze the entire handle! Damn, that's a dangerous design. You can set it off without really intending to."

"Possibly it's not so dangerous for the small Martian hand," Harri pointed out.

"We can't know it's Martian!" Joe repeated. "Don't you start in on that, Harri!"

"Oops," Harri said. "But I guess I'd rather it be a Martian than an Alpha Centaurian, wouldn't you?"

"It doesn't matter what we *want*," Jack said. "All that matters is what *is*. And we have to remember that these Martians or whatever they are have murdered General Douglas, so we ought to assume they're every bit the enemy the ACs are."

Harri pondered that. What if it were true? What if there were native Martians, somehow, impossibly, overlooked after two years of human exploration on Mars? What about those noises people had been hearing at night? What about those ruins in the Kilpatrick Desert? What if these Martians decided they'd had enough of an alien race despoiling their planet? Harri couldn't think. All he could do was follow Jack who was walking over to finger the remnants of the pine tree. Soon all the men were doing so, their EnviroFields permitting them to touch objects and get a decent feel of them. The fragments felt exactly like bits of glass to Harri. As he knelt, his EnviroField comm picked up scattered transmissions from civilians murmuring about what had happened to the tree. "Now the hotel can send you a bill for that pine *and* its EnviroField," he said, trying to push away his unease. "You know how expensive they both are."

"Huh," Jack said, barely acknowledging Harri's lame humor, transfixed by the gun in his hand. He carefully replaced it in the holster and stood up. "I shouldn't be taking any chances just holding it."

"That would certainly be a powerful weapon if we could duplicate it," Joe said.

"I don't know," the third Commer brother, Jim, put in. "We've had so much trouble reverse-engineering alien technology in Alpha Centauri. Still, I'll bet the Alien Tech Team would love to give it a try."

"But I wonder if the basic principle isn't similar to our EOS tech."

"That would be great, to get it instantaneous, like with that tree!" John said.

The sluggishness of Electron Oblivion Sequencing technology had galled the USSF for some time. The guns collapsed the electron cloud around any atom their rays encountered, wiping the chosen object out of existence. However, since its ray took anywhere from two to five seconds to take effect, the EOS gun was not a natural for personal combat. Too many Alpha Centaurian soldiers with heat blasters had killed too many USSF men with EOS rifles, and it didn't matter if a few seconds after the men were roasted, the ACs ceased to exist. Harri had tinkered with some of the pistols aboard the *Typhoon,* trying to reduce their effective time, to no avail. While EOS technology greatly augmented standard battle tactics, it wasn't what it could be. In fact, its only real success lay in how it had turned the criminal justice system on its head by entirely eliminating the *corpus delicti.* EOS technology was forbidden to civilians, but of course criminals eagerly sought it.

Yao eyed Jack holding the alien gun and said: "You're not thinking of removing that evidence from a crime scene, are you?"

"Yes, in fact, I need to," Jack said, wrapping the holster belt around his left forearm. "The USSF needs to see this gun as soon as possible, and I'd say it's too dangerous to leave in civilian hands."

Harri watched Yao briefly struggle with the concept that he was actually a civilian. Usually the police referred to citizens as civilians, as some sort of pets the fraternity of police were required to protect. Then along came a military officer who reminded him that, to the military, police were also mere civilians.

Yao shook his head with a small grin. "I suppose you'd remind me next that the USSF Code demands custody of all alien weapons."

Jack grinned back. "I knew I wouldn't have to go that far. And you helped me and Joe out of a jam earlier tonight."

"Well, then take it. And I'll be glad it's not me who accidentally shatters police headquarters."

CHAPTER EIGHT
Shattergun Terrorists

"This better not be the same smartass bus that blew us out earlier," Joe said as the eight *Typhoon I* crewmembers boarded the MATS bus in front of the Space Carpet.

"Hope not," Jack said as the men took their seats. To the bus, he spoke: "Eight of us, for the United System Building."

Harri had only gotten fragmentary details about the two punks who'd assaulted Jack and Joe earlier tonight while the rest of the crew was sacked out. Apparently one of them had almost singed Joe with a heat blaster. There hadn't been any time on the ride over to the Space Carpet to ask more, and everyone's mind was on General Douglas anyway. But, slipping into his ship's physician role, Harri found himself watching Jack and Joe. They hadn't had much sleep, and though the entire crew had experienced a major ordeal over the last twenty-four hours, Jack and Joe had fared far worse.

"Thank you, Captain Jack Commer," said the bus. "Eight fares have been charged to USSF account 3394514." A number of civilians saw the USSF men and whispered. Others pointed at the scene of confusion around the Space Carpet, and the blue force field keeping citizens out.

"Why are we riding the bus anyway?" John complained. "You'd think they'd've sent a jeep for us."

"This was faster all around," Jack said. "I can't believe we sneaked onto the bus without--"

"Without people hassling us about those *Martian marauders!*" John cried.

"Shhh, keep it down," Joe said.

"Martian marauders?" said some lady down the aisle. "Is that what happened?"

"Shhh!" Jack said again, then, seeing he was shushing a civilian, added: "Sorry, ma'am."

After the bus fully pressurized, a voice came from the speakers along the ceiling of the MATS bus. "Now for the *Three AM News!*"

"Oh no ..." Harri muttered.

"THIS IS ARESNET! This just in! VIOLENCE IN MARSPORT! COMMERS INVOLVED IN DEATH ON BUS! GENERAL DOUGLAS KILLED! Good morning! A few minutes ago police were called to the Space Carpet Hotel where two Martians have killed General John J. Douglas, the Alien Hunter specifically brought in from Alpha Centauri to deal with the MARTIAN MARAUDERS once and for all! Police report that two Martians infiltrated Douglas's hotel room, where he apparently killed one before DECOMPRESSING HIS ROOM WITH A PISTOL SHOT, killing himself as well as his second attacker! Douglas, back from Alpha Centauri, had been scheduled to investigate the KILPATRICK DESERT RUINS, scene of an ANCIENT MARTIAN CULTURE now out for BLOODY REVENGE AGAINST HUMANITY for invading their SACRED PLANET! Meanwhile, Jack and Joe Commer, the men who ended the Final War, were taken to Marsport Police Headquarters earlier this evening to be questioned in their role in the BLASTER DEATH of a Marsport citizen, Al Carson, 38, aboard a Marsport Automated Transport System bus! According to the bus: 'I was at the corner of Saturn and Ceres when four humans began initiating violence inside me. I had no choice but to depressurize and expel the violence. While I didn't actually witness Al Carson's death, I can say that Jack and Joe Commer did definitely brandish heat blasters while aboard me.'"

"Oh, jeez, listen to this," Joe complained. "The damn bus knows those jerks pulled knives first! And everyone keeps harping on this *Martian marauders* crap."

"Yeah!" John said. "That bus is *slandering* us!"

"WHAT'S THE CONNECTION?" AresNet asked. "Why did police release TWO MURDERERS? And why did they let them in turn investigate General Douglas's murder? What do they know of the MARTIANS MARAUDERS, and why are they covering it up?"

"I guess we should've known this would get out, once those civilians saw those Martian bodies!" John said.

"What? What bodies?" someone cried.

"Shhh!" Jack said. "*Damn*, John."

"It's the Commers!" somebody else shouted.

"What's going on? What about these *Martian marauders?*"

"Is the USSF going to do anything about it? Or is it gonna just let us all die like it always does?"

"What?" Joe shouted back. "We saved your stupid asses last year, you damn twits! We evacuated your worthless butts over here, and now you whine and complain!"

"Joe! Joe!" Jack cried.

"*You destroyed the earth is what you did!*" someone shouted.

"Screw you! Screw you!" Joe screamed, red-faced, storming out of his seat. Harri, across the aisle, tried to pull him back down.

"Watch out! They're trained killers!" someone shouted.

"You're goddamned right we are!" Joe snarled, hand moving to his blaster. "And if you think we're gonna take--"

"Joe, stop! These are *civilians!*" Harri grunted, wrestling with him as the bus jostled them in a wide left turn north onto Collins Boulevard.

"Then they can damn well stop insulting us!" Joe shouted, shaking a finger.

"Oh, God, look! *Martians!*" someone cried, pointing out the window.

"Oh, just crap on this *Martians* crap! I'm so sick of this!"

"No, there's something out there!"

Harri became aware of a purple strobe effect to his left. He turned to what appeared to be floodlights trained on the Armstrong Civic Center.

"Look!" Joe said, relaxing in Harri's grasp. "Someone's--"

"Someone's trying to laser the Armstrong Center!" Jack yelled, leaping from his seat. "Stop! Stop the bus!"

Harri stared. A small pink creature with a fin down its back trained a blue-purple ray on the sides of the Armstrong Center. Pieces of the building flew off.

"It's--it's a Martian!" cried Joe. "I mean, it's--whatever it is!"

"And behind him, it's that Hergs guy!" Jack said, pointing to a swarthy human in an ugly plaid coat hosing down the sides of the Armstrong Center with deadly gushes of blue-purple. "Stop the bus! USSF Command Override!"

The bus continued to cruise down Collins. Jack pounded on the door. Still the bus didn't stop. Jack turned to the CPU beneath the windshield and proceeded to wrench loose a large gray box.

"C'mon, Jack," Harri said, "you don't need to--"

"Yeeeooowww!" Jack cried, letting go. "Goddammit, the damn thing shocked me!"

"An electric shock was used to protect the CPU aboard this MATS bus," the bus said. "Violence is not permitted aboard MATS buses."

"Stop! They'll breach the Center walls and decompress the whole Civic Center!" Joe said. "Stop the bus, you stupid bus!"

"Obey USSF Command Override! Delta Sigma Theta Twelve!" Jack shouted.

"As persons of suspicion in a recent incident involving a MATS bus and the death of a Marsport citizen, Jack and Joe Commer are not authorized to stop a MATS bus," said the bus. "Furthermore, this MATS bus will detain the suspects in light of their attempt to tamper with the CPU."

"Forget it!" Jack snarled, yanking the strange ray gun out of the holster along his left forearm and squeezing off a blue-purple ray of his own.

"Damn, Jack!" Harri said as bright blue sparks shot from the CPU. Bits of metal flew off, but the thing didn't shatter as the tree had.

"*This bus will ... this bus will ... this bus will ...*" said the bus, still rolling along at thirty miles per hour.

"Damn, I wonder if the shock wrecked this pistol," Jack said, staring down the barrel of the ray gun. "It didn't *shatter* the CPU."

"Careful!" Harri shouted. "You shouldn't be firing an alien weapon in here!"

"*Bus ... bus ... bus ...*" said the bus.

"It's still not stopping!" John cried. "That Martian's getting away!"

"No, it's not!" Joe said, stepping forward with his heat blaster and firing a single ray that detonated the entire front of the bus in a satisfying sizzle of shattered AI brain wafers and roiling wires. Then he whirled and blasted out the doors of the bus. As air exploded out and the vehicle lost power, the eight men of the *Typhoon I* were flung onto the street followed by EnviroField-radioed shouts of:

"Those damn militarists!"

"Who do they think they are?"

Harri had a brief moment of worrying, as a surgeon, about the crunch the bus made careening into the statute of Neil Armstrong in front of the Civic Center. But the bus wasn't moving that fast, he reasoned, surely none of the passengers was seriously hurt, and up ahead, after all, there was a live Martian ray-gunning the Armstrong Center.

"They're using this same sort of gun on the building!" Jack said, charging the Armstrong Center with the alien gun raised.

"They've got Martian guns just like yours!" John cried, running.

"It's not a Martian! It's not a Martian!" Joe shouted.

"But they're not *shattering* the building," Jack grunted. "They're just crumbling it, like I was doing with the bus."

"Maybe they have more than one setting," Harri said. "Look! They've seen us!" He pointed to the man and the alien disappearing around the corner of the building. Harri was astonished that the little alien ran as fast and competently as the man. A couple seconds later the *Typhoon* men rounded the corner to see the two terrorists a hundred feet ahead, almost down to an alley behind the Center.

"They're getting away!" Ken Garrison shouted, pulling out his heat blaster.

"No! We'll capture that alien alive!" Jack yelled, raising the alien gun. "If this thing really is on a lesser setting now--"

He fired a purple ray. It connected, and the alien burst into a billion pieces of glass on the sidewalk.

"Oh my God!"

"No time to worry about it! Get that Hergs guy!" Joe cried, pointing to the man who'd ducked the ray and now spun to face his pursuers.

"No! We'll take *him* alive!" Jack shouted. "Hergs! If that's really your name! Lay down your weapon!"

The man in the ugly plaid coat and dark blue gym pants sneered, twisting a dial on his wristwatch.

And he disappeared.

"No!" Joe moaned. "He can't *do* that!"

"What did he do?" Craig Reynolds said. "What did he do?"

"I don't know! I don't know!" Jack said. "He *teleported!* Or something! That's not possible!"

"It happened!" Harri said, appalled. "We all saw it! He just *disappeared!*"

"My God! If he can do that--who *is* this guy? And he knows the aliens! They were wrecking this building!"

"He can teleport?" Joe said. "Is that possible?"

"He twisted a dial and disappeared!" John said. "We saw him twist a dial!"

"So it's technology of some sort," Harri said, struggling to order his thoughts. "I know our tech guys have been working on the possibility of teleporting objects. Like, there's Chamber's Theory of Force Field Inversions."

"No way, Chamber's Theory wouldn't apply," Joe said. "Ah, well, who cares?"

"The point is," Jack said, taking a deep breath and walking to the shattered remains of the alien, "this Hergs guy has this technology, he attacked us tonight, he knows the aliens, the same aliens that murdered General Douglas, and here he's trying to destroy the Armstrong Center."

"Didn't do a good job," Joe remarked as they stared at the scarred sides of the Civic Center. "Their blasters were just crumbling the surface, like you said. They never penetrated or decompressed the place."

Jack knelt by the remains of the alien and fingered the piles of tiny glass bits. Harri was reminded of a shattered windshield on an old-style automobile.

"Maybe the gun just works on organic materials," Jack said, aiming a test burst at a light pole fifteen feet away. The purple ray sang out as fiercely as before, but just seemed to bubble on the surface of the black metal. "Maybe only organic beings … *shatter*." He shuddered.

"It really is a shattergun, then!" John laughed. "A Martian shattergun!"

This time nobody contradicted John. Jack reached through the mounds of glass and pulled out the dead Martian's shattergun.

Harri scooped up a couple handfuls of shattered alien and filled a pocket. "Yao has more to analyze with those dead aliens back at the hotel. But this stuff might tell us something too."

The men stood on the sidewalk outside the Armstrong Center. Jack stared vacantly back and forth between the alien remnants and the place where Hergs had vanished. Harri regarded Jack nervously. Could their captain actually snap? He'd seen too much today. They all had. Then, to Harri's relief, Jack pulled out his USSF Comm and spoke: "Scott." He motioned to the men to tune their comms to his.

"Yes, Jack, bring me up to date," General Scott said over their comms. "Yao briefed me on your visit to the hotel and that strange gun you found."

"We have the gun here, sir," Jack said. "We're at the Armstrong Center and we just killed another Martian that was trying to decompress the place with another one of these ray guns. We have that gun as well."

"*Alien*," Joe hissed. "Not Martian."

Jack shrugged. "The alien was accompanied by the Sam Hergs guy who attacked me and Joe earlier. Hergs has some form of teleportation capability, sir. We all saw him vanish into thin air."

"Video of this?" Scott barked.

"Uh, no, sir. Sorry, in all the excitement, I forgot to set my comm video."

"Huh. And now I hear there's a second bus that has a

complaint on you. Said you were trying to destroy its CPU. Then MATS lost contact with it."

"Uh, yessir," Jack said. "Actually, the bus was preventing us from apprehending Hergs."

Of all people to start laughing, serious, straightforward Jim Commer was doubling up. Jack glared at him.

"Enough," Scott said. "Get some sleep, boys. The Kilpatrick mission is still on for 0800 tomorrow."

"What?" several men protested.

"C'mon," Jack said. "Let the general tell us."

"Gentlemen, in light of Douglas's death I've gotten another officer to replace him, Major John West of the Third Space Combat Group. We've called him back from Alpha Centauri just now. You may note he's done much of the combat training for the *Typhoon II* crew. And I'm also pulling in the crew from the *Typhoon II* project because I want them to start in on these kinds of special ops from now on."

Harri watched Jack nod reluctantly. The *Typhoon II* was a further refinement of the *Typhoon* series. Its crew had seen some months of combat in Alpha Centauri in training for the day when the faster-than-light *Typhoon II* could be inserted into the war and hopefully end it as decisively as *Typhoon I* had ended the Final War on Earth. Harri knew that Jack had mixed feelings about his *Typhoon* being superseded by a more powerful ship, even though he'd helped develop the *Typhoon* series from the beginning.

"Therefore," Scott continued, "you will proceed to the Kilpatrick Desert tomorrow with twenty men as follows: your eight-man crew, the four men of *Typhoon II,* and Major West and seven of his top commandoes."

"Uh, yessir," Jack said.

"I'm taking no chances at this point. It seems pretty obvious that someone or something wants to stop the Kilpatrick Desert mission. So I'm beefing it up because God knows what we might find there tomorrow in light of today's events. Although you of course outrank him, Jack, Major West will be in command. This will be a purely military mission. However, if anyone winds up speaking to reporters about the archeological aspects of this thing, it will be you, Jack."

"Well, yessir," Jack said. "But …"

"Your ship's physician/engineer studied archeology at the university. I'm sure you can rely on him."

"How'd he know that?" Harri whispered.

There was a long silence from the other end.

"Um …" Harri said. "I'm sure we can say things like *utterly fascinating discoveries,* necessitating additional research from the diverse community of scholars, etc., etc."

"Yes, I'm entirely sure that will soothe the troubled populace. Now out. Get some sleep, boys. We'll get to the bottom of these *Martian marauders.*" Scott cut off.

"No! He can't believe it too! Can he?" Joe said.

By way of answer Jack said: "Let's get walking. I'm not going to chance another bus now. We'll take Collins up to Neptune and cross over. And let's avoid that bus we crashed in the plaza. I'm not going to stand around and offer any apologies. We'll let Yao handle that one too if he cares to."

It took a while for the men to break free of the pile of broken glass. Harri's legs ached from all the standing around and running, even in one-third gravity. How must Jack and Joe be feeling on practically no sleep? Nobody spoke as they drifted down Collins towards downtown. Harri kept adjusting his EnviroField, but he knew it would never keep up with the deep cold of the Martian night. None of the men would question Jack's decision to walk, but Harri knew they all longed for the warmth of a bus and a chance to get off their feet.

They'd had it. They'd seen too much and their minds had shorted out, all except for the primeval part which had a hand hovering above a blaster holster and eyes flicking to every shadowy recess in every building.

What else was out here tonight? What other creatures? What other murders?

Harri tried to calm himself by focusing, as ship's surgeon, on the emotional state of the men. Was there anything going on in their minds that could endanger the crew? But he knew he wasn't really evaluating anything. He couldn't even assess his own mental state. What had he himself seen tonight? Had he perceived it properly?

Douglas is spoiled meat!

The Martians have fins! They look like human embryos!

Organic beings shatter!

Hergs twisted a dial and disappeared!

They all kept moving, on combat patrol, towards the tall black Marsport Hotel that promised a couple hours of edgy sleep before they had to face fresh insanity in the desert tomorrow. Then a new thought wedged into Harri's mind and he shivered. He didn't know where it came from and he was too exhausted to care.

This is not your planet anymore.

CHAPTER NINE
The Search
Friday, June 9, 2034, 1000 hours

Four desert rovers churned across the dunes. Major Phil Sperry was exhilarated at the speed, the wild bumps, the veers to avoid rocks. Klave, their driver in Rover 3, was one of Major West's commandos, a big blond muscled fellow, placid and competent, with three kinds of guns on his belt--heat blaster, EOS pistol, machine pistol--as well as a nasty-looking combat knife and six hand grenades. Phil had never met Klave before, but like West and the rest of his commandoes sent from Alpha Centauri for this mission, Klave was a fellow combat veteran and Phil knew he could trust him with his life.

It would be great to feel wind on his face as the jeeps shot across the landscape, but the suit's facial force field prevented that. Like all the men, Phil wore a full Mars suit designed for the desert. Its helmet had a visor that would pop down to seal and pressurize the head in case of trouble, but all twenty men trusted the force field.

Of course, since the Martian atmosphere was 1/100th that of Earth's, Phil doubted he would have felt anything anyway, even at the sixty miles per hour the rovers made over the dunes.

Riding Phil's rover in addition to the driver Klave were Phil's *Typhoon II* crewmates Patrick James and Lee Borman, plus Mickey Michaels from *Typhoon I*. Michaels had already filled them in on the mystery ship's attack on the *Typhoon I* yesterday, and the grisly scene at the Space Carpet hotel last night. *Martians*. Phil wasn't sure how to feel. He'd fought too many different AC species in Alpha Centauri to catalog them. One more species didn't mean much to him, except that this one was on humanity's new homeworld, and not very friendly. At any rate, as a physician he was eager for a chance to examine the bodies.

The fourth member of the *Typhoon II* crew, Will Connors, had talked Major West into letting him drive Rover 2. Connors, the *Typhoon II* navigation officer, had flown single-man fighter

71

aircraft in Alpha Centauri and was certainly qualified to handle a Martian desert rover. Riding with Connors were Jack and Joe Commer, *Typhoon I* turret gunner Craig Reynolds, and Harri McNarri, Phil's physician/engineer counterpart on *Typhoon I*.

Major West and *Typhoon I* crew Jim Commer, John Commer, and Ken Garrison cruised alongside in Rover 1, another stolid commando piloting that jeep. Right behind them came Rover 4 with five more thoroughly-armed commandoes.

All four rovers had been airlifted on a USSF transport and set down a few miles from the archeological site. It turned out there was a United System regulation about spaceships keeping a sensitive distance from archeological finds, and even though Scott's first exasperated curses concerned the fact that a transport craft was *not* a spaceship, he finally decided to make the most of it and have the four rovers charge into the civilian archeological site at top speed, their giant mounted EOS cannons unwrapped and ready for action.

They were within twenty miles of the spot where Scott and his friend Kilpatrick had crashed after the *Triumph* disaster two years ago, and Phil wondered how much it galled Scott that the Martian ruins lay so close to the Kilpatrick Monument.

Phil noted Michaels' anxious face and couldn't help but pity the *Typhoon I* turret gunner. The *Typhoon I* boys had finally experienced some real combat yesterday. Sure, all eight had gotten medals for their role in ending the Final War, but that wasn't really combat, was it? Now they'd seen their first taste of true danger and were absorbing the implications. Dropping bombs from spaceships wasn't all there was to war. Sometimes it was your turn to hunker down and absorb what the enemy felt like dishing out. Maybe now the Commers and their buddies would understand what the *Typhoon II* crew had been through.

Phil had completed three months of combat in Alpha Centauri in April. During the time the four *Typhoon II* members had been rotated off to combat duty, various tests and modifications had been made to the *Typhoon II*. When Phil returned to Mars two months ago as ship's physician/engineer, the project was back up to speed. Final selection of a pilot and copilot was imminent, and the *Typhoon II* might be shipped out to Alpha Centauri later this year. The four *Typhoon II* veterans knew how important their mission was. In comparison, this desert excursion was the classic walk in the park.

Phil suspected that Scott had sent the *Typhoon II* crew along to provide even more PR backup. People knew they were training for the AC war, after all, and Lee Borman was a certified war hero who'd been on the cover of that glossy paper *Mars Magazine* last December for destroying 4,068 AC fighters during his four-month stint.

Sure, there was a rivalry between the two crews. The Commers were more famous, the *Typhoon I* had eliminated the Central Asian Powers, and Jack's leadership had spearheaded the Evacuation. Then again, the *Typhoon II* was a much-improved ship designed to eliminate the much worse threat of the Alpha Centaurians.

If only they could find permanent pilots and finish a few more tests, they'd be ready. None of the civilian or military test pilots had impressed Phil. In the absence of pilots, Phil had emerged as unofficial leader of the *Typhoon II* group, also by virtue of his rank, the Navy equivalent of which would be Lieutenant Commander. He'd had a serious discussion with Jack in May about John Commer's obvious eagerness to pilot the *II*. To Phil's relief, Jack told him he thought John was completely unqualified. Their talk gently touched on the ongoing political pull of the Commers' father, Jonathan, and his relationship to the powerful senator Khamard from Acidalia Planitia. Both Jack and Phil worried that Jonathan Sr. might get John assigned to the *Typhoon II* anyway.

Over in Rover 2 Will Connors gunned his engine, crested a hill, and had his vehicle airborne. Jack and Joe yelped with surprise as the rover bumped to the ground a hundred feet down the hill. "*Dammit,* Connors," came Major West's hiss over the Mars suit mikes. "These Rovers are expensive, you know. Even in this low gravity their suspension won't take that sort of abuse."

"Yessir," Connors drawled. "Just testing this thing's

capabilities, sir."

Over in Rover 1 Major West stood in the front passenger seat like Washington crossing the Delaware. While Phil and the other three members of the *Typhoon II* crew undoubtedly owed their lives to West's vigorous training, they all considered him a grandstanding bastard they'd be happy never to lay eyes on again. West stood there with four pistols draped around his waist, all five-feet-six of him thrust into the nonexistent wind, his angry face a tanned block of muscle with a well-trimmed mustache above large teeth spitting out something that sounded to Phil like: "There! There! There!" as he jabbed a finger into the pink Martian sky.

All four *Typhoon II* men awaited West's final evaluation of their combat performance before they could be officially certified for the *II*. West had been sitting on their evaluations for months. Phil had no idea why General Scott didn't intervene. Surely he wanted his *Typhoon II* crew ready for combat, didn't he?

Phil wanted Will Connors for *Typhoon II* pilot and commander. Like Borman, Will was an Alpha Centauri war hero, the only true fighter pilot among any of the two *Typhoon* crews, scoring 2,500 kills in one-man ships. Yet Connors' was also the darkest story of any of the two crews: last year he'd been shot down at Barnard's Star and spent the last month of his hitch marooned on an asteroid, surviving in the wreckage of his fighter craft much the same way Scott had survived in this desert two years ago. Slender and fair-haired, Connors had a faint haunted look in his icy blue eyes. Phil had told Jack that he thought Will had some classic post-traumatic stress disorder to deal with. But while Connors emphatically said he didn't want to do any more piloting, Phil thought he'd eventually come back to it and would be the perfect pilot for the *Typhoon II*. Jack had been skeptical. To him, commanding a *Typhoon*-class warship and its crew required a lot more responsibility than piloting, however courageously, a one-man fighter. So Will would remain the navigation officer for now.

All twelve *Typhoon* crewmen had been part of the original

experimental *Typhoon E* project which had begun in 2028. When the first eight, including the four Commers, were picked for the *Typhoon I,* the rest had been miffed that they hadn't been considered good enough. Their placement in Alpha Centauri, scattered among different combat groups, had seemed like punishment for having failed. But the four rejects finally realized that a more powerful ship was being prepared for them, and that their combat training made them a tougher breed than the *Typhoon I* men. They knew their eventual crew of six would wind up more efficient, more talented, and more experienced than their sublight *Typhoon I* counterparts. No, they hadn't yet tested faster-than-light in the *Typhoon II,* but that day was scheduled for next month.

"Two miles! Two miles!" West shouted through the Mars suit microphones. "You can see the outcropping! That's where the cave is! We're right on schedule!"

Yes, Phil owed West his life, though he'd never fought alongside the major. During one drunken discussion deep one night when the two had chanced to be on the same planet awaiting transfer, Phil had blurted out his own trauma. Here he was a doctor, a licensed M.D., being used as a common soldier. From his heat blaster turret atop the heavy cruiser USS *Wrathspike* he'd blown away a couple hundred enemy spaceships, each one containing hundreds if not thousands of Centaurian soldiers. He was supposed to be a healer, but he was killing, if not people, then at least sentient beings. He hardly remembered exactly what West had said, but it wasn't the standard gibberish about following orders and doing your duty. Instead West had gone on about fate and karma and Phil's role in a cosmic struggle between the human passion to evolve into a higher understanding and the totalitarian insanity of the Centaurian race.

Somehow this talk saw Phil through the rest of his credited victories, 555 in all, and prepared him for the time when he'd ride with the crew of the *Typhoon II* back to that awful zone and sterilize it. Looking back, Phil had to admit that his stint in Alpha Centauri earlier this year, all the battles and every one of his kills, was the most meaningful thing that had ever happened to him. Much more so than what he'd previously considered the worst trauma anyone had ever faced, the Evacuation last year in which he, like all the *Typhoon II* crew, had played a part. The Evacuation, and humanity settling into a new life on Mars, seemed far away and unreal. No wonder he wasn't too concerned about *Martian marauders*.

He didn't know if the other three *Typhoon II* crewmembers also felt this way. Connors probably did. That month stranded on the asteroid had scarred him good. But Patrick James, an old buddy of the Commers from high school, might have come through AC relatively unscathed. James, the communications / sensors officer for the *Typhoon II,* had seen combat in AC but wasn't a fighter pilot or a gunner like the other three. He'd honed his technical skills and made innovative repairs to USSF computer networks fragmenting under combat conditions. He'd taken fire from AC ships and seen death and chaos, but Phil got the impression it hadn't sunk deep.

As for Lee Borman, the greatest blaster turret ace of all time, who the hell could say how the war had affected him? The guy was so extroverted as to be impenetrable. Like Major West, he was short, chunky, and aggressive, but without West's striking handsomeness. He'd certainly never said anything remotely metaphysical as West had that one night. It seemed to Phil that Lee Borman had treated his entire AC war experience as a big interactive computer game, with the score kept in dead bodies and exploded spaceships. Never yours, of course, since you were so hot with the blaster turret. What joy it must be to be so cocky and immortal.

"Down! Down the rill! Top speed! Let's blast right down on these civilians' heads!" West shouted, pointing to a hill to the left. "Show 'em who's in charge! Damn you Connors if you put it in the air again, though! You turn a rover over and I'll have your head!"

As the four rovers turned sharply left, Phil saw Harri McNarri grinning at West's obnoxious bravado and flashing Phil a thumbs-up sign. Phil returned it. There was another rivalry among the two *Typhoon* crews that nobody knew about but Phil and Harri, since they themselves constituted the secret society that truly was superior to the rest: the physician/engineers who did ninety percent of the ship's work, who knew machines and men more intimately and had more expertise than all the others combined.

Both Harri and Phil had come through the Air Force Academy, as opposed to the others, who were all Navy. Neither Phil nor Harri had ever understood the logic behind having one *Typhoon* crewmember be both ship's engineer and doctor. Their only conclusion was that the one out of a thousand candidates who survived the stress of their specialized training at the Academy and at medical school would be as formidable a weapon as the *Typhoon* itself.

Harri and Phil found that they could write their own tickets. All they had to do was *suggest* they be assigned to the *Typhoon* project and their wish was granted. Of course, the price they'd paid for it was having had virtually no life since then. McNarri was considered the old man of the group at thirty-five, but Phil, at thirty, wasn't far behind. But at least Harri could retreat under Jack's shadow if necessary, whereas Phil wondered how anyone could ever step forward to truly command the *Typhoon II*. For so long Phil had been considered the team's leader that it might be difficult for some young pilot to assert command. And Phil didn't want command. He'd rather do something himself than waste energy telling someone else to do it and then watching them screw it up.

For instance, he was content to let Major West make the idiotic decision to send four Mars military rovers swooping down the other side of the hill at sixty miles per hour into a crowd of civilian archeologists and AresNet reporters.

CHAPTER TEN
The Translator

"All right!" West shouted as he leapt from the rolling Rover 1. "Rover 4, I want you patrolling back and forth in front of the cave complex! All five of you remain in the vehicle! The rest of us, all out but the drivers! Leave the engines idling! Civilians! Reporters! Keep back from the vehicles! Back from the vehicles!"

Phil stepped from his rover. Further down the incline was a jumbled mass of rock forty feet high, with a wide cave entrance at the base. Around them were fifty or sixty civilians, including college students sorting through what appeared to be pieces of pottery. None wore Mars suits, apparently content to trust their personal EnviroFields in the open desert. Aggressive AresNet reporters shoved cameras at Jack and Joe.

"What's the story, Jack?" a reporter called out. "How dangerous are these ancient Martians?"

"We don't know," Jack grunted, obviously dismayed at the number of civilians pressing into the military group as they moved for the cave entrance.

"What about General Douglas's murder?"

"Do you have plans to Xon bomb these Martians?"

"Senator Barsdine has called for peace with the Martians! What's the USSF position on peace with the Martians?"

"Dammit to hell," Jack muttered.

"*Dammit to hell!*" the reporter yelled into a camera. "That's the official word from the Kilpatrick Desert this morning, as an edgy crowd of archeologists from the University of Mars assesses the USSF military takeover of their astounding discovery!"

"Militarist Jack Commer has arrived to take charge of the militaristic theft of one the universe's most incredible finds!" cried a woman wearing an AresNet gimme cap.

"Screw that!" Major West snarled at this woman, who also sported a transparent purple blouse with nothing underneath. Phil took a look but, like Major West, was too keyed up to care.

"I'm in charge here, young lady," West went on, "not Commer! Keep back! Reporters, civilians, keep back!"

"Hello, there, gentlemen!" said a pudgy little man in a Mars suit ridiculously camouflaged to simulate an Earth jungle. "What can I help you with today?"

"Who the hell are you?" West barked.

"Well, I'm Meintgeister, of course. Larold Meintgeister of the University of Mars, at your service, sir!" the man said, extending a hand. "I'm the leader of this team. Of course, I'm here to cooperate fully with the USSF in every regard."

West stared at Meintgeister's hand until the archeologist finally dropped it in embarrassment. "You can cooperate by getting these reporters off our ass before I have them all blasted down! And if even one of your little college girls gets in our way--"

"Uh ... of course, sir! May I ask what you might require here today?"

"We're going to *require* getting into that damn cave to take a look at your damn ruins. This where they are? Inside the cave, I take it?"

Meintgeister nodded. "Yes, yes ... although there are some more structures behind this outcropping. Buildings and so forth, many leading underground, how far we don't know yet. Fascinating, really! But the most astonishing treasures have been inside this cave here. Well, we've removed a few objects in order to get to others below them, you may have seen a few outside that our people are studying, but ..."

"Fine. We're going in. And if there's any interference--" West made a slashing gesture at his throat. Meintgeister blinked and ducked his head.

"Larold, you can't let the military desecrate--" some woman began.

"Shove it, ma'am," West said as he ducked into the cave. "We'll desecrate as we please." The cave entrance was low and ten feet wide. Phil looked back to the idling rovers surrounded by civilians and reporters. The cave lay at the bottom of what struck Phil as a natural amphitheater culminating in this odd little stage in the shadows of the rock outcropping, complete with cave mouth for actor entrances and exits.

Phil didn't like being at the bottom of a bowl. He was glad Rover 4 had also noted this problem and was moving to the top of the rill to take command of the entire amphitheater.

He entered the cave with the others. Red rock walls and ceiling were awash in lights never intended for them. At first Phil couldn't make sense of anything but the lights and the dark shapes of USSF men blocking them. From outside the cave came the muted sounds of faraway conversations, rendered through their Mars suit microphones to simulate actual distances and volumes.

"So what is this crap?" Major West said.

"Looks like Egyptian hieroglyphics to me," Harri McNarri mused. "That figure looks like it could represent a man. Or one of those Martian things."

"C'mon, we really don't know what those aliens are," Joe Commer said. "We can't say they're Martians just because we've found this old tomb or whatever it is."

The cave was fifteen by twenty feet and decidedly primitive. There was one pillar extending from floor to ceiling towards the back, and something like a table on either side of it, all apparently carved out of rock. The hieroglyphs were everywhere, on the pillar, tables, walls, and ceiling, and now that Phil nudged some dust aside with his boot, he could see they were even on the floor.

"Get that Mein Führer guy in the camo suit back in here," West snapped.

Ken Garrison hurried out of the cave and returned in a moment with Meintgeister the archeologist.

"Uh, yessir, and how may I be of assistance here?" Meintgeister said.

West pulled a heat blaster and aimed it at the wall opposite him. "What's all this crap mean on the walls and everywhere? You guys figure it out yet?"

"Uh, no, sir, not really, we only discovered the cave yesterday, and really haven't had time yet to explore all of it, or the ruins on the other side, and underground. Those ruins have been carbon-dated to a much later time period than this cave, which may in fact have been the original settlement at this site."

"You can't translate this stuff?" West said. "McNarri here says they're Egyptian hieroglyphics."

"Well, sir, I would venture to say that the likelihood of Martian hieroglyphics being at all related to Egyptian ... I mean, what I mean to say is, could you please not point your weapon at the hieroglyphics themselves? I would hate to think what a chance ray would do to them."

West grimaced, and Phil was surprised to see him holster his weapon in response. "Have it your way, dude. If you can't translate it, we'll have to do it ourselves. You there--Reynolds?"

"Yes, sir," said Craig Reynolds of *Typhoon I.*

"There's a USSF Translator in Rover 1. Bring it back here."

Reynolds nodded. "Yessir."

As he ducked through the cave entrance Meintgeister said: "The USSF has translators capable of ...?"

West shrugged. "Top secret, of course. We developed 'em to deal with thousands of AC languages, some written, some not. Sometimes it's pretty accurate. Other times, not so great. Let's just say this latest version just came out last month and it's the best we've got."

"You mean we're past Version 4.8?" Phil put in.

"Version 7.0. No combat units have gotten past 4.8 yet." Reynolds returned with a white box eighteen inches square and six inches high. "Sperry, since you're familiar with 4.8, you should be able to handle 7.0," West went on. "The interface is more or less the same."

"Sure," Phil said, moving to the box and unfolding its scanner, pulling out the control unit and taking measurements of the cave.

"I had no idea ..." Meintgeister babbled, staring at the display panel Phil unfolded from the back of the machine. The scanner dish panned the ceiling and walls as Phil calibrated the control unit, inputting every word he could think of to describe cave, drawing, language, pillar, table, and humanoid.

"And you'll continue to have no idea," West snarled. "You breathe a word of this and we'll have you shipped off the Alpha Centauri to study *their* archeological sites! You get me?"

"Of ... of course, sir!" Meintgeister said. "It's just that, with such a tool, what we could accomplish! Our own translation systems are so primitive."

"Oh, I imagine the technology will filter down over time," West said. "In a few years you'll have the equivalent of 7.0. Of course the USSF will have complete *telepathic* translators by that time, eh?" West slapped the camouflaged Meintgeister's back so hard and jovially that the archeologist stumbled and went down.

"Uh, yessir ..." Meintgeister said from his knees. "We'll look forward to it, sir."

From outside Phil could hear a woman's hiss: "Why is Larold sucking that moron's--"

Phil tuned that out along with the USSF men's chatter, their eager useless speculation about the hieroglyphics, and continued to adjust the translator. He'd been assigned translator duties on board the *Wrathspike,* and had sometimes been called on to obtain data from the wreckage of AC ships. Usually you didn't get much. Phil's greatest accomplishment was the small hinged panel he'd managed to decode as MASS RESTRICTION LEVEL FOUR.

"Not sure what'll come up," Phil grunted, "but I'm ready for a first run." He wasn't anywhere as excited as the others. He'd never been impressed by archeology, on Earth, in Alpha Centauri, and now here on Mars. A dingy little cave with some pictures, so what? He could imagine primitive Martian beings, maybe like the photographs of those finbacked things at the Space Carpet last night, simpering around this table, tossing their little pots about in some idiotic religious rite, obtaining some illusory sense of satisfaction so they could go on hunting Martian mastodons or whatever they once hunted here. What a tedious little life, led by animals.

The initial display seemed to confirm this sense of futility and self-delusion:

CAVE ... HOLY MEETING GROUND ... WE ... HOLY WE ... GREAT DESERT ROCK ... HOLY ROCK OF GL-JEEHLTAKK

"Sheesh," Phil muttered, even as his *Typhoon* crewmates, Meintgeister, and Major West whooped at the words appearing on the display.

Phil programmed the curved white scanner to rotate around the room.

CAVE ... DEDICATED ... HOPES ... WE ... HOLY PILLAR OF

"Man, this isn't much," Phil said.

OUR FONDEST GOD

"Huh," said Joe. "So this thing's really translating Martian?"

"Well, it's trying," Phil said. "It's taken every symbol on the walls and ceiling and it's trying trillions of possible word combinations every second. We can't really know if it's accurate, but you get to a point where there's a decent probability you've got it. But I can tell you this is nothing like any of the thousands of Centaurian languages we've got partially mapped in this thing's database."

"Hmm," West said. "Of course, nobody expected to find an ancient Centaurian site here on Mars, but still it does rule out *that* sort of alien." He stopped next to the pillar. "What about this? Seems it might have something more important to say than the walls, don't you think?"

Phil scanned up and down the pillar as Meintgeister said: "Well, sir, I'm not sure we can ever infer anything from--"

WAR ... CONQUEST ... EMPRESS FRA'LITH

"Crap," Craig Reynolds blurted. "I mean, sorry, guys. I was just hoping for some peace and love from these guys, y'know?"

Phil grinned. It was just like Craig to cover up all their unease with joking patter.

"Yeah, well, no peace and love after last night," Mickey Michaels put in.

"Look, we still can't connect this to *those* guys last night," Joe said.

FRA'LITH UNIFY ... REACHES FARTHEST ... WE AWAIT REINCARNATION

"Reincarnation?" John Commer said. "These Martians can't really think--"

"Well, that's what the translator thinks," Phil said in exasperation. "But I think it's starting to correlate a little faster now."

OF WHO WILL SET MATTERS ARIGHT BY THE BRAIN PIERCER, THE BLACK KNIFE OF *K'RERORR*

"Aw, *man*," said Patrick James.

West looked up and down the pillar. "We'll want to scan these other sides as well, then get the floor," he said, then: "Hey! Did you guys dust off these tables?"

"Well, no, sir," Meintgeister said. "We left everything as we found it, then photographed it, although, as I said, we did move some of the loose pottery-type objects out of the way."

"No, I'm talking about *dusting the tables*. Housecleaning, you know."

"Sir?"

"The table to the left of the pillar is thick with dust. But the one on the right--"

Meintgeister came forward, bent to the two tables, and said: "Well, I'll be. We simply didn't *notice*."

Phil moved over to the tables with the translator. Sure enough, the left table was clotted with the dust of centuries, with a few hieroglyphs faintly visible underneath, whereas the right table's hieroglyphs lay stark on a smooth clean surface. In fact, these symbols had no appearance of wear.

Phil blinked. The large central hieroglyph looked like an image of orbits around a sun.

FOUR PLANETS REMAIN

A sun with only four planets. Orbits drawn to scale for Mercury, Venus, Earth, and Mars.

AFTER DESTRUCTION OF GAS GIANTS

"I can't believe it! This stuff is *current* info?" Jack said.

"That can't be! It just can't!" Joe said.

"It has to be! These have to be the same Martians that killed

General Douglas!" John put in.

"This is *wondrous!*" Meintgeister said.

"Everyone stop yammering and read the display!" West yelled. "Our lives may depend on it!"

Phil shrugged off the major's theatrics and made adjustments to the translator as the group crowded around him.

PLANET CINDER NEW BASE FOR SCIENTISTS

PLANET MIST NOT HABITABLE

PLANET MARBLE NOT HABITABLE

"What are they talking about?" John cried.

"Cinder--Mercury! Mist--Venus! Marble must be *Earth!*" Jim Commer put in.

PLANET MARBLE IS DEAD

"Crap, they got that right," Craig Reynolds said.

INSANE APES DESPOIL THEIR OWN MARBLE ... INSANE APES NOW DESPOIL FIRST HOME

"Man, I can't *believe* this," Jack said.

"Commer, pull yourself together," West snapped. "You certainly ought to be able to handle a bit of scientific discovery."

"Listen, Major, I'm just fine. I'm just reacting like a normal human being if that's all right with you."

West expanded his chest and raised a finger. "Look here, man, Commer or no Commer--"

Jim the peacemaker cut them both off with: "First Home, that has to be *Mars!* And ... *insane apes?*"

"Don't ask," was all Craig Reynolds said, and there was a silence as the men continued to read:

EMPEROR COMMANDS MOVE TO CINDER ... ALL MOVE TO CINDER WHERE WE BUILD GIANT DEATH BEAM

"Damn," West said. "Sperry, this is all being recorded, right?"

"Of course," Phil said. "We have better scans of the walls and ceilings than the University of Mars people do, and of course this initial translation's being saved. We can refine it later."

TWO SETTINGS OF OUR SUN FROM NOW DEATH BEAM WILL FIRE AT FIRST HOME ... WE OF FIRST

HOME WILL DESTROY FIRST HOME DEFILED BY MARBLE INSANE APES

"Can this be? Are you translating *giant death beam* correctly?" Jack said.

"I don't know!" Phil snapped. "Why don't you try running this stupid thing? It's all guesswork!"

"Not 7.0!" West said. "It's state of the art. We used it to translate a weapons roster from an AC attack cruiser last week."

"Really?" Phil said. "Wow, I had no idea it'd come that far."

"If this is a real threat," Jack mused, "we'd better call Scott."

"I'm in command here!" West snarled. "I'll make that decision."

"Excuse me, but if this translation is at all reliable, and the threat isn't a bluff, we have two days, or less than two days, depending on when this carving was done, to prevent some sort of super weapon from being fired at us."

"Oh, you can't believe that, can you?"

EMPEROR ... HEE-ARR-GRGSSS ... COMMANDS WE DESTROY FIRST HOME IT SHALL BE DONE

"Hergs?" Joe cried. "Is that possible? Are they saying *Hergs?*"

"No! Of course not!" Jack said. "How could that be?"

"But he had that teleportation device! And he's working with the Martians!"

"So you believe there are Martians now!" John shouted.

"Yes! For God's sake, yes!" Joe yelled back. "The absence of dust on this table *proves* it!"

"If that's true, we may have a *second* space war on our hands," Jack said. "I can't believe it! There's been no evidence of Martians at all!"

"But what if they're part of the AC war?" Jim said. "What if the Martians are in collusion with the ACs? That might explain the saucer attack yesterday."

"Wait, don't get carried away," Phil put in, still coaxing word combinations out of the translator. "I saw the photos of the ship that buzzed Douglas's ship, and it matched the scans you guys took of the ship you blasted. Those probably aren't AC ships and I'll tell you why. They'd never do a saucer shape. They don't use circles or even like circles. They hate planets because they're round. ACs like jagged amalgamations. Their ships are all like that."

"Then what have we got?" Joe said. "*Martian* saucers?"

Jack cleared his throat. "Well, then, Major. Permission to contact General Scott, sir. I'm sure he'll want to send the *Typhoon* to pay a little visit to Mercury."

West sized up Jack Commer. "It can wait a couple minutes, Captain. I want a more thorough investigation before we start calling for help like little mama's boys."

Jack blinked. That was uncalled for, and everyone knew it. The only explanation Phil could think of was that West felt he was a hotshot combat veteran from Alpha Centauri and he was going to show that Jack Commer didn't know a thing about dealing with alien threats. Phil was ashamed of himself for feeling the same way towards the *Typhoon I* crew earlier. Hell, the *Typhoon* personnel were the top echelon of the USSF, and the two crews had to stick together. Hoping to defuse the tension, Phil said:

"Well, sir, it might be a really good idea to send both *Typhoons* to Mercury to deal with any threat that may be there. The *Typhoon II* could certainly use a shakedown cruise, and the presence of both *Typhoons* would boost morale here on Mars and maybe even prepare the public for when we launch it to Alpha Centauri."

West glared at Sperry, even as Sperry thought he felt Jack relax. After all, the tension between the two crews had sometimes gone from friendly rivalry to competition for resources, and Sperry knew he'd proposed an ingenious idea for team-building between the two crews. "May I remind you, Major Sperry," West said, "that your crew is quite understaffed at the moment? You have no pilots certified for combat missions, or did you forget that?"

"Uh, no sir, of course not, sir. I thought perhaps Will Connors could pilot."

"Connors! That man is brain-damaged!" West snorted. Phil looked for Will, realizing he must've stayed outside with the rovers. "And have you forgotten that the four of you are not yet properly certified for the *Typhoon II?*"

"Well, no, sir. Still, I think it would be a good idea to have the *II* ready. I think General Scott might really appreciate your going ahead and certifying us so we'd be ready to back up the *Typhoon I.*"

West folded his arms. "General Scott may wish to send a test crew of six to man the *Typhoon II.* However, until I certify you four, none of you will be among that crew. Is that understood?"

"Yes, sir, but may I just point out that, coming from you, the General would see--"

"Enough!" West bellowed. "Gentlemen, we are going to wait on all your foolish plans until I've determined--"

He broke off as they all became aware of a commotion outside. Then a scream.

Every USSF man instantly had his heat blaster out as an uncanny whine built up outside.

A college boy ran into the cave shouting: "The Martians are coming!"

"Okay, everyone out of here! On the double!" West cried, ducking out the cave entrance. "Get the civilians in here and let's--"

A blue-purple ray enveloped the major and he burst into shattered glass.

CHAPTER ELEVEN
Finback Attack

Jack hit the sand as rays sang above him. Up the slope of the hills all around the cave, scores of tiny naked finned beings sprayed the crowd with blue-purple light. People were *cracking apart, exploding*. Fighting the urge to gape in dismay, Jack cursed their poor position at the bottom of this bowl and noted with relief that Rover 4 with West's commandos was at the top of the rim, charging to the right.

"West is dead!" Joe shouted.

"I know! I saw it!" Jack yelled back. "I've got command! Get the civilians into the cave!"

"Civilians! Reporters! Into the cave! Retreat to the cave!" Joe ordered, turning up his Mars suit speaker.

"West--his fragments *hit* me!" Sperry gasped, writhing on the ground. Jack crawled to the *Typhoon II* surgeon and turned him over. Long slivers of *West* were embedded in Sperry's left arm, neck and cheek. Realizing his suit gloves were too thick for the task, Jack yanked them off and without caring for his own safety reached for the shards with bare fingers. He felt the buzzing of their merging EnviroFields but had no difficulty tugging out the slivers. Sperry's face and neck bled, but not too badly.

"Can you see? Eyes okay?" Jack shouted above the whir of ray guns firing everywhere.

Sperry blinked. "Yes! God! I'm okay, Jack. Just threw me, that's all!"

"Well, it ripped up your sleeve but the EnviroField's holding. And I think if West's pieces were *contagious* or whatever, you'd have--" Jack gulped. "You'd have *cracked* by now."

Sperry grabbed the heat blaster he'd dropped and threw himself to his feet. "Forget it! I'm okay!"

"Careful!" Jack turned to the hysterical crowd. "Civilians! Inside the cave! Now!" The USSF men hurled college students and AresNet reporters into the cave, but a dozen civilians lay in patches of shattered glass on the red slopes all around them. "Hey! Connors!" Jack cried as Will Connors drove Rover 2 up.

"The attack's coming from the west!" Connors shouted, pointing to the right.

"Charge them! Scatter them!" Jack yelled, clambering aboard with Joe and Sperry. "Blasters on kill! Rover 1! Follow us! Charge the hill!" One of West's commandos, *MacPhair* stenciled on his bright blue helmet, roared up in Rover 1, but with only Ken Garrison and Harri McNarri inside. Well, they'd have to charge with what they had. MacPhair swung close to the left and the two vehicles accelerated to sixty miles per hour up the hill, all the men firing hand blasters at the finbacks swarming up there.

Rover 4, manned with five commandos, three firing heat blasters and one grappling with the big EOS cannon in the rear, churned in along the top of the ridge from their far left. Yes, concentrate the firepower from two sides, break the attack, mop it up.

A finback--dammit, a *Martian,* there was no use denying it--popped from behind the hill, stood directly in front of the charging rover, and fired a brief blue-purple ray.

All five men shattered like chinaware. Jack gasped. The sound came through his EnviroField speakers like a two-foot stack of dishes dropped on a concrete floor. The rover mowed down the Martian and disappeared over the crest, snarling and pilotless, as a cloud of broken glass settled across the ridge.

"God!" Joe said. "It didn't harm the rover, but the *men--*"

"Charge! Keep charging!" Jack shouted. "Stay down and keep firing! When we hit the top of that hill we don't know what we'll find!" Behind him Sperry doggedly fired his blaster, and in an instant Jack knew everything the *Typhoon II* crew had gone through. He understood the wary look in Sperry's eyes, the dazed look in Will Connors', he understood the taut muscles, the *getting down to the business of slaughter.* These were war veterans. They'd follow him the same way they'd followed West, and together they'd exterminate these cockroaches who dared sneak up and murder them.

No, he wasn't going to underestimate the roaches. They were fanatic, no doubt about it. The way that one had stood in front of the rover, sacrificing himself for one clean shot, wasn't exactly admirable, but it was a factor. Jack was going to take all the factors into consideration. In fact, he'd welcome all complications from here on out as challenges to his ability to carve the one lucid path to victory. Yeah, he'd even welcome three more Martians popping from the crest in front of their two rovers.

To his astonishment three Martians did exactly that, training their ray guns on the vehicles when they got fifty feet from the crest.

Blaster rays from the rovers sliced two finbacks in half and then the third was down on his knees, firing his ray at the underside of Rover 1.

More demented shattering. Rover 1, tires disintegrating, seemed to cartwheel in eerie slow motion right at Jack's face. "Watch it!" he cried, noting the ray gun scars across the rover's white sides. He had time to muse that the rays seemed to work best on organic material, possibly the synthetic rubber in those tires would allow--

"Dammit!" Connors grunted, swerving hard to miss the rolling rover.

Jack was in the air. They all were. He came down on his shoulder, but in one-third gravity it wasn't too bad. Rovers 1 and 2 both lay upside down a few yards ahead. Sperry and Ken Garrison crawled to them for cover.

While Jack didn't like the idea of being pinned down behind wrecked rovers, this after all was one more of the complications he so badly needed to engage his deepest survival instincts. "Joe! Everyone up here! Take cover! Harri! Will! MacPhair! You guys okay?"

"Yeah--yessir," MacPhair said, dazed, dragging himself to the rovers. "If we could only get to the EOS cannons!"

"They're under the rovers now," Sperry pointed out. "And if I'm right these babies take five seconds to engage."

"Seven point five seconds, dammit. The bigger the cannon,

the more time it takes."

Jack turned to see Craig Reynolds, Mickey Michaels, Lee Borman, and his brother John advancing up the slope behind them. He grimaced. One more complication. Sure, those guys had missed getting onboard a rover, but why would they come up here to get pinned behind the wrecked rovers with the rest of them? They could've been held back for another attack. Jack berated himself for failing to note the positions of everyone on the slope.

"Keep down! Heads down!" he shouted. "Those shatterguns can reach all the way down to the cave!"

The four USSF men zigzagged the last few steps. But an AresNet reporter, a middle-aged man with a pot belly and full white beard, ran behind them yelling into his microphone: "Yes, there's no way to hide the *Martian marauders* from the public now!"

"Goddammit, get that man out of here!" Jack shouted, scanning the immense battle bowl and noting that while most civilians were off the slopes, a few remained cringing in front of the cave. "Civilians into the cave! Civilians into the cave!" he shouted at full amplification.

"Can the Commers handle this baby?" the reporter cried. "Or is this the beginning of the final Martian push to destroy us all? Live, from the Kilpatrick Desert, this is T. Jasper Mark--"

A shattergun ray flashed down the slope and skipped across the reporter's left shoe.

It seemed that everyone in the bowl stopped to watch as T. Jasper Marktholomew--Jack now recalled him as the host of the Monday Marktholomew Hour on AresNet--avidly studied the phenomenon of his toes cracking, his ankle cracking, his calf cracking, cracks racing up his thigh.

"God, I'm *cracking!*" Marktholomew broadcast to the battle. "*Cracking!* I'm cra--"

And the familiar sound of glass bursting.

"Yeeeeeee! Yeeeaaaahh!" came fresh cries from below, as if it took the death of a famous reporter to make people realize that they weren't immortal themselves.

More motion on the slope, and now Jack really was ashamed, for he'd forgotten the existence of Rover 3, which churned up fifty feet beside them and came to a halt. His brother Jim was at the wheel, firing a machine pistol up the slope, and beside him Patrick James of *Typhoon II* shot a heat blaster rifle, knocking off a couple Martians' heads as the finbacks dared to show themselves on the crest.

That rover's driver, the big muscled blond fellow who'd been draped with so many weapons that Jack had earlier wondered how the man could walk, stood behind the six-foot-long EOS cannon, grasping the immense black grips and swinging the cannon towards the crest of the hill. What did he think he'd hit over the crest? Jack wondered. For the Martians were securely hunkered down behind it. The blond guy abruptly reminded Jack of that Martian who'd sacrificed himself.

"Get down--" Jack called, but halfheartedly, as he saw what the blond commando was doing.

The Electron Oblivion Sequencer cannon emitted a colorless ray distorting the world into ripples. Its hum was much lower than the shatterguns', in fact it was a pleasurable bass murmur building in volume.

"Yeah, he's got it on wide dispersion!" MacPhair said in admiration.

"If he can just hold on," Jack said, counting the seconds. "If the Martians don't decide to charge them--*hey!* Dammit!"

A dozen Martians leapt over the crest, firing shatterguns at the EOS gunner.

"Blast 'em!" Jack ordered, as the men behind Rovers 1 and 2 opened up on the Martians. Several toppled but others kept a steady stream of shatter rays on Rover 3. Jack turned to it, heartsick. But the blond gunner stood, maintaining EOS fire that covered the entire hundred yards of the western hill. Jim and Patrick James rolled out of the vehicle and fired at their attackers, whose blue-purple beams attenuated and died two feet from their muzzles.

"My God! The EOS rays are *canceling* the shattergun rays!" Joe cried.

"Yes! That'd make sense!" Sperry said. "They must be similar technologies, and the EOS ray is active even *before* it's reached full potential!"

A second later, the entire top of the ridge ceased to exist.

The men stared. Jack stood incautiously. The gunner had taken off the last twenty feet of slope and everything behind it. They were looking at flat land stretching to a horizon of dunes. A handful of finbacks scampered away.

"We'll follow," Jack said, pulling an EOS rifle out of the back of a wrecked rover. "We'll keep the EOS rays on and just walk up to the Martians and blast 'em."

"We could probably capture a few," Joe said. "We might find out something."

"The hell with that. They're fanatics and dangerous. They won't surrender." How could he know that? It was uncanny, but he was sure of it. The same way he'd known those three Martians would pop up to shatter Rover 1's tires, the same way, as soon as he'd thought that more would charge Rover 3, they'd done so. He shook his head. Could battle somehow make you prescient? Or was it his imagination? How could being prescient really help if it was all hunches and guesses? What good did it do to wonder if another Martian attack was about to begin from the opposite direction?

He whirled to the crest on the other side of the bowl. Most of the men also turned. Hundreds of maddened finbacks swarmed over the top of that hill, then suicidally down the bowl to charge up the slope towards the rovers, blue-purple rays whining everywhere.

These roaches were putting up a great fight, Jack marveled. Yet he felt he could anticipate everything that was coming for them.

"Uhh!" moaned the blond soldier on Rover 3 as he swung the EOS cannon towards the new threat. "Hell!" he muttered at his cracking left wrist as the shatter crept further up his arm.

"*No!*" Jack shouted. He sure hadn't foreseen *that*.

The blond guy grimaced, pulled a ray gun and blew off his arm at the elbow. As blood exploded everywhere, the rest of the twirling arm shattered in midair.

"He's all right!" Joe cried.

The soldier flung his blaster aside and aimed his EOS cannon one-handed at the cockroaches before taking another shattergun bolt in the face.

CHAPTER TWELVE
The Prescience

Joe gaped at the messy cloud of sharp black particles tinkling all over Rover 3. "He was *there* just a second ago!" But how many of their comrades, how many civilians down there, had been *there* just a second ago?

The blond soldier's death made the battle real. For the past few minutes Joe had been all adrenaline and action. Now, as he watched several hundred little Martians scampering up the hill towards them, and more importantly, as he watched a dozen descend towards the cave opening and the frightened civilians retreating there, he understood they were in a fight for human survival.

Behind him Jack yelled: "Wipe out the remaining ones behind us, then shift to the other side of the rovers! Reynolds, Michaels, Borman, John--pursue 'em! Use EOS rifles, wide dispersal. Neutralize their rays!" The four newcomers grabbed EOS rifles and charged to the west, but Joe, without fully understanding how he'd arrived atop Rover 3, found himself grasping the big EOS cannon and firing it left and down, attenuating the shattergun rays the attackers were pouring onto the civilians and, seconds later, vaporizing the finbacks and a great deal of red sand into sundered atoms.

"Joe! What are you doing?" Jack said, leaping onto the rover next to him, firing his own EOS rifle to the center and right, covering Joe's exposed side. "Are you trying to get yourself killed?"

"Somebody needed to man the EOS," Joe grunted, swinging the cannon down at scores of naked pink Martians, who finally seemed to be aware that their guns no longer worked. Joe empathized with their frustration. The closer they got the more he fancied he understood them.

Demons from Marble! Must exterminate this infestation! But their evil is so great our shatterguns fail! We are doomed!

"Go ahead and kill them all! It's us or them!" Jack cried. Joe kept the EOS grips engaged and counted the seconds. A couple Martians threw down their shatterguns and pulled long black knives from belts, held them high.

But it didn't matter in the least what they did, because every one of them evaporated into nothingness in the booming gray ripple of the EOS beam.

"Damn!" Joe said as the beam cut off. "The cannon's totally discharged!"

Jack pointed to the cave entrance. "I don't see any new casualties down there. I'd say you saved their asses, Joe. And all of us. Good work."

Joe gulped for air, heart racing. "Thanks." By this time the four EOS riflemen sent behind them had returned.

"We EOS'd them all," Lee Borman grinned. "Thought they could outrun us. Sons of bitches."

"Look at all these shatterguns we got!" John laughed. "They just dropped them as they ran!" He held out a knapsack filled with the tiny weapons.

"We'd better search the entire area," Jack said. "Could be more of 'em lurking around."

Right, Joe thought, if he were as fanatic as these finbacks, he wouldn't give up so easily. He'd still be hiding behind the crest of this natural amphitheater, maybe attack from the center, off to their right.

Rover 3's tires shattered. Another swarm of Martians attacked from the center crest.

"I *knew* that!" Joe cried. "I *knew* that was about to happen!"

"Dammit! So did I!" Jack shouted, firing his EOS rifle towards the top of the hill a hundred yards away, then, as its low booming tapered off, threw it down in disgust. "This one's discharged, too!" He pulled out a heat blaster and fired.

A tall Martian urged other Martians into position. In contrast with the others, this one wore a golden robe through which its back fin protruded, larger than any of the others' fins.

"The leader!" Jack said. "God, how do I *know* that? Blow him away!"

Joe stared. The leader's eyes were two inches wide, unblinking, unfathomable, yet Joe felt locked onto them, understanding in spite of himself.

The battle grows desperate. We do not understand these killers from Marble. They have destroyed us, they have destroyed the emperor himself! And now, the new emperor ... we must worship filth!

A rattling distracted him. Lee Borman, Mickey Michaels, and Craig Reynolds were plunging fists into John's backpack and coming out with shatterguns.

"Hey, guys, those are artifacts," John protested. "The USSF needs to analyze 'em!"

"Screw it! Can't wait for the goddamn EOS guns to recharge," Borman grunted, throwing himself onto the sand, sighting down the shattergun barrel with a two-handed grip, and squeezing off a blue-purple ray as if he'd been firing shatterguns since he was a teenager.

"They'll protect him!" Joe cried as a naked Martian threw himself in front of the leader in the golden robe.

Borman's shot grazed the Martian's elbow, which started cracking. Everyone paused as the alien stood on one leg, bringing one hand to his forehead and balancing motionless as the cracking crept up his arm and then claimed his entire body.

Three more Martians stood in front of the leader, sheltering him as they blasted back at the USSF men. Borman, now Michaels and Reynolds on the sand, and finally John from a fully exposed standing position, fired answering rays. Shatterguns, heat blasters, half-depleted EOS rifles, and popping machine pistols with tracer bullets slashed deadly glowing lines across the hill.

While most Martians shattered instantly, or were cut to pieces by blaster or bullet fire, a few more received grazing ray hits, and to the men's puzzlement, again stood one-legged and touched their foreheads before they shattered.

"It must be some religious thing!" Jack marveled.

"Yeah!" Joe said. "Just what I was thinking!"

To accept the Grazing Shatter of Kl'alp'lor shows the truest courage.

"What?" Joe said. "*What* are they saying?"

"They're not saying anything! Are they?"

"I don't know! But I do know they're giving up!" Joe pointed to the increasing number of bodyguards pushing the Martian leader back from the battle.

"How do you know--" Jack began. "Right, they must have a *saucer* nearby!"

"But he'd rather die here than go back to--to what? I don't know! But his men want him to live!"

"How do we know all this? *How do we know all this?*"

"I don't know!" On a mad hunch, Joe turned back to the USSF men blasting away behind them and shouted: "*What happens next, guys?*"

"They raise their saucer from where it's buried in the sand!" Phil Sperry yelled back, then put his hand to his mouth. "How can I *know* that?"

Everyone stared at Phil. Hearing the deep whine build beneath them was anticlimactic.

"The saucer! Of course!" John shouted, waving his shattergun. "We all knew it!"

"How can that be? How can that be?" Jack gasped.

The sand shook. The crest of the hill across from them buckled. Several USSF men lost their balance as a gray, two-hundred-foot-wide saucer drew itself out of the sand behind the retreating Martians.

Yes, to withdraw! Unlike our brethren yesterday! They were so rash, so young, foolishly taking on the Marble death ship! Commander A'olfglnd sacrificed himself needlessly! But how could he disobey the direct commands of the emperor?

"Just like the one we blasted yesterday!" Jack said. "I can't believe it!"

"How can I know that? How can anybody know that?" Joe cried.

"Who gives a flip? They're trying to escape!" Jack said. "Mow 'em down!"

The men let loose. Six more Martians shattered, leaving just three around the leader. Joe pointed his heat blaster. The range was problematic, but Joe was fairly certain he could wing the tall one standing above his bodyguards. Yet all he could do was gape as all four Martians pressed devices strapped to their wrists. And disappeared. Then the saucer shot straight up so fast it sucked a cloud of red sand off the crest of the hill. Fierce gritty wind whipped around the men.

"*Damn* ..." Joe moaned.

"Search the area!" Jack shouted. "Kill any Martians on sight!"

"No, they're gone. They're all gone."

"We won! We won!" John said. "Give me back my shatterguns!"

Joe looked back and forth between his three brothers. "Are you guys all right? Is everyone all right?" He counted the eight men of *Typhoon I* and the four of *Typhoon II,* all standing. Plus the lone survivor of West's commandos, Rover 1 driver Embry MacPhair, who stood in a stupor, shaking his head and muttering: "We didn't have *this* in Centauri. Never saw *this* ..."

They got seven of eight highly-trained commandos, Joe thought, though six of those were by surprise. And the blond guy more or less sacrificed himself for them. Meanwhile, the *Typhoon* crews survived unscratched. Were they being groomed for something? By fate itself? And for what? Why was Joe still standing and the blond guy was broken glass?

"That damn coward!" Jack snarled. "That damn coward!"

"Who?" said Harri McNarri.

"The leader guy! Turning tail like that, just when we--when we--"

Just when they'd been about to administer the *coup de grâce,* Joe thought. But that made sense to him. He wouldn't stick around for that himself, not if he had a shiny new flying saucer and the means to run away and fight another day.

"And they have *teleportation*," Jack fumed. "What would *that* do in a battle situation?"

Joe shrugged. "It probably has. They probably just teleported onto either side of this amphitheater as needed."

Jack shuddered. "I didn't think of that."

The *Typhoon* crews and MacPhair stared around the

amphitheater, wordlessly taking in the AresNet cameramen below who must have recorded most of the battle. Jack winced at that but said nothing.

"Okay, men, let's clean up and get ready to move out. Pick up all the weapons, and any remaining shatterguns you find," Jack ordered. "We'll all be armed with them from here on out. As far as I can tell they don't need to recharge like our EOS guns. I'll call back our transport and we'll have them bring in a detachment of more troops to secure this area. Along with plenty of fresh EOS cannon. If that coward tries to teleport back here, we'll vaporize him *and* his saucer."

Phil Sperry grabbed EOS rifles from the sand. "Is this what it's like when a battle ends?" Joe asked, indicating the piles of shattered glass, the wreckage of rovers, and the civilians emerging from the cave to pick their way through it all. "Is this it? Everybody just stares at where it took place? Then we go get lunch?"

Sperry nodded. "Yes, except if you're on a ship your first duty is to spend a lot of time repairing it. But in fact I'm damn hungry now. Where did you say you were taking me to lunch?"

"Ah, man," Joe said, all at once exhausted. "All I know is, we oughta invite that Martian guy along, too. The big guy. Damn, I can almost *know his name.*"

"Don't say that, man. I'm feeling that way, too."

"We all are. Somehow we all *knew* them. It was in our heads somehow. I can't believe Jack's calling him a coward. Can't he see how noble the guy is? Man, the guy's thousands of years old! Although I don't know how I can *know* that."

Sperry placed the rifles in the rear of Rover 3. "Jack's in charge. He saw real battle today. We all did. Jack's now the one who has to order the killing to take place. He has to harden himself. He doesn't have time for that nobility stuff. But ... I know what you mean."

Joe pondered that. And he pondered his role as executive officer of the *Typhoon* in carrying out whatever Jack's new orders might be. This train of thought was interrupted by the noisy landing of the USSF transport a hundred yards off, archeological site be damned. Joe discovered that he'd had it. He didn't care anymore. He too was famished, and he found himself cataloging his options among his favorite Marsport restaurants.

CHAPTER THIRTEEN
Mission Briefing
Friday, June 9, 2034, 1400 hours

The combined crews of the two *Typhoons,* still in their dusty Mars suits, moved into General Scott's office on the 130th floor of the United System Building. John flung himself into a swivel chair in front of Scott's desk and laughed: "Man, you can't believe how wiped out we are!"

General Scott noisily cleared his throat. John met the unfathomable black eyes of the Supreme Commander of the USSF. How long and unkempt the General's gray hair was, despite its crewcut. It stuck straight up like a battered steel brush.

"*John!*" came his eldest brother's hiss.

"Huh?" John noticed that none of the others had taken chairs. In fact, there were only four chairs. "Who else wants to sit? We could take turns, I guess. We're all exhausted after that battle, I know!"

Jack jerked a cupped hand. Reluctantly John got out of his chair. Right, right, Jack was touchy about things like that. If only four people could sit, that wasn't fair, because eight other people didn't get to sit. Therefore, they should all stand, no matter how tired their legs were. John sprang to rigid attention and threw a salute that included everyone in the room. "Lieutenant Commer reporting for duty! Sir!" he yelled, feeling the flurry of excitement this caused in all the *Typhoon* men.

Behind his immense desk Scott made a weary answering salute. "Thank you, Lieutenant Commer," the general rasped. "At ease, men. Now let's get underway. You know it's rare that I would invite the entire crews of the *Typhoons* into my office, but I want to make sure every man here understands the importance of what I'm about to say."

John looked about to see the *Typhoon* men nodding somberly. "We're with you, sir!"

"*John!*" Jack hissed again.

"Hey, I'm only telling the General that we're with him!"

Jack shook his head. "John, let's just *listen.*"

"I hate it when you shush me in front of everyone!"

"John, for God's sake!" Joe cut in. "Jack gave you an order to shut up!"

"We just had a battle! We're still in our Mars suits!"

"Lieutenant Commer!" Scott shouted. "Attention!"

"Sir, if you'd just understand--"

"Come to attention, lieutenant!"

John took in everyone staring at him. He stood stiffly and threw out another salute.

"I didn't ask for a salute, lieutenant!" Scott roared.

"Sorry, sir, I thought, I thought--" John stammered, wondering if he should put his hand down, since this time Scott obviously wasn't going to return his salute.

"Silence!" Scott turned to Jack. "Captain, does your brother understand what coming to attention means?"

"Yes, sir, he does," Jack said. "It's just that, well, we had ground combat for the first time today, sir, and ship-to-ship combat for the first time yesterday, and so he may be, uh, a little excited, I think."

"Yes, sir, that's it, excited!" John said, gingerly dragging down his right arm. "Sorry, sir, I mean, I just got carried away, it won't happen again, sir."

Scott leaned back in his adjustable gravity chair. "I know you've all been through a lot."

"We have sir, really! It was *unbelievable,* those finbacks pouring down on us from all directions!"

"John! Silence! Right now! Don't say another word!" Jack snarled.

There was a long silence. Finally Scott said: "If I may proceed without further interruption."

"Yes, sir!" John cried.

Another silence. Scott sighed heavily.

"I was just trying to indicate that I'll follow your orders to the letter, sir," John protested. "Why is everyone so upset with that? That's what we're here for, aren't we? To follow orders to the letter in defense of humanity?"

"Captain," Scott said. "If Lieutenant Commer can't keep

quiet during my briefing, he'll need to leave the room. Is that clear?"

"Yes, sir," Jack said, then, as John started to agree, Jack's fingers executed a sharp gunshot snap pointed directly to John's open mouth. John slammed his jaws together so tightly his teeth ached.

"All right, then," Scott went on. "Let me just say that everyone's excited, flabbergasted, what have you. The news of these Martians is unbelievable. We had no idea, no idea whatsoever. No evidence of them in decades of exploration. I've scanned the report you sent on the way back here. Unbelievable."

Another pause. John knew it was a test whether he'd agree that it was all unbelievable, and then be forced to leave the room and hear nothing of Scott's reaction to all this unbelievability, or whether John could keep cool and calm and just stand there without agreeing that it was all unbelievable, and so gain further admittance to the secrets Scott was about to unfold.

John passed the test. Scott went on: "Our Alien Tech Team has completed the initial analysis of debris from the ship you boys destroyed yesterday morning near Earth. And they also had a chance to analyze material from the shattergun you obtained last night at the Space Carpet. They tell me the materials are the same, and they all seem compatible with Martian mineralogy. The scans of the saucer also match the photos and scans of the ship that buzzed General Douglas's ship on his journey here yesterday. So it looks like there really are native Martians, apparently out to wage war on us here on Mars and throughout what's left of the solar system."

"God, sir," John couldn't help but add, "after all we've been through since '28, it's a miracle people even dare to wake up every day!"

"John, *quiet*," Jack hissed.

"How can anyone really keep quiet about *the breakdown of the solar system?*" John cried. "I mean, I know I'm just like the rest of you guys, I push all those memories out of my mind just so I can go about my daily business! But every once in a while you really have to stop to consider the *horror* of it all!"

"Lieutenant, if you please," Scott said wearily.

"John!" Jack snarled.

"Consider it, gentlemen! 2028--and the four largest asteroids are *flung* into the sun! They just stop cold in their orbits! One every month for four months! They didn't spend weeks falling in, they *accelerated* in! Nobody believed those stupid scientists who thought they had some fancy explanation! It was *unknowable!* The world panicked! I remember the panic!"

"Lieutenant, I am giving a briefing here!" Scott shouted.

"No! We have to face the horror every now and then!"

"Lieutenant Commer, for your information we *did* face the destruction of the asteroids, and the outer planets, by creating the USSF!"

"2029--and Pluto is *hurled* from the solar system! Just shot out of its orbit into the unknown! I was *freaked,* if you ask me! And a few months later Neptune just *blows up!* Nobody knows why!"

Scott sighed. "Stop him, Captain. I know he gets excited sometimes, but I really am trying to conduct a briefing here."

"And exactly one month after *that,* Uranus drops out of orbit and accelerates just like those asteroids, straight into the sun!"

"John, quiet! That's an order!" Jack cried.

"Look, John," Joe said, "that's why we joined the USSF, to deal with this, to get to the bottom of it all."

"How could anyone get to the bottom of Uranus flying *right past the earth* on its way in? We all watched it happen! Two billion people died! All those earthquakes! And messing up the moon's orbit!"

John finished up staring at a dozen open mouths. There was a terrible silence in General Scott's huge office. It began to sink in that John had just committed treason to the USSF. "God, I'm so sorry ... I shouldn't have said anything. I know it's wrong."

Scott leaned back in his chair. "Lieutenant, are you all right now?"

"Uh, yessir, I know I did wrong to say anything, I'm so sorry, sir!" To make sure Scott knew how sorry he was, John threw off another snappy salute. Scott rolled his eyes by way of acknowledgement, and John hauled his arm down.

Scott cleared his throat. "All right, then. Let me just say that humanity was traumatized, Lieutenant. And I suppose we all have been. If you'll recall the defeatism of '28 on, all that superstitious fear that God or the Devil had come to take vengeance on us, you'll also recall the resurgence of hope that came from the founding of the USSF. A few of us decided to fight back, and that includes you four Commers."

"That's true, sir, quite true," John couldn't help but rejoin, "and believe me, I was astounded at how *fast* our tech started developing right then! We all were! All those spaceships we built almost overnight! Making a *Typhoon* that could do one-thirteenth light! And who would've ever guessed six years ago that now we'd have *heat blasters,* and *neural stunners,* and *EOS guns?*"

"*John!*" Jack moaned.

"Yes, yes, Lieutenant, we know," Scott rasped. "For your information it's quite typical of human ingenuity to come up with incredible solutions in the face of adversity. Now can we please get down to--"

"But what about adding *human folly* to the mix?" John cried, thunderous waves of eloquence rising in his throat. "We invent Star Drive in '30, and immediately start the whole stupid war with the Alpha Centaurians!"

"Enough, Mr. Commer. I think you've had more than your share of this discussion today."

"I'm just trying to say why do we all feel like we've been *reamed?* What about 2031? What about *July 15th?*"

"John, shut up! The general has ordered you to shut up!" Jack screamed.

"It's my fault, dammit," Scott snapped. "I shouldn't have made my own little speech back there. It just got him started up again."

"Jupiter and Saturn *blow up,* without warning, just like Neptune! At the *exact same time!* Who wouldn't think that God, or the Devil, or the ACs, might've done it? Didn't that set the stage for even worse despair than anything else? Don't you think it might've set the stage for the return of the Central Asian Powers? For the Final War, for *destroying the earth?*"

"I'll--I'll put him outside right now, sir," Jack said, digging into John's bicep.

"Forget it," Scott said. "He's part of your crew and he needs to stand there, shut up, and listen. Or else I'll have him court-martialed. Is that clear?"

"Perfectly clear, sir!" John said. "But now, to top everything off, *Martians!* It's unbelievable, is what it is, sir!"

"Silence!" Scott roared. "Not one more word, Lieutenant, or else!"

Everyone looked at the carpet. Another long uneasy silence. John took a tiny breath. But hadn't too many seconds passed for anyone to cashier him? Wasn't he probably okay? Didn't everyone know he'd only spoken the truth? But he saw he'd need to be careful from now on. For some reason they were all *against* his unique perspective.

"All right, then," Scott resumed. "Can we get back to the Martians?"

"Uh, yes, of course, sir," Jack answered with a warning glance at John.

"We now have, of course, the public to deal with in all this," Scott said. "Jack, you mentioned the AresNet reporters in your report, and I'm afraid to say your fears are true. The entire battle was captured on video, including the deaths of our people, transmitted live to hundreds of millions of Martian colonists, a few of which had the dubious honor of watching their loved ones get killed in action. That would be, in addition to our seven USSF dead, twenty-six archaeologists and six AresNet crew." Scott leaned back in his chair and adjusted his gravity a notch lighter. "A strange kind of battle, to yield no actual *wounded.*"

"Yes, sir," Jack said, checking John to make sure he didn't open his mouth again. "The slightest graze of a shattergun leads almost instantly to death."

"And while AresNet and much of the public were skeptical of what they called a *militarist solution* to the investigation of

Martian life, this battle has effectively turned public opinion around. Ninety percent of the population is now fully committed to eradicating these Martians by any means necessary."

"We saw some of that on the ride in from the spaceport, sir. Demonstrators, signs, and so on, but all *supporting* us."

"Except for your hysterical former comrade Vespertine," Scott said. "I assume you've kept up with his exploits?"

"Uh, no, sir," Jack said. "We haven't really had contact with him since the Academy."

"As I was waiting for you men to arrive, I perused his latest diatribe on AresNet. Not only was he nitpicking every action you took in the Kilpatrick Desert, as if he'd really learned a damn thing in his year at the Academy, he starts wailing about how he's getting married tomorrow and how militarism is ruining his marriage, what kind of future can they have, or some such nonsense. I didn't bother finishing it."

"Married?" Joe mused. "That's weird. I can't imagine anyone ..."

John too had trouble picturing anyone copulating with the bloated, cynical author of "To Die Honorably on Earth," a blog post Vespertine had published as the debate heated up last year about whether the earth's population should be evacuated off-planet. John had never known Huey Vespertine, who'd started the Naval Academy in 2022 but dropped out after a year, later flailing around in some academic study of Solar System Breakdown before turning himself into something resembling a wino.

"That wouldn't be important in itself," Scott went on, "except I wanted to ask you men, especially Jack and Joe who knew him at the Academy, whether you thought Vespertine might be working with this Sam Hergs character."

Jack shook his head. "I can't see that, sir. Unfortunately, I see Huey as just one more person who couldn't handle the Evacuation, and who's really flipped his lid since coming to Mars."

"He seems fairly harmless to me," Joe added. "Even if he's shrill and writes stuff that sounds treasonous. And anyway, I don't think that this Hergs guy, or that Carson guy, would be working with someone so famous on AresNet. Hergs has been pretty anonymous up to now."

"And there are hundreds of others spouting the same sort of nonsense on AresNet right now," Jack said. "They can't all be in league with Hergs."

"Hmm …" Scott said. "I'll take that under advisement. Even so, the USSF Interrogation Unit will shortly be paying a visit to Mr. Vespertine, marriage or no marriage." He shuffled through the papers on his desk as John grinned in admiration at the way his two older brothers laid out their opinions so succinctly. John had always wished he could speak as forcefully as those two. But now he saw that the very act of listening to them, instead of leaping into the discussion on his own, allowed him to appreciate the majesty of their words more than ever before. Yes, there was something to this *being quiet and taking it all in*. There was power here, to observe, to think, to understand.

"Then, of course, there's the matter of this Hergs character himself," Scott went on. "He does seem to be a bigger problem than we originally thought. His and Carson's assault on Jack and Joe on the bus was one thing, but his involvement in the attack on the Civic Center, in the company of a Martian, is very disturbing. And one has to assume that his proximity to the Space Carpet Hotel last night means he was also involved with the murder of General Douglas."

"And he has that teleportation capability," Joe put in. "All the Martians apparently do."

"And then there's Commander Joe Commer wondering aloud on live AresNet whether the USSF Translator's rendition of *Emperor Hee-Arr-Grgsss* refers to an *Emperor Hergs* of the Martians. You can imagine what various AresNet pundits have made of *that*. Half the populace of Mars now apparently thinks that Sam Hergs is the emperor of the Martians!"

"Was that live, too?" Joe complained. "I would've thought once we were in the cave--aw, of course! AresNet wouldn't have any scruples about that. Anyway, I'm sorry, sir. I got carried away. It sure sounded like it was trying to say *Hergs*."

"Well, this Samuel Jay Hergs is a cipher right now. And as far as we can tell he's currently not on this planet."

"*Wow!*" John said in spite of his new determination to listen and absorb. "Uh, sorry, sir."

This time Scott ignored him, which John supposed was for the best. "Well, we're pulling together all the information we can on him. I can give you the standard biography stuff right now, but once we finish tapping all the databases, we'll run it through the CogniSort program and upload it to the *Typhoon*. You can read the final report on the way to Mercury."

"Mercury?" Jack said. "You mean …"

"Tonight," Scott said. "You men will have a couple hours rest while the *Typhoon I* is readied for takeoff."

"*Man,*" someone whispered incautiously behind John.

"Now, I know you men are tired," Scott said. "Beat up, exhausted, all of you. I understand. But if we're to take this writing on that stone table seriously, if we can believe the USSF Translator's rendering of those symbols, we have only two days' warning of an impending attack on this planet from Mercury. And we don't know when that two-day warning begins. The Martians may have carved that message an hour before you men arrived at the cave, or forty-eight hours ago, or three weeks ago. We just don't know."

"I can't believe they'd sit down and carve out that sort of message in stone," Joe put in. "It seems like a silly way to communicate anything."

"Well, what do we know of their habits or their culture?" Scott snapped. "Maybe they carve out email to each other, who knows? It doesn't matter. We've seen the message, we've been attacked by a Martian army from a Martian saucer, an army that's apparently capable of teleportation, and we've got to investigate this Mercury connection immediately. If they do have the kind of death ray they're boasting of, we're in serious trouble."

"Yeah, but nobody could have a ray that could do any serious damage to Mars from Mercury," Lee Borman of

Typhoon II put in. "We're something like a hundred sixty-nine million miles apart now. We checked the navigation database on the way over."

"Lieutenant, I know you're an expert with PlanetBlasters, but I imagine that two days ago you would've similarly scorned the idea of a ray that shatters people like glass."

"Yes, sir, but over a hundred sixty-nine million miles any beam would be so attenuated--"

"I think we should assume the worst and act accordingly. These Martians are absolutely fanatic. They seem to feel that we've despoiled their planet and that the only honorable thing to do now is destroy the entire thing. I for one am not going to take the chance of watching all we've built here on Mars shatter into a trillion pieces of glass."

"Bravo, sir!" John cried, clapping vigorously. "Well said, sir! Bravo! Totally articulate, sir! See, I'm learning how to absorb it! We're with you, sir! All the way, sir!"

John saw he was the only one clapping. He took in the gaping faces of twelve other men, including the smoldering visage of the crusty Supreme Commander of the United System Space Force.

"We'll ... be ready, sir," Jack spoke into the silence.

"Captain, is your brother capable of carrying out the mission I'm about to entrust to your care?" Scott said.

To John's dismay Jack appeared to hesitate. "I'm sure it's just that we've all been a little stressed by today's ... situation, sir," Jack said. "Everyone's a little tense."

"Make sure you're all well rested by 1730 hours, which is the time the *Typhoon I* crew will board the ship. Liftoff is 1800."

"Eighteen hundred ..." someone whispered again. The same person. John saw it was Ken Garrison.

John checked the large gold clock on Scott's desk. "So, it's 2:30 now. If this meeting goes on for another half hour, and then we spend say fifteen minutes getting back to our rooms, that would give us--"

"*John!*" Jack hissed again.

"What?" John said. "I'm just trying to figure out our rest

time. If we slept to five PM and spent a half hour getting from the hotel to the spaceport, that would mean, from 3:15 to then, uh, an hour and forty-five minutes of sleep."

"Lieutenant!" Scott snarled.

"We can do it, sir! We can be rested in that time!"

"Lieutenant! Shut up!" Scott yelled.

"John! Shut up! That's an order!" Jack cried.

"Captain! *You* shut up!"

"*Sorry, sir!*" Jack yelled back, then put his hand over his mouth, finally whispering: "I mean, sorry, sir!"

Scott glared around the room. "Of course, if you'd all rather take a *nap* right now, we don't have to waste your precious time with the rest of this meaningless little briefing."

"Uh, sir, of course not!"

"I can do it, sir, Jack has complete faith in me!" John cried.

Another agonizing silence. Finally Jack looked at the floor and said: "Yeah ..."

"Look, men," Scott said. "All of you. I know it's been hard. Today has been hard. *Typhoon I's* battle with the saucer yesterday was quite a surprise as well. And these *discoveries* have been hard. For all of us. But we really don't have a choice now. We don't have the luxury of waiting around to see what the Martians might try next. You're just going to have to go straight to Mercury, find whatever base the Martians have created there, and destroy it."

"That's very clear, sir," Jack said. "We'll be able to do it. But before we go, there's something I think you should know about the battle, and these Martians. I mentioned this briefly in the report I sent ahead."

"Ah, yes, this *prescience* thing," Scott said. "I did note that. Don't let it worry you, Captain, and I appreciate your bringing it up, by the way. I'd say that during the battle you were *in the flow,* as we say. Many soldiers report that feeling in combat, that some divine guidance is protecting them."

"But all of us, sir?" Jack said. "All of us together, knowing exactly the same thing was about to happen?"

Scott frowned. "I don't see--"

"Some of us felt it more than others. Joe, for instance."

"Yes, sir," Joe said. "It was like there were voices in my head, telling me exactly how the Martians were about to behave. And then--bam!--they'd do exactly that."

"I felt it, too!" John said. "It was like they practically *wanted* us to know exactly what they were going to do!"

Scott briefly trained his glare on John and went on: "You were all dazed by the suddenness of it all, I think. Battle against an unknown enemy, one that really has no grasp of tactics, behaving most foolishly as I saw from the video."

"Well, sir, be that as it may," Jack said, "but the crew and I are concerned that the enemy may actually have various psychic weapons we'd have no defense against."

"Psychic weapons! C'mon, boys! Let's not let battle fatigue cloud our judgment now. You're imagining things."

"But--"

"Now I certainly don't mean to discount any valid concerns, but I've reviewed those videos several times already and I see nothing in them that would constitute any *psychic weapon.* They may have teleportation capability, and that may be mysterious to us, but it's not psychic for God's sake. Gentlemen, a few Xons lobbed onto the surface of Mercury will cure you of any worries about *psychic weapons,* I assure you."

John could feel the men wince. One Xon bomb had eventually led to the explosion of the moon, and Mercury wasn't that much bigger than the moon. Nobody wanted to think about lobbing "a few" Xons there and adding one more planet to the list of nonexistent solar bodies.

"Enough," Scott said into the silence. "I promise I'll take your concerns about psychic weapons into consideration. But before we end this meeting, I'd like to ask Major Sperry here to give a status update on *Typhoon II.*"

"Well, thank you, sir. Things are definitely coming along," Phil Sperry said. "We're able to sustain our sublight top end at one-fifth light speed, with none of the reactor problems that were bothering us in May. So we've stabilized the Augmented Nuke for sublight. As for the first faster-than-light test, that's set for

July 18th, and I'm sure we'll be ready for it."

"Hmm. Thanks, Major. And for this Mercury mission, I want the *Typhoon II* crew at the spaceport to act as operational support for *Typhoon I*."

"Of course. We'd all be glad to help out in any way."

"And I'm just thinking aloud now, Major, but is there any possibility the *Typhoon II* itself could assist in this mission?"

Sperry blinked. John noted the dried blood on his face where the jagged fragments of Major West had pierced him. "Well, sir, aside from a few dozen punch lists to go over before we'd be certified for combat duty, we still lack permanent pilots."

"Well, we have staff pilots Donnelley and Zang on standby. They're out in the Jovian Fragment Field now, but we can quickly recall them."

"Huh," Sperry said. "They'd do all right, I suppose."

"Oh, c'mon, Phil!" John cried. "You called them *pedestrian* the other day!"

"Lieutenant Commer!" Scott snapped. "I have had about enough out of you today!"

"John!" Jack snarled.

"We can't have *pedestrians* for the *II!*" John exclaimed. "That would be sacrilege! Only the best pilots should fly the *Typhoons!* Now, sir, you know that all this time I have been listening, and absorbing, all during this talk I've been listening and absorbing, and I think I know what needs to be done! Now if I were to take the *Typhoon I*--"

"*You* take it? You mean *pilot* it?" Scott said in disbelief.

"I've seen real combat twice now! I'm ready to pilot the *Typhoon,* sir! I'm almost certified as you know!"

Scott stared back.

"No, look! We'd have Jack and Joe piloting the *II!* I'm sure it's newer technology, not fully tested, but they'd be the guys for it! But for me, flying the *Typhoon I* would be old hat! I've spent hundreds of hours in the *Typhoon* simulators, I know what I'm doing, sir! I'd be a natural! And we'd have Will Connors along with me as copilot!"

Scott sat stunned. He finally managed: "And … and then who would replace Lieutenant Connors as navigator on the *Typhoon II?*"

"Get one of those staff pilots to do it! Navigation is nothing! A child could do it! It's all computer-assisted anyway! Just like my sensor duties on the *Typhoon!* Boring! I want to pilot!"

Scott closed his eyes. "Well, thank you for your suggestion, Lieutenant. I think I will stick with my original plan, thank you. Captain?"

"Uh … yes, sir?" Jack whispered.

"See that your sensor officer, and in fact, all your men, get their hour and forty-five minutes of sleep, then be at your ship at 1730 hours."

"Uh, yessir."

"Major Sperry, you do the same for your crew."

"Yes, sir," Sperry said.

"No! Wait!" John said. "Sir, I meant it when I said I'd do anything! Anything at all! I'll do anything to destroy that Martian base! I can pilot! I know I can!"

"Dammit, John!" came one more hiss and a corresponding punch at John's elbow.

"Dismissed," Scott said, turning to his papers. "Report to me while en route to Mercury."

The men filed out of the room. John waved his arms to catch Scott's attention. "Sir! Sir! You don't understand! I've listened! I've absorbed! And now I'm ready! Ready to do *anything!*" John cried, flailing, legs giving way as his eldest brother brutally dragged him out the door. "*Anything at all!*"

CHAPTER FOURTEEN
The Commer Brothers
Friday, June 9, 2034, 1830 hours

Jim felt the inertial dampers kicking in as the *Typhoon* broke from Mars orbit and accelerated to 49.8 million miles per hour. "We're on our way," came Jack's voice over the intercom. "Acceleration ceasing ... now." Another barely perceptible adjustment of inertial forces. "Harri--status of solar rechargers."

"Operational," came Harri's voice from further down the fuselage. "We'll have the Augmented back to full strength in one hour."

"Thanks," Jack said. "Jim, is our course to Mercury laid in?"

"All set," Jim said, finishing up a few keystrokes at his console. Of course, the navigation wasn't complex. They were flying a straight line to Mercury, or to be fussily precise, where Mercury would be in 3.4 hours. Still, they were aiming at a point of light near the solar glare and it was important to double-check the computer.

"Then we'd like to see you in the Control Room for a few minutes," Jack said.

"Who? Me?" Jim said. His work was essentially done for this mission. If anyone, they ought to be checking with John about how his sensors were going to locate the Martian base on Mercury. But he shrugged and set his console on locked mode. "Sure, I'll be right over."

He paused on the catwalk outside the Navigation Room and looked towards the rear of the *Typhoon*. The Communications, Navigation, and Sensor Rooms were aligned down the upper starboard quarter of the fuselage, balanced by the upper port quarter's equipment storage bins. The starboard catwalk zigzagged to the center of the ship for the two weapon turrets at the rear, so that the computers only had to cancel out a centered line of tail fin for PlanetBlaster fire. Below him, the escape craft squatted on the hull over its own exit hatch, and further back Harri attended to the Augmented Nuke at the rear of the ship.

Everything was illuminated in brilliant white.

"How's your landing gear, Harri?" Jim called down. "Rough takeoff, huh?"

Harri looked up. "Some jerk on the ground had *both* starboards underinflated. Despite what their checklist said. We'll be okay. I've reinflated 'em, but jeez."

"We don't usually have a one-day turnaround, though."

"We ought to be able to do it in four hours. Those guys are getting lazy, I tell you."

Due to the short turnaround time from their mission yesterday, the *Typhoon* had made a rare horizontal takeoff, though such a wheeled launch was slow and inefficient. The wheels were primarily used for landings, so Jim could see how the techs might've misjudged the inflation. The preferred method was to vertically blast off the launch pad, but this took more preparation time. The takeoffs were vertical 3G acceleration, as the inertial dampers didn't function well near the gravity wells of planets. But the good side of that was that the men could keep up their high gravity skills.

"Huh," Jim said. "Well, we'll put the screws on 'em when we get back. I'll see you later. Got a meeting with Jack."

He made his way past Ken Garrison in the Communications Room. Ken kept his hatch open, but like everyone else he was ready to slide it shut in a second if the main cabin depressurized. Jim moved past the Solar Recharger assembly and into the Control Room.

Jack and Joe swiveled to him. "C'mon in. Shut the door behind you and take a seat," Jack said, indicating the third seat at the rear of the Control Room.

Jim did so. "What's up?"

"Well, we've got three hours before we hit Mercury, not much to do. And, well, I'm sorry, Jim, but this is really the only time we can talk. I know it's awkward."

Jim looked back and forth between his two older brothers. Like him, they wore their red, white and blue ship uniforms. But they looked embarrassed. Jim tried to think what he could possibly have done to get dressed down by his brothers.

"So … what's going on?" he managed.

"Well, it's John," Jack said. "We have to do something about him."

"*Oh …*"

"I mean, I don't want to be ganging up on him, but really, this just can't go on."

"Are … are you sure we should be discussing it now? I mean, on this mission? I mean, with everything at stake?"

Jack sighed. "When else can we discuss it? We haven't had a second."

"I just don't think this is the time. We can't have loss of morale, you know." Didn't Jack realize that? Wasn't morale a major concern?

"I hate to say it, but I agree with Jack here," Joe put in. "John could've gotten us killed yesterday in that saucer attack. He just wasn't reacting, wasn't following orders. He gets so dreamy and out of it."

Jim looked away. Of course, Joe was right. Then again, it was just like Joe to stick up for everything Jack said. The two of them so tight, the command crew versus the commoners on the ship. Jim didn't want to go down that ancient path again, Jack/Joe versus Jim/John, the two older brothers versus the youngest. But Jim always had to play that role, had to be John's defender, even though he'd always found John childish and irritating and secretly wished the axis could be Jack/Joe/Jim, the mature ones, with John somewhere off to the side.

"You can't … *split the Commers,*" Jim whispered. "I can't believe you're saying all this stuff. I mean, *now.*" Was Jack so stressed by all these responsibilities? By the saucer attack, by the skirmish in the desert today? The skirmish Jim couldn't even think about yet?

"We have to say it," Jack countered. "I've got eight lives at stake on this mission. On every mission from here on out. John's not making it. We've given him all these chances, and now--"

"He performed well during the war," Jim protested. "And during the Evacuation."

Jack swiveled back and forth and crossed his arms. "He

performed poorly. We all know that. Everyone on this ship is always having to stop and hold his hand."

"But this is our *brother*." Jim wondered whether these two might size him up in the same tones as soon as he left this room, which he fervently wished would happen right now.

"And that's why he's been protected all this time. Because he's our brother, because everyone thinks it's cool how all four Commer brothers got into the USSF and are serving on the same ship. We have this media image to maintain and it's getting pretty silly if you ask me."

"But he's not bad at all. You know his IQ tested at 160." Jim pointed to the command console behind Jack. "I hope you have the intercom off for this!"

Jack glanced back. "It's off. Jim, look. We need your help on this. Joe and I have been discussing this for a while, but after John's performance in Scott's office today we knew something had to give. I mean, everyone heard me let him have it outside Scott's office, but did it do any good?"

"You were pretty harsh with him."

"And he acted like he just wasn't going to listen. Stuck his nose up in the air and pretended I wasn't there."

"Which enabled you to completely lose control of yourself right out in the hall," Jim pointed out. "I'm sure Scott heard everything."

"Yes, I'm sure everyone on the 130th floor heard everything. And yes, I'm ashamed for losing my temper. But don't you see, Jim? This is a military organization, not a family. Anybody else who talked back to me or Scott like that, they'd be cleaning toilets on what's left of Europa. But John gets this special protection, whether or not he's endangering the crew and the entire population of Mars. Don't you see the necessity of doing something? What would you do now?"

"I don't know," Jim said, agonizingly aware that he himself would not give John one more chance after what happened at Scott's office a few hours ago. Nobody had gotten their hour and three-quarters of sleep this afternoon, that was for sure.

"I don't know either. I considered replacing him with

Patrick James for this mission, but Pat doesn't know our routines. We can't train him in three hours, either. I do grant that John knows his sensors, and I'm really hoping he can just give me the data we need, we erase the damn Martian base, head home, and deal with this after that."

"This all seems so unfair. I'm sorry, Jack, I'm not being much help, but I can't help but think how hurt he'll be to be off the *Typhoon*. He was so good for such a long time."

"We all hoped he'd be good. But deep down, I think we all knew he just wanted to come into the USSF because the other three of us were here. I don't know, but I've always felt the three of us had a real calling to be here. Joe didn't get into the *Typhoon* project just because I did. You didn't just because Joe and I did."

Jim shrugged off Jack's feeble attempt to include him in a new axis. Nevertheless, there was truth in what Jack said. While the *Typhoon E* project had attracted Jim because it was the newest and most challenging technology of the time, he'd also assured everyone that if there was any other way he could serve in the USSF, staying apart from his brothers if that was thought best, he'd do it in a second. The breakdown of the solar system, the war in Alpha Centauri, demanded he not think of his own petty ambitions.

"John's been a bit off since October 8th," Jack said. "I think we all know that."

"Yeah, well I'd say we've *all* been off since October 8th," Jim shot back.

Jack and Joe both grimaced. "Yeah, you got that right," Joe finally said. "Still, it all comes down to: can we still go ahead and fulfill our duties? Until the *Typhoon II* comes fully online, all eight of us are responsible for the most powerful spaceship in existence. And the future of humanity on Mars is depending on us. Do you really want someone on board who's so rattled by October 8th that he can't function?"

"He can function," Jim whispered. "I know he can function."

"Really?" Jack said. "After yesterday and today?"

"Maybe ... maybe if he got his own command. He wants to

pilot, we all know that, he's trained for it, and maybe if he had his own ship, he'd have high energy, and enthusiasm, maybe he'd straighten out."

Jack and Joe shook their heads. "He can't command," Jack said. "We all know that. Yes, he's brilliant, IQ 160 and everything, but he can't focus on anything. He's so out of control and impulsive."

"So maybe he should be a fighter pilot. Those impulsive types make great fighter pilots."

Jack and Joe looked at the floor. As the silence went on, Jim reluctantly admitted that he was glad to be in the Control Room with his two older brothers. Despite the agonizing talk, he was comforted by the trust they offered. The Control Room was bright, the black wraparound windows showing apparently motionless stars as the *Typhoon* cruised at 49.8 million miles per hour, and Jim was shocked that he'd forgotten all about Martians on Mercury and a death ray being readied to destroy Mars.

And Jim did feel uneasy at the thought of one-eighth of the crew not being up for this mission. Wasn't it obvious that John decided to seek the Naval Academy in the fall of '27 just to stick with his brothers? By the time Jim was in as the third Commer, their father, an Illinois congressman and the eventual legislative sponsor of the USSF, was easily able to get Senator Khamard's appointment for John.

John had never distinguished himself at the Academy. About all Jim remembered of him there was John writing a few songs for a band called Nine Dollar Massage and singing a poor lead in it. Jim had had to babysit John through his freshman year. John barely made it through the Academy, but since he'd scored well on sensor systems, and the concept of "the four Commer brothers" had by then morphed into a minor media phenomenon, he'd been pushed into the *Typhoon E* project at the start of his junior year at USNA. When the Naval Academy was subsumed along with all other service academies into the USSF, John, class of '31, became in fact the only USSF Academy graduate of the four. By then Jack had little choice but to reluctantly allow John a post on *Typhoon I*.

Jim had been shocked when Joe told him last month that Dad was pushing for John as the command pilot for the *Typhoon II*. John who'd barely passed his piloting classes and never gotten his pilot's certificate. "Well, look," Jim finally said. "Whatever you do decide, if you at least maybe have a long talk with John, that would be good. Maybe just you, Jack, you know how much he admires you. Hell, maybe even let him copilot the *Typhoon* a few times on some routine runs. Show him you care. Then maybe you could get him into some non-military piloting or something."

Jack reached back for a cup of coffee at his console. "I've thought about all that stuff. Problem is, you have a two-hour talk with John and it looks as if everything's okay, that he perfectly understands what's needed. Then you turn around and he's whining about the NAV4 Cluster problem when we need him to focus on a battle situation, or he's cackling like a maniac in front of General Scott. It's like he's *daring* us to court-martial him."

Jim nodded reluctantly. "So you've made your mind up to kick him off the *Typhoon*?"

Jack winced. Joe took a moment to grab his own coffee from a cup holder on the side of the ship. Jim wished he'd brought his own mug to even things out.

"I haven't made a final decision," Jack said. "But it looks that way."

"I guess I never realized it was this serious. This is gonna break his heart, unless you do it right. And then there's also the *public relations* aspect of moving him off the *Typhoon*."

"*Man*," Joe said. "That was exactly what we were talking about as you walked in."

Jack nodded. They all understood that breaking up the fabled Commer brothers would have systemwide media impact. There was also Senator Jackson Khamard of Acidalia Planitia and political fallout to consider. And then there was Jonathan Commer, Sr. Some of the public relations considerations were actually *private* considerations.

"How are you going be able to able to tell Dad?" Jim said. "He's *committed* to the four Commer brothers on the *Typhoon*."

"I know, I know. It's not easy. But I report to General Scott, not Dad," Jack said, as if trying to convince himself. "I have to think of the ship, of what's best for the crew and for the USSF."

"It might be better to wait on all this until this flap with the Martians dies down. We could have a big loss of morale throughout the solar system if we split up the Commers now."

"I know," Joe put in. "It's like there's this myth about us. The four Commer brothers, who all decided to sign up for the USSF together."

"That's the official story," Jack agreed. "But we just can't be slaves to it. The Commer brothers can't be holding the solar system together. This all has gone on far enough."

Jim shook his head. But didn't everyone on the *Typhoon* know John had to go? "Dad's gonna have kittens," was all he could say.

Jack looked out the window at the stars, and the sun directly ahead, muted by the cockpit window's computerized tinting. "I know. And here I am crucifying *Junior!*"

There was a long silence. Jim was appalled. Jack had to be highly stressed to even allude to the painful family story. "Well," Joe said, "we do have to be careful, I guess. John's always been the most beloved son."

"Jonathan, *Junior!*" Jack spat. "Well, who cares? I finally took care of that!"

"You mean, when you were seventeen?" Jim blurted.

"What? What are you talking about?"

"The big argument with Dad, when you were seventeen!"

"What does that have to do with anything?"

"Because you told Dad he'd ruined your life! Because of the name change!"

"Forget it. I was just blowing off steam."

"You and Dad have never really talked since you were seventeen!"

"That had nothing to do with it!"

"Since the argument! When you screamed it was all Dad's revenge on you!"

"You were too young to remember!"

"Forget that! I was thirteen! Of course I remember! John tells me *he* remembers! The whole house was *shaking* with the argument!"

Jack folded his arms. "Crap on it. So I told him I never wanted to see him again. So what? Guess I didn't keep that promise, huh?"

There was another long silence. Finally Joe put in: "I know Mom's talked about how much that hurt Dad, to hear you telling the entire family that he'd ruined your life."

Jack stood up. "Why the hell are we discussing this? The problem isn't me and Dad, it's John!"

"So now it's *John* who's ruined your life?" Jim said.

"No, Dad did by taking away my name when I was five. Okay? Everyone happy now?"

"Shhh! Everyone in the house can hear you! I mean, the ship! The ship!"

Joe laughed. "I can't believe this! We're fighting it again!"

"Look, it's simple," Jack said. "Very simple, nothing to understand. I was Jonathan Commer, Jr. One day when I was five I made the mistake of telling Dad I liked my nickname better! That's all I did! That's all! I swear to God that's all!"

"I know, I know, you liked *Jack* better than *John*," Joe said. "But--"

"I know! I *violated* something! He turned *against* me! From that very day! I was only five, for God's sake!"

"Hasn't anybody ever said that the old boy must have been pretty touchy about all that?" Jim said, trying to grin and failing. "I know I for one never understood it."

"He must've been insane! He must've wanted a whole line of Juniors, Thirds, and Fourths, down to infinity! He must've known from that very instant that I'd never have a Third!"

"Why didn't Mom--"

"Because she was gone! Vacant!" Joe cut in. "She probably never even knew what Jack said when he was five!"

"She had to have known once John came along!" Jim shot back. "It's pretty obvious when the fourth kid is named Jonathan Junior!"

"Stop it! Stop it! Stop arguing over me!" Jack cried. "I can't stand it!"

"So Dad names the fourth kid Jonathan Commer, Junior," Jim said. "Jonathan is legally removed from *your* name. Sure, that would bum anyone out."

"But I was only five when that happened. How could I have cared?"

"Because when you were seventeen you screamed your entire life was ruined because of it!"

"That's stupid! How could anyone's life be ruined about that? Why would I have been so touchy about it? Especially when I hated the name Jonathan all along?"

"Mom says that Dad says that that means you *hate* him," Joe pointed out.

Jack threw himself into his command seat like a bag of garbage. "So what? So what? Yeah, I admit he always made me feel like a damn outcast! So what?"

"But we always looked up to you. We always worshipped you," Jim said.

"Yeah, but there was always this tension," Joe pointed out. "Always the sense we were rebelling, doing something forbidden, whenever we did that."

"Yeah, maybe. But what about John hero-worshipping Jack? How could the one who destroyed Jack's life turn around and hero-worship him?"

"Nah, forget it. John never destroyed anything," Jack said. "He was just there. Just came along and got the goddamn designation. Who cares? Maybe the oldest brother always gets hero-worshipped. Maybe the youngest always gets something else. I don't know. Look, all this speculation is pointless. We can always psychoanalyze each other another time. Right now we've just got to do what we have to do."

Another long silence. Jim finally said: "Sure, we all know that."

"None of this matters. It's just that … I have to tell him. Right after we blow the Mercury base to atoms, I'll tell him. I'll send a message on to Mars, I don't care how long it takes to get there, it'll be over and done. I won't have to hear his response, it'll just be a done deal."

"Huh?" Jim said, then realized who Jack was referring to. "Aren't you going to tell John first?"

"Oh. Yeah. Right," Jack said. "Tell John first. Right after we get the base. First John, then *home*."

"*Man*. I can't believe it."

"Some things just have to be done. You wish you didn't have to do it, but …"

"Well, it's not like you have to die in three hours," Joe put in helpfully. "It's just like sending an email. In fact, it *is* sending an email."

Jim stood up. "Look, I need to get back. Are you done with me here?" Joe's statement filled him with anxiety. How could they be bandying about these family issues, as if any of it mattered, when in three hours they'd engage the enemy above Mercury? Who knew what they'd be facing then? Jim saw Jack and Joe as tremendously unprepared for what lay ahead. But there was no way to say that.

"Sure, sure," Jack said, moodily sipping his coffee as if the email were really that important, compared to *death*. "Thanks for your input, Jim, I know this has been--"

"E'KAML … ERU'ULL KYLULK URRR!" reverberated from the metal beneath their feet. Frantic thumps followed.

"What the hell?" Joe cried, whipping out his blaster.

"It's coming from the storage room!" Jack said, also pulling his blaster. Jim quickly did the same.

"There's someone down there!" Joe yelled.

CHAPTER FIFTEEN
The Stowaway

Jim was the first down the ladder to the bottom of the ship. He whirled the wheel on the storage room hatch directly beneath the Control Room.

"Pull it open and stay behind it!" Jack ordered. "Joe and I will be ready to blast whoever's in there!"

Jim yanked the heavy hatch open and toward himself.

"Oh my God!" he heard Joe cry.

"Come on out! Hands high or we'll fry you!" Jack shouted.

"Dammit to hell!" Harri McNarri said, running up with an EOS rifle. "Those buttheads at the launch pad let this *thing* stow away? On the *Typhoon?*"

"YOOO DOO NAOAT SCARRE MEE EURTHMANN."

"What the hell?" Jim said, unable to resist coming out from behind the door and staring with the entire crew.

A man crouching behind a crate?

No, it was a Martian. A naked finback.

"YORR GRAVVITTEE ISS TOOO MUCHH! MAYKES MEE SIKKK!" the creature gasped. Jim met its huge unlidded catlike eyes. He felt sick himself, sick in his soul. How could he understand what the creature was saying? Yet it moved its lips, making croaking sounds approximating English.

"GETT BACKKK!" the creature moaned, waving a small black object. "I HAFFF SHATTTRRR RAAY GUNN HERRE, AND I WILLL USSE ITTT!"

"Crap!" Joe said.

The finback was experiencing three times its normal Martian gravity, Jim realized. USSF personnel were required to stay in shape in 1G, and despite long stays on Mars, all *Typhoon* missions kept interior gravity at 1G, except for the 3G vertical takeoff accelerations they endured. While their horizontal takeoff today had maybe only added another G to the mix, this unfortunate finback must have suffered six times its normal gravity at that point. No wonder it was freaked.

"Drop it! Drop it!" Jack shouted.

From behind its plastisteel crate, the Martian wrinkled its ungainly fish lips. "I KNOWW YOOO. I KNOWW YOOO ALL ... FRUMM THEE DESSEERRTTT."

"*No* ..." Jim gasped. Images of this morning's battle cascaded through him, all the death, the noise, the shattering, the sprawl of blasted Martian bodies up and down the sides of the desert amphitheater. Oddly, Jim experienced it as if he were one of the Martians charging up the hill towards the men behind the ruined rovers. He could see the faces of Jack and Joe--and himself--firing EOS guns and heat blasters down the slope towards *M'rrpla and his comrades.*

M'rrpla. The Martian's name was *M'rrpla.*

"WEE LAWWSSTT SOOO MANNEE SOLJERRS INNN THATTT BATTELLL. WEE WUNDERR WHETHERR WEE KANN SERRVIVVE."

"Drop the weapon!" Jack repeated. "Drop it!"

"BUTTT WEE SAFFED OURR LEEDERR DAR. WE SAFFED DAR FRUMM YOOO. SUMHOWW DAR WILLL KONKURR YOOO."

"The big guy! The Martian they herded away! The one who teleported back into their saucer!" Joe gasped.

"The thing's in my head! In my head!" John whined from behind Jim.

"It's replaying the battle! In my mind!" Ken Garrison shouted.

"DAR ISS OURR LEEDERR. ISS VARRY BRRAAVE. YOOO WILLL NEFFERR KONKURR HIM."

"His name is *M'rrpla,*" Jim said in wonder. "How can we know his name is *M'rrpla?*"

Jack's heat blaster wavered. "I don't know! You! How can we be speaking to you? How did you learn English?"

"We're getting some sort of mental *assist* from him," Joe grunted. "I don't see how."

"It's making me feel sick in my *mind!*" John cried.

"Shut up, John, and that's an order!" Jack snapped without looking back. "You there--M'rrpla! Who's this Dar character? Is he the emperor of the Martians?"

"Can we--can we talk to him?" Joe added.

"NEFFERR!" The creature stood defiantly behind the crate, its shattergun still raised. "DAR ISS OURR BRILLIANNTT MILLITARREE LEEDERR. NOTT OURR EMPURORR. OURR NEW EMPURORR IS HEE-ARR-GRGSSS--"

An image of a swarthy man with unkempt greasy black hair and puffy red lips shoved itself into Jim's mind.

"*Hergs!*" Jack and Joe yelled at once.

"Did--did you get that picture?" Jim cried.

"Yes! We all must have! I can't believe it!" Jack said. "Do you mean to tell me that Sam Hergs--a *human being*--is--is--"

"HEE-ARR-GRGSSS ISS OURR NEW EMPURORR. WEE WORSHIPP HEE HOO EMMBRAASES FURST PRINNSIPULS OF FURST HOMME, OURR PLANNETT. HEE ISS HYUMANN FRUM PLANNETT MARRBULL, LIEKKK YORRSELFFS, BUTT ISS ENNLIIITENNED."

"You're saying that butthole has turned traitor to the people of Earth and is working with you terrorist Martians?" Joe demanded. "Man, are we gonna fry his ass in a couple hours!"

"Quiet, Joe," Jack warned. "If these guys have telepathy, and can send messages to Mercury and warn them--"

"WEE OF FURST HOMME HAFFF YOONITTY WITH SOME OF YOOO HYUMANNS FRUM PLANNETT MARRBULL." More images flooded Jim: humans training with Martians, practicing with shatterguns and stolen EOS rifles in remote Martian deserts. Emperor Hee-Arr-Grgsss traveling to Earth in Martian saucers, recruiting soldiers from those disaffected individuals who so hated the United System, the USSF, and its plans for abandoning the ruined planet that they'd elected to die on Earth. But now they were coming back for revenge.

"HEE-ARR-GRGSSS AND WEE OF FURST HOMME WURKK TOOGETHHER TOO FORRM A SOOPER RAACE TOO KONKURR YOOO! DESSTROII YOOO!"

"Kill it! Kill it!" John cried, pulling his own blaster and advancing.

"No!" Jim said, jumping in front of the Martian and waving

his hand. "This is *M'rrpla!*"

The air sang. A blue-purple glow suffused the interior of the *Typhoon* and died. Jack and Joe dove for the hull.

"Ow!" Jim said, pulling his left hand down. Bee sting on the index finger? He brought it up to his face.

The tip. Bubbling and cracking like white-hot diamonds.

"Is ... is anyone else hit?" Jim managed, staring as the cracking began moving down his finger.

"YOOO WILLL DIIEE, TOOO BADDD," said M'rrpla, still training the shattergun on the rest of the crew.

"I ... I ..." Jim gasped, paralyzed. Fever blossomed in his brain. All he could do was trace the evolution of those cracks as they gathered speed. *Death*. To *shatter*. Incredible. Intoxicating.

Something flung him against the open metal hatch. He felt his arm spread against the metal.

Jack was there, dialing his blaster down to the narrowest possible dispersion, firing at the join of finger to palm. Jim gaped at the blaster burning the finger clean off, *the finger he'd had since he was a baby*--

The finger whirled away, shattering like a little champagne glass Jack might done target practice with.

Jim stared at his bloody, burned, ruined hand and collapsed in shock on the floor. "I--I--" he gasped. No, he couldn't give in to panic. He was needed for this mission. How could he pull himself together?

"Harri! Get Jim back!" Jack yelled. "Get him something for the pain and stop the bleeding! And somebody blow that little twerp's brains out! I'm sick of this crap!"

Harri undid the med kit he always carried at his waist. "God, I'm sorry!" Jim gasped as Harri got out a syringe.

"Quiet," Harri said. "I bet you're not feeling anything yet. This will guarantee that you don't. Or you won't care if you do." He jammed the needle into Jim's wrist and depressed the plunger.

"Wha's that ..." Jim said as ocean breezes and warm sunshine flooded his body.

"Alpha SynMorph, full dose," Harri said, grabbing Jim's

disfigured left hand. "Well, Jack's blaster cauterized the whole area, at least. I've got a bandage here and later I'll do you properly."

"Who cares?" Jim laughed. "Where's M'rrpla? I hope he didn't shatter anyone!"

"Jeez ..." Harri muttered, working a bandage onto the blank space between Jim's thumb and middle finger. "Nobody else was hit. The interior hull coating absorbed the ray. But the little bugger's hiding somewhere in the storage room with his damn shattergun. Nobody seems eager to climb over those crates and find it."

"All right, this is your last chance to come out and surrender," Jack shouted into the storage room, which wasn't that large but held six bolted-down crates the alien could hide behind. Jack turned on the storage room lights and motioned everyone else back but Joe.

"Let's move back," Harri grunted, helping Jim to his feet. Jim's legs were shaky but the shakiness was wondrous.

"M'rrpla, come out, buddy!" Jim sang. "We won't hurt you!"

"Sheesh," Harri said. "The SynMorph's gone to your head, man."

"JAKKK SAIDD HEE WANNTEDD TOO BLOWW MYY TWIRRPPY BRANES OUTTT!"

"But life is wonderful!" Jim laughed, waving his four-fingered hand at the storage room. "I don't care about a stupid finger! I really don't care!"

"*Man,*" Jack said. "Okay, M'rrpla, here's what I'm going to do. I'm going to close this door and lock you in here. You can try to shatter anything you want in there but the hull is protected. And then I'm going to go back up to the Control Room and do some acceleration without inertial dampers for a while, and we'll see how you like that."

Silence.

"For your information, we are actually coasting right now at 49.8 million miles an hour, as the solar rechargers replenish our nuke. But we've recharged enough that I can get a few minutes at 5G right now, and I can probably get 8G if--"

A pink blur flashed out of the storage room, under Jack's legs, and scampered up the ladder to the Control Room. Joe fired a blast that just missed the creature.

Jim had no idea how he came to be the first one up in the Control Room. "Good move, M'rrpla!" he laughed, pointing his bandaged stump at M'rrpla raising his shattergun to the command console.

"I DESSTROII YORR SHIPP KONTROLLS! I SHATTTRRR YORR HOPESS ANND DREEEMSS OF KONKWESTT!"

The waves of shock, fear, and desperation pouring out of the alien nearly knocked Jim down. Again he locked eyes with the Martian. "M'rrpla, no! There's nowhere for you to go! There's nothing left! You saw what happened in the Kilpatrick Desert! We can't be defeated! We just keep coming on! We just keep coming on forever!"

M'rrpla paused, staring into Jim's giddy Alpha SynMorphed eyes. "JUSS … KEEEPP KOMMING ON … FORREFFER?"

"Yes! That's how it's always been!"

"THENNN … THENNN …" M'rrpla pressed the barrel of his shattergun to his fishy skull and fired. His headless body fell against the control panel and shattered.

CHAPTER SIXTEEN
Towards a Socialist Solar System

The men went into the storeroom and pulled out eight folding chairs which they set on the deck behind the escape craft. Jim felt safe in this little circle. It had always been their makeshift meeting room. Eight pairs of feet pointed to the round auxiliary hatch in the center of the circle. This bottom hatch had been installed at the beginning of the Evacuation as the only ingress to the massive passenger shells that had been attached to the *Typhoon*. But the men preferred to enter and exit via the main hatch at the rear of the ship. Not only was it easier to use, it didn't remind them of five hundred Evacuation flights.

"How're you doing, Jim?" Ken Garrison said, nodding in the direction of Jim's bandaged left hand. They hadn't let him help clean up the shattered mess in the Control Room, though he'd wanted to. After all, he was the one who'd received the last thoughts of M'rrpla. He ought to be the one to clean up the broken glass.

"I'm … okay …" Jim said. He swallowed a wry chuckle he knew would turn into a crazed laugh. He was still flying. "It doesn't hurt. Nothing hurts!"

"Don't worry, Jim! You can still navigate!" John shouted from across the circle. "All you have to do is use a different finger for typing nav commands! It's not like you were a pilot and needed every finger alive on the controls!"

"Cut it, John," Joe said wearily. "If you hadn't panicked and advanced on the Martian, he wouldn't have fired his shattergun and Jim wouldn't have lost a finger."

"It's not my fault! That Martian was dangerous! He would've fired anyway!"

"No, he was panicked right then. We all knew it, we all could sense it," turret gunner Craig Reynolds said. "Sense what was in its head."

"It wasn't panicked! It was evil! Evil!"

"Hey, it's all right, John!" Jim laughed. "I didn't need that finger anyway!" Aware that he was making people uneasy, he tried to rein in his idiot's grin.

There was a brief silence. "Do you really think we're able to receive thoughts and images from them? From the Martians' minds?" Reynolds said. "I mean, that's *creepy*."

"And if so, what are the Martians picking out of *our* minds?" said the other turret gunner, Mickey Michaels.

"Good question," said Harri McNarri. "We all felt we could anticipate their moves in the Kilpatrick Desert. Are they also able to anticipate ours?"

Jim nodded. Harri was such a good guy. So brilliant. Such a caring physician. His Alpha SynMorph was incredible stuff. Jim had absolutely no pain in his hand. He soared in ecstasy, yet his mind was perfectly sharp. "I really don't care about my finger!" he laughed.

Everyone nodded awkwardly.

"I am sorry about M'rrpla dying, though. He seemed like such a nice guy."

Jack finally spoke up. Jim knew he'd been letting the men shoot the bull for the last half hour, say whatever was on their minds, release some of the tension. "Well, you were the one who probably saved the ship, Jim. You talked him out of wrecking the controls."

And talked him *into* committing suicide, Jim thought. He knew he'd probably live with that guilt for the rest of his life. But somehow, amid Alpha SynMorph ecstasy, that was just a messy concept someone else would have to deal with later.

"Well, he might not've been able to do much damage. We've seen that those shatterguns work best on *organic* matter," Joe said, looking away from Jim's hand. "It'd take a long time for the shatter rays to do any damage to the controls."

Jack laughed. It was a rare wash of sunshine that Jim hadn't seen in a long time. "Joe, you're the one who gets upset when I set my coffee cup on the console! Like I might spill a few drops into the electronics! Don't you think even a short burst of a shattergun ray would do far more damage? Who knows what parts of the system might've been knocked out? We might not've been able to complete the mission. Hell, we might not've been able to even decelerate, for God's sake. Jim saved the ship."

"Okay, okay!" Joe grinned back. "Thank you, Jim."

"Anytime," Jim said. "But you know, I'm still sorry M'rrpla had to ... to go. It was almost as if we were on the verge of ..." No, he couldn't say *becoming friends,* could he? How could anyone be friends with *Martian marauders?* Yet, beneath all the panic and hatred, deep in M'rrpla's mind there'd been something deep and warm and positive.

"Well, it was obvious he was sent to sabotage the mission," Jack said. "No explosives in the storage room, but I suppose he still could've been on some sort of suicide mission."

"Hell, I really don't think he could've done too much damage to the ship with that shattergun," Harri pointed out.

Jim smiled at the hatch at their feet. This little meeting was like sitting around the campfire on the eve of battle, except that, instead of a campfire, they had an ugly gray hatch that opened to the vacuum of space.

Jack shrugged. "I don't know, Harri. Maybe take a few of us out, cripple the ship somehow, who knows? Somehow this M'rrpla character was sent to sabotage us. All we know is that Jim somehow talked him out of it."

As everyone pondered this Ken Garrison said: "So Hergs must be teaching some of 'em English."

Harri winced. "Not very good English."

"Again, I think we were helped by whatever we might be seeing in their minds," Joe said.

"Well, all this brings us back to Hergs," Jack said, "which was the main reason I called this meeting. We received the CogniSort summary on him and I printed it out." Jack held up what looked like fifty sheets of paper. "Thought I'd familiarize you all with some of it before we get to Mercury."

"Fantastic!" Jim laughed. "This is just like story time around the campfire!"

"You know, a full dose of SynMorph might not've been necessary," Harri observed.

"Okay," Jack said, scanning the document. "Full name,

Samuel Jay Hergs. Born April 19, 1999, in Maine, specific town not known. Had a police record from fourteen: drug use, drug dealing, gang activity. Never made it through high school, and nothing more in the database on him after 2017 until 2032, when he was arrested for helping turn an anti-space protest in New York into a riot."

"Oh, so he was one of *those*," Joe observed. Jim remembered the massive protests when the USSF began grabbing bigger and bigger chunks of the federal budget by 2032. In the wake of the Neptune explosion, the Uranus flyby, and the destruction of Jupiter and Saturn, there was no way the USSF was going to be stopped. Nevertheless, there were significant numbers of people who thought exploring space was foolish and that the money should go to repairing the gravitational disasters caused by the Uranus flyby.

"Later in 2032 Hergs published *Towards a Socialist Solar System,* which advocated the violent overthrow of the United System, the deaths of everyone currently in power, and the rise of a 'solar proletariat' to govern the system," Jack went on. "He wanted any existing spacecraft to be used, and I'm quoting, 'for the people, not for the exploitation of space and whatever indigenous peoples we may find there.'"

"I somehow missed that book," Harri said.

"Cripes, what a loser," Joe added.

"He does sound a little bit like Huey Vespertine," Ken Garrison put in.

Jack winced. Jim knew that the rupture of that old friendship still hurt. "Yeah, same anti-space rhetoric, I guess, but I still don't think he could be in league with Hergs. Huey's much too passive for that." Jack returned to the report. "Hergs was one of the people opposing the Evacuation last year. He was even openly calling for sabotage of passenger shells and evacuation ships."

"Sheesh," Joe said. "It makes you wonder how many of those accidents were really accidents."

The passenger shells losses had hit Joe hard, Jim knew, maybe harder than anyone else on the crew. The *Typhoon's* record was better than most: only six shells lost out of 523. Still, losing only six thousand people wasn't anything to feel good about.

"The records show he evacuated Earth on November 14, 2033," Jack went on. "But then he disappears once he gets to Mars. He never registered a Mars address. His cohort Al Carson did the same thing."

"So what's he been doing all this time, recruiting disaffected Martians for the cause?" Mickey Michaels put in. "And disaffected humans, too, I guess. But how did he find Martians when nobody else ever has?"

"I haven't read more than a couple pages of this, but I'll bet the answer's not in here."

"If he, or anyone who was even slightly *psychic,* I guess, just tuned in to whatever thoughts were coming out of Martian minds ..." Ken Garrison mused.

"Yeah, maybe they could track the Martians down," Joe said.

"Weird!" said Craig Reynolds. "But why didn't more people tune in, or pick up those stray thoughts, or whatever we think we've been picking up?"

"C'mon, this is all speculation," Jack said.

"Because the rest of us have been busting our asses building a new civilization on Mars, that's why," Harri put in. "We haven't got time for this fancy psychic *tuning in* crap. I grant you we've all felt something out of the minds of those Martians we've encountered, but you know it's all faint and contradictory. But there must be some people who're more sensitive to that stuff. Like Joe here evidently was picking up more, or Jim here was picking up more from M'rrpla than the rest of us. Maybe Hergs was holed up in some pressure shack in the desert, high on drugs, and somehow started *finding Martians*."

"That's it! That's it!" Garrison said. "He's messed on something like AlphaFlare, lying around, totally screwed up, but *open* to alien minds!"

Was that why he'd bonded with M'rrpla? Jim wondered. Because he was higher than the Andromeda galaxy on Alpha

SynMorph? But what burst out of him was: "Wow, this really is just like a ghost story! We're all around the campfire, telling stories about scary things! That we know nothing about!"

There was another long silence. "Well, this really is all speculation," Jack said. "We need to get back to work, check over our systems, and get ready. I'm just hoping that Samuel Jay Hergs is at this Mercury base."

Jim shook his head. Bad idea. His mind felt like a toy balloon, blown up, released, and rocketing around the room.

"We definitely need to off that bastard ASAP," Joe added, to Jim's wonder. When had his two older brothers turned into such killers?

"John, we'll need you fully alert on sensor readings," Jack said. "This is your chance to really show us what you know about your systems. We're going to have to check the entire surface of the planet for their base, and we'll also check to see what might be in orbit around the planet."

"Forget it, I've got it all set on automatic!" John laughed. "I managed a hack on the sensor array that lets me just sit back and sip my coffee as all this data just *funnels in!* You can have any kind of report you want in seconds!"

Jack sighed. "Well, that's all fine, I guess, but we need you to be ready to perform any sort of sensor probe we need. The situation will be changing from moment to moment, and we'll need you to be on top of it."

"No, look, here's my plan! You're all tired, Jim's tired, hell, he had a finger lasered off! But I'm not tired! I could pilot the ship while everyone else rested! The sensors are running on automatic, I don't need to be in there!"

"John, if you only knew!" Jim laughed. "If you only knew!"

"Jim, that's enough," Jack warned.

"Let him pilot!" Jim laughed. "Pilot!"

"I don't see what's so funny," John sniffed. "I *am* a pilot, after all. It's about time I had my own ship!"

Jack stood so fast that his metal chair collapsed with a bang on the steel hull. "All right, that's enough. Gentlemen, we are now in a combat situation. This meeting is over. Everyone to their posts. John, pick up these chairs and put them back in the storage room. Then return to your post in Sensors."

All the men stood. Only Jack, Joe and Jim had any idea why Jack was so angry.

"I'm not putting up any chairs!" John whined.

"John. The chairs. Now," Jack said, pointing. "No backtalk. Not another word."

The ship got so quiet that the whir of the ventilation fans seemed overpowering. John finally scowled, put his head down, snatched up Jack's collapsed chair, and stomped back to the storage room. The other men gingerly stepped backwards and found their way to their posts.

Jim had the hardest time of all. It took every shred of his willpower not to cackle maniacally. But Harri hadn't said anything about not being able to perform his navigational duties, so he quietly ascended the metal stairs to his job.

CHAPTER SEVENTEEN
The Ice Ray
Friday, June 9, 2034, 2130 hours

"Deceleration complete," Joe said, punching in commands on his console as his words went over the intercom to the entire crew. "Taking up orbit ... now. Altitude 115 miles." He flipped the intercom off. "Want it nose in so we can see?"

Jack nodded. "Flip us around." Joe fired thrusters that swung the craft to orbit nose down. They were on the dark side of the planet, and Jack's console automatically lightened its images of the craters below. "Looks like the moon. You know, I still can't get over that."

"The moon being gone?" Joe said.

Jack nodded. "Somehow the concept of the earth being ruined is easier to accept than the moon being nothing but fragments."

"Yeah, but did you see that crackpot idea in *Mars Magazine* about actually moving Mercury out of its orbit and sending it to Earth to orbit there? Something about reestablishing tides as part of renewing the earth."

"Someone told me about it. I didn't read it," Jack said. "But think of the energy required to do that."

"It said we should revive the old Project Orion and fire a whole mess of Xon bomb bursts from the planet. We'd just need this spring-loaded thousand-mile-wide contraption on the surface that'd absorb the explosions and shoot the whole damn thing to Earth."

Jack wanted to share his brother's mirth, but the subject revived the uneasiness he'd tried to quell the entire trip. The Xon bombs. Yes, they could probably destroy the Mercury base with just their PlanetBlasters, but at wide dispersion it would take some time to complete the destruction. And who knew whether the Martians might be able to fire the death ray even as the *Typhoon's* PlanetBlasters began frying their facilities?

But the Xon, launched in stealth and accelerating to twenty million miles per hour, would obliterate the entire facility before anyone knew it.

Yet one Xon had blown up the moon. Jack had no doubt that one Xon would destroy Mercury, if not right away, then over the next few weeks as destabilizing forces built within the planet.

Jack had two Xon bombs aboard the *Typhoon*. If he really wanted to see Mercury explode within the next few minutes, he could probably do it.

But he was uneasy for another reason. He wondered whether Joe shared it. Because whoever wrote that article for *Mars Magazine* had to be thinking of whatever forces had flung asteroids into the sun, hurled planets like Pluto and Uranus out of their orbits, and blown up the other gas giants.

There were unknown forces at work in the solar system. There were so many things people simply didn't understand. And here they were charging around with Xon bombs slung in their torpedo tubes as they were really in control of it all.

"Man …" Joe said. "I can't believe we're really *here*."

Jack nodded. He felt that way too. He felt the dread in his gut of what they had to do. But there was only one direction for any of this. Get into the middle of it.

"Gentlemen," Jack spoke into the intercom. "The search for the Martian base is underway. I know you've all been sitting for three and a half hours and we're all tired, especially after our skirmish in the desert this morning and … our stowaway. But we all need to be on high alert now. With any luck we'll be able to knock this enemy base out shortly and head on home. You all have images of the surface feeding to your monitors now. Joe and I have turned the ship nose down so we can see out the cockpit window. Report anything suspicious immediately. John, what are your sensors picking up?"

"Scanning the entire surface as it comes into view," John said. "I'll be able to pick up anything artificial. I'm also rescanning our known older bases down there and comparing them with what's in the database, just to make sure."

Jack blinked. When John was on top of things, he was definitely on top. "Thanks, John. Great idea. I'm getting your data on my console now." Jack hadn't considered that the

Martians might disguise their facility among some of the old USSF experimental stations scattered across Mercury. A dozen of these had been set up over the years, none manned at present.

So John was over his sulk. Good. It had probably sunk into all the men, sunk even below their exhaustion, just what was at stake here. Jack knew everyone was shocked at his abrupt breakup of the meeting and the way he'd made John pick up the chairs. But they knew where the command responsibility lay on this ship and that there could be no challenge to it in a combat situation. Jack was shocked at how angry he'd gotten, but over the past couple hours he'd realigned himself. The John question was just another problem to solve. Jack simply had to tune it out, tune out sending Dad the email. They were all exhausted, but they simply had to perform.

Jack peered at the barren surface of Mercury. They'd passed the sun on the way here, and now, swinging around the planet, they were on the verge of seeing a sunrise over the dark rim. Jack bit back the urge to shout back to John about whether he'd found anything yet, but he knew a planet three thousand miles in diameter had a lot of surface area.

The sun popped over the horizon and Jack adjusted the cockpit windows to compensate. Before long the *Typhoon* floated over craters and mountains in full sunlight. Jack scanned crater after crater, knowing he'd never be able to find the base just by looking, that they'd have to rely on John's sensors. He drifted into considering the aesthetic qualities of the desolation below. Like Earth's former moon and much of Mars, the surface of Mercury looked as if unimaginable space wars had been fought down there. Jack could feel the scars of cosmic violence, the comet bombs and meteor bombs raining down. He could feel the millions of centuries it had taken to pummel the planet into this curiously static chaos. The craters were mathematically round. One directly below looked as if someone had deliberately added to the circle's perfection by scraping the walls to a uniform width and height.

"Hey!" John called out. "That crater right below us--it's not a crater! There's a huge doughnut shape in the center! With machinery!"

Jack snapped out of his trance. "Damn! You're right! I was staring right at it! Size?"

"Crater's forty miles in diameter. Diameter of the torus itself about half a mile! I have imaging on it. It's a gun of some sort! Pointing straight up!"

"That's the base!" Jack cried.

"But it doesn't have a shot at Mars yet, maybe not for a couple weeks until Mercury rotates into position," Joe said. "Mars is below that thing's horizon right now."

"Who cares? We've found the damn thing!" Jack said. "Right on the equator! PlanetBlasters! Target and destroy!"

Joe pointed. "Jack! Jack! Do you see? The entire tube's glowing!"

Jack gaped at the entire doughnut shimmering brighter and brighter blue.

"Energy output increasing exponentially!" John shouted.

"PlanetBlasters charging!" Mickey Michaels called.

"McNarri!" Jack ordered. "Come to the Control Room to the Xon targeting station. If we can't take this thing out with the PlanetBlasters--"

Jack's window filled with blue light and the Control Room crackled with energy. He felt every hair standing on end. Joe dove for cover.

Harri McNarri climbed into the Control Room. "Was on my way here anyway. Figured you'd need the--"

"We've been hit! We've been hit!" came John's voice. "By some ray!"

Jack peered through yellow afterimages to see the *Typhoon's* twin PlanetBlasters striking the planetary surface. "PlanetBlasters firing!" Michaels shouted. "But we've only got one-tenth power!"

"Even at one-tenth--" Joe grunted from the floor beside Jack. Jack couldn't make sense of what he was seeing. Was Joe really encased in *blue-white ice?*

"We're all right! We're all--" Jack said, or tried to, as he found he could barely move his mouth. He looked down. He was *also* covered with ice. "I--I can't move!"

"This--this is impossible!" McNarri cried, pulling out his med kit.

"*You're* okay--" Jack grunted.

"I wasn't in the room when it hit. What the hell's going on?"

"Base destroyed! Base destroyed!" Michaels called.

"Wow ..." Jack mumbled, managing a slight turn to the window where he could see a cloud of dust billowing where the Martian base had been. "We got it!"

"Man, I just don't understand," McNarri said, moving between Jack and Joe, taking readings from his medical monitor. "This is crazy!" He spoke into the intercom: "Anyone else have--have *ice* on them? Repeat: ice anywhere on the body?"

"No, not here," said Ken Garrison.

"None here," said Jim Commer. "What's going on there?"

"We don't know!" McNarri said. "Jack and Joe are covered with *ice*. The ray hit right on the nose of the ship. Maybe somehow it could penetrate the cockpit plastiglass? Turrets? You guys have any--any *ice?*"

"No, none up here," Michaels replied. "Did you say Jack and Joe are covered with *ice?*"

"Cold ... I'm so cold," Jack muttered. "Can't move at all, 'cept for my eyes a little." His entire body was sheathed in half an inch of ice. Joe looked almost as bad, but he had his left arm free and was trying to pull himself onto his chair.

"The turret glass has that deflector coating," McNarri said. "Why the hell the cockpit windows don't have it I don't know. Looks like the ray came in through the windows, but I don't see how it could affect PlanetBlaster power."

"Forget it," Joe said. "If all their damn death ray could do was coat two of us in ice, well, hell, I'm not worried. We'll just thaw out."

"Well, I don't want to alarm you," McNarri gulped. "But both your life signs are--are failing! Jack's more than yours, Joe."

"Is ... that why I'm so cold ..." Jack whispered.

"I got beneath the console when I saw the ray," Joe gasped.

"I can move a bit, but I'm cold, too."

"Hey! My PlanetBlaster's used up!" Craig Reynolds called down. "I don't even have one-tenth now!"

"Me either!" Mickey Michaels said.

"Maybe the ray shorted some of our systems," Jack said. "Doesn't matter. Can fix later."

"The important thing is to get you guys back to Mars right now," McNarri said. "We've gotten the base."

"No, need to … confirm that," Jack mumbled.

"I'll radio Mars to send more ships to confirm the destruction," McNarri said. "Meanwhile, sorry to say, Jack, but I need to assume command here. According to USSF regulation 645-80--"

Jack tried to smile. "Forget the regs, Major. I see the problem. You have command. What are your orders?"

"We're getting our pilot and copilot back to Mars right now," McNarri said. "I don't have the medical supplies here, or hell, I don't have the expertise, to deal with this."

"Aw, c'mon, Harri, you're the best, we know that," said Joe. He was turning grayer by the minute. Jack imagined he himself looked worse.

McNarri continued to take readings. "I just don't know. I've never seen--"

"WARR-NIINNG! WARR-NIINNG! WARR-NIINNG!" came a hideous shriek through the Control Room speakers.

"What the hell?" McNarri demanded, jamming his hands over his ears. Jack wished he could've done the same, but to him, the sound wasn't that loud. In fact, everything was getting quieter.

"DIIEE DIIEE DIIEE DIIEE DIIEE FOOLISSHH HYUMANNS!" came another scream. "I AM KLA'L-P'RT, SCIENTISSTTT OF FURST HOMME!"

"You! Where are you speaking from?" McNarri shouted.

"He can't hear you," Jack began, but was cut off by another screech:

"I AMM ONN PLANNETT CINDERRR BELOWW YOOO, EURTHMANN! HAKKINGG INTOO YORR

KOMMUNIKAYSHUN SISSTEMMS! YOOO ARRR DOOMMED! YOOO GOTT WUN OF OURR EISSE RAAY DEEFENSS BASSESS BUTT DOO WEE CARRE? NOO BECOZZZ WEE HAVE TWENTEE-NINE MORR EISSE RAAYS! HAA-HAA-HAA!"

"Damn you!" McNarri cried. "If you have twenty-nine more, then we'll destroy 'em all!"

"WITHOUUT ENERGEE? OURR EISSE RAAYS SUKK ENERGEE FRUMM YORR SHIPP'S SISSTEMMS! THEYYY FRYY ELECTRIKKALL SISSTEMMS AND TURRRN ORRGANNIKK BEINGGS INTOO EISSE!"

"Sheesh, these guys like to turn people into *glass,* and now *ice,*" Joe said. "They must like *shiny transparent stuff.*"

"God, that's it!" McNarri exclaimed. "You guys are turning into *ice!*"

"TAAKES ABOWTT FORR DAAYS TOO TURRRN YOOO INTOO EISSE! HAA-HAA-HAA!"

"Garrison, pinpoint that transmission!" McNarri shouted.

Ken Garrison came on the line. "I can't, Harri! It seems to be coming from everywhere at once. I've been sending all this back to Mars as soon as I thought of it, but it'll be several minutes before they receive it."

"Do we have any armament?" McNarri said.

"Just the two Xons," said Michaels. "Our PlanetBlasters are useless right now."

McNarri checked Joe's console. "We do have propulsion. Looks like one-tenth. We can still get around."

"WEE DONN'T CARRE IFF YOOO GETT AROUNNDD ORR NOTT! BECOZZZ WEE WILLL FIRRE THEE REALL DEATTHH RAAY NOWW ANND DESSTROII FURST HOMME, WHATT YOOO CALLL MARRSS!"

"Dammit, target--target *something,*" McNarri muttered, looking over both Jack and Joe's consoles.

"THE DEATTHH RAAY ISS ELSSEWHERR ONN THE PLANNETT, FOOOLLZ! BUTT I GIFF YOOO A CLOO--ITT ISS MUCHH BIGGGER THANN ANN EISSE RAAY! HAA-HAA-HAA!"

"I've got it! The death ray!" John cried. "My sensors are almost gone, but up ahead, in the sunlight, right before the terminator!" Jack craned at the image coming to his console.

A vast doughnut dominated the limb of the world.

"Five hundred miles in diameter! The doughnut tube itself is fourteen miles in diameter!" John called. "The central assembly is thirty miles wide! And the ray gun--"

They could all see it on the screen as the ship's orbit slowly brought the base closer. The gun seemed to stick ten miles into the blackness of space.

"It's pointed at Mars! Repeat, pointed at Mars!"

"WEE WILLL TURRN FURST HOMME INTOO RAYDEEOAKKTIV SLAGG! ENTIRRE PLANNETT INTOO SLAGG! EVREEWUN DIIIES HORRIBLEEE! EVREEWUN!"

McNarri snapped the speaker off. "We don't need to hear that crap. We can't even think! He's certainly not telling us anything we need to know."

"I'm so cold …" Jack whispered. "Feel so drained."

"I'm getting that way, too …" Joe grunted.

McNarri punched in a command that changed the ship's attitude to horizontal flight. Now they could see the immense base slowly coming to them. The doughnut glowed light purple.

McNarri flew into the seat at the Xon bomb command station behind Jack. Jack couldn't turn to see what McNarri was doing, but it was obvious the decision the ship's engineer had to make.

"Good choice," Jack whispered.

"Dammit!" McNarri spat. "The launch mechanism is fried! On both Xons! The ray hit the launch tubes right on the front of the ship!"

"Can we pull them out manually?" Joe said.

"Great. We could do a spacewalk and pull out the Xons, but they don't have propulsion either. Their Augmented Nukes are fried, too."

"How about their detonation electronics?" Jack said.

McNarri checked his console. "Xon 1's is gone, but Xon 2's

still seems to be online. Great, we could set it off if we could get it down there."

"I'll take it down in the escape craft," Jack said. As the only possible decision came into his mind, he felt a renewed burst of energy and well-being.

McNarri blinked. "Well, that's very noble of you, Captain Commer, but here's a better idea. Use Arkonsky clamps to lash the Xon to the escape craft, then send it down on autopilot."

Joe had painfully climbed back into his seat and managed to punch in some commands with his free left hand. "*If* the escape craft autopilot survived the ice-ray. Which it didn't. It still has some preset escape routes that look functional, but autopilot's gone. It does have 10.12 percent propulsion capability."

"That's two million miles an hour," Jack said. "I only need it for a second."

"And blow yourselves to bits too?" McNarri said. "Forget it, Jack, I've assumed command here, and I'm ruling that out. You're in no shape to pilot the escape craft anyway."

"That's why I'll be piloting," Joe said. "I have my left arm free and that's more than enough. Jack can sit in the back and navigate for me, call out the commands."

"Forget it!"

"We're dying anyway," Jack said. "We both know it." He managed to meet Joe's eyes. Yes, they both knew it, and this last adventure together was all that sustained them, all that fought back against the genocidal monsters below.

"I won't let you do this!"

"You're not used to command, Major. Let me tell you that when you're down to only one possible decision, you have to make it. It doesn't matter who dies at that point. The only possible alternative is to take the *Typhoon* itself down and detonate the Xon, and that means eight men dead and the loss of the USSF's best ship. Which just happens to be *my* ship, which I'm damned if I'll see lost to *them*."

"God, Jack ..." McNarri moaned.

John rushed into the Control Room. "I'm ready to pilot!"

CHAPTER EIGHTEEN
The *Typhoon I*

Everyone exchanged glances. As far as Jack could see, John had no emotion whatsoever on his face. But maybe John was coming into his own. Maybe John too knew that there was only one possible decision, and that it had come down to him to save the ship. That it didn't matter if his brothers died, as long as the mission was completed and the ship was saved.

"Harri, hoist me out of this chair," Jack grunted. "John, you sit there."

McNarri threw his hands up in the air. "I can't remember who's in charge anymore!" he snarled, pulling Jack from this seat and then hitting a button on the console that took them all to zero gravity. "If I've got to put two men into the escape craft and haul an Xon out of the torpedo tube, damn if I'm not gonna do it in zero-g. Still have the mass to move, but everything oughta be easier." He grabbed Jack.

Jack felt himself floating towards the Control Room hatch like a beach ball in a swimming pool. "Hold on," he said. "Turn me to John." McNarri did so. "John."

"Yeah?" John said, not turning back from the console.

"You're the pilot, Lieutenant. You control the ship while I'm not on board. But Major McNarri is now commanding this mission. Is that clear?"

John nodded. "I can pilot her. Don't worry. I've got command."

"Command of ship's *functions,* but you take orders from Harri as to the entire mission," Jack repeated. "You're the chauffeur for this mission. It's the only way to carry it out. Everything depends on you carrying that out."

"Sure, sure."

"We'll need to hover over the target. Don't try for geosynchronous orbit, that's gonna waste a lot of time and energy getting higher. Just use thrusters to hold us in position right over the target."

John nodded. "Makes sense. That's what I would've done

anyway. Sort of like a glorified helicopter, huh?"

Jack nodded back. There was something in John's eyes that said he finally understood that Jack and Joe weren't coming back, that all this wasn't just an excuse for John to get in some flight time. "I'm placing my full trust in you," Jack said.

*

The escape craft floated free. Joe tested the thrusters and found that, while the little ship was sluggish, he had full control. "You okay back there?" he called.

"Yeah, I'm here," Jack said from the seat behind him. "I feel stupid. I can't do anything."

"You can talk. Just keep your eye on the scanner and let me know if you see any hostiles, any more ice rays, anything."

"Thanks, I will. This all feels … I don't know, somehow appropriate. Can't say why."

"I know what you mean," Joe said, forcing his left arm through the necessary motions to thrust the escape craft away from the *Typhoon*. "We're here to do our duty. And that does feel good." He punched a button to talk to the *Typhoon*. "Hey, Harri!"

"Yeah?"

"When you get back, have them make an eight-person escape ship! I've always wondered why this thing only seats two people."

Brief silence from the other end. "Well, there are plans for a six-person escape ship for the *Typhoon III,* whenever that gets built," McNarri finally said. "That would accommodate its whole crew. Of course the *III* will be a lot bigger, too."

"Yeah, but the *Typhoon* oughta have an eight-man ship *now.*"

"C'mon, Joe, forget it," Jack said. "Let's just do the mission."

"Yeah, yeah. You know that's all I'm focused on. I don't care about anything else." Joe looked out the canopy where the Xon bomb, a little longer than the twelve-foot escape ship, was lashed to the side of the craft by seven mini-Arkonsky force field clamps. "We'll do it. I'm programming the Xon now to take our speed into consideration so that no matter how fast we're going, it'll detonate a millisecond before we hit."

"Sheesh," Jack said, "At least we'll never feel a thing."

Joe punched in commands. "Crap! What's wrong with this thing?"

"I don't know. You tell me."

Joe patched his radio to McNarri again. He was grateful the idiotic Martian scientist hadn't chosen to reappear on this frequency. "Harri! *Did we attach the wrong damn bomb by any chance?*"

"Great, that would be just like this whole day," Jack groaned. "Okay, Harri," he called up to the giant fuselage floating above them, beginning to move left of the escape craft as John kept maneuvering to keep the *Typhoon* directly over the enemy base. "Haul us back in and we'll get this straightened out."

"No, you've got the right bomb," McNarri called down. "You've got Xon 2, the good one. Running a diagnostic on 1 now. Nope, it's still fried."

"Well, 2 isn't responding to any detonation program commands," Joe complained. "I'll run a diagnostic on that--ah, man! It's out now, too!"

"Damn," Jack said from behind him. "So the Xons won't launch, they won't self-propel, and they won't detonate. I'd say we have two useless weapons of mass destruction on our hands right now. Okay, haul us in, we'll rethink this."

"This is Garrison! I took over Sensors!" came Ken Garrison's cry over Joe's headphones. "Something's building up down there! Power levels are a thousand times that of the ice-ray, and increasing!"

Joe looked down. They were directly above the five-hundred-mile-wide doughnut, the entirety of which glowed bright blue.

"WEE LAWNCHING DEATTHH RAAY! YOOO HYUMANNS DEDD! YOOO ISS DEDD MEET AS YOOO

SAAY!"

"Screw that! Take this ship down now!" Jack ordered. "Two million miles per hour! Rupture their gun barrel at least!"

"Got it," Joe said, maneuvering the escape craft to point directly at the giant barrel probing for Mars.

"New plan! New plan!" came the cry over the headphones.

"*John?*" Joe and Jack cried together.

"One escape craft can't knock that thing out! You'll only disable it! They'll just repair it and fire it again!"

"Forget it! We're going down!" Jack shouted.

"No, *we're* going down." Joe gasped as the *Typhoon I* expertly swung into a straight-on trajectory. "We still have one-tenth propulsion, 4.9 million miles per hour. I've set the Augmented Nuke to rupture one-thousandth of a second before impact. That'll take out the entire facility."

He was right, Joe knew. A *Typhoon*-class Augmented Nuke rupture packed about a fourth of an Xon blast. It never would've occurred to Joe to deliberately rupture his Augmented.

"No! John, no!" Jack screamed. "Let me talk to McNarri! Let me talk to Jim!"

"Goodbye, Jack--Joe--"

"You're not in command! McNarri is in command!"

"There's only one possible decision, Jack. Everything has come down to this one moment. Goodbye."

"Joe!" Jack whimpered. "Make him--"

Above them the *Typhoon I* flared into acceleration. Within an instant it was a dot of light sinking towards the center of the glowing blue torus.

"Jack!" Joe cried.

"*I forbid it! I forbid it!*" Jack screamed into the starfire engulfing the planet.

CHAPTER NINETEEN
Marooned

The canopy filters blocked the worst of the glare, but it was a long time before Jack could see. From the cramped seat behind Joe, he began to make out the thousand-mile-wide cloud of dust billowing towards them. He felt Joe firing thrusters.

"Don't know if it'll do any good," Joe muttered, "but I'm moving us to a higher orbit. Don't know if that crap will get blown this high or not."

"Well, who cares?" Jack said. "What the hell does it matter? Let's just jettison the damn canopy and finish this."

There was a long pause from the front seat. Finally Joe said: "I'll have us at four hundred miles in a bit. Think that'll be enough?"

"It doesn't matter. Nothing matters. We're finished." Some of Jack's ice had melted, and he found he could speak normally.

Their orbit carried them past the churning debris cloud and into Mercury's night. A bad orange glow at the base of the cloud slipped below the horizon.

"Okay, I'm checking our options here, and we've still got the preset escape routes," Joe said. "The rest of autopilot is out, but we've got escape routes to Venus, Mars, or Earth. So ... Jack? C'mon, Jack, we need to figure out what to do!"

"The ship's *gone!* They're all dead, every last one of them!"

"I know that! What are your orders, Captain?"

"John destroyed the *Typhoon!* He's dead, Jim's dead, Harri's--"

"Don't get like this! Don't get like this! The *Typhoon* completed its mission! We got the base! We saved Mars!"

"You ... you ..." Jack gasped. "Okay. Jettison the canopy. Those are my orders."

"That's very dramatic. But then your EnviroField would just kick in. And even though it won't last very long against hard vacuum--"

"I'll turn mine off!"

"Sheesh." Joe punched in something on the pilot console.

154

Jack saw he was shutting down command functions to the copilot seat. "Well, we're not gonna do it. I guess there's some part of the mission left for us to do."

"Then radio Mars. Tell 'em what happened, what John went and did."

Joe shook his head. "Radio's out, too, transponders out, the whole communications package. Don't know why. I just tried it. But Mars will know our telemetry stopped, and any astronomer will have seen the explosion. They'll figure it out, send some ships over."

"But they won't know to look for an escape ship. They won't know that two cowards abandoned the *Typhoon!*"

Joe shrugged. "I noticed your ice is melting. Mine's been for a while. I have both arms free now. You think maybe McNarri was wrong about the effects?"

"What does it matter? And why do these damn escape ships only have three days' rations?" Joe didn't respond. The top of the debris cloud sank below the horizon. The escape craft floated in darkness. "We could've ruptured our own Augmented," Jack grumbled. "We could've saved the *Typhoon.*"

"We didn't think of it," Joe said. "And you know an escape craft Augmented wouldn't pack the wallop anyway. It'd be like a BB gun compared to the *Typhoon's*. There was no time to delay. John was the one who thought of it. He acted within a split-second."

"It ... didn't really happen, did it?"

Another long pause from the front seat. "I know what you mean," Joe finally replied. "It doesn't seem possible. But it did happen. We can't just hit the replay button. There's no replay button."

"John blew up the *Typhoon!*"

There was a long silence. "You wanted to try the same thing with this escape craft," Joe said.

"I should never have left John in charge! I tried to leave McNarri in charge, but John took full command, and--oh, God!"

"And he took full responsibility. John did exactly what you would've done. He completed the mission the only way possible. I have to say … I'm damn proud of him."

"How can you say--how can you say--when they're all *dead!*"

"Jack, you have to pull yourself together! You just have to!"

"But everyone *died!*"

"Do you think it's easy for me? For me? Those were my brothers there too! And we spent the last conversation with Jim talking about what a jerk John was! I can't stand that, you know!"

"You--you--"

"And did you consider that maybe he sacrificed himself, and everyone, for *you?* That maybe he was trying to save your life? You know he worshipped you!"

"Dammit! Dammit to hell, Joe!"

"Okay, forget it. We can't afford to be arguing about this. Look, I have a plan. I'm gonna offer it to you, I assume you're still in command, but if you don't want command, just say so. Just let me know."

"Crap … crap on it …"

"I just don't see how you can give up your command."

Jack nodded miserably. "I can't, dammit! You know I can't give it up!"

"Well, there, then you have it. You need to assume command."

"Look, you're right. There's no way I can throw it away." He waved at the planet. "This is all *my* responsibility. Whatever's going on in front of my eyes, is *my* responsibility. That's what I swore when I became captain, after all." He took a deep breath. "Okay. Let me have your idea."

"Well, about all we do have in our favor is the fact that I'm still showing we have ten percent propulsion. That's a miracle. Two million miles per hour is a damn miracle. And we're maintaining air pressure and have three days' air supply. And the inertial dampers are online. We're maintaining 1G now and they should kick in fine for any acceleration and deceleration we need. On the negative side, we have no navigation system other than the preset escape routes. We don't have radio, communications, or sensors of any sort. So I vote we just stay in orbit and wait for one of our ships to do a routine scan of objects orbiting Mercury."

Jack sighed. "And get rescued like a pair of half-drowned kittens. Great. I can see the headlines: 'Captain and Copilot Sneak Out and Leave *Typhoon* to its Fate.'"

"Damn, Jack, if I could somehow just pop back into the past about half an hour ago, yeah, I'd have wanted to stay with the ship, too. But things don't work that way. Whatever happened, happened. Our mission as I see it is to survive, and offer our years of military training back to humanity."

"Great. Who'd want a captain who let his ship go down without him? And what about after our air runs out and they find this rusty little piece of crap with our dead bodies in it? They'll all know we were cowards!"

"Well, we're *not* cowards. And if we want 'em to know what happened, we better get to work leaving some sort of testament." Joe reached for a microphone. "Damn! Wouldn't you know it? The computer won't let me record anything. Even the QWERTY keyboard's offline."

"Hell, get yourself a pencil and a little notebook."

"I don't *have* a pencil and a little notebook! But if I have to, I'll carve out the story on the metal plating here!"

Jack shook his head. "Give it up, Joe. Just give it the hell up. We're *cowards*. We deserted the ship. Everyone'll know that."

"Jack, stop. Just stop. You're distorting everything. We need to keep fighting this to the end. Everyone on the *Typhoon* would want us to carry on. Destroying the Mercury base was just part of the job. There're still Martian marauders on the loose, on Mars, maybe around the solar system. We've got to get the rest of 'em."

Jack took a ragged breath. "Look, I know you're right. I know it's the only way, but I just can't believe ... *John* ..."

"I guess he saw the only possible decision. And he didn't hesitate for a second."

"There was so much more to him than we knew."

"The way everything was set up, the family ... I mean, it just wasn't possible. I mean, to really know who he was."

"Yeah ..." Jack nodded. "*Hey!* Down there!"

A circle of blue light glowed on the dark planet.

"Damn! We forgot about those other ice rays," Joe said. "We can't just stay in orbit waiting to be rescued."

"What are the preset options? Distances and times?"

Joe keyed in commands. "Okay. Mars, 169.5 million miles. At our top end, eighty-five hours. We don't have the air supply for that. We'd have to hope we get sighted and picked up on the way."

"Way too iffy. They probably wouldn't be looking for a tiny escape craft heading back to Mars."

"Okay, Venus is actually closest at 57.4 million miles. 28.7 hours there."

"And we'd better damn well hope we can decelerate two million miles per hour at the end of that," Jack said. "Hope the electronics hold out that long."

"Of course that's true in any case. So we take up orbit and wait. But would they look for us there, either? Pretty unlikely. Then there's Earth at 60.17 million miles. About a thirty-hour trip."

"Same thing. Mercury is the most feasible place they'd look, but we can't stay here." Jack eyed the glowing blue circle below, but it slipped away as they continued their orbit. It never got as bright as the one they'd seen on the day side. Had it just picked up a small object and concluded it was space debris? Were they out of its range if it decided otherwise? And up ahead another blue glow flickered to life. "Damn, there's another one."

"Look, we're about to swing into daylight again, and we can do two things: one, we fire our first burst to break us out so we're heading right for the sun. I can do that without the autopilot, even if it's not the most precise thing in the world. And then I manually jettison the Xon and send it into the sun. Even if the thing is fried, we can't take the chance of the Martians getting hold of an Xon."

"Yeah, right. Good thinking." Jack eyed the huge Xon

cylinder lashed to the side of the escape craft. "I'd forgotten about that thing. I know I'm just not thinking right."

"The other thing, we just hit the preset for Earth. It'll figure out how to cancel our heading toward the sun and accelerate us to Earth. A little over thirty hours."

"Earth ..." Jack muttered.

"If we head to Earth, we can park the escape ship inside the TerraProbe 5 sensor satellite. It has a little airlock for maintenance ships. We'll be able to radio Mars from there and we'll have supplies until they rescue us."

"Yeah. Okay. Looks like our best chance." And if they didn't do another orbit, they'd never have to look at that debris cloud again. The escape craft passed the second glowing blue circle without incident. The line of Mercurian sunrise was before them, but it dimmed in Jack's eyes and slipped out of focus. "Ah, man ..."

"Jack, are you all right?"

"Just feel so tired ... still freezing. Ice getting thick again ... can't see. All of a sudden I'm so sleepy I could just ..."

"I'm feeling pretty sick, too. I've had the cockpit heaters on high this whole time. I don't know if Harri was right or not, but we've got to keep trying, even if the ice ray has ..."

"Has already killed us ..." Jack yawned.

"Manually breaking orbit *now*," came Joe's voice from far away.

CHAPTER TWENTY
The Commer Crater
Sunday, June 11, 2034, 0445 hours

Thrusters firing … noisy … bumpy …

Arms and legs tangled themselves over the top of the pilot's chair. Some dark human form had come loose, jammed spreadeagled in the cramped space in front of Jack.

Yeah, it was Joe, dark, unconscious, eyes closed, mouth puffy. And there was so much *brilliance*. Was there a fire out there? A blue fire?

Jack moaned in his sleep. He sprawled half on the floor, his neck crammed further and further into the bottom of his chair. "Man, I'm so tired, jus lemme sleep …" The thrusters were kicking too hard. Shouldn't the inertial dampers be canceling that out? Damn, if the dampers were out they'd be squashed against the walls, the ship would disintegrate, and it'd all be over before they knew it.

A warning buzzer came from the pilot's console in front. The gravity was too high. It was a wonder Joe wasn't flung over his headrest and right onto Jack.

Jack pulled his head off his seat. Again, less ice. He could move his arms and legs. He strained against the gravity until he could peer over the rim of the fuselage. To his right and behind, a blinding blue sphere laced with thick gray swirls of death shot up at sickening speed.

"*Planet Marble* …" he groaned. "I mean, *Earth!*"

They were about to crash into it at two million miles per hour.

Now the main engine, pointed back at the planet, opened up in earnest. The earth stopped growing quite so fast, but the little ship shook madly. Jack felt himself pressed further and further into his chair. His neck, craned backwards at the approaching world, felt as if it would snap off. The warning buzzer was replaced by a stern synthetic female voice: "ATTENTION: DECELERATION EXCEEDING 5G … 5.5G … 6G …"

"Joe … *Joe!*" he grunted.

"7G ... 8G ..."

Well, the dampers had to be mostly working, or else the deceleration would've been orders of magnitude above a puny eight gravities. Unable to move, out of the corner of his eye Jack regarded Joe plastered against the back of his chair, twisted sideways, unconscious.

Maybe dead already?

Jack moved his eyes the other way. The entire glaring planet was upon them, filling the sky. What about the preset orbit? They were coming in way too fast. Jack recognized the upside-down coast of Africa as they hurtled east, coming down over--

Over the Commer Crater.

Was he really awake? Was such cruel justice possible? Wasn't he just delirious, hallucinating the last seconds of his life? Wasn't this all a dream?

Nobody had ever seen the Commer Crater. There'd only been radar maps. The clouds had never cleared like this since October 8, 2033.

The escape ship flipped over to point the canopy down. It demanded Jack experience this horror to the fullest. Five hundred miles wide, no clouds for a thousand miles in any direction, the entirety of the Commer Crater glowed psychedelic orange.

Two billion people right there, Captain Jack Commer, United System Space Force! That's what your Xon bomb did right there, Captain Commer! October 8, 2033! Just following orders, Captain Commer!

"God, *no* ..." Jack moaned. "Joe, we weren't meant to come here! It was all a mistake! Joe! Wake up, Joe!"

Would they have evacuated if it hadn't been for the Xon? Scott had always said yes, that the Final War itself had already polluted the planet far beyond repair. But Jack was the one who'd finished off Gaia. He was the one who'd carved that chunk out of her and wrecked her for good.

Gravity slacked off and the escape craft seemed to linger over what had once been the Himalayas.

"And you got us back, didn't you?" Jack gasped into the

glowing pit. "You got us back … got us right back. John and Jim, and Harri … and Ken and Mickey and Craig. You got us back, didn't you? Didn't we pay …"

Rounding the earth into darkness, the escape craft was rocked by new forces as they plunged into thickening atmosphere. Now the little ship would break and blow.

Jack felt himself going dark. Again he was fully encased in ice. Maybe the symptoms came and went, maybe it was all part of the process of turning completely into ice. Cold and sick, Jack longed for the last bright burn-through as the escape craft came apart. Even now it was flipping end over end.

*

Sunday, June 11, 2034, 1015 hours

Jack blinked into sunshine. Pine trees high above. The canopy was open. Shocking cold splashed across his cheeks and down his neck.

"Wake up, wake up!" Joe said. "Man, you gave me a scare there!"

"You--you're *alive!* You gave *me* a scare," Jack grunted at his brother, who stood outside the craft heaving handfuls of water at Jack's face. "Where *are* we?" Jack pushed himself out of his chair. "Ow! Damn!"

"That was my first response as well. I'm pretty banged up myself."

Jack took in a mixture of smells he hadn't experienced in ages: fresh wet air, dirt, and plants. He hoisted himself out of the escape craft and onto soft ground under tall trees, blue sky and sunshine. "Man--*ow!*" Behind the ship lay five thousand feet of gouged earth the tiny ship had dug. "We're on Earth? I can't believe it! Have … have we died by any chance? I know that's a stupid question, but is this …"

"I know. I thought that, too. But then I thought, what sort of paradise is it when you feel your spine's been snapped in fifty places?"

"Huh." Jack felt his feet ooze into the mucky ground. Joe

had been flinging this same filthy water into his face.

"This is all so *beautiful*. One second I was pressing the button to launch the preset, the next we're *here*."

Jack shook his head. He decided not to tell Joe what he'd seen over the Himalayas. Or whatever he'd thought he'd seen. Had it all been a dream? Nothing seemed real, not his footsteps on the soft earth, not the cool air coming down his throat, not even his aching back. In their smudged red, white and blue USSF uniforms, both still covered with patches of ice, he and Joe looked like a pair of muddy clowns.

"I can't figure out why we landed," Joe said. "Why didn't we orbit and link with TerraProbe 5?" He pointed to the escape craft. "There're huge holes in the fuselage now. Even if our propulsion systems survived the crash, we'd never make orbit."

"Ah, man! We never reprogrammed the preset! Back before the war, back before we evacuated--"

"Oh, right! The Earth preset would just take the escape ship back and land it on Earth. Man, is that stupid! All the other presets put you in orbit, but the Earth preset *landed* you."

"We forgot to change it. I'm sure we never thought we'd need it. I bet McNarri had it on a to-do list and just forgot about it. But it's my damn fault. I should've checked it. Dammit, I've screwed up everything from the beginning!"

Joe regarded the clearing, much of which had just been created by the escape ship. "Aaah, forget it. We're here, safe and sound. We really can't complain. But if that's really the case, why didn't the ship take us back to USSF Command in Nebraska?"

"Hell, I don't know. The software might've been damaged by the ice ray. Or maybe the ship was avoiding high radiation areas." Jack shuddered, thinking of the H-bomb hit USSF Command had taken.

"Then it should be easy to query the computer and see what it thought was the safest place. It's still running its EnviroProgram." Joe leaned into the command console and tapped the screen. "Southern coast of Alaska. Or at least that's what the ship *thought* it was aiming for."

"Is that why I'm so cold?" Jack pointed to his ice-covered uniform. "It seems to melt off, but then it comes back."

Joe inspected his own ice. "The computer says it's sixty-two degrees out here. It's summer here, after all. But I'm still freezing."

Jack was too weary to stand. He made his way to the root ball of a toppled pine and plopped down. "The hell with this. You know none of this matters. We've apparently landed in a pocket of livable environment, but so what? We have three days' rations, and then what? And we're dying of this ice ray thing anyway."

Joe blinked. "I think the main effect of the ice ray on you is to make you thoroughly depressed and negative, is what I think."

"Don't hand me that! We had no option to do anything but come here and die!"

"We don't *know* the ice ray will kill us. Here you are, abdicating command again!"

"I'm *not* abdicating command! I'm just saying that we have no realistic options!"

"Except to sit here arguing until we die, is that right?"

"You give me a better option, then!"

"Okay, here's one. We cut some of these tree branches off and make a lean-to, then we forage for food and water."

"That's crazy! Everything's polluted here! Anything we eat or drink will kill us!"

"You don't know that!"

"Yes I do! We screwed this planet over royally, and you know it!"

Joe's angry brown eyes locked with his own. They were both thinking about October 8th. But again Jack held back from screeching about the Commer Crater. Angry as he was, he couldn't hurt Joe like that. He'd always suspected that Joe's guilt about the Crater was a hundred times worse than his own.

Finally Joe trudged over to Jack and sat on the root ball beside him. "You know, this gravity is hard to take. Even with all our 1G rules on the *Typhoon,* you know you can turn it off at any time. But now I can feel this *massive planet* below us."

"I know. I can feel it, too."

"Yeah, I think Mars has spoiled me. That one-third G ..."

"I think of all of us, you were the one who transplanted the easiest."

Joe smiled. "I love Mars. I really do. But listen, Jack. I'm sorry. I really am. About what I said about you abdicating command. I know you'd never do that."

"No, I'm the one who should be sorry. I've really lost it here. I've been saying *crap* all this time. I *have* been abdicating command, and you're right to point that out."

"It doesn't matter. You're right, after all. We can't contact Mars, and we're marooned here. We missed our chance to get to TerraProbe 5. And now we're dying. You're right. I can feel it, inside me. I can feel myself turning to *ice*."

Jack patted his brother on the arm. They never showed affection like this. "No, maybe there's hope. And if not, well, we gave it our best shot." Moving his arm took a lot out of him. It did feel as if his muscles were freezing solid.

"Hell, I don't know if I'll be able to cut those branches down after all," Joe grinned, feebly pointing to the trees. "At first I thought I could climb up there and just hack them." Then his mouth dropped open. "Man, what is *that?*"

*

Jack followed where Joe pointed, in the blue sky beyond the pines.

"Something's moving in! A ship!" Joe cried. "But it's too big to be a ship!"

"No, it's--it's a *world!* You can see some of the moon fragments in front of it!"

Zooming in from the far right, a gray planetoid absurdly lurched to a stop amid the white fragments of the old moon.

"It--it just *came!*" Joe shouted. "Weren't we discussing *Mercury?* Could that goddamn planet really come *here?*"

"No, that can't be Mercury!"

"It looks just like Mercury! It *can't* have followed us here!

That's too insane! Are we losing our minds?"

"No, it doesn't have any craters! It's just a smooth round *moon!*"

Joe jammed his hands over his ears and fell off the root ball. "No, we're hallucinating! The ice ray is making us crazy! There's nothing up there!"

"There is! There is! Just take a look!"

Joe stared at the gray ball. "Oh my God! They're here! They're here!"

"*Who's* here?"

"They're in my head again! I can hear them! And they're as crazy as we are!"

"Who's--" Jack began, but then felt faintly, in his own mind:

DEFINE perigee = 225,744 mi., apogee = 251,966 mi.; INSERT routine moonOrbit, line 336,556, PUSH VAR X,Z; DEFINE period of revolution = 27.322 da.; GET Q,; IF Q=MOON GOTO line 7,367,777; ELSE--

"No, that can't be!" Jack said. "Those thoughts have the exact same flavor as--"

"I know! I know! The damn Martians! They're *here!*"

"They're moving in a new moon! It's the exact same size as the old one! You can *feel* the math in your brain!" The gray planetoid wobbled back and forth as if settling into a comfortable position.

"Why? Why?"

"I don't know!"

RECHECK mean radius = 1,080 mi., density = .605 of Planet Marble; IF Error > Z, GET routine reFashion, line 2,004,735--

"How can Martians be *here?* What are they doing?" Joe cried.

Jack launched himself off the root ball and jabbed his finger at the new world. "I don't know! But they built this one specially for Earth! I can *feel* their equations! I can feel what they're doing! What they want!"

But the equations were too much to sustain. Jack's legs gave way. Dark ice expanded in his brain.

CHAPTER TWENTY-ONE
The Boards Are Erased
Wednesday, June 14, 2034, 0700 hours

Joe opened his eyes to sunlight. At least he could still open them. He guessed that meant he still existed. He'd made it to another day.

He still couldn't turn his head. Where was Jack? There, just out of the corner of his eye. Jack's ice looked even thicker, maybe two inches. But Joe could see Jack's chest rising and falling. His brother was still breathing. Why were they still alive?

Joe guessed he looked about the same. But he didn't feel cold. He hadn't been able to move for the whole last day. Jack hadn't moved since the first day when he fell down. But Joe found he could at least blink. That had to be worth something.

It'd been three nights, he calculated, so this was their third dawn on Earth. He couldn't see that damn moon or whatever it was. But the last time he'd seen the thing, it had been full, which meant it would be setting about dawn, so it would be behind his head. Joe missed it. It had been fun watching it crawl across the sky just like old Luna. And if this new Luna was a hallucination, it was a damn regular one and maybe Joe would get to see it around sunset. If he was still alive. He was surprised he'd survived last night with all those crazy fever dreams. Was Jack having them too? Getting serenaded by that crackpot AresNet jerk who'd gotten himself shattered in the desert? What was his face, that T. Jasper Marktholomew guy?

AND HERE, LADIES AND GENTLEMEN, IS A THREE-DIMENSIONAL GRAPHIC OF HOW THE MARTIANS FUSED CHUNKS OF ASTEROIDS INTO A GIANT GRAY BALL, THAT'S RIGHT, LADIES AND GENTLEMEN, A GIANT GRAY BALL EXACTLY THE DIAMETER OF OUR DEAR DEPARTED MOON.

"No, forget it, man ..." Joe croaked, surprised to find that his mouth worked. Hey, this was great. He was awake, he could blink, he could talk. "Screw off, man, I'm not gonna sit here and take that crap all over again," he added, proud he could form the syllables.

HERE YOU CAN SEE THE MARTIANS ACCELERATING THE MASS TOWARDS THE EARTH. IT'S QUITE SIMPLY DONE, OF COURSE, YOU JUST CONVERT ENERGYMASS Z, CALL SUBROUTINE FUSIONWELD, LINE 34,556, AND IF RADIUS > S, THEN OF COURSE GOTO LINE 3,445,640, PUSH MASS Z, ACCELERATION = .4 Z, WHERE S = MOON AND MOON = 1.

"Naw, man, you're just a buncha fever talk, man. Gotta shake it off, man, it's morning, y'know."

THE BATTLE IN THE DESERT! THE MARTIANS! THAT HUGE SAUCER LIFTING FROM THE SAND TO SPIRIT THE MARTIAN GENERAL AWAY! I DIDN'T SEE THAT PART, OF COURSE, I WAS DEAD BY THEN, SHATTERED LIKE AN OLD BEER BOTTLE TOSSED ON THE CONCRETE!

"Forget it," Joe muttered. "You're not real. There's no T. Jasper Marktholomew. At least not anymore. I don't wanna hear any crap about--"

THE SICKENING IMPACT OF THE *TYPHOON* INTO MERCURY! THE DEATHS OF JIM AND JOHN! THE DEATHS OF EVERYONE, LADIES AND GENTLEMEN, SIMPLY EVERYONE! HARRI, MICKEY, CRAIG, AND KEN, ALL GONE! ALL BECAUSE JOHN WANTED TO PLEASE JACK! TO SHOW HIM HE WAS IN CONTROL!

"The hell with it! You don't know what you're talking about. You AresNet twerps are always the last to figure out what's going on!"

WE AT ARESNET KNOW ALL! WE KNOW ALL ABOUT THE IDIOTIC ADVENTURES OF JACK AND JOE IN THE ESCAPE CRAFT! HOW JACK PLEADED TO BE ALLOWED TO KILL HIMSELF! HOW DEAD PLANET EARTH WAS ASSIGNED AS THEIR TOMB! IT WAS ALL IN VAIN, ALL IN VAIN!

"It wasn't in vain! It wasn't! Aren't there *any* AresNet

reporters who have their heads screwed on straight?"

ASSUREDLY, THE NAYSAYERS ARE ONCE AGAIN WRONG. WE NOW KNOW THAT *TYPHOON'S* SACRIFICE WAS NOT IN VAIN.

"Scott? General *Scott? Sir?* How can *you* be on AresNet?"

THE MARTIANS' MERCURY BASE WAS A REAL THREAT, AND ITS DESTRUCTION A CAUSE FOR REJOICING THROUGHOUT THE UNITED SYSTEM. YET WE DO FEEL SORRY FOR THE IRONIC END OF JACK AND JOE COMMER, AND SADLY SALUTE THEM FOR TRYING TO CARRY OUT THEIR DUTY TO THE BITTER END.

"Yes, sir! Thank you, sir! I accept your judgment, sir! I'm sure Jack would too! But see, he can't right now, he's out cold, sir!"

FORGET THAT! IT'S BEEN SCIENTIFICALLY PROVEN THAT JACK COMMER FELL APART AND FAILED MISERABLY! COMMER IS IN FACT A *TRAITOR* TO THE HUMAN RACE! THAT'S CORRECT, A TREASONABLE TRAITOR! WE SHALL NEVER FEEL SORRY FOR HIM OR HIS BROTHER!

"Huey? Huey *Vespertine?* Dammit, that's just like you with all your cynical crap! You weren't there, what do you know? Jack never snapped! It was just that he was way overstressed by the whole day before Mercury! Doesn't anyone understand the pressures he was under?"

JACK COMMER FAILED TO UNDERSTAND HIMSELF. FAILED TO HANDLE THE PRESSURES. HIS BROTHER JOE JOINS HIM IN TOTAL, IRREDEEMABLE DEFEAT.

"We're not dead yet, you jerk! We're both still breathing. This ice isn't such a big deal, Jack and I can handle it!"

YES, EVEN AS HE WAITS FOR THE END, JOE COMMER UNDERSTANDS THAT THE ICE IS SOMEHOW A PRESERVING FORCE. FOR INSTANCE, EVEN THOUGH HE HASN'T BEEN ABLE TO MOVE TO GET FOOD OUT OF THE ESCAPE CRAFT SINCE DAY TWO,

JOE FEELS NO HUNGER AT ALL. HE FEELS NO URGE
TO URINATE OR DEFECATE, HE FEELS NEITHER COLD
NOR HOT, IN FACT, HE FEELS NO BODILY
DISCOMFORT AT ALL.

"Oh, so it's the end, huh? You think you're gonna preside
over my death now, Huey? Get outa my head, man! I tried to be
your friend, I tried to make things right, even after you and Jack
fell out, even after he said he never wanted to see you again!"

ONE HAS TO ASSUME THAT IT'S THE SAME FOR
JACK. JACK COMMER MIGHT BE IN A COMA, BUT HE
MUST BE DYING PEACEFULLY, AS JOE IS. THE
MARTIAN ICE RAY GUARANTEES A SLOW DEATH,
BUT LET'S JUST SAY IT'S PROVIDED SOME
ADVANTAGES.

"Name one, you jerk! And bring back General Scott! *He*
knows what's going on!"

THIS IS SCOTT. PROBABLY THE BIGGEST
ADVANTAGE IS THAT JOE GETS TO LIE RIGHT HERE
AND JUST THINK FOR DAYS. THINK ABOUT HIS
ENTIRE LIFE. HOW MANY PEOPLE ARE EVER GIVEN
THREE DAYS AT THE END OF THEIR LIVES TO JUST
THINK? SURE, IT'S FRUSTRATING NOT TO BE ABLE TO
MOVE, BUT WHAT DOES THAT MATTER? ISN'T
EVERYTHING FOR THE MIND?

"Well ... well, sir, if you put it that way, I guess I agree,
sir!"

JOE COMMER GETS TO REVIEW EVERYTHING,
AND ISN'T IT OBVIOUS THAT WHEN HE FINALLY
FINISHES REVIEWING IT, HE'LL SHUT DOWN? AND
WON'T THAT BE ALL RIGHT? IN FACT, WON'T IT BE
APPROPRIATE TO SHUT HIS LIFE DOWN, ONCE HE'S
REVIEWED IT ALL? ONCE HE BECOMES A COMPLETE
HUMAN BEING FOR THE FIRST TIME IN HIS LIFE?

"Wow ... yes, sir, I'll get right on it, sir! The review! The
review of everything, sir! And may I just say in parting, sir, that
it's been an honor serving under you, sir?"

THIS IS T. JASPER MARKTHOLOMEW, CUTTING TO

THE CHASE! THERE WILL BE NO SUCH CALM APPRAISAL OF JOE COMMER'S WORTHLESS LIFE! HASN'T MR. COMMER BEEN EVEN A LITTLE SUSPICIOUS ABOUT THE ORIGIN OF THESE HALLUCINATORY DREAMS? DOESN'T HE KNOW THEY'RE SIMPLY A CLEANSING AGENT? THAT THEY'RE HERE TO WIPE JOE COMMER'S BLACKBOARD CLEAN? JOE'S OWN PRECIOUS BLACKBOARD WITH HIS PRIVATE SET OF PSYCHO-PHYSICAL EQUATIONS THAT HAVE DEFINED HIS LITTLE LIFE? THE FEVER DREAMS WIPE ALL THAT CLEAN!

"No, man, bring back Scott, I liked what he was saying."

THE HUEY VESPERTINE REPORT CONTINUES! THE ESSENTIAL EQUATIONS HAVE ALWAYS REVOLVED AROUND THE PEOPLE IN JOE'S LIFE, AND WHETHER OR NOT HE'S SCREWED THEM OVER!

"Aw, crap, Huey, you oughta talk, you turned your back on the whole human race!"

CONSIDER THE TANGLED THICKET OF ENERGIES RELATING TO THE FOUR COMMER BROTHERS AND THEIR FATHER. IT PROBABLY CAN'T BE NAVIGATED BEFORE SYSTEM SHUTDOWN. FOR WE SUSPECT IT ALL GOES TOO DEEP TO BE DEALT WITH IN THIS LIFETIME. PERHAPS IN A COMING LIFETIME JOE WILL MANAGE TO FIND THE TIME TO DEAL WITH IT.

"I don't believe this! Don't give me this coming lifetimes crap!"

THE NEED FOR COMING LIFETIMES COMES FROM THE TWISTED DESTINIES THAT DEMAND RESOLUTION, NO MATTER HOW MANY EONS IT TAKES. CONSIDER THE WOMEN JOE COMMER OWES SO MUCH TO, AND ALL OF WHOM HE'S WRONGED ONE WAY OR ANOTHER. DID HE REALLY COME UNGLUED DURING THE HORRORS OF THE FINAL WAR AND THE EVACUATION? THE LAST SIX WOMEN CAME DURING THAT TIME, AFTER ALL. DID THEY

SOMEHOW RELATE TO THE BREAKDOWN OF HUMAN EXISTENCE? HUMANITY ITSELF HAVING ITS BLACKBOARD WIPED CLEAN?

THIS IS GENERAL JOHN J. DOUGLAS, THE ALIEN HUNTER, TAKING OVER THIS LINE OF INQUIRY!

"Oh, no!" Joe groaned, desperately trying to turn his head to confront his new tormentor. But all he saw was bright blue sky.

OH, YES, YAH BAHSTAD! AS I HAPPEN TO BE AN EXPERT ON THESE MATTERS, IT'S MY DUTY TO INFORM YOU OF YOUR SERIOUS SEXUAL TRANSGRESSIONS!

"Me? You're accusing *me?*"

YES, CERTAINLY, JOE! YOU DON'T MIND IF I CALL YOU JOE, DO YOU, JOE? BECAUSE WE MIGHT AS WELL GET UP CLOSE AND PERSONAL IF WE'RE GOING TO DISCUSS THE SHAME OF YOUR SEXUALITY!

"*Shame?* You jerk! Get out of my head! You're just a fever dream!"

CARLA AND AMY AND CHERIE, AND HANNAH AND SHAN AND LUCIA, ALL WONDERFUL WOMEN, AND YOU JUST USED THEM ALL.

"Look, I know, I've thought about that myself, but it's been a really stressful time, you know?" Joe babbled. "I mean, Carla, Amy, and Cherie, sure they all came and went during the Final War, I mean, like everyone was so afraid, you know, I mean, who could stick together? And Hannah was during the Evacuation, I mean I always wondered if Hannah wasn't somehow the one, but it was like the Evacuation tore us apart, you know."

YA BAHSTAD! WHAT TOTAL BS! YOU NAVY BOYS ARE SO GOOD AT DELUDING YOURSELVES! THEN CAME SHAN, YOUR FIRST GIRLFRIEND ON MARS. LASTED ALL OF TWO MONTHS, DIDN'T SHE? YOU TWO WERE SO FOREIGN TO EACH OTHER THAT--HOW DID SHE PUT IT? "THE WHOLE THING WAS LIKE A MERGER BETWEEN A CITRUS GROVE AND A CEMENT

PLANT!" WOW, YOU MISSED OUT ON A CHANCE TO MARRY A POET!

"Damn you! Get out of my head!"

WHEN YOU TOLD SHAN ABOUT LUCIA FROM GANYMEDE, THE RELATIONSHIP COLLAPSED IN AN INSTANT, AS YOU NO DOUBT INTENDED IT TO.

"Stop it! Just stop! I'm *not* having these thoughts, I'm not having them!"

LUCIA TRONDZ, LIEUTENANT ON GANYMEDE OUTPOST IN THE JOVIAN FRAGMENT FIELD. AND A FANTASTIC PIECE IF I SAY SO MYSELF! IN MARCH, THREE MONTHS AGO, DURING A *TYPHOON* LAYOVER AT GANYMEDE, YOU MEET LIEUTENANT LUCIA IN THE CAFETERIA AND IMMEDIATELY ASK HER TO BED! WAY TO GO, YA BAHSTAD!

"Well … well … I still don't know why I said that! Sure she was gorgeous, but--"

AND WHAT FOLLOWED FOR HOURS IN HER QUARTERS COMPLETELY UNHINGED YOU. THIS ONE-NIGHT LUCIA AFFAIR HAS CONSUMED YOU FOR MONTHS, EVEN THOUGH YOU STILL TRY TO PASS IT OFF AS MEANINGLESS COPULATION. BUT THE REVERBERATIONS ARE OF PASSION! PASSION AND DESTINY! DAMN, I'M TURNING INTO A POET MYSELF!

"Look, I know, this is all crazy, I really haven't had time to think about any of it!"

YOU PROMISED TO EMAIL HER, BUT YOU DIDN'T UNTIL MAY. AND THAT WIMPY UPDATE ON *TYPHOON* REPAIR SCHEDULES WAS SOMEHOW SUPPOSED TO HINT THAT YOU WERE STILL INTERESTED? AND HER RESPONSE, YA BAHSTAD?

"I know, look, I *know*."

"IF YOU CAN'T KEEP A PROMISE ABOUT EMAILING ME, WHAT CAN YOU KEEP?"

"I just didn't know what to make of that, I'm sorry I never replied!"

THEN AGAIN, IT DIDN'T NECESSARILY MEAN SHE

WANTED TO CUT OFF ALL COMMUNICATION, YOU KNOW.

"You can't be serious! That'd mean Lucia might have really wanted to--to--"

TO LOVE YOU? DO YOU THINK THAT'S POSSIBLE? ISN'T LOVE AS ALIEN TO JOE COMMER AS THOSE *MARTIAN MARAUDERS?*

"God, do you think I really hurt her?"

SHE WAS THE LAST ONE YOU HAD. AND YOU BOASTED CRUDELY ABOUT HER TO THE ENTIRE *TYPHOON* CREW. WELL, YOU HAVE YOUR LADIES' MAN REPUTATION TO MAINTAIN, DON'T YOU? REMEMBER THAT DRUNKEN NIGHT WITH THE BOYS?

"Listen, I'm sorry, but if you'll just get lost, stop all this fever talk, I don't know, I'll try to make it up to her somehow!"

IT'S TOO DAMN LATE, JOE BABY. LUCIA'S KARMIC PAYBACK IS GOING TO BE RELEGATED TO ONE OF THOSE COMING LIFETIMES. THINK OF ALL THOSE COMING LIFETIMES, MY LITTLE BAHSTAD NAVY COMMANDER, THOSE WEARY COMING LIFETIMES SOLELY DEVOTED TO CLEANING UP ALL THE MISTAKES YOU MADE IN ALL YOUR PREVIOUS LIFETIMES. WHAT AN ENDLESS LOAD OF WORK!

"Dammit, this is all just fever! You're all just hallucinations! Yeah, I can see you walking around me, so what?" In fact, boots now clomped beside Joe's head. The hallucinations had finally come to take him away. Everything was swirling fog. "So what if this is the end?" he gasped. "So what? Damn you, so what?"

THE END, WHERE ALL THE BLACKBOARDS GET ERASED AND THE BLACKBOARDS THEMSELVES ARE DISMANTLED? YA BAHSTAD! I DON'T THINK SO!

*

Furious blinking was the only way left to shake off General John J. Douglas and all the other hallucinations. Joe could see them moving away, angels or devils, ten or fifteen of them, pink feet in silver slippers, scampering around the escape craft, jumping over Jack's head, jabbering high, hypnotic, lovely nonsense.

Why, the fever dreams had conjured up *finbacks.* Yes, Martian finbacks scurried here and there, pointing little devices at Jack, then Joe.

One finback in particular caught Joe's eye. Taller than the rest, in a glowing golden robe. Funny that Joe had been thinking about Lucia with her perfect body, because here was a finback parodying that perfect body. The dazzling robe wrapped snugly around long thighs and a high firm ass, tightly outlining wondrous handfuls of breasts. These fever dreams were so clever. Finbacks didn't have breasts, or long black hair, or--

A young woman with dark eyes and full sensuous lips inspected the ice-covered form of his brother.

"Now don't you worry your pretty little head, honey," came a rough deep drawl out of Joe's visual field. "Ice death is pretty ugly, I know."

"It's really not so ugly," she replied. "The ice is *preserving* them. But aren't the Martians going to fix them?"

"I suppose, so we can interrogate 'em and torture 'em later!"

Joe flicked his eyes towards the dark nasty voice. He wanted to laugh. The fever dreams had concocted a hallucination of Sam Hergs. Sam Hergs and a beautiful woman and Martian finbacks. It was a party at the end of Joe's life. All these themes that defined him had come to the fore: beautiful sexy women, unknowable aliens, and monstrous human evil.

Is it adjusted properly? came a voice in his mind.

Two finbacks pointed to the gray moon in the sky.

It should be rising one hour local time later each day, came a voice. *Get T'rfigg and the others over here and we'll coordinate an AT to fix that.*

Some bustling about. Presently there were a dozen finbacks over there.

Done, said--T'rfigg? In Joe's mind?

Meanwhile the Sam Hergs hallucination rubbed his groin

into the back of the young woman's perfect golden-robed thigh.

"Mmmm … hunnee …" Hergs groaned. "Now I know why I took you on this mission! You feel so damn good! Make me wanna just come right in my pants!"

Yuck, Joe wanted to say.

The finbacks also seemed to be radiating *Yuck.*

The young lady bore Hergs' rutting with a strained, bored smile.

The Consort to the Emperor has many duties, came a voice. *Yet consummation must be delayed until the Feast of the Wedding.*

And that includes ejaculation in the presence of the consort.

"Huh? Wha'?" said Hergs. "Aw, ya damn things with all your damn rules!" Nevertheless he pulled off of the young lady, who again bent to Jack.

"He's barely alive," she whispered.

We have made the initial measurements and have the healing ray here. A finback approached Jack with a black cylinder and fired a blinding purple pulse.

The other is awake!

Pulse him now.

The cylinder came to Joe's face and everything turned white-purple. He felt heat throughout his body, penetrating to every cell. Then the purple faded into dark blue, then deeper and deeper into black.

These fever dreams are so thorough! he had time to think. *They erase everything in existence!*

CHAPTER TWENTY-TWO
You Are My Prisoners!
Wednesday, June 14, 2034, 2200 hours

"Joe! Wake up! C'mon, Joe!"

Something from outside dared interfere with wondrous total absence of existence. Joe had to resist. Hadn't he been ordered to sleep forever?

Nevertheless, *something* was receiving all manner of data uploads. Somehow identity was being assembled.

"C'mon, Joe, wake up! Don't die on me, man! We've lost too many already!"

Love and concern poured out of that voice. Jack's voice. At once Joe Commer solidified. "Jack! You're alive! What the hell happened? Where are we?" Joe sat on a cot in a dark cramped room. The air tasted like hot metal. Machinery rumbled through the steel grating beneath his feet. Across from him his brother sat on another cot. Even in the dim light Joe could see Jack radiating health and vigor. "Man, I thought you were dead! I thought we were both dead!"

"I don't know. I've been gone for hours, maybe. I just woke up."

"We're--on Earth? For three days?" Joe leapt off the cot. One wall of this room was vertical steel bars. The whole space was only six by six feet. "Dammit, did any of this really happen?"

"All I can remember is falling down, and lying there, and dreaming the strangest stuff. I knew I was dead, I knew I was having all these dreams, and I just didn't care."

"It went on for three whole days! I was awake the whole time!"

Jack checked his wristwatch. "You're right. It's the fourteenth. It's ten PM."

"Man, if we crashed on the eleventh, and it was three days, then I can remember this morning! I had all this fever, I started seeing the strangest stuff, and then I lost it! Now we're in this *room*." He pointed to the hinged door in the wall of bars. "Man,

178

this is a jail!"

"All I remember is that I was getting colder and colder, and I didn't care. The cold was okay. But at some point, I felt this *heat*. This weird purple *heat*."

"That's it! Purple heat! The healing ray *cured* us!"

"The what?"

"The Martians! They had a healing ray! They pointed it at you and you were nothing but purple light! Then they pointed it at me! And here we are!"

Jack shook his head. "No. The *Typhoon* destroyed the Martians, Joe. That much I do remember."

"But not all of them! I don't know how I know it, but those hallucinations must've been real! There were these finbacks, and they said they were adjusting that gray moon's orbit, and there was this beautiful woman dressed in gold!"

Jack grinned. "Great! Now I *know* you were dreaming."

"No! It has to be true!"

Clanking reverberated down a long metal hall. Their cell shook with approaching footsteps, and in front of the bars a short man in a black trench coat stood silhouetted against dim light.

"You are my prisoners!" shrieked Sam Hergs.

Jack and Joe stood so fast that Hergs drew back with widened eyes. "Gnrrr'flu! H'razgz/m! Shatterguns at the ready!"

"YESSZSIR!" came a screech.

"YESSZ, MEE LORRD!" came a second.

Two finbacks leapt from the shadows, mouths painfully working to force out these ugly sounds. Again Joe had that queasy feeling that they didn't have to speak aloud. Somehow he already knew what they were saying.

He looked into the barrels of shatterguns trained on him and his brother.

"Shoot these losers if they show any aggressive behavior at all," Hergs snarled. Pale ochre light behind him framed his blunt little body. Joe could make out the wet glint in his little black eyes.

"ITT--SHALL BEE AZZ YOOO WISSH," one of the finbacks painfully said/thought.

They didn't really want to fire shatterguns at living beings, Joe realized. It was morally painful to them. Yet both Gnrrr'flu and H'razgz/m would do it in a second. They seemed like attack dogs on a leash. Very, very unhappy attack dogs.

Joe looked over to Jack, who nodded back, obviously picking up the same concept.

Jack turned to Hergs. "Well, I have to say I can't believe this turn of events. Of all the nasty jerks to be captured by!"

"Hey, watch it, I could consider your language *aggressive behavior,*" Hergs taunted, raising a hand as if to signal the attack Martians.

Jack folded his arms. "We have certain rights as prisoners of war."

Hergs rubbed his sweaty, stubbled face. Joe could see bits of gray meat in his big square teeth. "This ain't no war, Captain Jack," he sneered. "It's a damn final cleansing of your goody-goody USSF BS once and for all. And as Emperor of the Martians I reserve the right to torture anybody I damn well wanna!"

"Emperor? Crap, so it's really true!"

"Damn right!" Hergs laughed. "I made myself emperor! These guys love me! They'll do anything for me!"

Joe stared at the Martian guards. Concepts that made no sense floated out of their minds.

The tradition has been broken but we must repair the tradition by adhering to the tradition

We cannot resist dare not resist do not think to resist

We love the emperor must love

"Is this guy crazy or what?" Jack said.

"Careful, Jack," Joe said. "He's serious about blowing us away."

"You're damn right I'm serious!" Hergs hooted. "Although it's not really the kind of torture I wanna do on you damn Commers!"

"Buzz off, twit!" Jack shot back. "We could care less. We got your Mercury base and unless I miss my guess we've totally crippled your little terrorist plot."

"Jack!" Joe cried. "There's no reason to just rile this guy. Look, I know what the *Typhoon* meant, but don't just throw everything away!"

Jack took a breath as Hergs motioned Gnrrr'flu and H'razgz/m up to the bars. "Forget it, Joe. I know I freaked out back there. I know we're both completely wracked over the *Typhoon*. But I'm back now. Somehow all those days in ice added up to something. I don't know what it is, but I'm okay."

"Yeah!" Joe said, flexing fingers that had been crippled a couple days before. "I feel that too. Like all those aches and bruises from deceleration are *gone*. I feel great!"

Hergs held up a hand to prevent Gnrrr'flu and H'razgz/m from adding shattergun fire to this discussion. "If I may have a word here, gents. To answer your rather smartass assertion that you harmed our cause in any way, Captain Jacko, yeah, you got our main Mercury base, dude, with our Mad Momma Death Ray and everything. Very good. Why, it may take us all of three days to build it back!"

"Aaah, you're full of it," Jack said.

Martian concepts oozed out of the dim light. Gnrrr'flu and H'razgz/m looked away, apparently embarrassed.

Amplified Thought?

Hergs shrugged.

"No ..." Jack whispered. "That's impossible!"

"Do the math," Hergs sneered. "Of course it's possible!"

Although the math would short-circuit your puny human minds.

"That's enough, H'razgz/m!" Hergs spat. "Try to damp it down, will ya? That's a damn standing order around here, y'know! Damp it down, damp it down! I don't wanna have my head cluttered up with all your stupid damn thoughts and opinions! Jeez Louise!" He turned back to the Commers. "Well, it don't matter if the secret's out or not. Both you boys are gonna be tortured into total insanity, and then chopped into hamburger, so what do I care if you know what was your damn downfall?"

"So we're on *Venus*," Jack said.

"You pick a lot of stuff outa these buggers' heads," Hergs

said. "They leak all over the place. Well, like I say, so damn what, since you're gonna die horribly."

Joe lifted one foot, then another. "Hell, I wondered if we were back on Mars, by the gravity."

"We keep the gravity in the dome at .38G to keep these guys happy. Can't say I haven't grown accustomed to it as well. But what the hell. Yep, we're on Venus, boys! This is our main base. Mercury was really just a diversion. But I guarantee ya, we're gonna rebuild Mad Momma One and fry Mars once and for all! Like I say, it only took us a coupla days to build that five-hundred-mile-wide monster. That's why your regular probes didn't ever see it being built, or any of our ice ray defense bases. 'Cause we can do it in a *second!* So what if we lost the damn base? We'll just rebuild it in the twinkling of a damn eye with Amplified Thought!"

But seven hundred of First Home lost their lives there.

"Aw, who cares? They died in the service of the emperor, and they should be damn happy floating around in your damn Martian afterlife!"

Leaving only thirteen hundred of us left--facing extinction!

"Shut up! Stop thinking! That's an order! That's classified info!" Hergs shrieked. "And it's gonna be twelve hundred ninety-eight in a minute if you two don't stop *thinking,* damn you!"

"Let me get this straight," Jack said. "These Martians can *think together?* They can link themselves, and manipulate matter?"

"Yeah, they can build whatever they want. Or destroy whatever they want! Just depends on how many of 'em are linked."

"ITZ REALLEE KWITE FAZZCINNATING!" squealed Gnrrr'flu, working his mouth spastically in an approximation of English, though the meaning was quickly filling Joe's mind to capacity. In fact, the more he aligned with the creature's thoughts, the more lucid the Martian's speech began to sound. Gnrrr'flu continued: "Since the entire universe consists of information quanta--"

"*Classified, classified!*" Hergs shouted, thwacking Gnrrr'flu across the rounded bump that passed for a Martian snout. "Sheesh! Double, triple sheesh!" He turned to Jack and Joe. "See what I have to put up with? At least I can have an intelligent conversation with you guys. Before I kill you, that is!"

"We found you via Amplified Thought!" H'razgz/m croaked. "We tracked your escape ship as it broke out of orbit around Planet Cinder. We knew your ship was harmless and that's why the other ice rays didn't fire. But one of our ships followed you to Planet Marble!"

"I've tried to get 'em to rig up an AT that'll plug up their own damned *mind leaks,* but will they? No way! They say it'd gut their entire central nervous systems! Cowards!"

"You were there? Martians? Watching over us?" Joe cried. "See, Jack, I was right! I saw Martians there!"

"Actually, our ship's main purpose was to coordinate the arrival of New Marble Companion One," H'razgz/m went on. "It was trickier getting it into the proper orbit than we'd initially supposed."

"Wow!" Joe said. "Jack, they put a replacement moon into orbit with Amplified Thought!"

"I know, I know!" Jack said. "My God! Think of the possibilities!"

"When its captain saw you two had survived the journey," Gnrrr'flu said, "they notified our emperor."

"Okay, okay!" Hergs yelled. "I know you guys can at least shut your damn mouths, even if you have to leak your silly little minds all over the place! So just shut your traps before I order you two to shatter each other!"

"And Hergs came over, too!" Joe said. "And he brought this incredible woman with him! The consort!"

That is correct, came leaking mind only.

"She was gorgeous! I can see her perfectly in my mind!"

"Okay, boys, you can stop your drooling," Hergs said. "You have no idea how hard it was to convince the Council I needed an Earth woman! I sure as hell wasn't gonna stick it in one of those Martian bitches!"

There was no comment, telepathic or otherwise, from Gnrrr'flu or H'razgz/m. All Joe could sense from either was a sense of hot bile rising in their throats.

"Don't know why I let her come," Hergs went on. "Said she was bored here in the Dome. Women! But if I have to have an empress, first she has to be the consort, and it's all horribly complicated. Martians are *weird* about sex, y'know. All their rituals revolve around it. I never woulda taken this emperor job if I knew how much sexual trouble it was gonna be. So I figure, I'll get the best, most perfect babe I can. Even so, I hadda adjust her to have no real personality at all!"

Everyone let this laugh die on the dark metal all around them. Joe could feel the Martians trying to avoid this entire line of thought. Instead they seemed to be focusing on the new moon's tidal effects on the earth.

"Hey!" Joe cried. "You're *repairing* the earth? Why?"

Well, Gnrrr'flu and H'razgz/m radiated together, *because it's fun to create!*

"Well, it keeps 'em occupied, so I let 'em," Hergs said. "But the real reason is simple. Martian soldiers are *wimps*. They don't know how to fight worth crap. I need a breeding ground for a fanatical following of human soldiers whose minds don't leak to you goody-goody USSF'ers. But I won't need Earth very long. Once I have my army, in twenty years or so--" He shrugged. "Hey, screw Mother Earth is what I say."

Jack shook his head. "I don't know how to tell you this, Sam, but the USSF is gonna fry your ass no matter what your stupid plans are."

Joe braced for shattergun rays, but not only did he know that Gnrrr'flu and H'razgz/m would probably argue and delay until the moment had passed, he could also see that Hergs himself somehow enjoyed Jack's insolence.

By way of answer Hergs pulled a computer pen out of a shirt pocket and flicked it at the cell door bars. Blinding sparks followed, and the pen plopped to the floor grating, glowing red. "Try grabbing these hundred-thousand-amp bars, Jacko. That's exactly what'll happen to you if you touch 'em. They're courtesy of Amplified Thought. So you can see that with AT, I'm sure not impressed by any of your nasty little slurs against the emperor."

"I wondered why my hair was standing on end," Joe remarked. "For some reason I haven't been very keen on grabbing those bars."

"Me, either," said Jack, placing his hand a few inches from the bars as everyone watched the hair rise off the back of his arm. "But look, how can a second-rate thug like yourself become emperor of an alien species? It doesn't make sense. Last time I saw you, you were setting fire to the Armstrong Center. Do Martian emperors really go around doing petty acts of terrorism?"

"Aaah," Hergs said, "I like to get in on the action, be a common dude and all. If I can pull off some stunt like that, wow, what a rush is what I say! Too bad we didn't decompress that place! You'da seen all sorts of dweebs gunking themselves right and left. Most of 'em'd have their EnviroFields off inside the place, listenin' to their pretty music or whatever they do in there. We woulda seen 'em blowin' outa the side of the building, turnin' to *gunk!* Man, I like to see people turn to *gunk!* When me and Carson jumped your guys, we wanted to rip off your EnviroFields and watch you *gunk!* Maybe that's what I'll finally do to you guys! *Gunk* you outside!"

"Sheesh," Jack said.

"Hey, it's nine hundred degrees out there," Hergs smirked. "But piss on this whole mess, is what I say. It's late, and I'm sick of you guys. I'm gonna go upstairs and call up the nude 3D holos of my little consort. These twits say I can't even touch her yet, but I sure as hell can see the application holos, can't I? So bye-bye! Any complaints on room service, by the way, before I say goodnight?"

"Yeah, crap on you."

"Don't forget, we'll start torture tomorrow morning at eleven sharp. I have a Council meeting at ten, but I'll be sure to be on time. I see my boys have done a bang-up job on restoring you to perfect health, but that'll make the days of torture last so much longer! Bye-bye!"

Hergs swished away in his trench coat. Joe caught the eye of one of the Martians.

Cannot pretend to understand/question emperor's unfathomable wisdom

Yet stomach/guts mourn

Need bad to get to Recycle Hole

The Martian guards scampered after their dark emperor. As the figures moved down the long metal corridor, the ochre globes spaced ten feet apart extinguished themselves behind them. Hergs' heavy clomping and the skittering of the guards' boots finally died away, and the entire hall as well as their cell plunged into blackness.

"You know what I think?" Joe said. "I think this is one giant prison, and we're the only two people in it."

"I think you're right," Jack's voice came out of the darkness. "I sure haven't heard a peep out of anyone since we've been awake. And I saw that the floor and ceiling gratings were showing cages above and below us. When we had light I could see several levels of 'em. Hergs may have built this with political prisoners in mind."

"So how are we going to get out of here?"

"I don't know yet. But I do know we need to destroy this entire base."

"Well, we're both well-rested and wide awake." Joe was so thrilled to have the old decisive, confident Jack back that he didn't care that their odds of survival were astronomical. "Looks like we have twelve-plus hours to plan something."

"Yeah, but I'm sure Hergs has this place bugged. He'll expect us to try to escape, although he feels confident we can't. So for right now the plan will be concocted all in my head as we turn in for the night."

"But I'm not tired. It's like morning for me."

"We have to follow Hergs' schedule now. He's tired, he wants to moon over some pictures of that consort of his, so that's giving us our time to rest and plan. So sleep is an order right now, Commander. You're also ordered not to roll over and grab those bars in your sleep."

"Well, yessir," Joe said, settling back in his cot. Jack was back. Joe had no idea how much he'd missed him. Tomorrow he and his brother would fight for their lives, but they'd do it together, gloriously. The outcome absolutely didn't matter. And although Joe was too excited to sleep, somehow he found himself effortlessly transplanted from this tiny room to Lucia Trondz's quarters on Ganymede, where he worked on his karma with her, in light blue light, for endless hours.

CHAPTER TWENTY-THREE
Serving His Majesty the Emperor
Thursday, June 15, 2034, 0930 hours

Jack awoke to a wave of dim lights clicking to life in concert with clomping footsteps. Human footsteps down the long corridor, no skittering of Martian finbacks. Judging from the clangs on the grating, a fairly heavy human. Beside him Joe's dark figure shot upright.

"Damn! I'm sorry! Man, I can't believe I *slept.*" Joe heard the stomps and mouthed: *Plan?*

Jack made an okay sign and whispered: "There's really only one weapon we have."

Joe nodded. "I realized that, too."

As the footsteps came closer Jack reached behind him and yanked off the tiny security camera disguised as a rusty bolt dangling from the bars. No wires trailed out, but of course the thing would be radio. He'd noticed the bolt yesterday when he'd checked the cell out during the light from Hergs' visit. Why would a rusty bolt serving no obvious purpose be attached to the bars of a new jail facility? And why would it be placed exactly in the center of the cell, giving a panoramic view of the two bunks?

No doubt someone would soon notice an absence of video from this cell--Jack hoped audio as well--but it gave them a few minutes.

Yellow light flooded the cell. Before them stood an obese man in gray uniform, his nametag reading MCBOERLAND--SERVICE LEVEL 3. He also had a round green pin: *Serving his Majesty the Emperor with a Trouble-Free Smile!*

But McBoerland's expression was anything but trouble-free as he jerked a set of keys off his flab, blearily puzzled about which one to use, and finally stuck a key into a metal box in front of Jack. As the lock clicked open Jack felt the immense electrical current shut off.

"Don't even think about arguing with this here shattergun," McBoerland said as he raised the alien weapon. "I been up all

night with a damn cold, I don't need this crap. I'm sick and I
hate this. I got the okay to shatter ya both if ya try anything."

"Not me," Joe said, backing away as McBoerland pushed
the cell door open. "But, sir, has anyone told you your breath is
enough to knock a guy down? I mean, I could smell you coming
thirty feet away! Man, that is *foul*."

"Piss on ya," McBoerland said, tossing two silver bags onto
Joe's bunk. "I don't need your crap. Ranblon was supposed to
have this shift but the turd has a damn hangover. So I get stuck
with it. But I'm the guy who's sick. I hate this place! Always so
damn cold and damp down here at the damn bottom."

"Huh. I wonder if that's the cause," Jack said. "Your breath
really is bad. To be completely honest, it's enough to make us
puke."

"Crap on that. I ain't here to give a crap about what ya think.
That's your grub there, ya better eat it. Ya get fed once a day,
the first two days that is. As the Torture goes on, ya don't get
fed none at all. I watched Hergs break a few guys in the Torture
Room so I know what I'm talkin' about." McBoerland carefully
backed out of the room, shifting his shattergun from side to side
to cover them both. He shut the door and reached for the key in
the box.

Jack pulled his sleeves back to expose bare arms to the
elbows.

McBoerland turned the key and the amp field came on.
Again Jack's forearm hairs stood on end.

"*We said, your breath makes us want to puke!*" Joe
screamed.

McBoerland froze. Jack met his bloodshot pig eyes, then
deftly stuck his arms between the hot bars, jerking the guard off
balance towards him and releasing his grip just as McBoerland
plunged into the hundred-thousand-ampere bars in a blinding
sizzle of light and smoke. The guard shook rigidly against the
cell as Jack carefully reached through the bars to find the key,
still inserted in the box, and twist it to OFF. McBoerland
slumped to the floor, grilled by the bars like a slab of swordfish.

"Sheesh, that was almost too easy. What lousy security,"

Jack muttered as they swung the cell door inwards and stepped over the guard's body. "Well, we probably have a few minutes to see what we can wreck."

"Hopefully that will include Sam Hergs," Joe said.

"I'm taking Mr. McBoerland's keys. And his shattergun. They might come in handy. In fact, look down there. Some sort of maintenance door."

Thirty feet down the dimly lit corridor was a steel door marked VENT SHAFT 333B. Machinery hummed behind it. Unbelievably, McBoerland had a key marked VENT SHAFT 333B.

Jack unlocked the door. "Watch your step here. There's no floor. Just get onto the rungs." He and Joe climbed inside a cold shaft four feet on a side. Dim white walls extended above and below them. Climbing rungs ran the entire height, little yellow lights dotting the way.

"Where to?" asked Joe.

"Up," Jack said, shutting the maintenance door behind them. "Everything anyone's said so far has indicated we're on lower levels." He checked his watch. "I've got 0950. If we can get to wherever Hergs is holding his Council meeting at ten, we can at least shatter the bunch of 'em." He patted the shattergun he'd stuck in his thigh pocket.

Climbing wasn't too bad in one-third artificial gravity, but Jack could tell that he and Joe were both winded after coming up what he guessed were twenty levels, if he was correctly counting the half-sphere lights appearing every twelve rungs. Before long they began finding one vent per level, a three-foot-wide grating that looked out onto sometimes darkness, sometimes incomprehensible factory scenes, sometimes bleak gray halls. Jack memorized which levels they might want to return to and check out later. He was all action now, simply here, alert to any opportunity, flowing effortlessly from moment to moment.

"Damn!" came from below him. Jack turned to see Joe flailing, hanging by one hand, feet windmilling. In an instant Jack reversed himself, scooting down the left side of the rungs and securing Joe's left arm.

Joe found the other rung and hung on. "God!" he whispered. "If you hadn't caught me, I'd still be falling! I lost my grip. I swear these rungs are getting *wet*."

"Yeah, I was noticing that myself," Jack said, feeling the slimy wall of the shaft.

"We must be close to some Martians."

"Huh? How do you know?"

"It's the water they release through their breath. When they're excited, it can really be a lot."

Jack stared back. How could Joe know that? But didn't it make sense? Of course Martians did that. Jack knew that himself. But how?

The next light was much further above them, fifty or sixty rungs instead of twelve. Could this mean a multi-story space, deep and open? Yes, of course, that broad grating way up there led to the Chamber of the Martian Council to the Emperor.

Dammit! How do I know that?

"Come on!" Jack said. Joe climbed behind him, both careful to establish full command of a wet rung before relinquishing it for the next. Presently they came to the ventilation grating, four feet wide and two high. Jack hung to the left of the rungs, Joe to the right. Fifty feet below, a horseshoe conference table seated twenty ornately dressed Martians, with Sam Hergs at the apex.

"All right, Council boys," Sam Hergs barked from a big red leather chair marked M.E. "Let's get this damn meeting done, 'cause ya know I got some torturing to do! You dudes are gonna give me your latest update on Amplified Thought. So Mr. Leader of the Council, if you will please make it snappy?"

A Martian glided from the horseshoe to stand at its open end, facing Hergs sprawled in his chair. The creature was the largest Martian present. Jack immediately understood that his long thick fin, protruding through a slit in his golden robe, was a distinction of maturity and wisdom in contrast to his smaller-finned peers.

"It's that Dar guy!" Joe hissed. "The leader of the Kilpatrick Desert raid!"

"Yes, I know!" Jack whispered. "Quiet! Listen!" Why did he have the urge to shout: *We're saved?*

CHAPTER TWENTY-FOUR
Strange Mental Vibrations

"I beg the Emperor of First Home and the Solar System to forgive my unworthy report," Dar began in a high-pitched yet resonant voice. His two violet eyes, each two inches in diameter and unlidded, moved to the floor of the vast chamber for a moment in a gesture of obeisance, then returned to gaze at Hergs. "However, from my humble position may I extend every member of the Council's supreme benefaction upon our savior, the emperor." The rest of the Martian retinue, like Dar, wore the golden robes signifying status as Martian elders. Jack knew that each of these Martians was at least one thousand years old. They were the wisest of the wise. All the Council members lowered their huge eyes to the floor and then resumed gazing at the emperor as Dar had.

"Right, right, thanks for the glorious benefaction and all," Hergs snapped from his red swivel chair. He pressed a button at his waist. And disappeared.

"Damn!" Joe whispered.

Hergs reappeared standing beside Dar. "But I asked for the damn report, my good man! Instead you waste my time spouting your typical Martian clichés!"

Again, Hergs vanished.

Dar took a deep breath. "Sire, if you will please--"

Hergs reappeared in his leather seat. "If I will please what, Mr. Dar?" He vanished again, this time winking back into existence behind other Martians on the horseshoe. It was exactly like special effects in movies from a few decades back. Before Jack knew it Hergs was popping up and disappearing all over the Council chamber, which seemed to extend for acres into the shadows. The horseshoe in fact only took up a tenth of the vast space, so that several images of Hergs were blinking in and out of existence all across the blank volume.

"Well, sire," Dar said, "your teleportation pack only has limited storage, and its recharging time is about three days. I suggest you save it for when you truly need it. While it is capable of storing a few of our AT subroutines, they are not extremely stable stored in such a manner. We would certainly hate to see the pack overheat and become unable to reassemble your components."

"Aw, crap!" Hergs said, reappearing in his leather M.E. chair. "Can't a damn Martian emperor have a little fun? It feels so *good* to teleport! But of course you Mars dudes have all your little rules! Sheesh! But let's get on with the report, boy. I haven't got all day. I've still got the Commers to torture, and for all we know my fellow Earthmen might be sending a whole fleet to blow us to kingdom come any minute now."

"As you wish, most exalted Emperor Hee-Arr-Grgsss," Dar said, and Jack wondered if he wasn't mocking Hergs. These Martians certainly seemed a hundred times more cultured than the thug leaping from his red chair shaking a fist.

"Pronounce my damn name correctly, damn you! Hergs! *Hergs!* Can't you stupid Martian twerps even talk straight?"

"We try … Emperor Hurr … gaaassss," Dar managed, mouth straining to form the word. Why did he bother speaking aloud? Jack wondered. The meaning was absolutely clear, after all, coming straight out of his mind.

"Sheesh! Sheesh it to hell!" Hergs muttered. "Aw, who cares? I'm surrounded by imbecile finbacks! No wonder I'm depressed! How you guys ever ran an empire is beyond me!"

"Well, my liege, over the course of eons we evolved--"

"Crap on it! Just crap! I've heard enough of your damn history! It goes on damn near forever! Just tell me about the weapon! That's what we're here for today! Focus, boys! The weapon!"

"Well, sire, the Amplified Thought Mega-Program is almost completed. As you know, by linking the minds of Senior Martians in a series, if you will, we can amplify--"

"Right, right, I know all that BS. You guys have been foolin' around with all that BS on Earth the last few months."

"We've actually been experimenting with Amplified Thought for a number of years," Dar went on, "but only now have hit upon the precise means of full control. The Earth Project helped us immeasurably in refining the technique. Of course, we don't expect that you would be able to follow all the intricacies."

"You're damn right I won't follow it!" Hergs hooted. "You Mars dudes come up with more weird BS than I can possibly follow! But get on with it, my man!"

Dar exchanged what Jack felt was a small bitter smile with his comrades. It was hard to tell when a Martian smiled. You had to look closely at the tiny folds of skin by the mouth.

"Amplified Thought," Dar continued, "gives us the ability to harness the naturally resonating power of the Martian mind and amplify it a hundred, a thousand, a millionfold. While our earliest experiments tended to end in … various unfortunate disasters, since we at first did not have the ability to contain the resulting energies, we have since developed software feedback mechanisms that allow us full control. Our work on Earth the past few months has demonstrated the potential of fully controlled Amplified Thought on a small scale. We believe that with the Mega-Program, we can achieve virtually unlimited powers. We could gather the remnants of the great outer planets of this solar system and fuse them into a new sun."

"Or we could destroy any planet we choose!" Hergs cried. "Instantly! With a thought! Isn't that correct, my good Dar?"

Dar nodded. "Yes … complete destruction, with a thought."

For some time Jack had been eagerly awaiting Dar's next turn to speak, and he'd been cursing Hergs' foul interruptions of Dar's high musical tone. The lovely essence of Dar reverberated in Jack's head. Joe was smiling, also enthralled.

Jack shook his head. He hadn't been himself in days. The *Typhoon* had been destroyed, their brothers and friends killed, he and Joe had almost died on Earth, and now he was spying on the Council to the Emperor of Mars and understanding every word. A few days ago Jack had denied the possibility of Martians. Yet here he was, fully conversant with Martian speech and culture.

"We've been reading their minds all along," he whispered. "Ever since the Desert, when we always knew what they were about to do."

"All along we've been *attuning* ourselves to them," Joe said. "We can understand them better now because we're getting more and more used to them. Before we could only crudely feel their thoughts."

"High mental energy. It's their nature to radiate all their thoughts *outward*. They don't need to speak, that's just a convention."

"Telepathy, but probably one-way, or they'd have picked up on *our* thoughts by now."

Jack nodded. Somehow the Martian mind radiated in all directions. In fact, Jack was receiving confirmations of this theory from the Martian minds. When they spoke, he wasn't understanding what they were saying. He understood what they were thinking *as* they spoke. The music of their voices carried the thoughts out of the Martian brain. Jack realized that Hergs was actually speaking in Martian, and Jack was understanding him by hearing the Martians listen to Hergs. No wonder he recoiled at Hergs' speech. He felt the revulsion the Martians themselves did for Hergs' mangling of their language. Jack further saw that Hergs probably had an easy time teaching himself to speak Martian from feeding off Martian minds. Jack himself had probably picked up enough of it already to make himself understood.

And Joe was right. It was all one-way. Although any human could hardly help but read the fully open Martian mind, the Martians could not read a human. Their new emperor, Sam Hergs, was closed to them except for the pathetic, barbarically Anglicized Martian that came out of his mouth. And yet, and maybe for this precise reason, the Martians, while positively hating Sam Hergs, were *addicted* to him.

"So tell me," Hergs cut in, "how soon can we use this Amplified Thought contraption of yours to destroy Mars? From what you tell me we don't even need to rebuild the Mercury death ray. That sorta weapon is obsolete now. Am I right? Huh?"

Now the thoughts coming out of the Martians made Jack want to throw up. Dar mastered himself and said: "My lord, Amplified Thought is not a *contraption* as you refer to it. Rather it is a program, similar to your human computer programs, linking our minds in a series, stepping up the amplitude. And yes, we no longer need the death ray from Planet Cinder." *Unspeakable sorrow/mourning for seven hundred of First Home killed on Planet Cinder, and for what? For nothing! For madman's lust to destroy! For nothing! Nothing!*

"Huh? Whazzat, boy?" Hergs snarled. "I didn't quite catch that last there."

"Oh … nothing, my liege. As I was saying, it will take approximately five hundred of us so linked, and we are in the process of training the last hundred now." *Only thirteen hundred of us left in the solar system! Well over a third of our population will be required to carry out these insane orders to destroy everything!* "It should be ready in about a week."

"*Sire!* It should be ready in about a week, *sire!*" Hergs flashed, bringing his fist down on the arm of his swivel chair.

"Sire …" Dar finished weakly. "I'm sorry, sire, I suppose I've perhaps had enough of your air for a while. I think that's it … not thinking well …"

"Crap on it, my good Dar!" Hergs shot back, playing with his belt, disappearing, then reappearing in his chair. "You know the tradeoff. You guys breath *my* air, I take *your* gravity."

We can take your gravity better than we can take your thick, highly pressurized, oxygen-rich air. I need to get back to my chambers, my First Home chambers with just one percent of this annoying cloud of toxins.

"Ya damn wimps!" Hergs laughed. "What kind of Council of Martian Elders *is* this?"

"We … we must protest …" said another member of the Council, a slightly built Martian with a much smaller fin. "We feel it is *wrong* to destroy. Especially our mother planet. Earthmen, yes, we can destroy Earthmen as you wish, for they have despoiled our planet. But is there truly reason to destroy our ancestral home? Perhaps we could reclaim it, as we're doing with your Planet Marble? That is, demolecularize the ugly structures with which humans have despoiled our planet, returning First Home to its sacred--"

"Aw, listen to this," Hergs said. "Kner, your planet is BS, you know that? It's just a bunch of red sand! It died off a coupla billion years ago! It's BS, man! I hate the place! Just forget the dump heap and live here on Venus. In a few years we'll have the place completely terraformed!"

Jack felt the Martians' revulsion at the word "terraform." Yet it was plain they were all afraid of Hergs. Why? For some reason the Martian minds were literally closed on this subject.

"Piss on this!" Hergs said. "You twits yourselves agreed with me just last week that since Earthmen have despoiled your planet, it's not worth saving! Don't forget there're something like two billion goody-goody Earthmen running all over the place like a buncha damn ants! The only way to sterilize the place is to blow it the hell up!"

"What Kner is trying to say," Dar cut in, "is that Amplified Thought should never be used to destroy. Instead, as on your Planet Marble, your own Earth--"

"Sire!" Hergs bellowed, coming out of his chair with clenched fists. "Sire! Sire!"

"Sire ..." Dar squeaked, stepping back. "I do not wish to offend, sire, but it would be so much more beneficial to ... to terraform *Earth,* to use your phrase. To clean that planet up, rather than destroy First Home. I'm quite sure that your fellow humans would eagerly wish to return to their mother planet, and that way we could return to ours." He sighed. Jack could feel the wistful longing of all the Martians for a glimpse of their home planet.

"Hmph!" Hergs said. "What I'm quite sure of is the new spirit of defeatism in the Council of Elders! My Martian warriors on Mercury sure wouldn't be spouting this cowardice!"

Dar blinked. Again Jack could feel the mourning for seven hundred of their fellows killed on Mercury. "Sire, those who volunteered for duty on Planet Cinder were the younger members of our populace, what you might call *hotheaded.* Yet we loved them."

"Give me one saucer pilot with balls like A'olfglnd over this entire pissy Council any day of the week!" Hergs cried.

"Wimps! Wimps all of you!"

"Our saucers were developed for exploration, not military purposes! And A'olfglnd, yes, he was courageous, but so foolhardy, to attempt a head-on attack against the famous *Typhoon I.* He paid for it, and we feel his loss most bitterly."

"*Most bitterly!*" Hergs mimicked. "Sheesh! This is what I get to take into the Final Battle! This wimpy Council of Elders in their golden robes! Sheesh it to hell!"

"Well, sire, we of the Council do wonder if your present course of action is indeed the most prudent. You must remember that we of First Home are a peace-loving people, although I beg you to recall my recent loyal service in the battle of the Desert of Doom."

"Forget it, Dar! It's all BS! You're in the fight of your lives here, and there's no turning back. What's coming up is gonna make your little skirmish in the Kilpatrick Desert look like a damn picnic! Earthmen are *not* gonna go back home to Earth and leave Mars for you. No damn way! Just look at their damn AresNet! Read all those new bestsellers out the past few months! They all say the whole Earth disaster was necessary to push humanity out of the cradle. That's the kind of BS they wanna believe. They're space-happy! They believe they gotta keep pushing outwards. Well, look at the trouble it got 'em in Alpha Centauri. I don't buy that BS! They'll never leave Mars, even if they do send ships to the stars from there. They like the idea of it as a base. It feels alien to 'em, and they like it. And if they hafta do a genocide number on all of you guys, well, so much the better. It keeps their adrenaline going."

"Is ... is this really true?" Kner asked. Jack's heart sank. He too would have done a genocide number on the Martians a few days ago. He couldn't believe the nobility and intelligence in these Martian minds. Already he was picking up some fascinating concepts of Amplified Thought. "You know," Kner went on, "there are those among us who say that humans are perhaps capable of understanding our sorry position."

"Forget it, Kner! That's BS! Almost treasonable BS, I might add! See it don't come outa your mouth again, boy!"

"Uh ... yessir ..."

Hergs disappeared. When he blinked back, he was pacing around the Martians. "For your information, kiddoes, my fellow humans are *insane*. They're out to fry your asses, if you get my drift. I'm the only damn one of 'em who had the sense to quit the mess. That's right! I quit my planet, why can't you jerks quit yours? Huh? Huh?" He pulled out a ceremonial riding crop and rapped a senior Martian's little pink knuckles with it. "Now, all of you guys, forget the BS and let's get that Amplified Thought deal in gear now! Whaddya say, boys?"

"Well, sire ... it will be done ..." Dar said.

"That's right! I'm the Emperor of the Martians, and you guys are just the peon Council! Right?"

"Uh, right ..." said Dar. Jack recalled what he'd picked out of Dar's mind in the Kilpatrick Desert: *We do not understand these killers from Marble. They have destroyed us, they have destroyed the emperor himself! And now, the new emperor ... we must worship filth!*

But Dar suppressed his thoughts as best he could in the presence of his emperor. Jack could look deep into these Martian minds and know that it was impossible for them to disobey Hergs, who'd killed off their old emperor P'nal last December and assumed the position himself. The Martians had given him the job because they couldn't read his mind. Hergs was a numinous unknown, to be worshipped as a god. He was already the most powerful Martian emperor who'd ever lived, and their history stretched back 40,000 Martians years, twice as long as human years.

"And when I say that in one week, we are gonna use the Amplified Thought deal to waste the planet Mars, then that's what we'll do, right?"

"Uh ..." Dar swallowed. "Right. But, if I may point out, we could easily forcibly put humans into their spaceships with the Thought and bodily remove them from First Home. We could send them back to Earth whether they wanted it or not ... sire."

"Forget Earth! I admit I have some short-term uses for it, but once I've got my master race of trained human killers, then--poof! We Amp-Thought the earth as well!"

"Sire!" said Kner. "That will leave just what you call Venus and Mercury left in the solar system!"

"That's right, baby! Then we zap out Mercury, too, 'cause it's such a nothing planet. There'll be only Venus, which'll be renamed Hergs and made completely livable! What an Empire we'll have here, boys!"

"But, sire--"

"Shut the hell up!" Hergs bellowed. "By the way, Dar baby, have we heard back from the damn Alpha Centaurians yet? Those bastards make me nervous. That's another reason to have only one planet in this solar system. Easier to defend. I think those pigs are gonna try to take us out once they wipe out the USSF over there."

Dar cleared his throat. "Your human spy smuggled aboard one of the Earthmen's Star Drive ships finally did return. But there was nothing left of his mind. All we could obtain from him was a list of demands, including the destruction of our sun itself, that appeared quite insane."

"Crap! We're gonna hafta keep trying," Hergs said, pulling the scrambled data out of Dar's mind the same way Jack did now. "I'd rather have those bastards on *my* side. They can keep the USSF fleet occupied while we take *this* system." Jack saw Joe wincing at the news of Hergs' men trying to negotiate with the ACs. But above all came the Martian mental radiation: *We cannot mix with that race. They are insane, they are Group Mind, totally devoted to destruction.*

"Well, all this means we have to keep refining Amplified Thought so we can repel any AC attacks if they come," Hergs went on. "And if we have to Amp-Thought the entire Alpha Centaurian Empire, well, we'll just hafta do it! They better not mess with Sam Hergs is what I say!"

"Sire, I confess all this talk of violence and killing makes us all weary," Dar said softly. "Destroying First Home, destroying Planet Marble, using this wretched Planet Mist as some sort of last-stand fortress against attack from outside the solar system--"

"Well, then, listen up, my good Dar, and all the rest of you coward wimps. That's the damn plan, and anybody who doesn't like it can just commit one of your fancy Martian shattergun suicides! Just remember, as you dudes die off, I replace you with specially-trained human Council members!"

Jack could feel an edgy contraction of Martian thought and feeling. The possibility of having another numinous Earthman on the governing Council was too much to bear. The only way the Martians could deal with Hergs' various human guards was the fact that they acted like slaves around the emperor. They were like somebody's pet leopard brought into the living room for the nervous guests to admire.

Even now one of these human slaves bowed behind Dar. Rather than interrupt Hergs' fresh playing with his teleportation belt, Dar uneasily let the guard whisper into his huge pink ear hole. Instantly there was a commotion among the Martians. Hergs was so busy disappearing and rematerializing that he didn't pick up the message now known to everyone, including Jack and Joe.

Problems with the video/audio system in the Commer cell on Level Three. Security sent to investigate. Guard 33456-Z McBoerland does not acknowledge.

"Crap!" Joe cried, jerking up and banging his head against the vent.

In disbelief Jack and Joe watched the heavy grill dislodge and twirl free, sliding through space to clang on the parquet floor below.

"Aw, dammit to hell!" Joe gasped.

Twenty Martians and their emperor turned to Jack and Joe. Hergs strode forward.

"Spies! Traitors! Guards, annihilate them at once!"

CHAPTER TWENTY-FIVE
Flight Hanger A

Joe felt blaster heat and shoved Jack back from the vent. The vent hole glowed blue-white and began to melt. Through the hole Joe saw scores of gray-uniformed guards, human and Martian, firing blasters and shatterguns.

"Thanks," Jack muttered from a couple rungs down the shaft. "Although for a second I thought I was going all the way down."

"Hey, sorry! But we definitely need to get out of here."

"No, we need to take care of Hergs first," Jack said, climbing back to the hot vent, the right half of which had melted closed. He pulled the Martian shattergun from his thigh pocket. "Damn! They've hidden him!"

"Keep down! All they need to do is graze you!"

Nevertheless Jack stuck the shattergun out the vent and flexed the grip. "Aw, man! I can't believe this!"

"What now?"

"Look at this piece of crap!" Jack held the shattergun down to Joe. A panel on the side of the weapon glowed with moving Martian symbols. Joe realized he'd picked up enough of the Martian language to understand them:

PALM PRINT IS NOT THAT OF RAPPOL MCBOERLAND, GUARD 33456-Z. PLEASE RETURN THIS WEAPON TO CORPORAL RAPPOL MCBOERLAND.

"Damn!" Joe said. "I didn't know they could code shatterguns to individuals."

"Well, apparently they can just like we can. We just haven't seen it before." Jack jammed the gun back in his pocket. "The hell with it. I'm not gonna give it back to Corporal McBoerland. Maybe we can bluff somebody with it later. Let's get going."

Joe swung a leg down.

"No, not down," Jack said, quickly climbing past the melted side of the vent hole. "We need to go up. Hang off to the right like this, where the vent melted, so they can't see you."

"Huh? Why?" Joe said, following Jack.

"First of all, they won't expect us to go up. They made that hole too hot to climb up that way, but they'll be in this shaft any second. It may buy us some time if they're scanning down, not up, for us." As they climbed another level Jack went on: "The other thing, I saw in a Martian's mind that these shafts can be flooded with poison gas, and I'm thinking the gas will tend to be less dense the higher we go."

"Yeah, that's probably--wait!" From far below Joe heard the sound of boots clambering up the rungs.

"I'm betting those guys have gas masks," Jack went on. "Now if I understand that Martian correctly, we'll hear a little *chink-a-chink* sound when the gas outlets open. And then we'll have to hold our breath the rest of the way."

"Hold our breath? The rest of the way? To where?"

"To Flight Hanger A," Jack said. "It's only ten levels above us. If I read that Martian right."

"What Martian?"

"The general from the Kilpatrick Desert. Dar, the one that wants us to escape."

"Look, Jack, I don't know how to say this, but I'm already completely out of breath as it is. How'm I gonna--"

Chink-a-chink!

"Here's your chance to find out. Ten more levels, Joe."

Joe clamped his mouth shut as clouds of phosphorescent gas shot from hundreds of red holes up and down the length of the shaft. Already his lungs were tight and empty. He wanted to scream: *Jack, you idiot, let's get off at the first level here!* But Jack scrambled faster above him, pulling away. A good idea for him to lead, Joe thought dimly. He'd totally collapse if Jack weren't here. Maybe he could ignore his lungs if he could just concentrate on his brother. Sure, Jack had cracked after John sacrificed the *Typhoon,* but who wouldn't have? It had been pure grief and shock. They'd lost the ship, two brothers, and four of their best friends. Joe knew he would've cracked too if he hadn't been so dinged out from the ice ray.

Anyone could see that Jack was back, fully in command and ready to ruthlessly exploit every last possibility of survival. And who knew? They might pull it off one more time.

Except there was no way Joe could make it. He knew he'd have to gulp for air any second. His stomach knotted, his vision narrowed, and his hands grew numb on the rungs. The gas was so thick that Jack, climbing four feet above him, glowed like a neon sign. Joe decided to grab one more rung to prove he'd tried his best. One more, then he'd stop and take in a delicious gulp of whatever was already burning the hairs off his forearms. One more grab and then he could gulp and drift through space. Peace …

The eerie singing cry of a Martian shattergun cut through the gas, embroiling it with a thousand hues of violet and crimson. The two-foot-wide ray struck the rung Joe was about to grab. Like most inorganic materials the rung merely crackled instead of shattering. Joe gazed dully at it and wondered if that meant he couldn't gulp the air as planned.

But above him Jack was writhing. He'd been hit. Joe opened his mouth to shout.

No! You can't! You can't breathe the poison!

It was only with the greatest difficulty that he closed his mouth and it took all his will to expel the gas that got inside. He felt dizzy and knew he'd taken in toxins. What a brutal death that would be, your insides corroded like that.

But Jack had taken a shattergun bolt. The ray had only grazed his brother's left rubber boot heel, and it was taking a long time to disintegrate, but when it did the chain reaction would spread through the sole of Jack's foot and shatter his entire body. Jack furiously tugged at the tight boot.

Joe quickly moved up past his damaged handhold. Hooking his left arm through a rung, he grabbed Jack's boot with both hands, carefully avoiding the shattering heel. He yanked the boot loose. The gray sock beneath looked all right, but Joe decided it had to come off too. He let the boot slip into space, pulled the sock off, threw it into the shimmering gases, and watched it float.

Six guards in gray uniforms climbed the rungs fifty feet below. Four humans and two Martians. As the lead one aimed a shattergun, Jack's boot struck him square in the chest. With a wild cry the guard lost his hold and fell, whipping his shattergun beam in wild arcs, splashing all five of his comrades with its deadly light. In seconds the guard fell from sight, accompanied by the shattered chunks of his buddies.

Joe felt a tap on his shoulder. He looked up. Jack signaled to keep climbing. Joe waved a hand to indicate: how many more levels? His heart sank when he saw Jack holding up five fingers.

But he climbed. Somehow his mouth wouldn't obey his desperate commands to open up. Soggy with sweat, he climbed whether he wanted to or not. It took centuries. Rung after rung was sighted, challenged, and conquered, and still there was no end to it. But they were both climbing faster now, almost running up the rungs.

Abruptly the gas thinned. Joe stuck his face right in Jack's bare left foot. Jack had stopped to work several nuts off a big black panel with his pocket wrench. Here? Finally? Jack hoisted off the panel and slung it into the void. He threw himself into the hole beyond and Joe climbed in after him.

They stood gasping on gray concrete, sucking in fresh cold air. For several minutes that was all Joe could do. Then Jack tugged his sleeve.

Joe looked up. They stood at the right rear corner of a spaceship hanger, a cube five hundred feet on a side. Dozens of ships stood poised on numerous levels of launching decks. The far wall consisted of giant yellow hanger doors secured against the high-pressure Venusian atmosphere.

Several human technicians clustered around a silver ship on the nearest flight deck, peering into a service hatch. It was a Mercedes luxury saucer, the ultimate recreational vehicle for the utterly rich. The only nonmilitary spaceship capable of interplanetary flight, the Mercedes had a small but efficient Augmented Nuke that could get you between planets in a few days. And it was pretty, a saucer thirty feet in diameter, twelve feet high, with a polished mirror finish.

Joe knew what Jack was thinking. They didn't have to say it. They were running.

"Lady, I don't care who you are," growled one of the technicians. "If we can't get this unit up to one hundred percent, I won't clear this ship for takeoff. Got that?"

"I don't understand why you just don't replace the whole unit," came a petulant female voice from the open crew hatch.

"Because they cost four million apiece, that's why. Now press down on Communicator Button A on your right console while Ernie and I--hey!"

Joe landed a clean punch on the technician's face and the man collapsed. A second man with the nametag ERNIE stuttered: "It's those guys that escaped! The Commers!"

A third pulled out a shattergun. "In the name of Hergs--"

"Saboteurs! Saboteurs!" Ernie shrieked. Two more technicians produced shatterguns.

At the open hatch, Jack wrenched out a young woman and threw her to the metal deck. She glared in indignation. Joe wanted to laugh. A society girl--a debutante--at Hergs' Evil Dome! Her shiny long black hair whipped around her face and she sprawled on the flight deck in her gold minidress and her thick fur jacket and her giant red rings, fuming at her ruined outing. Jack stared incredulously at her.

Joe jumped into the Mercedes and took the right copilot seat, saving the command position for Jack. "Hey, come on!"

"I--I'm sorry--I didn't mean to be so rough!" Jack stammered.

"C'mon, Jack! We haven't got a second!"

Jack finally turned back to Joe. "I--she--"

The girl charged him, screaming: "That's my saucer, you monsters! Get away from it!"

She fell inside the saucer atop Jack as three shatter rays bounced off the side of the Mercedes. Joe reached over the two sprawling bodies, yanked the hatch down and secured it.

"Okay, baby, you asked for it," he muttered. The ship's engine had been on Standard Warmup for at least half an hour. The girl had probably been preparing for a pleasure cruise when some fastidious technician decided he didn't like what he saw on his monitor. Joe had dealt with that kind before. But he could see perfectly well from the control panel that all was well.

"It's--my--ship!" the girl grunted, pummeling Jack.

"Look, I'm sorry, but we need it!" Jack shouted.

VARRRRRR! Joe fired up the main reactor and cut in the side maneuvering thrusters, unsure how big a hanger door he'd have to maneuver through. He felt guilty for taking Jack's job, but time was wasting. Too bad about the maintenance crew, too bad about everyone in the hanger, but they were Hergs' men, after all. He pressed the button on the panel marked "OPEN HANGER DOORS." The technicians scrambling for the safety of their airlock weren't going to be fast enough.

The hanger doors wrenched apart and the thick Venusian air, at a pressure over ninety times the inner atmosphere, blasted in with hurricane force. Joe expected it and had already applied the computerized stability thrusters as well as maximum power to the main drive. The technicians hadn't expected it and were crushed to pulp. The well-built Mercedes shot out of the hanger, accelerating across the blistering Venusian wasteland at twenty-two thousand miles per hour.

CHAPTER TWENTY-SIX
Confrontation

Jack pulled himself into the left chair as Joe transferred ship's command to that console. "What's this thing's top end?"

"About a million miles an hour," Joe replied. "We're still accelerating. It'll take a few minutes to top out."

"And is one-fourth artificial gravity all we have?"

"Yeah, that's all this thing's got."

"Well, it'll have to do. You've set the autopilot to Mars?"

"Yep. But at this speed we'll need a hundred thirty-six hours to get there, counting acceleration and deceleration. Over five and a half days."

"We'll have to radio ahead for the USSF to come get us," Jack said, looking over the console for the communications program.

"Wait up a bit, Jack." Joe listened on a headset. "I'm picking up some reports. There's still no sign of pursuit. But--" He grinned. "I can't believe it! They think they got us, Jack! They found all those crystals at the bottom of the shaft and they think that's us!"

"Probably some fool wants to believe they got us. Hergs'd probably have him killed if he admitted we got away. But how're they going to explain away this saucer? We just blew out their flight hanger."

"They--whoa!" Joe laughed. "They're treating it as unrelated! Looks like it happened once before. A girl launches her private Mercedes off the deck without pressurizing the hanger, destroys the whole thing and all its ships!" He swiveled to the girl, who sat stonily in one of the four chairs behind the pilot seats. "You wouldn't be called Amav, would you?"

The girl looked away. "Am I in trouble? Is that what they're saying?"

Joe shrugged. "What happened last time you blew out the hanger?"

"They--they told me never to do that again. But they didn't really care, I guess. The Martians just rebuilt it with Amplified

Thought." She tossed her head, dark brown eyes glaring, arms tightly wrapped around her black fur coat. "Who cares? It's just a lousy old hanger. But I'm gonna get blamed for it. They'll probably take my license away. All thanks to you guys!"

"Correction," Jack cut in. "You're coming with us to Mars, where you will face charges of treason for collaborating with the enemy." He found himself in a staring match with her.

And only now was he hit with how beautiful she was. She might be a spoiled rich girl, and God only knew how a spoiled rich girl had made her way to Hergs' hideout on Venus, but this Amav was nobly, haughtily beautiful. She held her up exquisitely chiseled face like a case of jewels Jack Commer could never afford.

"Huh," Joe said, still listening on the headset. "Looks like we destroyed a bunch of their attack saucers. No--all of 'em! All fifteen Martian attack saucers were in Hanger A. Hanger B just has some freighters, they're saying. I don't think they can touch us. And even if the Martians can make new ships with Amplified Thought, it's probably still gonna take 'em awhile."

"But whatever ships they do get up here, they're gonna be faster than this Mercedes," Jack said. "A freighter could throw a damn steel girder at us and rupture us, for God's sake. This thing has no armament whatsoever. We need to radio ahead for an escort."

"Okay, I'm trying--damn!"

"What?"

"Well, I can pick up the Venusian frequencies, but the transmitter doesn't--oh, no!" Joe punched in command after command. "Jack, what those technicians were repairing on the side of the saucer--"

"You mean we can listen, but not transmit?"

"Yeah, I'm sorry."

"That was the problem I was having yesterday," said the brunette vixen behind them.

Jack whirled. "They were repairing the comm unit just now?"

She nodded. "I guess that ruins all your little plans for

stealing my ship, doesn't it?"

"Dammit! So we just have to creep along like a sitting duck! Their saucers do ten million miles per hour. I imagine they've got something left that can come after us. Why haven't they launched anything yet?"

"They will," Amav said. "They'll come get me. They won't forget me."

Jack turned from those smoldering eyes. Why were they stuck with this absurd female? "Of all the damn *luck*," he muttered.

"It may take 'em a little while to figure out this isn't just a pleasure cruise," Joe said. "How far do you normally go after blowing out a flight hanger, I might ask?"

The girl pursed her lips. "About five million miles, if it's any of your business."

"Huh. We might have as much as five hours, then," Jack said. "Maybe time enough to repair the transmitter before they even launch."

"You won't get away with this," Amav said. "They'll never allow it."

"Quiet! You … traitor …" Jack whispered, again locking eyes with her. Mistake. There was something intoxicating in those eyes. Dangerous.

"You should hear these guys crowing about shattering us," Joe said, still listening to his headset. "Now they're saying the hanger implosion was a *planned celebration*. That they're so happy to get rid of us that they decided to destroy all their attack saucers as a work of art! I guess they need to explain it all away somehow. And there's something about this Mercedes. For some reason people are talking about it being important."

"Who are you saucer thieves, anyway?" Amav demanded. "I demand you take me back to Venus." Her voice, low and clear, musical and direct, was as intoxicating as her eyes.

"You--you--" Jack gasped.

The girl narrowed those eyes and smiled. "It gets so damned hot on this ship. The environmental controls haven't been right. That's another thing they're supposed to look into." Then she wriggled out of her fur coat, thrusting her torso until Jack gasped. Her golden minidress, composed of thousands of gleaming metallic disks, tightly followed the contours of generous breasts and slender hips. She crossed endless legs in dark gray hose to present ninety-eight percent of her thighs. Diamonds and rubies hung from soft earlobes and her long elegant neck. Her smile penetrated to Jack's core. He couldn't breathe. He couldn't remember where he was.

"Dammit, that's a Martian Elder's robe!" Joe burst out. "You've made it into a *dress!* Why, that's--that's--"

"It's a very, uh, imaginative use of, uh ..." Jack stammered.

"Thank you," Amav said. "I had the Court Seamstress tailor it to me personally."

"Y-yes, I can see that. It's all very ... lovely ..."

"God, Jack!" Joe said. "Didn't you read the Martians' minds about these robes? Don't you realize what she's *done?* These robes are sacred! A Martian Elder only gets to wear one after practicing the Mind Discipline of *K'Thoti* for four hundred years! Can't you see what she's *defiling?*"

All Jack could see was Amav's deep brown eyes and her long dark hair that came halfway down her back, so silky that it floated in the air every time she turned her head. And her smile. Her special smile for Jack.

"You stole that robe! Jack, I can't believe it! You know about the Mind Discipline, and what it means to a Martian to wear that robe!"

"Well ..." Jack muttered. "Well, I mean ..." All he could think about was what a perfect fit that robe made as a minidress on this impossible female *force.*

"C'mon, Jack, this is serious! Don't you remember how we felt listening to the Martians? I vote we take her back there and let *them* deal with her!"

"No. Out of the question. We'll just proceed on to Mars."

"But they'll know something's wrong when I don't circle back," Amav said. "They'll follow us. Your friend's right. Take me back. But I assure you the Martians won't say a word about this dress. I requested it through Hergs."

"Hergs?" Joe said, leaning forward. "Who in blazes are you, anyway?"

"Are you kidding? You don't know? I'm Amav! The Emperor's Consort!"

"What?" Jack said. "You mean--Hergs?"

"Precisely! You idiots!"

"Whoa, this is getting interesting!" Joe leered. "I can't believe we picked us up Hergs' *whore* on this trip! Might make the next five days real interesting, yessirree!"

"Joe, that's out of line!" Jack snarled.

Joe shrank back. "Gee, sorry, Jack, just kidding and all." But his eyes roamed up and down Amav's golden body. "I just mean, if the emperor has the pick of any woman he wants, then, well, I guess he got the best, all right."

"Joe, we will treat Miss Amav with respect on this flight. This is a flight just like any on the *Typhoon I.* Is that clear?"

"C'mon, Jack, loosen up a little."

Jack let the comment go. They all sat in embarrassment. Jack's face was hot. Dammit, he'd fallen in love again. Just like all the stupid times he'd fallen in love.

Another meaningless one-sided passion that lasted a few weeks and led nowhere. And this time, for a *whore*. They'd hijacked *Hergs' whore's* spaceship. No wonder she was perfect. It was her *job*. And they'd take her to Mars and drop her off at the United System Justice Department to be tried for treason and executed. And Jack would grieve for her for weeks. Then he'd forget it, fall in love with some other girl. All hopeless. Why did he bother?

He forced himself to speak. "It's time ... to begin the interrogation, I think."

"What interrogation?" Joe and Amav cried together.

"The official ... preliminary USSF debriefing. Necessary protocol, in cases like these."

"There's no protocol like that!" Joe said.

"Known only to ship's captains, of course. Perfectly official and all. We ... we need to concentrate now. We need focus, after all ..."

Amav shook her head. Jewels tinkled and lustrous black hair swirled about her impassive face. "Well, then, by all means, let's focus, then." She took a moment to yawn and stretch her golden arms wide, breasts tight and high again. God, those were her *nipples,* clearly pushing up some of those tiny golden disks in the center of those taut mounds.

"Well ..." Jack gasped. "Well, then, Miss, uh, Amav, first, uh, what is your full name?"

"Amav Frankston, Mr. Consort Kidnapper Numero Uno."

"And ... and your age?"

"Twenty-one, if you must know."

Jack blinked. She didn't seem that mature to him, more like sixteen. "And exactly how did you come to be this ... this consort of ..."

"First of all, I'm not officially his consort *yet*. Hergs decided to bow to Martian custom in this case, since to be a Martian emperor means respecting above all the sexual laws of the Martians."

"I ... see ..."

"In fact, Hergs has never had any sexual contact with me. But I've been informed I've been scientifically selected to be the perfect match for him." She dropped her eyes with endearing shyness. "The Martian custom is to train the woman in the secret Erotic Teachings for six months prior to actual consummation."

"Wow!" Joe burst in. "Jack, if you'd read that part of the Martians' minds, you'd know, I mean, you'd *know!* Martians are *obsessed* with sex. Since they live to be thousands of years old, they have plenty of time to learn how to do it right!"

Jack regarded Amav in growing horror, and she returned another sunny open smile, eyes lingering meaningfully on his. Although he thought he'd never be able to open his mouth again in his life, he found himself blurting: "So what do you do, get lessons from all these husky security guards we saw everywhere down there?"

Amav looked at the ceiling.

"No, Jack, they do it all in their heads at first, through telepathy," Joe said. "But believe me, they learn *everything,* down to the minutest detail. They might be totally virgins but a thousand times more experienced than humans! They just let the energy build for *months,* and then finally, when they're ready to *explode--*"

"Did you find all that in the Martians' minds as well?" Jack snapped.

"Yeah, Jack, I had to look, after all."

"Yeah, you had to look." Of course his brother would have taken the opportunity to explore all the back corridors of the Martian mind while Jack hung at the vent and contemplated the complexities of Martian language and Amplified Thought. In fact, it was probably because Joe was so intent on Martian sexual practice that he'd knocked the stupid grating onto the Council floor in the first place. Damn it all. It was just like Joe.

His younger brother dated scores of girls in all the colonies, on the barren asteroids and the surviving moons of the major planets. Joe knew all about girls, and women, and the difference between them. And he'd sit in the copilot seat on those *Typhoon* missions and crack insipid off-color jokes for hours. The old adage, "Those who talk about it, don't do it," apparently didn't apply to Joe. He talked and did, and talked and did. Occasionally he'd get semi-seriously caught up in an affair at some outpost-- Lucia from Ganymede was the last big one Jack recalled--and be moody and silent for a few weeks, but soon he'd shrug it off, contact one of his numerous girlfriends, and the putrid sex jokes would crank up again.

Was Joe one hundred percent devoted to duty? It wasn't just the sex talk that bothered him. Every once in a while Joe would burst out with some enormous emotion that embarrassed every crewman on board, like declaring the earth was a death trip and he was glad to have left it behind. Sure, sometimes it turned out that Joe had broken a lot of buried tension with that sort of wild remark. McNarri had once said that Joe was the unofficial spokesman for the group's emotions. But what the hell did that mean? How could Joe indulge in all these emotions and sexual escapades and still focus on the job of copiloting the deadliest spaceship ever made?

Sure, men had feelings. But wallowing in them like that? All that talk about women's breasts and asses and clitorises, those crude jibes about every female body he saw?

Jack didn't talk. And he didn't do. He never had. Well, at least he wasn't a virgin anymore. That curse had followed him up through last year, at age twenty-nine. The cleaning lady at USSF HQ on Titan, blowsy, big-boobed, and drunk, had followed him to his room, asking what the famous space pilot might possibly need …

That had been the last day of May 2033, over a year ago. Jack later attributed the whole disaster to his tension about the upcoming first test of the Xon bomb. In fact, they'd gone to Titan to retrieve some new components for the bomb. Joe and the boys were off by themselves getting smashed, and … there was the cleaning lady.

She hadn't stayed long. After strapping herself back into her stiff blue custodial uniform she'd told him the whole thing had been worthless, that he hadn't done a thing for her, that he was worse than her emotionally crippled husband. Jack tuned her out. What did he care what she thought? Basically he was relieved he'd been able to perform the required docking operations.

He'd almost gone down to the hotel bar to boast to Joe and the others that he was no longer a virgin, but instead he wound up getting drunk by himself, alone in his room, drowning in shock and shame. He'd probably only thought about the whole situation four times since. He couldn't remember the woman's name, only that her name tag began with "Eso." Somehow he'd tagged her as "Mrs. Esophagus," and he'd never been able to shake off that name.

Joe knew that Jack had never had a serious date in his life, but they never spoke of it, and Joe never backed off the sexual gibes.

And if Jack were to admit he was becoming increasingly despondent, well, what good did that emotion do him or anyone else? He was the captain, after all. For six years he'd been integral to the development of the *Typhoon* series. With General

Scott he'd helped organize the Evacuation. And he'd commanded the spaceship that won the Final War. What an impressive résumé.

Yet the captain was desperate. He had to admit it. That's what all the bestsellers counseled, wasn't it? Admit those feelings? Sure, he'd read the bestsellers. Secretly, on his own USSF Comm, no printed copy for Joe to discover. *Explore Your New Martian Feelings* and *The Asimov Foundation's Guide to the New Relationships on Mars*. They hadn't helped a bit.

And being the solar system's greatest space pilot actually worsened things. It brought him into contact with hundreds of beauties throughout the remnants of the solar system, but where girls swooned over Joe and to some extent the rest of the *Typhoon I* crew, Jack had never been able to take advantage of the situation, or any of the girls.

Because he always kept falling in love with them. They sensed it and backed away. Once it had gotten back to him that one of the beauties had said: "Jack looks so good, but he's so *damaged*." And if they didn't care about damage it was because--he sighed so audibly that both Joe and Amav flinched--they turned out to be space whores, like this Amav thing.

Amav and Joe had been conversing for some time.

"You're the Commers?" Amav gasped. "I can't believe it! They said your ship was destroyed over Mercury!"

"That's a sad story," Joe said. "In fact, I know it hasn't really sunk in yet. I still can't feel anything, and I can hardly remember why Jack and I were outside, in the escape craft, when John decided to take the ship down and blow up the death ray. Somehow we made it to Earth, but we were captured and brought to your dome on Venus. But we knew we had to break out."

Jack hung on every word Joe said. Though it was a garbled account, it nevertheless seemed like the most eloquent statement he'd ever heard. Why was that? Why was he feeling these things? What was this *female force?* What was she doing to him?

"I had no idea you were on Venus!" Amav said. "Imagine,

the Commers on Venus!"

"Yeah, well even your tech crew knew who we were and that we'd broken out," Jack said roughly, hoping to break the spell. "You really need to keep up with things, you know. That's absolutely necessary for survival these days."

"Well, I guess I don't follow this stuff as well as I should. I was just set on taking a morning outing, and there you were! I can't believe it! The Commers! I mean, I know we're supposed to be enemies and all, but … you're Jack Commer?"

"That's right." Jack cleared his throat. "That is, Jack Commer, Captain, United System Space Force, at your disposal, that is."

"Captain of an entire Space Force!" Amav said with wide eyes.

"No, not really. I'm just a ship's captain, that is, General Scott is the actual Supreme Commander of … well, who cares?" But, mortified to have blasphemed the USSF, Jack babbled: "I mean, I just command the *Typhoon I,* that's all. Or did, I guess."

"Hmm. I guess I always pictured you as maybe taller, or maybe more dashing, or something."

Jack looked at the floor, face burning.

"Is he always like this?" Amav giggled.

"Sometimes," Joe said. "He gets real moody when faced with a gorgeous doll like you, for instance."

"Shut up!" Jack snapped. "I mean, I'm sorry, I guess I've been pretty uptight lately for some reason. Why don't we … resume the interrogation?"

"What interrogation?" Joe said. "I'm Joe Commer, by the way," he added, easily stretching out his hand to Amav.

"Pleased to meet you, Mr. Joe," Amav said, shaking his hand briskly. "Yes, what interrogation, Jack?"

"*The* interrogation!" Jack cried, unhinged by the sound of his own name pronounced by that inexpressibly lush voice. "We've got to find out about this traitor here."

"All right," Amav said, again smiling at Jack. Jack swallowed and once more found his eyes locked into hers. Gazing into her eyes was like a long, loving kiss. Mrs.

Esophagus on Titan definitely didn't count, that was like plunging a toilet. Amav ... wasn't like plunging a toilet. She was ... she was ...

God, I love her! That smile! Oh my God!

"All right, Mr. Commer," she said. "You can continue your interrogation, if you please."

"First of all," Jack gasped, "your ... background. What you did on Earth, how you came to Venus, and your ... present position."

Amav sighed and stood. She began to pace the room in the slow motion of one-quarter gravity. Jack followed her long gray-hosed legs in ecstasy. Yet he was aware of a change in her mood. Something somber was rising and Jack was falling deeper, further, faster in love. And now Jack felt that *she* was in control of the entire situation, that he was *her* prisoner.

"Listen, do you really think they're not gonna rescue me? I mean, they have to, don't they?"

"Well, maybe they'll try," Jack said, "but we're definitely headed for Mars."

"I'm sure I can rig up the transmitter for us," Joe said. "I do all sorts of electronic work. Sort of a hobby of mine. Then we'll get us some help."

"What you're going to do is get all of us killed!" Amav burst out. "Don't you see Hergs *has* to follow me?"

"That's right," Joe said. "She's the damn consort of the emperor, after all."

"And tomorrow's the wedding!" Amav cried. "I finish the six-month Erotic Teachings tomorrow!"

"*Tomorrow?*" Jack groaned. "The--the *wedding?* To be *married* to that jerk?"

"Yes! And then we *do it* in full sight of the entire Martian Council! Oh, God, he's such a slimeball! He's been after me for so long! He's wanted to circumvent the Customs for months now!"

"The--the Erotic Teachings?"

"Wait!" Joe said. "Hergs! You and Hergs! Now I remember! I've seen you before! It was on Earth! With Hergs and the Martians!"

"Are you crazy?" Amav cried. "I never leave Venus! Well, I might go on a little cruise, but I never leave this area."

"No, you were there! When the Martians came to rescue us! On Earth! Yesterday! Hergs was trying to molest you, but the Martians intervened and said he couldn't! But you were there, you saw Jack needed help, I remember that. You were afraid he was dying!"

"That's crazy!"

"What's going on here?" Jack shouted.

"And the Martians had these heat rays and they *cured* us," Joe insisted. "I could feel the heat from their purple rays *healing* me. I knew then we were gonna be all right."

"That's crazy!" Amav repeated, stamping around the Mercedes control room. "I wouldn't go to Earth! Would I? I don't think so, but what you're saying seems *right* somehow. I've *wanted* to go to Earth, but ..."

She stopped three feet from Jack, who tried to concern himself with her pensive mood but found himself admiring her golden body all the more.

"It's funny, I know I must have a whole past on Earth, but I really can't remember it!"

"Huh," Jack said. Was this how the traitorous mind operated? You just didn't care about the earth anymore, about your own past? Yet Amav's obvious treason to her home world was fascinating. In fact, it was exciting.

"You must think I'm nuts. I know I'm not making any sense!"

"No, you're not making any sense," Joe said.

"Quiet," Jack commanded. "Let her talk."

"I mean, normally I just think about today! But--but when you mentioned being on Earth ... oh God, what's *wrong* with me?"

Jack stared. The beautiful, luscious Amav was *upset*. How could that be? Wasn't she supposed to be in control? Jack had never seen a girl upset before. What did it all mean?

CHAPTER TWENTY-SEVEN
Planetary Engineering

"I can't remember!" Amav cried. "This whole life I have is like some stupid movie! It doesn't mean anything!" Again she locked eyes with Jack, but now anxiety flooded out of her. He held this scary gaze way too long. He began to feel her feeding off him. What did she want? What could he possibly have that she wanted?

"Jack," Joe cut in sharply. "Her *eyes*."

"Huh?" Jack said.

"Dilated. I'm thinking B-drugs."

"B ...?"

"Maybe something that limits her memory to the last day or so."

"No, that's impossible," Amav said. "I can remember all of the last six months. They've been training me. I can remember all the goddamn Erotic Teachings."

"Or you just remember all the programming you've been stuffed with the past six months," Joe said. "Yeah, I'm thinking Hergs has really brainwashed you."

Jack gaped. The brainwashing drugs that could program the subject any way one wished? With the endless series of garbage in, garbage out failures that had led them to be outlawed throughout the United System?

"Could that be the case?" Jack said. "B-drugs?"

"No, of course not! I ... I need ..." Amav flew to a console by Joe and yanked open a small refrigerator. "I just realized ... I'm so thirsty ..." She pulled out a cold can of Saturn Suds and popped the tab.

Instantly Jack was on her, ripping the Saturn Suds from her hands and scattering most of it around the room in lazy one-quarter G arcs as he fought off her desperate grasp for the bright green can.

"Hey, what are you doing?" she grunted. "Give me that!"

"No way!" Jack shouted. "This is the B-drug!"

"Idiot! That's just Saturn Suds! I always have one after I

221

take off!"

"Forget it," Jack said, handing the can to Joe. "Joe, this ship ought to have some sort of analyzer, I would think."

"I'm sure it's got a little one," Joe replied, hunting beneath the copilot console and flipping open a small compartment. All USSF ships had material analyzers in case they should encounter any items of scientific interest, including alien life forms. Even pleasure ships were required to have simple models and report back all findings to the United System. Joe poured the can's contents into a bowl and punched in commands on his console. The machine hummed.

"You're crazy!" Amav said. "That's no drug!"

"But you wanted it as if it were a drug, didn't you?" Jack said.

"Are you kidding? You guys make me talk all this time! I'm not used to it, and it made me thirsty!"

Jack pulled open the refrigerator door. The two-foot by two-foot compartment was filled to the top with Saturn Suds cans. "I expect you drink these all day just because you're thirsty, huh?"

She shrugged. "I like my Saturn Suds."

"Analysis of liquid," came the mechanical voice from the analyzer. "Fifty percent water, thirty percent sugar, nineteen percent artificial flavor, one percent unidentified chemical."

"That'd be right," Joe said. "B-drugs sure wouldn't be registered with the medical databanks. But we can compare its molecular structure with the typical B-drug configuration." Soon he had a display of the chemical's molecular structure alongside images from an AresNet article on illicit drugs. "Yep, similar to classic B-drugs. Ninety percent match with a fairly mild, short-term program. Probably not any sort of total personality change. Something real light and subtle, and that needs to be repeated a lot."

"How can you be sure it's a B-drug?" Amav said. "I can't believe this!"

"It's a B-drug, all right, and I'd say it's probably wearing off about now."

"You think I've been on drugs all this time? But I've had

Saturn Suds since I was little!"

"They probably knew you were addicted to the stuff in the first place. So they kidnapped you to Venus, and started you in on it. My guess is that it affects your memory. Maybe just wipes it clean. Then they write whatever they want into your brain."

Amav sat down, stunned. "Kidnapped? I can't believe it! But I do know I haven't thought about Earth ever since ..." She looked into Jack's eyes. "Joe's right! I was kidnapped! I'm just remembering! How could I have forgotten that? But, God, *my father's still back on Earth!*"

"You're father's still back there?" Jack babbled. "No, that's impossible!"

"No, it's not!"

"No, nobody can be alive back there," Joe put in. "Earth is *dead.*"

"He's *there!* Haven't you ever heard of Stewart Frankston?"

"Are you kidding?" Jack cried. "The environmental kook?"

"He's not a kook! I'm his daughter! He's on Earth! They made me forget him!"

"The guy who refused to be evacuated?" Jack turned to Joe. "Is she hallucinating on the B-drugs or something?"

"No, he's my father!" Amav shouted. "Stewart Neal Frankston, you idiots! God, this is so *weird!* I've forgotten all about him! They *made* me forget him!" She leapt from her chair, breasts bouncing in that tight minidress. Jack knew he was done for. He was ready for some B-drugs himself. He wanted to forget everything, forget the *Typhoon,* forget Hergs, forget their own imminent deaths. Nothing mattered except *having this woman.*

"You're right, Joe," Amav continued. "I was on Earth. I'm just *remembering* it. This is *insane.*" She resumed pacing. Jack stared in ecstasy. "You're right, I did see you there. I'm remembering everything now! Hergs knew you'd crashed there and wanted to personally pick you up. I remember going into the middle of some Council meeting and demanding to go too. The Martians were shocked that I got into the emperor's presence without my Martian sex chaperone!"

"S-sex chaperone?" Jack gasped.

"You can't believe what I promised Hergs if he'd let me go along! The Martians were *shocked*. The only time they hear a woman saying anything like that is during the Great Erotic *J'thath!*"

"Wow!" Joe laughed. "I can just imagine what you promised!"

"*No* ..." Jack gasped. "You--you can't ..."

"C'mon, none of that matters," Amav said. "Don't you understand how ridiculous all this consort crap is? The drug must have worn off for a while, if I was really on a drug, because I did think of my father. I knew he was on Earth, I knew Hergs was going there, and he let me come, but he must've gotten me back on the drug because I never remembered asking about Daddy again. Even though we went right to the Alaska Demonstration Project. You guys crashed right in the middle of the Project!"

"But how can anyone be alive there?" Jack said. "All our instruments have shown the whole planet's *dead*."

"But it was clear in Alaska," Joe said. "Don't forget. We were amazed it was so clear. And our computer chose Alaska as the best possible spot to land."

"But that was just an aberration. We know the radioactivity levels, the amount of dust in the atmosphere--"

"Forget it. My father's in Alaska," Amav insisted. "The Alaska Demonstration Project. That's where the Martians have been testing this project of theirs called Amplified Thought."

"Yeah, we know about that," Joe said.

"Daddy was determined not to abandon the earth. He didn't want to go to Mars, even though he designed all these plans for terraforming it. So when the Evacuation started, I decided to stay on with him. We built a base in southern Alaska."

"You were *helping* the Frankston kook?" Jack gasped.

"Yes! And for your information I'm working on my Ph.D. in planetary engineering with that kook!"

"In ... in planetary engineering? A *space whore?*"

Amav folded her arms beneath her golden breasts, pushing them high and taut, grinning at Jack's obvious inability to spew his inept lust all over her. "God, I'd forgotten all that!" she laughed. "I can't believe it! All my studies! I really do know a hell of a lot about planetary engineering!"

"Look, I'm sorry I called him a kook. I know he's done some important stuff, but I just can't believe this!"

"Well, so many people do think he's a kook! But it was near the end of November when the *saucers* landed at our base."

"Martian saucers?" Joe said.

"Six of them! We were freaked out! But then we realized we could understand the Martians, and that they wanted to test Amplified Thought along with Daddy's Demonstration Project."

"No, wait, wait!" Jack cut in. "That would mean Martian saucers were landing on Earth even as we were starting the Evacuation!"

"Well, that's exactly what happened. Apparently you were so concerned with evacuating *outwards* that you didn't realize saucers were coming *in*."

"Damn!"

"I think the Martians were naturally drawn to the earth after the war, because their hearts went out to see a damaged planet. But they weren't familiar with its ecological relationships like Daddy was. So after we got over our freakout, we went into a partnership with them. The Martians used their thought control to help us start to clean up Alaska."

"You know, we always kept coming across Alaska as unusually clean," Joe mused. "We kept flying the *Typhoon I* over every so often to check things out. Of course we knew damn well that Earth was still unfit for human life, but I guess it was sort of nostalgic."

Amav wearily dropped back into her chair. "But a couple weeks later one of the supply saucers landed and we found out that this guy Hergs was the new emperor. The Martians couldn't believe it. In fact, some of them were hoping *Daddy* would be named emperor. There's something about human beings that *ensnares* the Martians."

"Yeah, we've seen that. So Hergs became emperor around, say, early December?"

Amav nodded. "And apparently he'd just realized that an emperor needs an empress. He needed to select a mate fast. He had the Martians search through as many human databases as they could find. But I gather that with the Evacuation, everything was in flux, and here I am, a human woman, just sitting in front of them in Alaska."

"The perfect match for Sam Hergs," Jack groaned. How could that be? Wasn't Amav Frankston the perfect match for *Jack Commer?* How could she be slated for sex with Hergs? Did that mean that Jack and Hergs were somehow the same?

"They just grabbed me. They told Daddy I'd keep working on Venus. That he'd hear from me in six months. What crap! That just gave Hergs six months to have me complete the Erotic Teachings. The Martians told me that Daddy was furious, but Hergs keeps posting more and more human guards at the Project, and it's more and more fascist all the time. Daddy's a prisoner there. We have to help him!"

"There, there," Jack said, patting her shoulder, daring to touch the goddess. But it was like patting the side of an armchair. No reaction at all. "We'll do something. If we can get to Mars, I mean, we can go back to Earth. We'll do anything …"

"Thanks. I'm so sorry. You must think I'm some sort of deranged person, brainwashed, flying around in a pleasure cruiser, being the consort of …"

Jack stared into her brown eyes. "N-no … we think you're wonderful …"

He heard Joe sigh. So Joe knew Jack had fallen in love again. Disastrously in love. Joe had seen Jack Commer transform Amav Frankston from traitorous whore to brainwashed planetary engineer to ultimate goddess within three minutes.

"Thank you," Amav said, holding his gaze. "You're a very thoughtful man."

Need flooded out of those deep brown eyes. Deep brown eyes that went on forever. She was *rearranging* Jack with nameless need. And all he had to offer in return was a certain need of his own, but now it shamed him. Here she was in tears, emerging from months of brainwashing, and all he knew was his own foul desire.

"You know, I've only been able to live in the present day. I've only remembered things from the last few hours. I was ripe for all the indoctrination. I believed it all. The only good thing has been the friends I've made with the Martians, even though they're still mad about this silly dress here." Jack followed her fingers brushing the golden discs. He took it all in, her thighs, her hips, her breasts ...

To his dismay Joe also followed her fingers exploring her own body. "Hmm," Joe smirked, "I hope you didn't forget the *other* good things you learned on Venus."

"Well, besides knowing the Martians, I don't think there's any good that's come out of this."

"What about the Erotic Teachings? Too bad if you forgot *them*."

"Joe! Enough of that!" Jack snarled. "After all she's been through!"

But Amav smiled. "No, the Erotic Teachings are geared to your basic personality. All they do is fully bring out your own style of lovemaking."

How could she sit there in that golden minidress and say such a thing? And *nod* at Jack? Ever so slightly? Almost imperceptibly? But definitely?

"*Wow!*" Joe crowed. "I can see they geared the Teachings *perfectly* for you!"

"Joe, knock it off right now!" Jack shouted. "Or so help me--"

"Aw, Jack, ease off. It's no big deal. I mean, I bet we could all use a dose of the Teachings. It's a basic urge. We all have it. So why deny it?"

"It's not right! Just--just to jabber about it like this!" He threw his hands up. Blood rushed into his brain. He had no idea how he wound up hobbling for the door to the rear compartment. Damn if his left foot wasn't still bare from Joe yanking his boot off in the shaft. "You--you--" he began, shaking a furious finger at his brother. "You think you know so much about--"

"Jack!" Amav called out. "Don't! Joe means well!"

"*What?*" Jack ripped open the door to the rear. "*What* did you say? What did you mean, Joe *means* well? Does that mean that you want--"

"No! Are you crazy?"

"Well, I suppose if the two of you want to sit around and discuss *sex,* well then, goodbye!" He turned, slammed the door behind him, and groaned.

The entire rear of the ship, half the saucer, was bedroom. The walls were sensuous folds of deep maroon velvet. A circular bed, black cover turned down to expose pale satin sheets, occupied most of the floor. A black marble bathtub leered off to the side.

Jack slammed his eyes shut. He'd never have her. His brother would move in and despoil Amav Frankston. She wanted it from *Joe.* Maybe she might have taken it from Jack. Maybe what he saw in her eyes wasn't entirely confusion and need, maybe it was also lust for a man. Any man.

But he'd blown it. Now they both knew he was a goddamn wimp. He spun on his remaining boot heel and banged open the door to confront the illicit lovers. He expected Amav to be in Joe's lap, slurping it up, but they were talking quietly.

"--gets uptight," Joe was saying. "He's got so much to worry about that--" He raised his head, genuinely grieved. "Hey, Jack, I ..."

"I'm ... sorry," Jack said. "I'm just ... I don't know ..."

Amav stood with tight lips, gathering her fur coat to hide her torso from the eyes of horny teenage boys. "Look, as you might imagine, I could use some rest. I've got a lot of sorting out to do."

"Well ... well, of course," Jack stammered. Where was the *sex?*

Amav jammed a hard finger into his chest. "And if it hasn't sunk in," she snarled, "I've been brainwashed! Kidnapped! While you two prattle about God knows what! My God, I thought you were space heroes! Why don't you two just fly the ship or something? I'll wait back there for you to save the damn day! Is that all right with you?"

Joe shrugged. Jack nodded numbly. The goddess stomped past him, hair flying, oval face taut. The bedroom door snapped shut and Jack heard a bolt thrown.

CHAPTER TWENTY-EIGHT
The Spacewalk

As Joe monitored the Venusian frequencies, Jack checked the primitive Mercedes scanners and the crude autopilot system. They hadn't spoken in ten minutes.

"I'm running diagnostics on the radio problem and it's definitely going to require a spacewalk," Joe finally said. "The problem's outside at that panel they were working on."

"Yeah, thanks. Look, Joe, I know I've been out of it. Haven't been making good decisions, I guess. And I'm sorry I got upset."

"I know. Don't worry about it. We don't want to think about the *Typhoon*. Let's try to forget it, Jack. Let's just get this crate back to Mars. Then we can ride in with the fleet that blows Hergs to kingdom come."

"I mean, maybe I haven't been thinking *enough* about the *Typhoon*."

Joe shrugged. "Maybe there's nothing much to think about. Maybe we just have to do our duty now. Just dwelling on the ship won't help. Second-guessing John won't help."

"No, I mean I need to apologize for the way I've been treating that girl back there."

Joe grinned. "Forget it, Jack. I'd say you were treating her like a proper gentleman. And I sure didn't mean to denigrate her or anything. I was just joking about--you know, just joking."

"Sure, that's no problem. But ..." Could Jack really confess this? Or could he tiptoe around it but still bleed some of the pressure off? "I mean, maybe I'm just using the girl as a way of forgetting the *Typhoon?*"

Joe nodded. "Maybe that's not such a bad idea for you."

Jack shook his head. Was Joe saying it was all right? All right to love Amav Frankston? Someone who'd been brainwashed into being Hergs' empress? But she was short-circuiting him. It wasn't fair. How could he proceed with anything if his mind was scrambled? His soul? Whatever you wanted to call it?

"Look, if this ship was ever in compliance with United System law, she oughta have a spacesuit and air pack in here somewhere," Joe said, standing up.

"You mean, go out and fix it? Do you really think it can be done?"

"Sure. We can always hotwire something. Get a simple message out to the USSF. They can be here in a couple hours or less, depending on what they can send."

"Well, I'll do it."

"Naw, let me, Jack. You know I used to help Ken with the *Typhoon* communication diagnostics. I'm sure I can fix it."

"But what if they launch while you're out there?"

"Look, if they catch us out here by ourselves, it won't matter whether I'm inside or out." Joe opened a storage locker and pulled out a simple gray suit made for an aristocrat's idea of gamboling in space. Jack helped him slip into it and secure the helmet. Joe put together a silver pack of tools and spare parts and went into the airlock.

It took several minutes to pump the air out. It made such a racket that Jack expected Amav to stamp out and tell them to knock it off.

On the other hand, she hated him so much now that she surely wouldn't say a word anyway. He'd probably never even see her again. At the end of this folly, USSF Security would just take custody of her and that would be that.

Soon he could see Joe's bulky figure maneuvering on tiny suit jets past the front saucer window. Jack put on the headset and punched in the spacesuit frequency.

"--moving over the top of the dome now," Joe said. "Yep, it's the radio unit, all right. We lost the hatch panel when we blasted out of the hanger. And the antenna is almost twisted off. It's a wonder we can even receive Venus. Say, Jack, try fiddling with the directional controls for the antenna."

"Right, Joe. I'm turning it ninety degrees. Any change?"

"Jack, try the directional controls. Jack? Jack, are you there?"

"Crap," Jack muttered, realizing the problem. He came up

with a second helmet from the storage locker, then put it over his head and switched on its radio. "Jack here. I'm using another spacesuit's radio. The main one's offline, obviously."

"I figured that. Did you try the antenna control panel?"

"Yeah."

"Well, there's no result here. We may just end up maneuvering the saucer to point the antenna at Mars. But a lot of wiring got ripped out of the back. I can have it all repaired, but it looks like it'll take a couple hours. I have air for four, just in case."

"Need help out there?"

"Negative. Just take it easy, Jack. I just need to rewire this and get the antenna freed up. I'll call you back when it's time to test."

"All right, sounds good."

"And look, Jack. Just talk to Amav. Try to calm her down. Tell her everything's gonna be all right. And that I'll call you guys in a couple hours when I'm done. If I need any help I can buzz the console comm system. Okay?"

"Sure. Okay," Jack said, with a shiver. Possibly he could call Amav from this space helmet, but he was not about to knock on the tiger lady's door.

*

Okay. Get hold of yourself. You are in fact the captain of this silly pleasure ship. It's time to do this mission strictly by the book.

The mission. Jack had to get this ship back to Mars. In line with that, Joe's spacewalk to repair the radio transmitter was the most important factor here. He studied the control panel, noting that Joe had properly secured his safety/data cable to the ship and that all his vital signs were normal.

Jack Commer was the captain. The mission was not complete. Any distraction from the goals of the mission could cost not only the lives of the three onboard, but also the destruction of the planet Mars and the extinction of humanity.

There was no possibility of anything like romance with this Amav Frankston in any case. Yes, emotions were important to human beings, but they were secondary in this situation. The captain of this ship couldn't afford to mix up his feelings about the *Typhoon* and a silly flirtation with a brainwashed refugee. He had to get control. A captain was all about control.

Command override established. Good.

He strode to the bedroom door the way he strode to any USSF meeting, except that one of his feet was embarrassingly bare. Rapped on the wooden door. A wooden door on a spaceship, he marveled. "Miss Frankston," he spoke through the door. "I'm here to apologize for any misunderstandings back there. I hope you'll understand that Joe and I have certainly been stressed over the past few days. I guess you could say ... *thrown off* by the events of the past few days. But I want to assure you that, as a fully trained combat space captain, I understand my primary mission and will execute it. That is, to get this ship back to Mars and warn my superiors about the threat posed by Hergs on Venus."

No answer.

"Um, I'm sorry, Miss, uh, Frankston, could you hear me?"

Silence.

He knocked on the door again. "As captain of this ship, you need to know ..." Wait, that was a dangling modifier, old Mrs. Nortel had always been on him for that in AP English.

He cleared his throat as noisily as he could. "As captain of this ship, I need to know ... uh, what I mean to say is, I need to inform you that what you are is, well, you're a passenger under my care. I mean, I know this is your ship, or Hergs gave it to you, or, well, that doesn't matter, I guess, but it has to be *my* ship now, that's all. I'm the captain. *Me.* That's all I wanted to tell you. Guess I have to run things now. I'm sorry about everything. How I acted back there and all. I've been so wiped out by ... by losing those men ... my *brothers* ..."

His voice broke. His eyes were wet.

Command override now!

He heard something in there like bedsprings shifting.

"Look, I know you hate me, and I'm sorry, but that's the way I am. That's the way I live. It's the way I've always lived."

Silence.

"You'll be safe. Joe's doing a spacewalk to repair the transmitter. Says it'll take a couple hours. I think we'll be well within time parameters for being rescued."

Still no answer. "Okay, don't accept my apology! Thanks! Thanks so much! We're *trying* to save you! I know you've locked the door, I know you hate me!"

Finally, a tiny voice: "It's not locked."

*

Amav stood frozen against the curved saucer wall behind the bed. Dark anguished eyes challenged him. Parted lips challenged him. Long gray-hosed legs challenged him, miniskirt two-thirds up her thigh.

Hands behind her back, she stood with hunched shoulders, breasts pushed wondrously between them. Jack had no idea how he'd come through the door. When he shut it behind him, then locked it, he knew he'd taken an axe to the tidy dank future he carried around like a dog-eared ID card in his wallet.

Nevertheless he babbled: "Miss Frankston, please accept my apologies for--"

"Shut up! Shut all that talk up!" Amav cried, hunching against the curved side of the saucer wall. "You know it doesn't mean anything compared to what *we* have!"

"To ... what *we* have?"

Head down, glaring, she pushed herself into the wall, scrunching her shoulders further, compressing her golden breasts all the more.

"Or do you just mean, like, all the suffering we've been through? What's happened to you, to me? This war, all this craziness, and we're just, like, unable to control ourselves? So we kind of lose control, sort of?" He took in the vast black bed between them, a divine circle of soft warm black and satin pillows rumpled by this young woman's body, by her suffering.

"I mean *you!* Don't you dare try to explain it away!"

"You--you can't mean--"

"Yes! I mean!"

Amav's shout yanked him around the circle.

And when he grabbed those mysterious shoulders she burst into his arms, opened her mouth to his kisses, the length of her body merging into his.

Completion! Success! All channels open!

She pushed him back, reached to her thighs, and yanked her miniskirt all the way up over her torso as thousands of golden disks burst about them.

She wore nothing beneath.

"Oh my God ... *Amav* ..." Jack gasped, reaching for those smooth taut breasts, then, out of his mind, kissing them amid a shower of spangling golden orbs.

"For ... for you ..." Amav sighed, shreds of cloth wafting down. "Robes ... fragile ..."

"Yes ... yes we are ..."

"It's all for you ..." she gasped, working at his belt. "Get me--get me to bed *now!*"

"But I'm not like you! I don't know anything! You know everything!"

"Forget it! You know *everything* about me! I could *feel* you from the moment I saw you!"

"You *felt* me? This isn't just the Erotic Teachings coming out?"

Amav laughed. "No! Forget the Teachings! And just *practice* with me! Get all these clothes off! Let's *practice* forever!"

Her words were just like Martian outradiance, blasting her life essence into his deepest and most unknown recesses. The room, the spaceship, and the entire universe were scarlet with the core energies pouring from both of them.

Uniting them forever? Was this possible? How could this happen to two people randomly thrown together?

CHAPTER TWENTY-NINE
Stalemate in Space
Thursday, June 15, 2034, 1815 hours

The ensign escorted them up to the USS *Andromeda's* observation blister and gently shut the hatch behind him. "Wow," Joe muttered, settling onto a black swivel chair around a circular table. "Henderson's damned gracious to let us sit alone awhile. I'm so wasted. I really didn't think we were gonna make it for a while there."

Amav and Jack took chairs across from Joe. "I knew we'd make it," Amav said. "All along I knew we'd make it."

"When we saw those Martians ships coming at us on the scanners, I thought it was all over. We knew the fleet was close, but still ..."

"Well, what's done is done," Jack said. "I agree it was touch and go for a while."

"*Freighter* saucers," Joe said. "I'm kinda sorry Henderson had to blast 'em. Top-ending at 10.6 million just like a regular saucer. But they were defenseless."

"Except for Amplified Thought," Amav said. "Who knows what they could've done to us?"

"Oooh, that's right, I didn't think of that." Joe noted that Amav sat a little too close to Jack, and they both looked a little too relaxed. Then there was the fact that she'd changed from her golden miniskirt into a long gray dress that clung to every curve of her body. Joe had earlier noted the numerous golden disks scattered by the entrance to the Mercedes bedroom and concluded that something semi-violent must have happened to that former Emperor's Robe. Well, he'd been hoping something like that would happen while he was out repairing the transmitter.

But it was true that the Martians could've taken the Mercedes by Amplified Thought alone. They could've paralyzed the ship's systems, forced the airlock, kidnapped Amav, then left Jack and Joe inside the ship with no air. Simple. It would've taken them five minutes.

Four freighters full of *wonderful beings*. Joe had felt their thoughts across the distance, stronger and stronger as they closed, jumbled transmissions of love and war and death, and honor and despair.

"Henderson said there was a port up here I could patch my USSF Comm into. Yeah, here," Jack said, punching in a code on the communications port.

Joe leaned back in his big black chair. He couldn't believe how knotted his forearms were. He'd been running at a hundred fifty percent, constantly exposed to danger for a solid week. And so many people had died.

But the observation blister conference room was cozy and relaxing. It had just enough room for the conference table and eight chairs. Out the blister he had a 360-degree view of the gray spaceship around him, and, above, nine other USSF battle cruisers outlined against billions of stars.

Rescued by *Doomboats*. Of all the ironies. The *Typhoon* family, the designers, crew, technicians, and support staff, had had a long rivalry with the *Doomboat* class of battle cruisers, which were the second fastest ships in the USSF at 35.5 million miles per hour. Second of course to the *Typhoon* at 49.8 million.

"Man, I'm beat," Joe muttered.

Jack nodded. "I know. We all are. But we need to get our version of this off to Scott ASAP." He placed his comm on the conference table and spoke. "Message for General Scott from Captain Jack Commer. Contributing to this report will be Commander Joe Commer and ... a human refugee from the enemy base on Venus, Amav Frankston.

"Captain Henderson's Special Ops 10th Fleet is now three hours from Mars, about one hundred nine million miles out. We're aboard the flagship *Andromeda*. I realize this message will take almost ten minutes to get to you, and that you've already received a brief report from Captain Henderson. However, here's the gist of our own report.

"The *Typhoon I* was ... destroyed at Mercury. Repeat, destroyed. Systems malfunctions due to a Martian ray attack prevented deployment of the Xons. Joe and I went out in the escape ship to manually take an Xon down to the surface to destroy the enemy base. However, in the interval Lieutenant John Commer elected to ram the enemy base with the *Typhoon*."

Jack took a breath and closed his eyes. Joe looked away from the sight of Amav taking Jack's hand. Joe had no one to take his.

"Entire crew dead. Repeat dead, except for Joe and myself. Joe and I were able to take the escape craft on a preset course to Earth. We were captured by the Martians and imprisoned on Venus. In breaking out we managed to take with us one Amav Frankston, the daughter of Stewart Neal Frankston, the planetary engineer. Ms. Frankston was apparently being groomed to be the … consort of Sam Hergs.

"We stole a pleasure craft, and en route to Mars we managed to fix a broken transmitter and get a distress call out at 2.5 million miles distance from Venus. We now understand that you launched Special Ops 10, which had been on standby, within a few minutes.

"Apparently the Martians waited until 1640 hours, about six hours after we escaped, to launch a fleet of four nonmilitary saucers at us. However, at approximately 1720 hours Special Ops 10 arrived, engaged the Martian saucers as they overtook us, and destroyed them. We were then taken aboard *Andromeda*. Captain Henderson made a brief survey of the area, but on hearing what we knew of a new Martian development called Amplified Thought, and hearing this confirmed in an ultimatum broadcast by Hergs, Captain Henderson decided to return to Mars, awaiting further instructions en route."

"I have to add that Jack was magnificent all through this!" Amav cut in. "Absolutely magnificent! I mean, Joe was great, too! He fixed that transmitter and that saved our lives! But Jack really held us together when those saucers were closing in!"

Jack smiled. "Well, we'd been talking with Captain Henderson for some time as our range was closing. Computers calculated all the proper decelerations and engagements, really. I knew we'd be able to pull it off."

Joe cleared his throat. "Weren't you going to include Hergs' threat?"

"I thought Henderson had already done that in his message."

"Maybe we'd better add it, to make sure."

"Hell, I'm not sure I want to hear his damn voice ever again," Jack muttered, but keyed in commands on his comm. "Okay, General, here it is."

"The damn Martians kept me waiting for six hours!" came the slurred voice. "Else I woulda had the damn *whore* back here, back on her damn *sex drugs* where she belongs, and those pretty Commer boys'd be piles of guts floating in vacuum! Damn that Dar! Kept delaying and delaying, said they didn't have any damn ships after the damn Commers blew out their damn flight hanger, but I said launch damn *freighters* if you hafta! Yeah, I thought Amav was out on a joyride at first too, but after a coupla hours, I knew! I told 'em all, the Commers've escaped again! My so-called Council to the Emperor just sat there and *delayed!* Finally I yelled they better get somethin' goin' or I'll pull their pants down and whip 'em all, but by then it was just a hair too late! Dammit to hell, but I don't think it matters because we just about have Amplified Thought figured out to where we can blow your stupid Mars up just by *thinking* about it! Whaddya say to that? Huh? Huh? You back off your damn spaceships right the hell now, or else I'm gonna blow up whatever I can right now with my Martians! I bet your damn Commers picked up a helluva lot about AT outa the Martians' heads, they leak all over the place, they can't help it, the dumb sucks! Anyway, so Jack baby and Joe baby know it's for real. Hell, the Martians blew all the outer planets just experimenting with the stuff! AT's damn dangerous, I tell ya! So just back off, boys, lemme be here on Venus, I'll let ya be there on Mars, we'll have peaceful coexistence for a while, huh? Hergs out, babies! My final word is this: mess with me and die, die, die!"

Jack sighed. "Well, that's Hergs' message if you haven't already gotten it. What Joe and Amav and I can add is that yes, we can apparently read Martian minds, one-way only, and this stuff about Amplified Thought is real. They've been experimenting with it for the last six years or so, and apparently it's been *them* behind the destruction of the outer planets."

"We don't think the total destruction AT will be ready for a few days," Joe added. "From what we can gather, the only way the Martians could emotionally bring themselves to destroy their home world would be to completely wipe out the planet all at once. Reduce it to vapor instantly. They couldn't bear earthquakes, explosions, fragments, all that stuff. No violence. Apparently the process requires five hundred Martians wanting the exact same thing, thinking the exact same computer program in their heads, with no qualms."

"And the program's over eleven million lines long!" Amav put in. "It's unbelievable. You can see some of it in your head."

"We don't know whether Hergs can mandate five hundred Martians doing this," Jack said. "He does have a powerful emotional hold on them, why we don't really know. But it appears that even a handful of Martians could probably set up the kinds of stresses that exploded the outer planets, or sent Pluto or the asteroids flying every which way."

"I keep thinking," Joe said, "that maybe I can reconstruct some of the code in my head, but I don't understand whatever kind of computer logic they're using. And even if we could reconstruct it, we sure as hell don't have the Martian outradiance."

"The *outradiance*," Jack sighed. "I'd forgotten about it."

"Yeah, it's everything," Joe said, pleased to see both Amav and Jack nodding.

*

Captain Daniel Henderson opened the hatchway from the *Andromeda's* Control Room below them. "Finished your message, gentlemen?"

"Just finishing now," Jack said. "It's hard to know what to say to describe it all, to collect your thoughts."

"You'll have plenty of time to chat with Scott back at Marsport. Meanwhile, got a surprise for you gents."

Jack nodded pleasantly but Joe again found himself irritated by Captain Daniel Henderson. The guy seemed more like a butler than a ship's captain, alternatively servile and snooty, with an Eastern USA accent that seemed a bad satire of upper-class British. The Commers had known Henderson for years. They'd met his young son Roger, who already seemed to be grooming himself for butler school. Joe imagined the Hendersons had been butlers for generations.

When Henderson decided to head Special Ops 10 home for Mars after hearing Hergs' diatribe, Jack and Joe had exchanged a disdainful glance. They both knew they themselves would've instantly launched every Xon from all ten ships. It would've surprised Hergs and at least one Xon would've gotten through any Martian AT defense. Now the surprise was lost and they were heading back to Mars with their *Doomboat* tails between their *Doomboat* legs.

"Yes, gentlemen, one of our ships, the *Cosmic Dust,* has docked beneath us," Henderson went on. "Some important passengers, civilians actually, who happened to be on board when we had to break out of Mars orbit."

"Must we climb these steep stairs?" came a female voice from below. "Couldn't we have met elsewhere?"

Amav came alive at the alarm on Jack's face which had to mirror Joe's own.

"*M-Mom?*" Joe blurted.

"Ma'am, I think you'll agree that the view from the observation blister is magnificent," came an unmistakably junior lieutenant tone from below. "And Captain Henderson could tell our guests were rather, well, shellshocked I suppose you could say, and needed to be alone for a while, so they've been up here relaxing."

"Shellshocked? Did you say *shellshocked?*" barked a man. "Do you dare use the term *shellshocked* to describe my sons? My sons, who're trained USSF combat pilots?"

"Oh my God!" Jack cried. "Dad!"

Joe watched in dismay as first Joyce Commer's head came up the hatch, then the almost unrecognizable strained and mustached face of Jonathan Commer, Sr. They seemed like roaches burrowing out of a crack in the baseboard.

"Dad!" Jack moaned. "I can't believe it!"

"Dad! Mom!" Joe echoed. "How can you be *here?*" He saw Amav Frankston at near military attention in the face of this invasion. The junior lieutenant also climbed up into the now crowded conference room.

"Had to get up to the *Doomboats,* Joyce was all pissed off, she insisted on coming, I told her it was damn dangerous, had to jump all over Scott politically," Commer Senior yapped. "We happened to be on this stupid ass *Cosmic Dust* when the order came to break orbit. So we couldn't get off. I told this Henderson twit that anything happens to her, it's on *his* head."

Jack's eyes were wide with shock at the sight of Jonathan Commer, who appeared to have aged another ten years in the month since Joe and Jack last saw him. He was only fifty-five, but he seemed even smaller now, his shoulders ever more stooped after his heart attack last year during the Evacuation. He had a new mustache, but more of his wispy hair was gone and he seemed to be straining to breathe. Some character actor had been sent in to play the part of their father. Could this be the same man who flew fighter jets for the U.S. Air Force back in the teens? The congressman who'd helped start the USSF in '28?

It took a moment for Jack and Joe to realize they were supposed to hug their mother and father. But they were good hugs, emotion pouring out of everyone. Then it hit Joe why they had to be here.

To remind them of the deaths of their brothers.

Joe pulled back to stare into his mother's wet eyes. At fifty-four, Joyce Commer was dark, trim, round-faced, still young, lovely, fashionable and alluring, as Joe could verify from a glance at Captain Henderson who, though almost twenty years younger, was having trouble keeping his mouth closed and his eyes off her slender torso and the tiny red dress clinging to her petite legs. Joe was surprised she hadn't already reduced Henderson to babbling with her trademark mixture of flirtation, high humor, and quick spite, all nonchalantly twirled into the world like poisoned-tipped Ninja throwing stars.

"My God, my God," Jonathan Sr. muttered. "We just can't believe it. John, my boy John, oh God … and Jim …"

"I know, I know, nobody can believe it," Jack whispered. "This is Amav here, my friend Amav."

"The *Typhoon* gone?" Jonathan blubbered. "Gone? The best spaceship ever made, *gone?*"

"Gone …" Joe said, staring at the ugly new mustache. "Just--we can't explain it."

"Had to come up. Scott finally gave us permission. Sensors recorded the crash on Mercury. We thought you were *all* gone. Ten ships here on standby the last few days, then they got your message a few hours ago and they just blasted off, we were stuck here on board but damn if I wasn't going to ride in anyway."

"Okay, it's up here!" came another voice from below. Everyone turned to the sound of objects banging their way up the metal stairs.

Another cockroach emerged. Huge fleshy face, loose lips, loose jowls, blackened eyes. Raw obesity squirmed through the hatch.

"Huey! Huey Vespertine!" Jack cried.

"What are *you* doing here?" Joe said.

"Get--get off this ship! Get outa here!"

"Hey, guys," said Huey Vespertine, pulling himself free from the hatch. The conference room now held eight people, and was decidedly close. And Huey seemed to be following his old practice of returning to his *natural scents,* as he termed it.

"Couldn't shake this bastard, followed us to orbit," Jonathan Commer snarled. "I thought the USSF had rules about AresNet correspondents being on military ships, but evidently they screwed up royally on this one."

"Well, I'm sorry about that, sir," Captain Henderson put in, "but Mr. Vespertine did invoke the Freedom to Report Act, and we weren't technically on an actual mission at that moment."

"Crap! You were on standby military alert!"

"I'm sorry for any inconvenience, sir, but the same rules that allowed you and your wife to come aboard--"

They all broke off as two more roaches crawled out of the hatch, beefy guys dragging up wires and equipment, including a camera emblazoned with ARESNET. Ten people jammed in here now.

"Damn stupid name for a ship, anyway. *Cosmic Dust!*" Jonathan spat.

"Hello, everyone!" Huey Vespertine chortled. "Welcome to the Huey Vespertine Report! If we can just continue the interview--"

"The *what?*" Jack cried.

"Bastard was interviewing us when we broke out of orbit to come here," Jonathan gasped. "Filming every damn thing, hoping to get us to cry! Well, Joyce obliged 'em, that was for damned sure!"

To this Joyce merely smiled. "Darling, don't get so worked up." She launched fresh hugs on Jack and Joe. "Oh, Jack, Joe! At least you two survived! Now I know *I* can survive!"

"Great! Great shot!" Huey laughed. "The mother will *survive!* Great!"

"Damn, I'm not recording yet," one of the techs grunted. "What's wrong with this damn thing?"

"Look, can you two hug again, and Mrs. Commer, you talk about surviving again?"

"Get out of here!" Jack yelled. "I told you years ago I never wanted to see you again!"

"I detest this man!" Jonathan shouted. "For the record, I detest Huey Vespertine! He's a traitor to the United System!"

"Dad, all he did was drop out of the Academy," Joe said.

"Don't you defend him again!" Jonathan Sr. screamed. "I won't have it!"

"This is great! Great!" Huey laughed. "The tearful reunion, live on AresNet!"

"No way," Amav cut in. "It's ten light minutes to Mars. It can't be live."

"Screw it, it's live enough for me and our audience," Huey sniffed. "We'll blast it out to the entire solar system and it'll get there sooner or later! And who might you be, anyway?"

"Don't give your name!" Jack said.

"Amav Frankston!" Amav yelled.

"It's so *crowded* in here," Joyce Commer complained. "Can't some of these peon junior officers just *leave?*" she added, pointing to the junior lieutenant as well as Captain Henderson. Yet, transfixed by her remarkable body, neither made any move.

"Damn you, Huey, promise me you'll edit out anything that embarrasses the USSF!" Jack cried.

"Recording," said one of the techs.

CHAPTER THIRTY
The Huey Vespertine Report
Transcript of "The Huey Vespertine Report," broadcast on AresNet June 15, 2034

Jonathan Commer: No, stop it! You bastard! Just stop this! Everyone, listen! This man is a *traitor* to the United System!

Huey Vespertine: Ladies and gentlemen, welcome to the *Huey Vespertine Report, Special Edition: Death of the Martian Fantasy!* We're here aboard the spaceship *Andromeda* to record the emotional reunion of Jack and Joe Commer with their stricken parents, who just lost their two other sons in the USSF's foolish attempt to dominate the nationalistic uprising of the native Martians!

Jack Commer: Shut up! I can't believe you'd do this! That you'd be here!

Joe Commer: How'd he get here anyway?

Jonathan: He *followed* us here! Joyce and I got to the *Cosmic Dust* this morning, then the next thing we know this Vespertine character's showing up in orbit with us!

Joyce Commer: We just wanted to be on hand if they, you know, *recovered* anything.

Huey: Then the force of historical necessity intervened! Me! Hell, guys, I didn't wanna come up here, either! But my editor said I hadda!

Jack: Forget it! We know you broadcast lies! We've followed all your slimy Internet escapades over the years, then shamelessly plastering it all over AresNet!

Huey: No, really! Didn't you guys know I got married a few days ago? Man, I sure as hell haven't wanted to give up my honeymoon, I tell ya!

Jack: Yeah, we heard something about that from Scott.

Huey: Scott! I *knew* it was him behind those USSF goons who hassled us the second day of our honeymoon! What a paranoid old fart! Having goons question me, question Jackie too, just because they don't like what I say on AresNet! I thought we had freedom of speech on Mars!

Joe: Jackie?

Huey: My wife! Like I say, I hadda give up Jackie for a day to do my job! Man, if you met her, Joe, you'd know! You'd *know!* My own wife's a *piece!* And have we ever been gettin' it on the past few days, if you know what I mean and I think you do! I know I shouldn't be sayin' this on AresNet, but hey, it's part of this whole *confluence of fate* we're all in now! The fact that I'm gettin' it on with a fantastic babe who happens to be my wife! I can have it any time I wanna! So why shouldn't I stick it right in this report?

Jack: Jeez, listen to this!

Jonathan: It's disgusting!

Huey: Why you old fart, you have a piece yourself, I think! Mrs. Commer is looking quite *yummy* today, I would say!

Jonathan: You son of a bitch! I'll kill you!

Captain Daniel Henderson: There, there, sir, we can't have any disturbances aboard *Andromeda.*

Jonathan: Get your hands off me! Get off!

Huey: Just paying a good-lookin' woman a compliment, sir! Don't have a heart attack! And look, Jack has a piece today too, I might add! He was always so shy around the ladies, as I recall. And here he has this lovely young thing, the consort of the Martian emperor himself, trained in all the secret Erotic Teachings, so I hear.

Amav Frankston: What? Who are you? Where'd you hear that?

Huey: Why, it was all in Captain Henderson's first report out to General Scott a few minutes ago.

Captain Daniel Henderson: Excuse me, sir? I don't believe I gave you any such report.

Huey: Oh, don't be silly! AresNet cracked your USSF code six months ago! We read all your top-secret stuff!

Jack: *What?*

Amav: Captain Henderson, you really didn't pass along all that stuff I was saying about the Teachings, did you?

Henderson: Well, we recorded the first conversations as a matter of protocol, you know, preserving the evidence, and, well, every scrap might help General Scott, you know.

Amav: That does it! I'm outa here!

Jack: Amav--

Amav: You locked the hatch!

Huey: Quite a piece you got there, Jacko! Nice ass if I may say so! Same perfect bod as Jackie, but you know Jackie's a *wicked* flirt! If she was here right now every man in this room would be standing at attention!

Jack: Crap! Henderson, open this hatch immediately! We're all leaving!

Henderson: Captain Commer, you will recall that I have *five weeks seniority* on you and you will address me as *sir!*

Jack: Aw buzz off, jerk! You there! Lieutenant! Open this damn hatch right now! I've had enough!

Lieutenant Marsden Kralik: Well, sir, yes, sir.

Henderson: Kralik, don't obey his commands!

Jack: Open the hatch!

Kralik: It--it appears to be stuck, sir!

Huey: Oh, this is priceless! Get a shot of that boy wrenching that lever back and forth!

Joyce: I'm *suffocating* in here!

Jack: Huey, you stink, I might add!

Jonathan: What woman would want to f--oh, the hell with it!

Huey: Hey, I'm happy, I'm getting laid, Jackie's *fantastic!* She jokes she used to be a prostitute! I don't think she really was, but you know I can never be sure about her! She sure knows all the tricks! What a woman!

Jack: Wait a second! We're losing sight of the important thing here! If AresNet has broken the USSF code--dammit, Huey, you tell me straight out or I'm gonna pop you one! Are you in league with Sam Hergs? Are you really such a traitor? Because if you're passing our stuff to him--

Huey: Hey, Jack! Take it easy, man! I don't know the guy! Not at all! I just happen to sympathize with the native Martians, who've been reamed by the USSF occupation! Hergs is just one more two-bit dictator who's gotten power over 'em, just like *we're* trying to do! We've got to liberate the Martians from *everyone!*

Jack: Okay, then! So you work with *us* then, and not give aid and comfort to Hergs! You got that? You stop this interview crap right now!

Henderson: Captain Commer, you will please cease and desist acting as if you're the ranking officer here!

Jack: Danny, you back off or I'm gonna paste *you* one! As far as Joe and I are concerned, you've jeopardized this entire mission through your cowardly refusal to attack Hergs head-on a few minutes ago!

Joe: That's right! That's right!

Henderson: You--you--that's it, I've had it! Gentlemen, I will be in my quarters! Don't you dare attempt to speak with me for the duration of our journey to Mars! There's been enough disrespect here today to your commanding officer who saved you, I might add! Uhhh! Uhhh! Kralik, open this hatch!

Kralik: Sir, the latch's busted!

Henderson: Damn you, Kralik! Damn you all! Vespertine, stop recording this immediately!

Huey: Forget it, sir! The Freedom to Report act specifically guarantees--

Jonathan: We ought to just kill him! Invoke any USSF reg you need to, but kill him!

Henderson: Aw, shut up, old man! I don't take orders from you, either! How the hell I got stuck with you coming along on this mission I'll never know!

Jonathan: Why, you--

Joe: Look, Dad! Just cool it! Dad, Jack--why don't we try to work with Huey here? If he's not on Hergs' side, maybe we can sway public opinion.

Jonathan: That's idiotic! Just take him out and shoot him! Huey was a traitor to everything we stand for the day he dropped out of the Naval Academy!

Joe: All I'm saying is that seems to want to *understand* the Martians, just as we do!

Jonathan: Drop it, son! He's a traitor! Everything he's done on AresNet years proves it! And don't think I don't know you've been in contact with him since he dropped out!

Joe: Aw, Dad, it was nothing! I've seen him a couple times, but that was years ago! The three of us were buddies at the Academy! You just can't drop it like it never happened!

Jonathan: Oh yes, you can! And I hope you've stopped emailing him like I told you to!

Joe: Look, Dad, I've just wanted to know what went wrong. There's nothing wrong with keeping in a sort of distant contact just for karma's sake!

Jonathan: Is my own son a traitor, too? Did John sacrifice himself for *this?*

Jack: You haven't still been emailing Huey, have you, Joe? We talked about that!

Joe: Not since the Evacuation!

Jack: Dammit!

Joe: We had a friendship! All of us! At the Academy!

Huey: But I was the only one who saw through the militaristic BS, and I got my ass outa there! But I hafta admit some of my training came in useful. How do you think AresNet finally broke the USSF code? We've been reading everything as if you're broadcasting right in the clear! We know all your military secrets!

Jonathan: That does it! Execute him!

Henderson: *I* give the orders around here! Me! You're not even in the USSF, old man!

Joyce: You leave my husband alone! Don't you dare upset him! Can't you see we've just lost two of our sons? Don't you have the decency to just shut your mouth?

Henderson: Well, well, if everyone continues to treat me with such disrespect--

Huey: Haw, haw, haw!

Henderson: Then consider me in my quarters now! Stuck hatch be damned! I'm not here! I'm simply not here!

Jack: Listen, none of this is important. If Huey really has broken the USSF code--

Huey: Then you know I have the entirety of your last message to Scott! The Venus threat to Mars! Amplified Thought! The fruit of native Martian wisdom, about to be directed in a holy annihilation of our mad species!

Jack: Dammit, Huey, I told you to be on *our* side!

Huey: I'm on the side of the Martians! And right now, they're with Hergs, and Hergs is holding all the cards, so I say, play ball with Hergs!

Jack: You'd capitulate to that monster?

Huey: Yes! Any sane person on Mars wants us to capitulate to him! He can fry us with a single thought!

Jack: This can't go out to AresNet! Henderson, can't you put a lid on this?

Henderson: I told you, Captain Commer, I am not here! I refuse to answer nitpicking questions from a junior officer!

Technician: If I might point out, if we've been talking here for ten minutes, the opening part of this interview is now reaching Mars.

Jack: Crap! Crap!

Henderson: Even your *Crap! Crap!* is attempting to assert authority over me! I can't stand it! You're acting as if *you're* running the show!

Amav: Jack *is* running the show! Can't everyone see that?

Huey: No, *I'm* running the show, little lady! The media drives everything, you know! And I'm sure AresNet will soon be putting out peace feelers to Mr. Hergs, and that we can reach an accommodation with him.

Jack: Great! An accommodation that reduces Mars to atoms! That kills two billion human beings!

Huey: Hey, don't think I'm not suffering over all this, too? My wife's back there, you know! Jackie! Jackie, can you hear me? Get on a ship now! Get off Mars! We're all gonna die! Meet me in space!

Jack: You coward! You there! Lieutenant! Open this hatch! Henderson, I'm taking command of this fleet. We'll turn it around and Xon Venus right now.

Joe: Jack, we really have to wait now. We've lost the element of surprise. The Martians would just vaporize any Xons they see coming. They're waiting for them, I can feel their thoughts!

Jack: You can't feel their thoughts from millions of miles away!

Joe: I can! I can! It's faint, but--

Amav: I can, too! Jack, we've got to find a better way! We can't destroy the Martians!

Huey: I've suffered, too, you know! I'm still suffering! I lost a friend of mine in your stupid Kilpatrick Desert battle! T. Jasper Marktholomew died because you militarists just wanted to fling Xon bombs everywhere!

Jonathan: Oh, I saw that live on AresNet! Marktholomew was a pansy and he deserved to get shattered!

Joyce: Jonathan, watch what you're saying, this is being beamed everywhere on Mars!

Jonathan: Well, if this traitor has the right to free speech, then so do I!

Huey: And I'm suffering because I'm up here in space when I want to be right in my wife's--

Amav: Can't we get this hatch open? Can't you radio someone from below to free it up? It *stinks* in here!

Henderson: Why should I? When you all piss on me? Well, this is *my* ship! *My* fleet!

Huey: All you militarists are alike! You destroy everything you touch! Let AresNet handle the negotiations is what I say! And since I'm the closest AresNet rep to Venus, I say turn this ship around and let's go to Venus and *talk* to Mr. Hergs!

Jack: There will be no such negotiations! Scott will give us new orders, and we'll figure out how to wipe this threat out!

Amav: But Jack, remember the Martians! Remember the nobility in their minds!

Jack: I'm sorry, Amav, I know what you mean, but the threat they present--

Huey: Destroy! Destroy! Just like the Final War, eh, Jacko?

Jack: Piss on you, jerk!

Huey: Let's set this all in perspective, shall we? You and Joe were the prime agents of the destruction of our planet! *You* dropped the Xon that finished off the earth!

Jack: Forget it, man, we had to! We had ships bombing CAP's factories for months, but CAP was too damn deep in the mountains. They were cranking out a hundred H-bombs a month!

Huey: Yeah, well we got most of 'em before they did any harm!

Jack: Most of 'em? Sheesh! They *landed* twenty-nine! Like New York, Paris, and Berlin! They wrecked the moon with *their* Xon, and then threatened *us* with it! What the heck would *you* have done, man?

Huey: Forget it, Jack, it's been well-documented that the Central Asian Powers were ready for negotiations!

Joe: Look, Huey, Scott finally just decided enough was enough. I mean, we can't care that he circumvented the United System and all that political crap. Those people were doing *nada*. So we got the order to go and we went!

Huey: You dropped an Xon bomb on Gaia!

Joe: I know it! I damn well know it!

Jonathan: *My sons destroyed the earth!* I've had to *live* with that! And now there's no John, Jr.! Even *that* legacy's gone now!

Jack: Dad, look, I know, I'm sorry we're here, surrounded by jerks, and we don't have time to *feel* anything!

Jonathan: Would you like that designation, back, officially? To make the family whole again?

Jack: *What?*

Jonathan: I mean, you … become John, Jr., again? Officially? I give the name to you, again? You drop this *Jack* business, and we forget the past troubles? John is reborn … in *you?*

Joe: Oh my God!

Jack: Are--are you serious?

Jonathan: Yes, I'm serious, Jack! I mean, John Jr.!

Jack: Forget it! That's insane! I am who I am! I'm Jack Commer!

Jonathan: God! You can't reject me!

Jack: I'm not rejecting you! Listen to me! John is *gone!* And *Jim's* gone, who you don't even seem to care about!

Jonathan: You … you don't care about the *family!*

Joyce: Jonathan, please!

Jonathan: John died a hero! He saved Mars! While you and Joe slunk off like cowards in your escape ship!

Jack: Dammit, I knew you'd say that! I reject that! I reject it totally! John should never have been on board the *Typhoon* in the first place! My fault was letting him pilot when Joe and I went out in the escape ship! He didn't even ask Harri, who was in command, what to do! He should've known there were other options than to take the ship down in a kamikaze run!

Jonathan: You've broken the family!

Jack: Forget it! Joe and I trust ourselves first!

Jonathan: Aahhhyyyiiiee!

Joe: Look, Jack, this--this is *Dad*. Dad, look. We're not out to break the family, or anything like that. It's just--

Jonathan: It's just that Jack here has managed to find the perfect solution to the John problem in his own way, I see! Don't think I don't know you were plotting to have him removed from the *Typhoon* all along!

Joyce: Jonathan! Stop this at once! I won't have it!

Henderson: You see, sir? You see how Jack Commer operates? He *usurps* authority as he sees fit! The only solution is to ignore him! Go underground! Go to your quarters! He'll never find you there!

Jonathan: I ... I ... my heart ...

Jack: Oh, forget it! You're playacting again! You've faked four more heart attacks since the real one! Every time we come to visit, as a matter of fact!

Henderson: Let's see Captain Jack Commer deny the rumor that he decided to Xon the earth all on his own! He *usurps* authority!

Jack: Damn you to hell, Henderson! To your quarters!

Henderson: Gladly! Kralik, open this hatch!

Jonathan: I'm sorry about everything ... I won't interfere ever again ... I just don't care ...

Kralik: Sir, this latch! This damn latch! I'm so sorry, sir!

Joyce: I'm *concerned* about him! Jonathan, just sit down here, in this chair. Would you move, you oaf?

Technician: Sorry, ma'am--

Huey: Close up on her face! Yeah!

Amav: Well, Jack Commer, your family is perfectly crazy! But I still love you!

Jack: You--you *love* me? But--I love you too! I knew it all along! I was just afraid to say it!

Huey: No, cut that, cut that! This is a militarist talking, after all!

Technician: We can't cut it, it's all spewing out to AresNet.

Amav: Jack, there's so much stuff to do! Ignore this idiocy here! My God, my brains are coming back! Listen to me! I'm almost done with my Ph.D.! And the Martians have taught me even more about planetary engineering. They know how to repair the earth! We can work with them!

Huey: Sorry, missy, but it looks as if Scott is simply going to send Killer Jack back here with another world-destroying Xon!

Henderson: You can bet your ass on that, ma'am. I got a message back from Scott before I came up here, and that's precisely what he's thinking about. He knows Hergs is insane and there can't be any negotiations.

Amav: No, that's stupid! We have to figure out some new channel.

Joe: You know, I think Amav's right. There's got to be some way to spring the Martians loose from Hergs.

Jack: Forget it, Joe. Remember what was in their minds. Absolute obedience to the ruler. If we could assassinate Hergs, maybe it'd work. But we can't get close to him when they have their Amplified Thought.

Amav: Jack, we need to try!

Jack: Well, I know what you're saying, but--

Amav: Jack, when you radioed General Scott earlier, I know you had to make a proper report, but didn't we all notice you left out everything we've felt from the Martian minds? That sense of wonder and awe? And maybe even friendship?

Jack: But they're fanatics. They can kill with a thought. We can't possibly imagine we really understand them!

Huey: We should all just step aside for them, and die! Just get out of their way! Our whole culture is militarist! We deserve extinction!

Amav: Jack, I love you! Together we can make everything right!

Huey: Aw, cut this! We'll edit it later! So Jack finally got a girlfriend! I hope for his sake she's decent in bed!

Amav: I am, thank you! Because I love him!

Huey: The consort of the emperor! I'll bet Hergs is pissed that Jack Commer stole her! *That'll* complicate negotiations! The very guy that lusts to Xon Venus is screwing the emperor's consort! But AresNet can broker a deal!

Joe: The only thing that matters is preserving the Martian culture. They have so much to teach us!

Amav: That's right! The possibility of us ever returning to Earth depends on the existence of the Martians!

Joe: God, what's happened to us, Jack? The *Typhoon's* gone!

Jack: I … I know … we'll get a new ship, Joe. We'll get by somehow.

Joe: Jim and John are *gone!* And all the rest! They aren't coming back!

Jack: Don't … don't cry, Joe, please.

Amav: Let him--let him--

Huey: Jeez, this is supposed to be *my* interview! *I'm* in charge of it!

Joe: Jack, we've tried to pretend it didn't happen! But it did! They're *gone!* They're all *gone!* Why did *we* survive?

Jack: I don't know. There must be some reason, but maybe we'll never know.

Joe: They were blotted out! They're gone! Everything's *gone!*

Jack: I know, but we're *alive* somehow. Everything's gone, but we're *alive*.

Amav: Joe, it's okay, just let it out, let it all out.

Joe: You have Amav, Jack! I don't have anyone!

Kralik: I--I don't mean any disrespect, everyone, but I've finally got the hatch open.

Huey: Sheesh! This has screwed up totally! Just pack it up, guys! Pack everything up!

CHAPTER THIRTY-ONE
Conference
Thursday, June 15, 2034, 2145 hours

General William Scott sifted through four inches of papers. Strength issued from the old man behind his infinite titanium desk, and, eyes half-closed, Jack took pleasure in Joe's calm recounting of their mission as if it had all been a movie they'd seen a few weeks ago.

Jack slumped in his chair, drifting in the cool office. Outside the thirty-foot-wide black window, the unmoored, multicolored lights of downtown Marsport glided with him. Sure, the mission wasn't complete. Maybe it would never be complete. But Jack would drift through it now, drift with the dream of the beautiful Amav Frankston.

"Then Dad and Mom showed up," Joe was saying.

"Ah, yes, I apologize for that," Scott rejoined. "Henderson was out of line to take your parents along on the mission. I okayed them visiting the *Cosmic Dust* but I thought it was understood they'd be transferred to one of the nearby service ships if the fleet needed to move. And as for letting AresNet on board a top-secret USSF mission ..." He scratched his stubble beard and searched for a paper. "Ah, yes. As a reward, Captain Henderson will be flying meteor sweep patrols in the Saturnian Fragment Field effective Monday."

"Oooh," Joe winced.

"Unfortunately, I have no similar jurisdiction over Mr. Vespertine."

"It's all right, sir," Jack said, lazily cruising into the movie of himself saying this. "We don't care."

"You don't care that Huey Vespertine embarrassed you on AresNet?" Scott said, oddly gently. "That the interview is being replayed over and over again across Mars?"

"Well, no, sir, not really. I guess we're all grown up, we can handle that sort of thing."

"Well, how about the embarrassment to the USSF itself?" Scott barked. "About the fact that Huey Vespertine's leaked top secret military information to the public? That the public is panicking, out of its mind with fear that the whole planet is about to *vaporize* any second?"

"Oh! Well! Sir!" Jack stammered, fully upright in his chair.

"Do you have any idea, Captain Commer, how the spaceports of this world are being jammed with millions of would-be refugees this second? And that the panic keeps growing?"

"Well, sir, no, to tell the truth, I hadn't thought ..."

"Do you really think I've been spending the last three hours sitting here relaxing over a cup of tea? No, I've been wrapped up in hours of planning, trying to figure a way to save this sorry United System! Do you think the United System Council has even bothered to call me? No! They're all glued to their AresNet feeds, out of their minds with panic! So they're leaving it all to me! As usual! Me! *I've* got to come up with the damn plan! But certain other important people seem to think it's time to sit around and fall asleep!"

"Uh--sir! No! Not me! I'm ready! What are your orders, sir?" Jack cried, springing from his chair into a full salute.

Scott grinned. "At ease, Captain. Please resume your seat. I would just like your full attention at this time. I'm sorry if I gave the impression that, by wanting to hear Joe's account of your mission in detail, I've turned my office into a little teahouse where we quaintly gossip about literally *world-shattering* events."

"Uh, no, sir! No teahouse! Understood, sir!"

"As for my orders, I imagine you could begin to infer them from the gentlemen sitting behind you."

Jack turned to the four men in armchairs behind the Commers. He could feel their power. These comrades were well-trained. They were the best.

"Uh, yes, sir. I mean, I didn't know for sure," Jack said, resuming his seat. "I do know that Joe and I are exhausted at this point, we've been fighting for several days, and probably aren't at the top of our form right now, I'd say."

"Hmmph," Scott said. He found another memo. "By the

way, I want you to know that Ms. Frankston is at the USSF Spaceport Clinic having a thorough checkup by our best physicians. Not only do we want to make sure she's in good health, but unfortunately we also have to check for any implanted communication devices or even, God forbid, weapons."

"Right." Jack gazed out the dark window at the glowing thin skyscrapers of Marsport. Amav was only a few miles away. Jack slid into a dream ... General Scott officiating at his wedding to Amav, the most beautiful and noble woman in the universe ...

But wasn't that crazy thinking after all? Wasn't she too much for him? How could he ever win such a beautiful, noble woman? If they survived all this, what would happen? Another mission, some weeks separated, and wouldn't she move on? Was Jack just a bit of space fun for the experienced consort of the Martian emperor?

But hadn't she said she loved him? Hadn't he said the same thing back?

Glancing at his papers, the general went on: "I did have time during the past three hours to award you both the Humanity Cross for your bravery during this mission."

"Wow ..." Jack muttered. The Humanity Cross was the highest award that could be conferred upon a member of the military.

"Well, thank you," Joe said. "But I have to say it means nothing in the light of ..."

"Yes, I understand," Scott said quietly.

"Our crew," Jack finished. "Our brothers. We just can't believe they're gone. We're both numb. We feel one thing, then we feel another completely opposite thing, none of it adds up, then we go ahead and feel all those things *again*."

"I understand, son. I know the feeling. When I was aboard the *Triumph* ..."

Jack nodded. "Yes, sir." Scott had won his own Humanity Cross for his ordeal on the *Triumph* two years ago. Rescued after two months of being marooned on Mars, the visionary Air Force colonel, who'd been so instrumental in creating the USSF in

2028, had become an international hero. His subsequent appointment to four-star general, and to the newly-created position of Supreme Commander of the USSF, had come as no surprise.

Scott *was* the USSF. There'd been other factors in the lightning evolution of the space force over the past six years, including the legislative genius of Congressman Jonathan Commer, Sr. of Illinois, the worldwide panic caused by the destruction of the gas giants, and the Final War right alongside unexpected conflict with previously unimagined Alpha Centaurians. Over half the world's financial resources had been funneled into the USSF by 2032. But Jack always suspected it was those bleak two months alone on Mars after the death of his friend Kilpatrick that had truly hammered William Scott and the United System Space Force into a single incontestable entity. No one disputed his right to rule the USSF as he saw fit.

"It may mean nothing right now," Scott went on, holding another memo, "but I hereby issue the Order of the Earth Award to each of your fellow crewmen, and the next six planets discovered will bear their names."

"Thank you," Jack whispered. The Order of the Earth was the highest human award possible. It was like sainthood. He'd never realized Scott could just issue these awards. He'd always thought they had to be ratified by the United System Council.

Scott took a deep breath. "Gentlemen, I don't know if I should reveal this or not, but I'm well aware of the stresses and strains you men have lived under for so long."

"Well, sir, I'd say our entire civilization had been under stress and strain for the past few years," Joe put in.

"True. But I want you to know I've been monitoring your medical records and psychological profiles since October 8th of last year, and I have complete confidence in you. Now don't look at me like that! It's not as if I've had the crew of the *Typhoon* on suicide watch, but one of our physicians accused me of precisely that. To drop the Xon on our mother world, well, I can't imagine what that would be like."

"Unless it would've been to *order* it," Jack said. "So who's watching out for you, General?"

"There was absolutely no choice ... no choice. But at any rate I do need some time to think, maybe write my memoirs. So I've been planning my retirement for some time now."

"Sir! No!" Joe cried. "You've only been SCUSSF two years! We can't do without you! Not now!"

"Not with the Martians and Hergs about to destroy us," Jack said. "Not to mention the Alpha Centauri war."

"Easy, boys. I won't retire until I know things have quieted down," Scott said. "And of course if we live through this next crisis." He glanced at his watch. "But time is pressing. It's time we moved on to completing this mission."

"Yes, sir. We'll offer any help we can."

"I've decided we must move tonight against Hergs. As you've probably guessed from the four men behind you, you and Joe will pilot the *Typhoon II* tonight at 2300 hours. That's an hour from now."

"But we just got here!" Joe gasped.

Jack straightened up. "Yes, sir. We're ready to move out. We couldn't ask for a better crew." He turned to the four men behind them: Patrick James, Will Connors, Lee Borman and Phil Sperry, the crew of the *Typhoon II*.

"We'll ... be ready, sir," Joe said.

"According to what you've told me, the completed Amplified Thought program might be ready in a few days," Scott said. "However, it's obvious Hergs already has some Amplified Thought capacity, and the Martians can apparently blow this planet right now if they choose to, except for this finicky aesthetic sense they have about not actually wanting to *see* the violence." Jack could all but hear the general think: *Wimps!*

"They could easily have blasted Special Ops 10 out of space, for instance," Scott went on. "They could've split the hulls of all ten ships in a second, from what I gather from your reports. I have no idea why they didn't intervene in that."

"Well, in spite of all the battles and terrorism we've seen, the Martians apparently have this injunction against violence,"

Jack said. "I know that some of the younger Martians were easily incited against us in the Kilpatrick Desert, for instance, but I don't think the elders want to do it. But at the same time, they know they have to obey Hergs. Once he got to be emperor, no matter how crazy that sounds, they have to worship his authority. I think there was probably a lot of arguing going on about whether to pulverize Special Ops 10 with the Thought. Maybe that kept just enough Martians from forming an AT group to really do anything. They waited six hours to come after us with those unarmed saucers. That gave Henderson enough time to find us."

"Well, maybe they'll continue to vacillate, and we can make use of that. You know, boys, I would've had trouble believing any of this stuff about Amplified Thought if we hadn't seen evidence of it firsthand."

"Evidence?" Joe said.

"The earth's new moon. We've already named it New Luna. A couple days after the destruction of the *Typhoon*, during which time we were convinced you were all lost, our astronomers were going nuts. They saw material aggregating in the Outer Planetary Debris Field and couldn't find any explanation for it. This whole planet was watching in absolute horror as a body the size of the earth's moon shot at incredible speed towards the earth. I don't have to tell you that this echoed the disasters of the twenties in everyone's mind, and it's one more reason why everyone on this planet is panicked out of their gourds."

"The gray moon!" Jack gasped. "I'd completely forgotten it!"

"We were on Earth just as it came in," Joe said. "I forgot it myself!"

"And when it took up a perfect orbit around the earth, right among the remnants of the old moon, these same astronomers started raving about the Second Coming. Half the planet was behind 'em on that, too. But, as usual, there's a rational explanation for everything. I was damned relieved to hear of Amplified Thought. First the *Typhoon* and you boys, then this New Luna thing. I thought *I* was going crazy. Now it turns out the Martians must have done it."

"So they made us a new moon," Jack mused. "Why would they do that?"

"Dr. Frankston's project," Joe said. "It makes perfect sense. The Martians were helping Dr. Frankston restore the earth. Amav was right. He was starting this project in Alaska and the Martians were going to help him extend it to the whole planet."

"But why would they do something like that?" Scott said.

"Well, two reasons. Maybe three. One, Hergs wants Earth at least partially restored so he can train his squads of human goons there. Second, Amav said the Martians are, like, *sad* at the sight of the earth being wrecked and have this urge to help it. And then there's the self-interest that if they fix it up for us, maybe we'll go back to it."

"So what have they been doing the past six years, wrecking the outer planets and dropping asteroids into the sun? Jack reported it was *them*."

Joe shrugged. "I don't know, sir, but it sounds as if those were all *mistakes*."

"Hmmph. Well, boys, that's interesting speculation, but I think we have to stick to Plan A, which is to assume they're hostile, and that our mission is to prevent them from hurting us. For whatever reason they may want to restore the earth, we still don't know that they won't use the Thought against us here on Mars at any moment." Scott cleared his throat. "I do want you to know I'm sorry this is all again devolving on you boys. We were all shocked at the loss of the *Typhoon,* but we really thought you'd wiped out the Martian threat. Special Ops 10 was being held in readiness in Mars orbit simply as a precaution, but in reality we all thought the enemy was defeated on Mercury. We had no idea Hergs had a base on Venus, or this Amplified Thought, and when we got your message a few hours ago, well, it's been a big reversal here, especially after that damn Vespertine character spilled all this on AresNet and riled up the entire planet."

"We understand, sir," Jack said.

"Boys, at this time the *Typhoon II* is the only ship that can handle Hergs and the Martians. I can't risk sending a whole fleet out now, as the enemy is sure to detect it and this time the Martians may be persuaded to use the Thought. But sending in our best and fastest ship, which has the best cloaking technology we have, may bring it off. The *Typhoon II* now has a full crew, with the two best pilots in the United System, and I've got to gamble on it."

"She's a good ship, sir," Jack said. "But Joe and I really haven't trained on her new technology. I've only been on board her a few times."

"Oh, forget it, Jack. You've spent years working on the *Typhoon* technology. Except for the crew of six instead of eight, the layout's almost identical to *Typhoon I*. Aside from not being officially debugged and commissioned, it shouldn't give you any problems. It's run perfectly in all tests. For this first combat mission, though, Sperry here recommends you run at only sixty million miles per hour as opposed to the possible 133.9 maximum sublight."

"One-fifth light speed," Jack mused. "That is damn fast. And with Star Drive on top of that. But the thing is, Joe and I don't have Star Drive certification yet, sir."

"Well, that's a matter for the future. You won't be using Star Drive on this mission."

Jack nodded. The *Typhoon I* had refined the Augmented Nuclear Drive technology, but its top speed was only one-thirteenth light. The *Typhoon II,* mating Star Drive to the superior *Typhoon* tech, was the most formidable human weapon ever developed. Jack had been eager to fly Star Drive for some time.

"Gentlemen, the *Typhoon II* was designed to be sent into the Alpha Centauri war and end it. I want you and Joe to understand that I've considered you two to be my *Typhoon II* pilots from Day One."

"Thanks, sir," Jack said.

"Yeah, and we didn't know how to handle Star Drive in the first place," Joe muttered, "and look what happened. Cromwell blunders right into the middle of the Alpha Centaurians with the

12th Fleet and he starts that whole stupid war!"

"Young man, you're way out of line!" Scott flared. "For your information, we're fighting an implacable enemy in Alpha Centauri, one that's blocking our further spread into the galaxy. Now it may not happen in my lifetime or yours, but someday we'll populate this galaxy, young man! And if you don't feel up to populating it, then I--then I--" He brought his fist down on his desk. "All right, so what if nobody can clean up this damn military bureaucracy! If Cromwell had been an Air Force man, he'd never've crossed me like that! Dammit to hell!"

Everyone looked at the gray carpet. After six years with the USSF, and two as its supreme commander, even William C. Scott hadn't been able to streamline the bureaucracy. Though as a rising colonel he'd been influential in the amalgamation of all branches of the United States armed forces into the USSF in 2028, the lines of command, spheres of power and influence, personal kingdoms and petty rivalries had if anything grown more tangled since then. The former services refused to cohere, and Scott had long since given up trying to standardize the ranks. Chief petty officers flew beside master sergeants, and admirals and generals commanded fleets side by side.

At least Scott, who'd come out of the Air Force, and the Commer brothers, who'd gone through the Naval Academy, understood each other well. Scott had often said that the passing of another generation would straighten out the USSF, but Admiral Cromwell had demonstrated that the bureaucracy itself might well finish off humanity before any alien danger did.

Finally Joe whispered: "I'm sorry, sir. I guess I just can't get over the *Typhoon*. It won't happen again, sir."

"See that it doesn't, Commander." Scott's eyes narrowed. "Do you have the slightest suspicion that your feelings will interfere with the execution of your duties? If so, speak up honestly now."

Joe shot upright. "Sir! I mean, no sir! Of course not. I'm ready to fly now."

"Does any man here question his ability to execute the orders I'm about to give?"

No one spoke. Scott smiled grimly. "All right. Jack, here are the orders for the *Typhoon II.* Your ship is now equipped with four Xon bombs."

"*Four* ..." Jack gasped.

"That's right, four. Probably more than enough to turn Venus into dust."

"But ..."

"Easy there, gentlemen. I have my own strategy here. It actually came about when that jerk Vespertine revealed that AresNet had broken USSF Authorization Code 3-310. I was so angry at first that I thought of having Vespertine arrested the moment he set foot back here. What a defeatist, willing to make the first deal he can with Hergs! Peacefully coexist with that slimeball while he waits for the perfect moment to vaporize us! Incidentally, gentlemen, pass over your USSF Comms to me."

Puzzled, Jack and Joe handed their comms across the desk to the general, who inserted what looked like an old-fashioned ball point pen into the bottom of each unit.

"There," Scott said, handing them back. "I've already updated your other crewmembers' units. Fortunately we've been developing USSF Authorization Code 3-330 for a year now, and we were just on the verge of releasing it, so we went ahead and did that tonight. They tell me this one is impossible to break, which probably means it's good for a year or two. Anyway, you're all on 3-330 now. But I've left 3-310 up and running, with a few ineffectual patches tacked onto it after the news broke this evening, to make AresNet think that *we* think it's secure now. Of course these patches are nothing their computers won't break in half an hour. Meanwhile, we've been flooding our 3-310 channels with all sorts of disinformation, mainly backing up Mr. Vespertine's theory that the USSF has no choice but to accept Hergs' idea of peaceful coexistence. 3-310 is actually ordering all USSF units to stand down militarily to appease Mr. Hergs, whereas of course 3-330 is ordering select units to do exactly the opposite. I even had our computer boys use 3-330 to hack into AresNet and edit certain technical documents to make us look less powerful than we are.

"My aim is to make Huey Vespertine and his cohorts more and more popular. We're even seeing that with the United System Council paralyzed, AresNet itself is broadcasting peace feelers to Hergs. My God, a private company taking the initiative! What a riot! So I say, let it go on. Let's lull Mr. Hergs into thinking that *we* think we're doomed. All this will be cover for our attack."

"Wow," Jack said. "Seems pretty risky, though, sir."

"Well, there's another element of risk here as well. You see, Jack, you're going to issue an ultimatum to Hergs, the text of which is stored in your ship's computer. Basically, you'll tell him that he must relinquish the emperorship, release the Martians from any allegiance to him, and surrender himself to us immediately. That is correct, immediately. There's no time limit for him to consider. He must surrender immediately or else we will immediately destroy Venus. Do I make myself clear?"

"But Hergs won't buy that. He's a monomaniac. He'll try to stall, anything to keep his power. And then we'll have to destroy Venus. And the Martians."

Scott smiled bitterly. "You know your duty well. I know that you *will* destroy Venus, and the Martians, and all hope of us ever returning to Earth, if Hergs rejects the ultimatum. You know, we're taking an extraordinary risk even issuing an ultimatum. Some of my advisors want to bomb Venus with no warning. I say, perhaps we can free the Martians and profit from their friendship. You have convinced me, incidentally, that this Amplified Thought might really be the key to restoring the earth."

"Excuse me, sir," Jack said. "But once we radio the ultimatum, they'll just pinpoint us even with our cloaking systems, and then a simple Amp-Thought, and poof! Or we launch our bombs and they vaporize them."

"That's another risk we're taking. But in addition to the cloaking, the *Typhoon II* won't be flying a regular orbit around Venus. We've installed an autopilot program that causes the ship to career wildly, at random, all over Venus, at varying altitudes. Thank God the ship's inertial dampers are a hundred times more sensitive than on the *Typhoon I*. You'll never feel a thing. You'll swear you're sitting in your living room. The Martians will receive your signal but its source will appear to be from all directions at once. The chances that even five hundred Martians could think their way onto your random course, locate your ship, and destroy it, are, I think, infinitesimal. Likewise their ability to lock on and destroy your four bombs, launched without warning from four different points along your random path, and each equipped with a small augmented nuke that'll boost their speed to one-fifth light. No, they'll have less time to react than you'd have if I activated my personal chair lasers right now."

Jack winced at the old joke. Scott always joshed visitors about the anti-assassination lasers mounted in the seats of chairs in his office and all along the walls, programmed to lock onto and destroy any living being that was not Scott, if and when certain mysterious AI software detected potential violence. Everyone assumed he was kidding until a disgruntled admiral had started a shouting match a couple months ago and made the unfortunate mistake of raising a clenched fist. The lasers took his arm off at the elbow.

"It doesn't seem like enough time," Joe said. "What if Hergs does stall, but meanwhile the Martians secretly want to kick him out?"

"Believe me, we're giving the Martians a chance for survival," Scott said. "If they don't realize that and take it, if they don't depose Hergs in that case, well, they'll pay the price. And you know it has to be that way."

"Yes, but ..."

"No buts. And the rest of the ultimatum says that even if they somehow destroy the *Typhoon II,* we'll go ahead and complete Hergs' little dream of destruction, but we'll get Venus as well. Are you men familiar with Donald Parker's recent paper, 'An Artificially-Induced Supernova'? About engaging Star Drive near a solar mass? The USS *Zeus* is now inside the orbit of Mercury, on its own random flight path--"

"No!" Joe cried. "Not the *Zeus!*"

"--ready to aim straight for the sun and engage its Star

Drive. Hergs will realize we'll get him one way or another. We'll all go supernova and that'll be that. Those Martians will see we've got our own version of Amplified Thought."

"I call it Amplified Stupidity. If we had half a brain we wouldn't think of destroying the sun!"

"Commander, I've had enough out of you for one day!" Scott turned to Jack. "Jack, does your brother see the necessity of our actions? I can't have a doubter on this flight."

"Uh, yes, sir, I'm sure he knows," Jack said.

Scott softened. "Men--all of you--I understand how you feel. I don't believe it'll come to that. But Amplified Thought in Hergs' hands could mean the end of every civilization that might possibly exist in this galaxy. We've got to stop it now. Is that understood? Joe?"

"Uh ... yessir," Joe said, eyes to the floor.

"Everyone?"

The rest of the men murmured their assent.

Scott turned back to his papers. "You have fifty minutes until liftoff. Dismissed!"

CHAPTER THIRTY-TWO
Amav
Friday, June 16, 2034, 0030 hours

WE KNOW THE SHAPE OF YOUR LITTLE CRAFT. WE KNOW THE SHAPE OF YOUR LITTLE CRAFT, sang the voices. YOUR LITTLE CRAFT IS FLYING PERFECTLY.

Amav shook her head. There was no way to clear her brain. She stared blearily at the velocity indicator on the Mercedes control panel. Unbelievably, it read 49.2 million miles per hour. She'd been flying for two hours and at this rate she'd arrive in forty-six minutes.

THE UNKNOWN FEMALE WILL COUNTERACT THE UNKNOWN MALE.

THE EMPEROR CANNOT FAULT US FOR BRINGING THE UNKNOWN FEMALE TO HIM. SHE WILL MAKE HIM SEE!

PARTICULARLY AS HE HAS NOT YET EXPERIENCED INTERCOURSE WITH CONSORT AMAV. SHE CAN CONTROL HIM AS LONG AS INTERCOURSE IS WITHHELD.

ADMITTEDLY THIS IS A STRANGE HUMAN CUSTOM.

TO WITHHOLD INTERCOURSE?

NO! TO EVEN ATTEMPT INTERCOURSE WITHOUT OUTRADIANCE! WITHOUT TELEPATHIC MERGING!

INCREDIBLY DANGEROUS IF YOU ASK ME!

Amav had gotten accustomed to the tones of different Martians. One voice had complained about how exhausting this precise work was, especially with only ten Martians involved. Over the past couple hours, there'd been nothing to do aboard the Mercedes but speculate about which tones might correspond to which Martians she knew. She was certain that three of her favorite Martian Elders--Dar, Fulr, and Kner--were involved.

She studied a magnified view of the hot cloudy planet ahead, worrying whether the Martians had properly protected the ship against micrometeors. At this velocity even a grain of dust would rupture the fragile pleasure cruiser. She knew faster military craft had special shielding methods, but what would the one million mile-per-hour Mercedes have? But maybe the Martians figured 49.2 was safe. They wanted this craft to arrive safely, didn't they?

Amav still wasn't sure why she'd followed the crazed commands. At first, alone in the chilly examination room at the USSF clinic, she'd thought she was hallucinating, then, pacing in her paper dressing gown, she'd panicked. Where was she really? Had the Martians kidnapped her again during a minute of comatose sleep? But she had to be on Mars, safe with the USSF, didn't she? Weren't these just voices in her head? Wasn't it simply that she was cracking up?

WE KNOW THE SHAPE OF YOUR LITTLE CRAFT. Somehow the voices had navigated into her head by endlessly repeating that phrase. IF BY SOME CHANCE WE COULD FEEL THE SHAPE OF YOU ALONE INSIDE THE SHAPE OF YOUR LITTLE CRAFT ...

"Who are you? What's going on?" Amav had gasped.

WE KNOW THE SHAPE OF YOUR LITTLE CRAFT.

It had taken several minutes of shouting back at the voices to convince her that whatever was infiltrating couldn't respond. Then she knew she was dealing with the one-way telepathy of Martians, astoundingly broadcast across a hundred thirty-six million miles of space. "Dar! Dar!" she'd shouted, realizing he couldn't hear her but finally recognizing his frequency.

WE KNOW THE SHAPE OF YOUR LITTLE CRAFT.

IF BY SOME CHANCE WE COULD FEEL THE SHAPE OF YOU ALONE INSIDE THE SHAPE OF YOUR LITTLE CRAFT ...

WE COULD TRANSPORT IT HERE! TO US!

There was no reason given. Were the Martians brainwashing her long distance into fleeing back to Sam Hergs' greasy arms? In despair, Amav felt the odd and beautiful Martian outradiance compelling her obedience.

And when two nurses, hearing her shouting, burst into the examination room followed by a doctor holding a

DermaPenetrator full of something blue and undoubtedly narcotic, she'd been ready for this development, yanking her purse from beneath the long gray dress piled on a stool and producing her golden empress shattergun.

Everyone on Mars seemed to know what a shattergun was. Jack had told her of the universal horror at its effects in the Kilpatrick Desert skirmish, as broadcast live on AresNet. The nurses and doctors didn't protest as Amav took their USSF Comms and locked the entire med staff in the exam room. She'd changed into her gray dress in the reception room, charming a young USSF lieutenant who tried unsuccessfully to look away from her naked body as the paper gown hit the floor.

WE KNOW THE SHAPE OF YOUR LITTLE CRAFT.

Amav found that female USSF personnel responded more readily to her commands when she waved the golden shattergun in their faces, whereas male personnel seemed to need only the sight of her tight gray dress unbuttoned to her crotch. The coffee-colored brassiere casually draped around the gun was an added erotic tease. In truth the empress model was a newly developed cryogenic design with a power source hovering a few millionths of a degree above absolute zero. Theoretically the gun never needed a recharge, but the exterior metal always felt as if it had just come out of a freezer, so the bra came in handy.

IF BY SOME CHANCE WE COULD FEEL THE SHAPE OF YOU ALONE INSIDE THE SHAPE OF YOUR LITTLE CRAFT ... YOUR LITTLE CRAFT ...

WE COULD TRANSPORT IT HERE ...

AND THE UNKNOWN FEMALE WOULD COUNTERACT THE UNKNOWN MALE!

Amav could hardly remember how she'd escaped the USSF spaceport unmolested. What had struck her most was the panic everywhere. Wild-eyed USSF hanger crews carelessly babbled to the half-naked stranger that the Mercedes was being trucked to the other side of town to Marsport Commercial Spacelines, which had facilities to thoroughly dismantle a private saucer. And the obese taxi driver slicing through the jammed Upheaval Freeway kept jabbing a thick disfigured middle finger at the receding concrete plain of the USSF Spaceport, with the silver *Typhoon II* wreathed in vapor on its launch pad, yelling that if the *Typhoon* didn't bomb Hergs right now they were all gonna die and so would the lady like to perform oral sex right now or what? Fortunately, that line of inquiry died as she peeled back her coffee lingerie to expose another inch of golden shattergun.

Cutting through the commercial spaceport, Amav broadcast numerous ID and credit frequencies from the USSF Comms she'd taken off the medical personnel. She'd distributed beguiling smiles in all directions, flashing boobs, bellybutton, or bra-covered shattergun as necessary. But most useful was a tone of command that reduced panicky minds to worshipping subservience, though they never guessed that this aura of command was the end result of ten Martian voices careening in her head.

Amav was in the flow. Anything she did was the right thing to do. She was no longer just obeying the voices, she was collaborating with them. She met the Mercedes on the tarmac just as USSF handlers signed it over to Marsport Commercial Spacelines. Claiming she was a USSF investigator taking over the ship's dismantling, she'd shooed out the technicians, secured the hatch, strapped herself in, and waited.

Within a few seconds she was pressed into her seat by explosive acceleration. She knew she wouldn't be shot down, but didn't understand why until, watching her velocity unreeling into the millions of miles per hour, she again began paying attention to the voices.

THANK YOU FOR BEING ALONE IN THE SHAPE OF THE LITTLE CRAFT!

WE HAVE SHIELDED ITS SHAPE FROM DETECTION.

NEITHER HUMANS NOR THE EMPEROR KNOW IT'S COMING.

AN UPGRADE CREATED BY KNER!

AND KNER HAS SHIELDED OUR OWN THOUGHTS FROM THE EMPEROR.

MARVELOUS!

WEIRD!

BUT UNSTABLE! DECEIVING THE EMPEROR IN THE NAME OF MAKING THE EMPEROR HAPPY BY BRINGING HIM HIS CONSORT TO CONTROL HIM SO THAT HE WILL NOT DESTROY FIRST HOME!

CONFUSING! MORALLY STRANGE!

TEN MARTIANS RUNNING ONE HUNDRED SIXTEEN SUBROUTINES SIMULTANEOUSLY!

EXHAUSTING!

CAN MAYBE HOLD FOR ANOTHER HOUR!

Amav only hoped she was still sane by the time she got to Venus.

CHAPTER THIRTY-THREE
The *Typhoon II*
Friday, June 16, 2034, 0100 hours

Phil Sperry pulled his tall, bony body into the third seat behind the Commer brothers as a telescopic image of Venus on Jack's monitor showed a steadily growing half-sphere of light. Joe requested a position update from Will Connors in the Navigation Room. Soon it would be time for Phil to take up his upside-down position at the ventral turret with its reversed gravity.

"All right," Jack spoke to the crew. "Final checks. We're going to deceleration, then to random course, in fifteen minutes, repeat, fifteen minutes. Sensors?"

"All systems functional," replied technical wizard and AC war veteran Patrick James from the Sensor Room. "No sign of enemy activity. No unusual radio communications."

"Roger," Jack said. "Navigation?"

"All systems go," said Will Connors, the former fighter pilot in Alpha Centauri. "Updated information feeding into autopilot. Ready for random course insertion."

"Roger," Jack replied. "Dorsal turret?"

"All systems go," replied Lee Borman, the best turret gunner in the galaxy with over four thousand enemy spacecraft shot down in Alpha Centauri.

"Check," Jack said. "Ventral turret?"

"Right behind you, Jack," Phil said lazily. "I'm just finishin' up my coffee break."

Jack turned. "I knew you were there, you skunk."

Phil grinned and stretched his legs. "All right, all right, I'm going."

"No hurry," Jack said. "I'm sure Lee can take care of enemy ships all by himself. We don't really need you, you know."

Phil laughed. "Tell me about it. I'll just go back and take me a catnap."

"Go ahead, sleep through the entire mission," Joe said. "We'll all just hate you from afar. I'm practically asleep as it is."

275

"Tell me again why they gave the P/E even *more* duties than on the *Typhoon I?*" Jack said. "It's always seemed insane to me."

"Hey, I always assumed the they in this case was you, Captain Commer," Phil said. "I thought you were behind all those design decisions."

"Not me," said Jack. "That was the Personnel Office. Everyone knew we'd have to double up on some duties when we went from eight crewmembers to six, but whoever decided to give the physician/engineer the ventral PlanetBlaster had to be nuts."

Phil shrugged. "Maybe they just assumed our technology was so foolproof that I'd never need to repair anything. Or that nobody would ever get sick."

"Yeah, right," Joe said. "Sheesh."

Even the genius Harri McNarri had been overwhelmed by his tasks on the *Typhoon I,* yet when the planners had reduced the second ship's crew from eight to six, they had, incomprehensibly, placed an even greater burden on the physician/engineer. In addition to maintaining the physical and psychological health of the entire crew along with every technical system onboard, including computers, weaponry, and propulsion, Phil had to train on all types of PlanetBlasters and see three months fighting in Alpha Centauri before he could take up his additional duties as ventral turret gunner. Phil didn't have the luxury of hours of free time sitting in his plastiglass turret scanning the stars, as Lee Borman did. He was generally expected to attend to this or that all over the ship.

But not until today had Phil felt he was flying on a true USSF ship. The test pilots on the shakedown runs had never imparted the feel of a real spacecraft. But today the *Typhoon II* finally had its pilot and copilot, the best in the USSF.

"Hey, seriously, how are you guys?" Phil said. "You both look pretty wasted."

"Well, earlier this morning we were climbing up that horrible shaft without even getting to breathe," Joe said. "This day has seemed like forty years."

"Yeah, but the ship is keeping us awake," Jack said. "Joe

and I have been taking turns flying this thing. The acceleration is unbelievable. And the controls are so responsive!"

"Yeah, I can't wait to fly it in a real planetary atmosphere," Joe said. "I bet she handles real well. Mars' air just doesn't have the bite."

"Well, we've flown it to Titan," Phil said. "It's always performed perfectly. Of course that's no comparison with how it'd do on Earth."

"Earth ..." Jack said. "Yeah, I'd like to fly it over, say, Nebraska."

"It's incredible, isn't it? We still can't believe the earth is worse than dead, in a way. I mean, if we'd just blown it to pieces, like say happened to the outer planets, that'd be one thing. We'd know we couldn't go back. We wouldn't be so homesick."

"Hell, I'm not homesick," Joe said. "I don't want to go back."

"Really? *I* feel homesick. *I* want to go back."

There was a silence as Jack refused to vote along with the other two. "Anyway, we very nearly did blow it to pieces," Jack finally said. "I heard one scientist say that four Xons probably would've done it, but it would've taken a few years to actually tear the planet up. Apparently you'd need a couple dozen to blow it all at once. But to drop even one ... you know, when Scott told us to drop it, well, I really did question whether I could go ahead and obey that order."

Phil blinked. This was more than he'd ever heard from Jack on the subject.

"Man ..." Joe said. "There've only been three Xons ever used, at least in *this* solar system."

Phil nodded. The *Typhoon I* had assisted in the first test of an Xon bomb a year ago: a detonation in the asteroid belt lit up the nighttime earth like day. Then came the September Central Asian Powers Xon, which blew off a chunk of the moon and caused its explosion two months later. The third bomb was the one the *Typhoon I* had given to Central Asia to end the anxious months of the Final War.

Planetary engineers later determined that the earth was still a stable body, although it had been slightly shifted off its axis. But people on the streets of El Paso had been knocked down by the force of the explosion. The planet lost a large quantity of its already poisoned atmosphere, and earthquakes had followed for weeks. And in place of the Central Asian Powers, there was a crater five hundred miles wide and a hundred deep.

Several thousand Xons had been shot off in Alpha Centauri, to little effect, since the Centaurians rarely lived on planets or concentrated their shipbound populations. It made Phil weak to think about the *Typhoon II's* four Xons. His ship could choose to destroy any body in the solar system. By engaging its Star Drive, not operational on this voyage, it could destroy the sun as well. It was unreal. Phil went about his duties and tried not to think about the destruction his ship carried.

"Well, I'd better be getting to my turret," he said. "Are you going to keep us posted?"

"Sure," Jack said. "When we send the ultimatum I'll broadcast it over the intercom, so we all know what it says. I'll put on a reply if we get one."

Phil nodded. They all knew what had to happen if no reply was received. "You guys sure you don't need some amphetamines, something to keep you going?"

"No, we're fine. I want to keep my head clear for any decisions that need to be made." Jack checked his console. "0116 hours. Standard deceleration procedures, Joe, followed by random course program."

"I'm on it," Joe said. "Damn, this is *easy,* Phil. Just now we went from sixty million to four thousand miles per hour, and into random course, and I didn't feel a thing!"

"It's a smooth ship," Phil said. "Although maybe I should go check the Augmented Plus now that you've abused it."

"Yeah, get on back to that fancy upside-down cage of yours and leave us alone," Jack grinned.

"Okay, I've overstayed my welcome." Phil turned to the hatch. "But if you--"

"Hey!" Joe shouted, arching over his console. "Pat, can you--"

"That's what I'm feeding you now," Patrick James called over the intercom. "Let me check the configuration. God, *that's* weird."

"What's weird?" Jack called. "What is it?"

"It's a ship, but too small to be military, and it's decelerating tremendously. It's nearing the clouds. Estimate it was moving one-thirteenth light speed. God, that deceleration's *amazing.*"

"On such a tiny ship?" Will Connors cut in. "How can it take the stress? And how could it be going one-thirteenth anyway? Before us, only the *Typhoon I* could do that."

"I've got it on the configuration program," James said. "It's a Mercedes PleasureCraft, four-person model. Can't be capable of that speed, unless it got a boost somewhere."

"Trace back its probable course!" Jack shrieked, eyes bulging.

"Damn! *Mars.* I trace it back from *Mars.*"

"It's Amav!" Jack screamed, leaping out of his chair. "She's leaving me! She's going back to Hergs! Oh my God!"

"What in the world's going on?" Phil shouted. "Who is this--oh, that's right, that girl whose ship you took. You think that's *her* again?"

"It's her! It's her! Oh God, it's her! She's left me! She's left me!"

"My God!" Joe cried. "I can *feel* their thoughts!"

"What the hell are you talking about?" Phil said.

"The Martians! I think! I mean, I can feel the *outradiance!* Jack, can't you feel it?"

"No!" Jack screeched. "Are you *crazy?* God, how could she have launched from Mars without anyone knowing about it? We haven't received any report!"

"I can *feel* the outradiance!" Joe insisted. "It's very faint, but the Martians are *exhausted!* Something about their *programming* not holding. The ship can land but it'll be rough."

"What are you *talking* about? Amav's *left* me, and Joe's worried about what a bunch of stupid Martians are thinking!"

"What is *everyone* talking about?" Phil said. "This isn't making sense!"

"Something about a core group of the Martians," Joe gasped. "Ten of 'em. They're exhausted! Can't keep up the *shielding* anymore? Can't control the *little craft* anymore?"

"Forget that crap!" Jack yelled. "James, why didn't anyone tell me Amav was going back to Hergs?"

"Uh, sir, we just now received a message from General Scott," James called. "Apparently the Mercedes is, uh, unaccounted for."

"*Unaccounted for?* Why didn't you pass that report to me immediately?"

"It just came in a minute ago! I had my hands full with the sensors! It's not in real time anyway. We're twelve light minutes from Mars. Scott says it's all confused. The people at the commercial spaceport are swearing a woman from the USSF signed for it."

"No, that was Amav! She wanted Hergs all along! I was a fool to think I could hold onto her! I knew it! I knew it! I knew she'd leave me! I'm such a damn idiot!"

"Jack, get a hold of yourself!" Joe shouted.

"Kill me now, Joe, and put an end to this!"

"What's going on here?" Patrick James said, poking his head through the door.

"Pat, back to your post!" Joe snapped. "Monitor that damned thing!"

"What's it *doing?* Oh, what's it *doing?*" Jack moaned, pointing to the blip on his console.

"It's just decelerating down. Now sit down, Jack, please!"

"No! She's gone! She left me! She must hate me!" Jack turned to Phil. "Phil! She *left* me!"

"*Jack* ..." Phil gasped. "We've got to issue the ultimatum! A stupid pleasure craft can't interfere with that!"

"*You* issue it! I can't, because *she's* there now! I can't blow her up, Phil, I just can't!" Then he hurled himself into his chair and punched buttons. "Or what the hell, maybe I can! Phil, go to console B and arm the Xons!"

"What?" Phil protested. "You know damn well it's too dangerous to arm those things until just before we launch 'em!"

"Well, yeah, we're gonna launch! You stupid jerk! We're gonna launch and that'll be the end of that! Scott'll get what he wants, and Hergs'll be dead, and so will--oh, Amav! Darling! Oh, God!"

Phil had to use every ounce of his will to overcome his shock. So Jack had finally cracked. But the mission was too important to allow anybody, including the Captain, to jeopardize it. "Captain Commer," he spoke evenly, "as ship's medical officer I find you unfit for command. You will retire to the ship's kitchen immediately." Phil was unsure about the wording of that last sentence. Usually a commanding officer would be confined to quarters, but the only nonmilitary parts of the *Typhoon II* were the small kitchenette and the lavatory, and it didn't seem right to send Jack to the lavatory.

Jack whirled out of his chair, red-faced, sputtering.

"You can't do that! This is *Jack Commer,* you know!" Joe yelled with all the arrogance of the experienced pilot to the neophyte crewman, forgetting that Phil had fought in more battles than the Commers and knew this ship better than either of them.

"Commander," Phil said, "you will assume command of the *Typhoon* immediately. Jack is unfit for duty. The mission is too important--"

"Forget it! I *countermand* your orders, effectively immediately! Immediately!" Jack shrieked. "You and your cowardly meathead buddies can just go straight to blazes!"

"Jack! Jack!" Joe cried. "For God's sake, get hold of yourself! Please!" He whipped his brother around and shook him until Phil could hear Jack's teeth clattering.

"Joe!" Jack sobbed, collapsing in his chair. "Do you think she's left me?"

"Jack! It doesn't matter! She's just a girl!"

"She's *everything,* Joe," Jack whispered. "She ... she ..."

"He's really cracked," Phil ventured. "Joe, you really need to assume command."

"The Mercedes is in the clouds," James called. "Being knocked around by the atmosphere. I don't know if it'll make it."

"Why would she risk her life like that," Jack moaned, "unless she wanted *sex with Hergs?*"

"Jack, *please* ..." Phil found himself chanting in unison with Joe.

"She's *linked* to him! Joe! Everyone! Can't you see? It's the Erotic Teachings! They *brainwashed* her into loving him! And now she has to *unite* with him! It's canceling out everything! It's canceling out *me!*" Jack slumped out of his seat. Phil considered catching him, but decided to let him flop onto the floor.

Joe shook his head. "Jack, look! Hey, look what we can do! We can be on top of that thing in a second! With our cloaking they'll never know! We just go to full power, swoop down on that Mercedes and Arkonsky-clamp it, pull it up underneath us! Then we come back out here and do the ultimatum!"

Jack closed his eyes and groaned on the floor. "Yeah, yeah, good idea, Joe. Oh my God, oh my God ..."

"Yeah, Jack, we'll catch her. We'll bring her back. Now, please, just straighten up."

"I'm sorry, Joe. I don't know ..." Then Jack threw himself to his feet. "Hey, Phil, I'm sorry. I'm all right now."

"Uh ... yeah," Phil said dubiously.

Jack shook himself. "All right, then. Sperry, back to your turret. Crew, prepare for maximum sub-light power."

"Jack, we shouldn't try for 133.9 just yet. I recommend we keep it at sixty."

"Forget it, Major. We'll need every millisecond, and we'll do the whole 133. We've got to intercept that craft before we carry out the rest of the mission."

As Jack made his way to his command chair Phil felt the shipwide upsurge of activity as Joe prepared to bring up the power. Phil resumed his seat at Console B. "Jack, I should be up here. To monitor the engine and all. I mean, we've never gone to full power like this before." In reality he knew he had to keep an eye on Jack, and that Jack knew it.

Jack cocked an eye back to Phil. "As you wish, Major." Then, to Joe: "All right, let's go for it!"

Joe punched for maximum. Phil braced himself.

A muffled explosion came from the back of the ship.

"Damn!" Jack said. "Of all the stupid crap! Sperry, this is all your fault!"

But Phil was already flying out of the Control Room, down past the escape craft and back to the engine area. As he'd suspected, the main and auxiliary power thruster units were smoking. They smelled like melted plastic.

The entire crew had abandoned stations to see the problem. "It's not fatal," Phil said. "The reactor's still putting out full power. We just can't thrust with it."

"You mean we can't go anywhere?" Jack cried.

"Not for at least ten hours. I can repair these units. They must not've been ready for a full power surge."

"Sperry, what the *hell* is wrong with this goddamn ship?"

"Take it easy, Jack," Joe said.

Jack took a deep breath. "It's all right. I'm in command now." He turned to Phil. "What about the cloaking system?"

"Still in operation. As are our life support and other systems. We can still send the ultimatum and launch the bombs, but we don't have the random course to protect us."

"Let's just launch the bombs and be done with it," Lee Borman put in. "I don't see any other way."

"Forget it," Jack said. "We have to deliver the ultimatum or else we lose the chance of saving the earth. But we can't deliver the ultimatum, or they'll pinpoint us and Amp-Thought us. And now this damn Mercedes has alerted them that something's up." He frowned. "Okay. Here's what's going to happen. I'm going after her in the escape craft. Prepare to seal off and depressurize the launch cabin. If I'm not back in an hour, destroy Venus!"

"Jack, I'm coming with you!" Joe said.

"Negative. She's my problem, and I'm going to take care of her my way."

"Jack, the escape craft's too unstable for a Venus landing without two people piloting. You could never handle it by yourself."

Jack hesitated. "All right. Come on. Just--this isn't going to be a repeat of Mercury, you know!"

"Dammit, I wasn't thinking that! How can you say that?"

"Because it feels exactly the same! You volunteering to come along, the *Typhoon*--God, the ship killing itself!"

"Forget it! Get a hold of yourself, Jack! We have a mission to accomplish. I'm coming along because I'm needed!"

"Dammit, I *have* hold of myself! Okay, okay, forget it! Just get in the damn ship and let's go!"

"Look, exactly what is this supposed to accomplish?" Phil cut in. "I don't see that finding this girl means a hill of beans to this mission."

Jack looked him in the eye. "I know what I'm doing, major. Now all of you out of this area at once. Depressurize via standard procedure."

"Jack, really," Phil said, alarmed by the cold fury in Jack's eyes and his rude references to his old buddy as "major." And the fact that he was insane.

"Major, you will not question my authority, especially during wartime. You will follow my orders without delay. If one hour from now we're not on our way back, destroy the planet. Is that understood, major?"

"Yes ... sir."

"Major, I leave you in command of this ship," Jack said. Joe opened the bubble hatch on the escape ship and the two of them climbed in. "Begin depressurization."

Phil watched Jack and Joe strap themselves in, then motioned the other crewmen back to their stations. When the launch area was safely sealed and the air had hissed out the belly of the ship, Phil sat at Console B in front of the four Xon arming buttons. He listened to the Commers run through an abbreviated preflight checklist.

"Done," one of them said. "Ready for launch."

Phil felt the *Typhoon II* shudder as its fuselage doors opened and the Commers slid into space.

"This time," said the other, "we'll do it *right*."

CHAPTER THIRTY-FOUR
To the Boudoir

The escape craft chugged along the unending dome wall in the darkness. The ten-mile-wide dome set up odd turbulence patterns in the thick Venusian atmosphere, and Joe had a hard time controlling the ship at five miles per hour, ten feet from the wall, 457 feet off the ground. Every few hundred feet a dim green light on the concrete to their left marked a spigot exhaling waste gas from Hergs' vast fortress.

"What we need is something like a small service airlock," Jack said from the auxiliary controls behind Joe. "But how we'll get 'em to open it is beyond me." He warily eyed the gray metal sides of the ship bulging inward along with the plastiglass canopy. "How're we doing on outside temperature and pressure?"

"You don't want to know. Outside temperature: 912 degrees Fahrenheit. Pressure: 1,310 pounds per square inch. I've got our interior pressure cranked up to four atmospheres. High as it'll go."

"God, yes, I feel like someone's *strangling* me," Jack grunted. He'd been tempted to nudge the metal plates back to their proper shape, but that was suicidal. There was no way he could push back over ninety atmospheres of pressure, and the slightest stress crack he made might shatter the ship.

"Our cooling system's losing ground against the outer temperature, but I think we can hold it at bay awhile."

"We're at 129 degrees as it is," Jack said, reading his gauges. "Correction: 130. *Man ...*"

"You know, Jack, when we get back, we oughta make sure future escape ships can withstand something like Venus."

"Yeah, good idea. Listen, Joe, do you think the Mercedes made it through this?"

"Yeah, probably. It did well on Venus before. I mean, she was always taking cruises out of the dome in it and all."

Don't think about her. Don't. "Look, Joe, I just want to say I'm sorry. About the way I acted back there."

"It's all right, Jack. I really understand. I really do."

Another green light came up, along with more outgassing shoving the little ship sideways. "Thanks. I don't know what got to me, I guess."

"It's all right," Joe said. "Really."

Jack focused on his sensors. The same barely curving wall to the left. "I just don't understand why we haven't been detected. An escape craft has minimal cloaking, after all."

"I don't know. I keep getting this sense of the *Martians* again. Something about that core group of ten of 'em. I think including that Dar guy. All *exhausted*."

"I don't know, Joe, I still can't believe you could be reading them from out in space."

"No, really, Jack, somehow I could *feel* their thoughts. I mean, if five hundred of 'em can blow up Jupiter and Saturn, you'd think I could probably feel the thoughts of ten of 'em."

"Well, maybe you're more sensitive than I am, or something. I'm not feeling them at all."

"Even now, I can feel how *exhausted* they are."

"So what's this exhaustion thing? Why would they be so tired?"

"Because of the mental energy they spent dragging the Mercedes here to Mars. That's what they did. And now they're so wiped out, they can't feel *outwards*."

"Okay, okay, I believe you. I felt their thoughts myself last time we were here. And that's probably the only possible explanation for how the Mercedes could've covered a hundred thirty-six million miles in a few hours."

"Man, I'm getting that they could pick up the *Typhoon II* right now, even with our cloaking, if they weren't so blasted."

"Wow, we didn't consider that. But it means we have to move quickly, before they recover." There was a beep on his scanner. "Joe! Three hundred feet ahead! Radar's picking up some sort of entrance. And it's open!"

"An airlock?" Joe said.

"I think so. A little one, obviously adjusted to Venus pressure. And now I'm picking up a small craft, bearing for it.

Not much bigger than us."

"I've got it on my scanner now," Joe said, accelerating. "I'll just sneak us in right behind it."

A patch of brilliant yellow appeared. Jack made out a square entrance ringed by bright yellow floodlights. "Okay, there it is. Now where's that ship?"

"I only hope they haven't got us on *their* radar."

"I'm sure they're paying more attention to their own docking. Wait!" Five feet to their right loomed a slim black submarine with portholes, through which Jack saw several humans gaping at the Commer craft. Enemy humans in Hergs' gray uniforms.

Jack reached over Joe to pull the small forward laser around and flash a half-second burst at the other ship. The ray looked harmlessly narrow and brief, but the slight scratch of the laser ruptured the already strained walls of the other ship. In a second it collapsed like a crushed paper airplane, falling noiselessly out of sight.

"Wow," Joe said. "Did you have to--?"

"Couldn't chance it," Jack said, dropping back into his seat. "They looked ready to report us. We'll just slip into the airlock in their place."

"If we don't need any special access code." But Joe turned the ship left and swept into the tiny airlock below a sign in English: LEVEL 65 KITCHEN LOADING DOCK B.

"I don't think they'll bother us here," Jack said as Joe guided the escape craft onto metal gridwork and put the thrusters on idle. "It's just a kitchen." Behind them a massive door slid shut and they heard pumps working to expel the ninety-atmosphere pressure. Jack relaxed as the airlock cleared, the exterior pressure indicator steadily went down, and the walls of the ship gradually straightened out. He felt lessened weight, and remembered that Hergs kept his dome at Martian gravity. As Jack and Joe grinned in relief, two gray-uniformed men came through a door and moved toward the ship.

"One atmosphere outside," Joe said. "I hope we can fast-talk these guys."

The space around Jack's head shrieked. Roaring chaos blew the gray men down.

Thousands of pieces of plastiglass tinkled to the floor. Jack blinked. They'd failed to reduce their high internal pressure and their plastiglass canopy, weakened by the Venusian atmosphere, had bulged in the opposite direction.

"Man, we exploded!" Joe gasped.

"Yeah, but all outwards, thank God. I don't have a scratch. How about you?"

"I'm fine. What a dramatic entrance!"

"Hmm," Jack said, climbing over the side of the craft, noting with horror that several metal plates simply crumbled off at his touch. He pointed to the gray-uniformed men sprawled on the floor. Flying glass had severed the jugular veins on both of them. Instantly Jack was on top of the bodies, loosening the uniforms. "These guys are about our size. Help me get these things off before they bleed all over 'em."

Joe knelt to help. "Uh … Jack? Isn't this a little … I mean, can we really pull off impersonating these guys?"

Jack met his brother's brown eyes for the first time since they'd left the *Typhoon II*. "We don't have much choice, do we? Have you got a better plan?"

"Well, no. I guess you're right," Joe said, beginning to work on his own man.

"Listen, I may have lost my cool back on the ship, but don't think I don't know what I'm doing. If you think I'm really crazy, why'd you bother to come with me?"

Joe flushed under the rebuke and made no reply.

"Look, Joe, I'm sorry. I acted like a jerk, and I yelled at Phil, one of my best buddies. Okay, I admit it, I've been really messed up over this Amav thing. It's gotten to me, I guess. But I promise it hasn't interfered with my command capabilities."

Struggling with his man's body, Joe finally nodded. "Well, I suppose I can understand it. I guess you've never been in love before, Jack."

Jack paused from working off his man's trousers and was on the verge of telling his younger brother how off base he'd always been about Jack's romantic life. Jack knew all about love. Hell, he'd fallen in love fifty or sixty times. He knew all the stages, how everything was supposed to go. But then he sighed. "I guess you're right. I've never met anyone like Amav." He pulled boots and socks off, then slid the man's pants down. "I guess she's really thrown me."

Joe grinned. "Believe me, Jack, I understand. I really did think you'd cracked. But it's just a girl."

"Yeah, maybe you're right."

They put on the gray uniforms, discarding everything of their own but the USSF Comms and heat blasters they hid in sleeve pockets. The uniforms fit well and the blood stains weren't obvious. Satiny black trim highlighted the deep gray of the uniform, and yellow armbands read CS in lettering evoking the fluid script of the written Martian language. Both also wore knife sheaths on their belts.

"Let's go," Jack said, pushing open a heavy steel door. They found themselves in a white corridor next to a large silver serving cart. Two chrome domes rested on the top level, various silver utensils and a silver bucket took up the middle level, with folded black cloths arranged on the lowest.

Footsteps behind them. Outradiance filled Jack's mind. An unusually tall Martian strode forward in a gray uniform with a CS armband like their own. Jack felt the Martian's power and maturity. He was some thirteen hundred years old.

"You two!" the Martian snapped. Or rather, Jack read the Martian's mind, superimposing thoughts over the spoken words. "Do you not salute the Senior Chef?"

"Ah ... ah ..." Jack said. This was Ywer, Senior Chef to the Emperor. Both he and Joe flung right arms in stiff salute. Jack could easily see that Ywer was an exception to the rule of the timid Martian. His devotion to his culinary duties was so intense that he bossed everyone around, Martian or human.

"Sir," Jack tried in his clumsy Martian, "we were just--" And it hit him exactly what this chrome service was doing in the corridor. "We were just picking up the emperor's special order that just arrived from Mercury!"

"Ah, yes, the Mercurian Pheasant," Ywer nodded. "Absurd that two Grade Tens of the Chef Service should be sent to this damned airlock when you have better things to do. But it probably has to do with all that unpleasantness on Planet Cinder. And of course, the emperor is expecting his Mercurian Pheasant for the wedding feast."

"The wedding feast?" Jack gasped.

"Yes, yes, of course!" Ywer snapped. "You will deliver the wedding feast to the emperor immediately." He made to lift one of the chrome servers.

"Sir!" Jack said. "Do--do you not recall that Mercurian Pheasant can only be viewed by the emperor himself?"

"Ah, right, right you are," Ywer said. "Of course, I just wanted to savor its smell. It's been so long since we Martians were free to hunt Mercurian Pheasant and enjoy its hallucinogenic properties. Of course, Hergs has forbidden us that pleasure." He stiffened. "Well, I'm sure you humans do not understand our religious rites!"

"Believe me, sir, we ... do understand." Jack was awestruck at the knowledge flooding him: that a species resembling an ancient Earth pterodactyl was native to Mercury, and that for centuries the favorite pastime of the Martian aristocracy had been to vacation on that planet, hunt these beasts down with shatterguns set to "large chunks," set the pieces on the open airless cracked ground of the Mercurian day, let simmer for two weeks, and then gorge themselves into psychedelic stupor. Curiously, since the Mercurian Pheasant was glasslike in composition, a shattergun ray paradoxically turned it into edible, hallucinogenic meat, the only known instance of this phenomenon in Martian experience.

And the Mercurian Pheasants *desired* to die in shattered ecstasy. The hopping, twenty-foot-tall glass bird things were drawn from all across the planet to the cool Martian outradiance and their own transcendent demise. Over the ages this hunt had become a deeply religious ritual for both Martians and the semi-sentient Pheasant. Yet for some inexplicable reason Hergs had ordered that Mercurian Pheasant was strictly reserved for the emperor. He'd forbidden the Hunt except for the gathering of hallucinogenic meat for his own purposes.

"We really do understand," Joe echoed, mouth agape. "We really do."

"Hmmph," said Ywer. "Well, carry on, then."

"God, Jack," Joe whispered as they pushed the service down another corridor, "how did you know we were supposed to deliver Mercurian Pheasant to the emperor?"

"I picked it out of Ywer's mind, of course."

"So you *are* reading their minds again!"

"Sure, I can't help it when they're this close. But the next question is, where the hell are the emperor's quarters?"

"That's easy. We just navigate by tapping into various Martian minds." Joe indicated three Martians down the corridor. Jack nodded, sorting outradiating concepts until he found ones he could use. One Martian might only know that Hergs was "several floors up," another knew Hergs was "near the Central Solarium." Another didn't know where Hergs was, but knew where the Central Solarium was. Piecing the clues together, Jack and Joe wheeled the chromed service with apparent purposefulness through the corridors and up the elevators.

They also picked up the fact that Hergs considered the Chef Service to be the most useful branch of his military forces, and that Chef Service crew from Grades Ten up were expected to double as the emperor's bodyguard if and when the need arose. That was why they wore the Black Knife of *K'rerorr* at their waists.

Finally Jack spotted a Martian woman in the deep blue uniform of Personal Attendant to the Emperor. She was five hundred years old, but despite her youth her thoughts were bitter. *So the traitorous Mistress Amav has come home to face justice at the hands of the emperor, and on her wedding night, no less!*

"Dammit!" Jack muttered.

"Shhh!" Joe said. "I got that, too! But don't let on that--"

"No! Isn't it obvious that June 16th was the actual wedding date all along? She told me she started the Erotic Teachings December 16th last year. Then on June 16th she officially becomes the empress. It just turned June 16th! She must've wanted this all along!"

"No! I can't believe that!"

"A June wedding! She wanted it all along! To *Sam Hergs!*"

"Jack, we've got to be *quiet*. We're on our way to Hergs now. We have to *focus*."

"Right ... you're right, Joe." Jack sped the service at steel doors beneath a great archway. "Focus, dammit, *focus*." The doors parted.

The emperor's bedroom, forty feet wide, receded another sixty feet into darkness. Walls of velvet forest-green rose from burgundy shag carpet. The canopy bed was thick black fur. Scores of blinding chandeliers hung from the twenty-foot ceiling.

And Sam Hergs, Emperor of the Martians, sprawled nude on a white loveseat.

CHAPTER THIRTY-FIVE
The Ritual

Jack gasped. Hergs had a huge hard body with no flab anywhere. Every square inch of his skin was covered in wavy, oily, glistening black hair. He had a three-day beard and his eyes glittered.

"Ah, the Mercurian Pheasant," murmured the emperor. "Just the thing for a mating feast, don't you agree?"

Jack stared. Beside him Joe ineffectually tried to clear his throat. Why hadn't Hergs recognized his enemies? He had to be on drugs, Jack saw, and from the way he rolled his head, intense pleasure drugs, the kind banned throughout the United System. In fact, Hergs' eyes were so dilated they were entirely black.

"You know the Ritual, gentlemen! Prepare the feast for my love and me!"

Jack hesitated. Should he roast Hergs with his USSF blaster or should he reveal himself and deliver the ultimatum? The problem was that he'd never seen the ultimatum and wasn't sure he should try to deliver something he'd only heard summarized by General Scott. If he killed Hergs now, perhaps the Martians, freed of his control, would surrender Venus immediately. On the other hand, killing Hergs might produce chaos in the Martian government that could lead, in less than an hour, to Phil Sperry launching the Xon bombs. He said slowly: "Yes, sire, we shall prepare your feast."

Hergs struggled to stand, but his legs wobbled and he flopped back on the loveseat. "You fools! I won't have you messing up the Ritual! Don't you know the correct words?"

Joe and Jack glanced at each other. There was no mind-reading their way out of this one.

"Well," Joe tried, "we just thought you might like a chance of pace, that's all. Maybe get tired of the old Ritual and, you know, want something a little different."

"You idiot slobs! There can only be one such Ritual in an emperor's lifetime! The mating with his bride in the emperor's bedroom! Don't you fools realize that this entire scene is being broadcast to the Martian Council? You can't change the Ritual! You've already blasphemed it!"

"Hey, sorry, guy."

"Damn you, you were not the first to speak. The other there--you!"

"Yes?" Jack said.

"You were the first to speak. You were to say: 'I deliver these portents of fine lovemaking straight to my emperor.'"

"Well ... I, uh, deliver these portents of fine lovemaking straight to my emperor."

"And now you, the second one, who was never supposed to open his mouth in the first place, you bow and leave, and the first one serves the meal."

Joe wavered. "It's all right," Jack whispered. "I'll take care of this. You wait outside."

"Get lost!" Hergs screamed. "And close the damn door!"

Joe backed away. The door clicked and there was silence in the vast boudoir.

"All right, then, fool, now push the cart forward while I don the Helmet of Pleasure." Jack wheeled the cart to the loveseat while Hergs pulled on a heavy gray helmet studded with glowing knobs. Jack strained to search for the purpose of this device from whatever he'd already pulled from the Martians. He got the impression that the Helmet intensified emotions to unbearably intoxicating levels. First the pleasure drugs, now the pleasure helmet. The emperor tried to stand and inspect the service, but again collapsed on the loveseat. His fingers writhed at empty space. "My God! It's so fantastic!"

Jack stood by the service, placing his hand on the first dome the way he hoped a Chef Grade Ten would. "And would m'lord the emperor like to add some hallucinogenic *meat* to his already addled state?"

"No, damn you! Not now! Serve the champagne! You dolt!" He was having trouble peering through the thick visor. "Where are you, fool?"

"Right here, sire," Jack said. He'd already spied the two bottles of champagne in an ice bucket on the second level and proceeded to open one, reeling in disgust with the concept of Jack Commer, the United System's foremost space pilot, pouring champagne for humanity's worst villain. Hands quivering in anger, he slopped champagne across Hergs' outstretched fingers.

But Hergs was too far gone to notice. "Champagne, champagne ..." he burbled, settling back on the couch. "One for me and one for my love! Behold, she comes!"

A panel opened to the right. There, framed in brilliant white light, stood Amav, tall and slender in a crimson teddy, long dark hair shining. She smiled down at Hergs. Jack dropped his mouth. He could see everything--the breasts, nipples, belly, smooth thighs--that had so recently been his, and now belonged to the Emperor of the Martians. Jack thought he would scream, but no sound came out.

Eyes locked onto Hergs, Amav glided to the loveseat. "My emperor, I am here," she purred.

"So the Martians brought me a present without telling me! Thought they could keep it a secret! But of course all I hadda do was read their minds! I knew ya'd come back!"

"So did they," Amav whispered, caressing his oily chest. "They knew how much I wanted to be your empress. They delivered me from those awful kidnappers."

"Damn! You are so *fine!*" Hergs burst out. Jack glanced down. Hergs was fully, shockingly ready to take her.

"*You* are so fine," Amav smiled at his groin. "You are the Emperor of Everything. No emperor before has ever been so ... *big.*"

"And you're ... damn, girl, you're *incredible!* I just gotta ..." He scrunched her breasts in his strong hairy paws. "Baby!"

"Sire! Shall we execute the traitoress?" Jack screamed.

His huge gray Helmet of Pleasure obscuring Amav's face, Hergs tugged off the right strap of her crimson teddy with his teeth. "Forget it, dude, I ain't gonna execute her. She's no traitoress! Damn, she's so *fine!*"

"Sire! The traitoress consorted with the enemy! With the

notorious Jack Commer! She went all the way with him!"

"Huh?" Hergs said, turning. "Chef, you're out of line! You're not following the Ritual at all!"

"Neither are you!"

"But I'm the emperor, I'm exempt!"

"She not your woman! She's *mine!*" Jack pointed at Amav's stunned face. She recognized him in dismay. "Amav, you loved *me!* Not him!"

"I'm warning you, Chef, serve the Mercurian Pheasant *now* or face the consequences!"

Jack leapt to the two chrome domes and flung their covers clattering into the wall. "There's no Pheasant! There's nothing!"

But Hergs had returned his attention to Amav. Pawing, kissing, crawling on her, yanking down her teddy to expose her breasts. Amav writhed beneath him with a terrified glance at Jack.

"You--you--" Jack gasped, pulling out his USSF blaster. "You're both under arrest!"

"Mmmm ..." Hergs murmured, kissing and licking, dreamily eyeing the ray gun. "Good thing I've got force fields in here that neutralize any blaster but the emperor's."

Jack's power indicator flashed DRAINED. "You--you--so be it!" he screamed, dashing down the weapon. "Hergs, prepare to face the Black Knife of *K'rerorr!*"

Hergs pulled away from Amav's delightful chest. "This is definitely not part of the Ritual, you pipsqueak. I'll have you know--"

Jack pulled the Knife of *K'rerorr* and lunged. Instantly Hergs was on his feet, swiping his own heat blaster off a bedside table.

Jack raised the knife, but was astonished to see he held no blade, only an empty hilt.

He searched the files he'd downloaded and found out that a Chef, whether Martian or human, had first to be implanted with the Orb of *K'rerorr,* deep in the small intestine, for the energy field blade to operate. Jack threw the knife to the floor in disgust.

"It's you, Commer!" Hergs cried, peering through the thick

Helmet of Pleasure. "I should have guessed!"

"Listen to me, Hergs! If you don't surrender right now, my ship is going to Xon bomb Venus! Your only chance to stay alive is to surrender!"

"Surrender? When I hold the blaster? And pass up a chance to fry the famous Jack Commer? Not on your life, baby!"

Hergs crouched with the Helmet of Pleasure framing his twisted, bearded jaw and his stained wolverine teeth. His rage was amplified by the Helmet of Pleasure, feedbacking out of control. And, shaking in anticipation of his kill, Hergs was still fully aroused.

This was the end. Jack had failed. The final vision before the Xon bombs ripped this world was the hysterical frothing of this naked man in full sexual heat. Humanity would never return to Earth. The home planet was gone forever. For the first time since October 8th Jack felt how much he missed that gorgeous blue marble.

His enemy curled his thick finger around the blaster trigger--

And the space between them filled with a high-pitched whine and shivering blue-purple light. Jack fell to the carpet, assuming he'd just had his chest burned out. But he was whole, gaping at Sam Hergs who ripped off the Helmet of Pleasure and stared at Amav half-naked on the loveseat.

She held a golden shattergun. "As you may know," she said, "the empress' personal shattergun by definition bypasses your security system."

"You--you'd kill *me?* The emperor?" Hergs wheezed. "You can't!"

"Looks like I already have."

"You missed!"

"Look to yourself."

Hergs peered down. The tip of his passion glowed, it was slowly, now faster and faster, turning to glass. And crumbling. "You--" he gasped. He swung his blaster at her, shook his head feverishly, then turned to Jack. "You--" he tried again. His lust was cracking all down its length and he had but one chance to save himself. He trained the blaster at the root of the problem and swallowed. But before firing he sneered at Jack as if to blame him for everything that had ever gone wrong in his life.

The moment of hesitation proved fatal. In the next second the accelerating process claimed his entire groin. Then Sam Hergs was a pile of broken glass on the burgundy carpet.

Jack stood shakily, transfixed by the multicolored bits of the monster. He felt Amav's hands on his shoulders and stiffened.

"Amav ... you smell great ..." was all he could think to say.

"Jack," she said, silky hair on his shoulder, "did you really think I came here to do anything less than assassinate Hergs before your silly little USSF messed everything up?"

"I ... I don't know what to think." Dizzily Jack faced the bride with the crimson teddy tugged away from her taut breasts. *"Amav,"* he gasped, nodding in the direction of the furry black bed. "I ... we ..."

"Oh, no, not in front of the Martian Council!" she laughed. *"Our* wedding night will be quite private!"

"You--God--" Fresh outradiance flooded Jack's mind as hundreds of Martian minds surged to extraordinary levels. They'd been trapped in this dome, enslaved to the mad emperor, but now they were *popping free.*

"Focus, Captain Commer," Amav whispered. "Time to contact your friends on your ship and have them call off their Xon bombs, don't you think?"

Jack checked his watch. "Hey, we have twenty minutes."

"Focus, dear husband," Amav repeated, taking him into her arms, kissing him lightly, and pulling back with his USSF Comm aloft in her slender fingers. "Call."

CHAPTER THIRTY-SIX
Return to Earth
Wednesday, June 21, 2034, 2130 hours

Jack sipped a mug of jasmine tea on the porch in the silky evening. Bright grass glowed in the last rays of the sun. Beyond a line of bushes Martians and humans slung a Frisbee, their hearty yells carrying back softly. Behind him the screen door creaked open.

"Hey," Amav said. "I thought you were at the base checking on the *Typhoon*."

"Well, I decided not to go after all. Guess I like it better here." The smell of rocket fuel, the camaraderie of men bending themselves to crucial concepts, the instructions and injunctions he'd gloried in for so many years, had palled on Jack. The Southern Alaska Resupply Port, five miles to the south, had been built in less than a day with Martian help, and had already brought in two hundred engineers and scientists from Mars. The Frankston research station to the north had grown into a small city. But Jack shunned that as well, preferring Dr. Frankston's old house on the outskirts, and this same porch where Stewart Neal Frankston had sat for months sketching on legal pads his vision of a restored Earth.

The sun neared a ridge of fir trees on the horizon. Amav sat beside him. "Anyway, Joe and the rest can handle things," Jack said. "I'm on vacation, you know."

"Hey, I'm not forgetting it. I'm just sorry you had to bring the *Typhoon* over on it."

"Well, it just worked out that way. And I know you and your father wanted to be together. So, anyway, I'm just doing nothing now, just enjoying the sunset. It's incredible that it's so late."

"Well, it's the summer solstice, and we *are* way north." She snuggled into him. "Daddy says he's following Daylight Savings Time mostly out of nostalgia. He likes the long summer evenings."

"We'll I've been off military time this week. Somehow 9:30 seems better than 2130 hours all of a sudden."

The Frisbee players ended their game and headed towards the house, laughing and talking. Most continued past to their new apartments, but several came up onto the porch.

Jack rose from his bench. "Dar!"

"Captain Commer!" Dar smiled, holding out his dry pink-scaled hand. "I'm glad I finally got the chance to properly meet you."

"I--I hear you've been named emperor," Jack stammered at the sight of the great Martian with the huge head fin wearing cut-off jeans, sneakers and a blue Rice University T-shirt bulging over his hard chest. Dar's powerful pink biceps and thighs glowed in the last light of the sun.

"That's an old T-shirt of mine," Dr. Frankston interposed, noting Jack's confusion.

"Yes, it was already torn in the back, so Dr. Frankston just enlarged that a bit to accommodate my fin," Dar said.

"We were having a conversation about the physics of Frisbee flight, and several of his comrades said they could fly it by thought alone. So we had a little match."

"I ... see ..." Jack said, noting the similar dress of the other Martians and humans, male and female, on the porch. "I just thought the emperor and Council had to wear the golden robe at all times." But he could pick up Dar's thoughts: *The old files have been updated.*

"We decided to dispense with all that jazz," Dar elaborated. "It just wasn't working out, the ritual, the robes, the Council, all that. We'd been refining it for thousands of years to the point where it got totally sterile. But now that we're developing Amplified Thought, we see the old forms are holding us back. We even decided to abolish our government. We don't need it anymore, although we're keeping the emperor and Council as a sort of figurehead setup."

"Huh," Jack said, astonished at Dar's casual English diction. "That's amazing." He nodded to the rest of the Martians. "You all seem to be taking the higher gravity pretty well."

"Oh, yes," Dar said. "We can handle it for short periods. I myself like to work out in your gravity. Keeps the leg muscles strong and all."

"But over the millennia we've evolved certain natural functions similar to the EnviroFields you humans wear," said another Martian whose name floated into Jack's mind as Kner. "We can adjust ourselves to many hostile environments, and we can damp down the G forces to a degree. We can even breathe your rather thick air here. But it all takes a certain amount of energy expenditure to maintain."

"But that poor stowaway on the *Typhoon*. He was so upset about the gravity!"

"Ah, yes, M'rrpla," Dar said. "The son of one of my generals. Well, the younger the Martian, the less developed his control over this natural EnviroField, if you want to call it that. M'rrpla was only 157. Many of our younger comrades, especially the ones who were so eager to go to war, simply couldn't control their functions in stressful situations. Which is the reason many of our younger ones simply couldn't fight well, even when they thought they wanted to."

"God, I'm sorry," Jack said. "I didn't mean to bring up ..."

"Oh, no," Dar said, "we need to discuss these things so we know each other better. Just so you know, we Martians tend to strengthen and develop this environmental control sometime around our two hundredth year."

"Two hundredth ..." Jack whispered. "You know I'm sorry about M'rrpla. Sorry about everyone. We just didn't understand."

"No one understood, and many died. Now we do understand. I know that you yourself lost two brothers, and four other friends."

Jack nodded. "Yes, now we do understand. The hard way."

Dar took a bench opposite Jack. Frankston and the others also found chairs and benches on the large porch. "Yes, we have all been through a great deal of painful understanding."

"We should never have been at war with each other. We simply had no idea that there was any sort of life on Mars, and when we saw it, we panicked, I guess."

Dar managed a humanlike shrug. "Well, we of First Home

had long ago abandoned cities and structures of any sort. In fact, as we began living in caves our prime aesthetic pursuit became eradicating all former physical traces of our civilization. About the only evidence of us your spaceships would have been able to detect from the sky over the last few of your decades would be our footprints, and I gather you missed those."

"You're right, we definitely did."

"We knew about your various explorations to First Home over the last few decades. Basically, they didn't concern us. We paid them about the same attention you would have paid to your migrating birds. But then, in your timeframe of what you call last November, we became aware of a more massive migration underway. And since we couldn't obtain any mental radiance from you, at first we assumed you were ..." There was a polite attempt on Dar's part to suppress the concept, but it floated into Jack's mind as *termite infestation.*

"You can imagine our consternation when we saw you building your city of Marsport atop what was in ancient times an important temple to the Empress Fra'lith. We wondered if you were sentient beings after all, capable of knowing that fact via some mental wavelength we couldn't access. And then, when Sam Hergs and Al Carson first contacted us ..."

Dar didn't have to go on. Jack felt all the guilt and confusion that came from the erroneous conclusion that the unreadable thugs Hergs and Carson were gods who had to be worshipped. Hergs made himself emperor, Carson was given the title of Grand Marshal of First Home, and when Carson died it was a religious tragedy that spurred the more quarrelsome younger Martians into ever more fanatical revolt.

"Acceding to Hergs as emperor is only part of our guilt," Dar went on sadly. "The other part is our experimentation with Amplified Thought. We spent the last several years learning how to control it, but not without untold damage to this solar system. We did try to resist Hergs' orders to use it to destroy First Home, yet we built his death ray on Planet Cinder, knowing full well this would give him the power to press the trigger himself and bypass us."

"You were all … in *thrall* to him," Jack said.

"And that's a mistake that will never be repeated. How an entire culture can be hijacked by one madman is impossible to explain. But apparently fate has made me emperor precisely for the purpose of making sure it never happens again."

"Wow." Jack stood up. "Listen, let me get all of you some of this jasmine tea. Just the thing after a Frisbee workout. Amav and I made a vat of the stuff." In truth he was unable to stand the outradiance from the Martians. Their guilt was too intense, and he knew he'd start saying something like *There, there, it was just a little mistake, don't worry about it.* He didn't want to say that Jim and John's deaths were a little mistake.

"That sounds fine. We can ingest your food and process it."

Jack went back to the kitchen and got out cups and ice. Amav came back as well, ostensibly to help, but in reality for a long kiss in the dark kitchen.

"You looked upset back there," she said, breaking off.

"I'm not upset now," Jack murmured into her dark eyes.

"About how they were feeling? They're wonderful beings. How could we ever have fought them?"

"But it's so hard to take what's in their minds right now. And anyway, it's weird to read somebody else's mind in the first place."

"Oh, you and I have been doing that since we first laid eyes on each other!"

"But you know what I mean. I just wish we could talk trivia with them. How they feel about their deserts, their moons, all that. Just chat, get to know them slow."

Amav held him for a long time in the darkness. "I'm getting that they're curious about how this tea will taste."

"You and Joe. I can't really read them very well unless I'm in the same room with them. You two seem to be able to sense them across millions of miles."

She shrugged, disengaging from him and putting the tea tumblers on a tray.

"So what does your father really think about our marriage?" Jack said.

"Are you kidding? He's proud to have Jack Commer for a son-in-law. Amav Frankston-Commer! What a mouthful!"

"I hope he's okay with it. After all, I'm the one who wrecked this planet."

"Jack, we've all come to an understanding. The Martians understand us, we understand them, Daddy understands you and everything that's happened. We've all just got to move on and fix everything we broke."

"Yeah, I guess that's the only way to look at it." Dr. Frankston had already received United System approval to turn his Alaska Demonstration Project into the Earth Terraforming Project as of July 1st. The top scientists of two worlds would first focus on repairing the earth, and eventually consider how Amplified Thought could rebuild the outer planets. Jack was awed that anyone would consider repairing so much damage. He focused on arranging ice in the tumblers as Amav poured a pitcher of jasmine tea. "Are twelve glasses enough?"

"That's how many people are on the porch, counting us." At Jack's raised eyebrow she grinned. "Kner counted everyone on the porch, and I'm picking that up now."

"Huh. I've definitely seen there's an art to sorting through all that outradiance." Jack carried the tray to the porch. They handed out cups and resumed their seats.

"It appears I must also congratulate you, Captain Commer," Dar said. "Dr. Frankston was just telling us that when General Scott retires next year, you'll become Supreme Commander of the USSF."

"Well, I'm not certain I'm going to take it. First of all, I'd prefer flying to a desk job. Second, I'm not certain I'm going to want to even do that. I may just decide to settle down here on Earth with Amav."

"Are you kidding?" Amav said. "You didn't tell me that!"

"Well, I was just thinking that as I've been sitting here this evening. Maybe I've come to the end of all that. I was thinking that up to now, I've never really lived. I've never really known what this planet is really like. And now that you all are going to be working so hard to clean it up, I'm really appreciating it for the first time, I guess."

"But you're a pilot! You wouldn't last two months here!"

Jack flushed. The humans politely ignored what threatened to be a private discussion between the newly engaged couple, but the Martians leaned forward, eagerly digesting whatever emotions might pop from the unreadable interior of the human mind. Jack had expected Amav to be delighted with his decision to remain on Earth. "But I'll be helping out here. Your father was telling me that even with Amplified Thought, there are so many complexities to pay attention to. I suppose I could fly some on Earth here, like maybe transport."

"Transport!" Amav spat.

"Well ..."

The Martians were staring. "I thought you were supposed to take the *Typhoon II* to Alpha Centauri in a couple months," Dr. Frankston said.

"I know. I hope this doesn't sound too strange, but after all the misunderstandings we've been through with you Martians, I really have to admit I don't really know what to do about the Centaurians. I mean, could we be misjudging them somehow? I know they seem insane, but is there any way of reaching an understanding with them? Or should I just go in and start slinging Xon bombs? I just don't know."

"Do your other crew members feel like this?"

"If you mean conflicted, yes. Joe feels the same way. He's also not inclined to take command of the *Typhoon* if I left the program. The other four have fought in AC, and they're ready to fight again if necessary, but they've also seen firsthand how stupid the whole thing is. So you're sending in a ship, designed to win the war in one blow, but my fear is that we're not really up for the task."

"Maybe you're all just exhausted right now," Frankston said gently.

"I don't know. Scott won't listen to me on this. And he's right when he talks about the dangers if we don't act. The Centaurians have gone *crazy* recently. Like black-holing Barnard's Star last month just to get a handful of our ships. An entire solar system, just *gone!* There's even talk that they want to try to get to *our* solar system and destroy the rest of it."

"I can confirm that," Dar said. "Unfortunately, Hergs had a human spy smuggled aboard one of your Earth freighters to Alpha Centauri. Hergs proposed that we Martians link up with them against you. The Centaurians did receive this spy but sent him back insane. He kept babbling hysterically about what he called the Head of the Emperor destroying this solar system, and finally one of Hergs' underlings killed him. We Martians were disgusted at this talk, but at the time we were unfortunately in no position to protest."

"We knew Hergs had contacted them," Jack said. "But that's interesting."

"Can it really be, I wonder," Dr. Frankston said, "that here we have an entire race, spanning several solar systems and hundreds of planets, and apparently having as its basis *total insanity?* How can that possibly be? How can they function as a race?"

"There's only one way to find out," Amav said. "Jack, take the *Typhoon II* to Alpha Centauri. And instead of just blindly blowing things up, find out exactly what's going on."

"But I can't do that," Jack protested. "Scott's orders are to give a demonstration of the *Typhoon's* power."

"Delay. Say the *Typhoon* needs more tests. Wait until January 1st, when you're head of the USSF."

"But--"

"Combine the functions. Be head of the USSF *and* pilot of the *Typhoon*. Sort of a player-manager. You'll be able to do anything you want."

The Martians experimentally sipped their tea, their emotions flooding out: fear, grief, and concern. And curiosity, fascination, and hope. "But, Amav, what about you and me? And our life here on Earth?"

"C'mon, Jack, we'll always take the earth with us wherever we go. We'll never lose it."

"*We?*"

"Well, of course I'm coming with you. You're going to

need my skills. We and the Centaurians have ruined a lot of planets out there, and I'm a damn good planetary engineer. And we'll need a few good Martians, too. Dar was telling me they're developing a streamlined program for Amplified Thought that needs only three Martians."

"Myself, Kner, and Fulr here," Dar said. "When shall we leave?"

"Are you kidding?" Jack said. "I can't fit four extra people on the *Typhoon!*"

"Of course you can," Amav said. "We'll need the Martians to help us get to the bottom of this mess."

"But Dar's the emperor!" Jack cried. "And Kner and Fulr are Council!"

"Certainly we're coming," Dar said. "And I can be--what is your phrase--a player-manager as well. Besides, there's nothing for me to manage anymore. Our government is just a formality now."

"But you're the wisest of the wise!"

"All the more reason for you to listen to me, Captain Commer. And I also want you to know that your new bride possesses far more wisdom than I do."

Jack reeled with the cascading resonance of Martians broadcasting *friend ... brother.* The humans eagerly nodded. "So!" Jack laughed. "You want to use Amplified Thought to end this war, is that what you're saying?"

"Precisely. By ending this war, you humans and we Martians, and even the Alpha Centaurians, can continue our explorations. We Martians have been sitting in our caves with our rituals for thousands of years. Now we're ready to explore again. This war is the first obstacle to that. We need to get it out of the way."

The sun spread through the fir trees to the west. Chilly night was upon the top scientists of two worlds. Everything had been destroyed, Jack thought, everything had been turned on its head, the sun was going down, but they'd rotate into it tomorrow whether they wanted to or not.

For thousands of centuries this same setting sun had meant

despair. Maybe the sun god would get tired of running across the sky, maybe he'd have a temper tantrum and never come back. Even today people were afraid of the dark. All you had to do was look at all the little nightlights they had outside their houses, all along their streets.

But how many hundreds of sunrises and sunsets had Jack flown above the four inner planets? You looked up and there was the sun, the core of everything. They were all in orbit around it. There was no night and day. It was all day.

And this same sunlight had seeded the planets with life. That was why Jack was here. That was what he was supposed to get involved in. Life that expanded out to new suns.

"All right, then, ladies and gentlemen, let's get our little war out of the way," Jack said, turning to face the darkening west.

About the Author

Michael D. Smith was raised in the Northeast and the Chicago area, then moved to Texas to attend Rice University, where he began developing as a writer and visual artist. His Jack Commer, Supreme Commander science fiction series is published by Sortmind Press. In addition, Sortmind Press has published Smith's literary novels *Sortmind, The Soul Institute, CommWealth, Akard Drearstone,* and *Jump Grenade.* All titles are available from Amazon.

Smith's web site, https://sortmind.com, contains further examples of his novels and visual art, and he muses about writing and art processes at https://blog.sortmind.com/.

Amazon author page
https://www.amazon.com/author/smithmi/

The Jack Commer, Supreme Commander Series

The Martian Marauders
Jack Commer, Supreme Commander
Nonprofit Chronowar
Collapse and Delusion
The Wounded Frontier
The SolGrid Rebellion
Balloon Ship Armageddon